PRAISE FOR PHILIP FRACASSI

"[*Sarafina* is] a fairytale like no other, Fracassi has crafted a nightmarish story weaving together threads of mythology, history, fantasy, and horror that explores the bonds of brotherhood through a terrifying landscape of war, religion, and the supernatural."

—*Scream Magazine*

"[*Boys in the Valley*,] the most frightening novel of the year."

—*Esquire*

"[*Gothic*,] a literary treat that delivers what it promises to horror fans."

—*Fangoria*

"A tale that will truly frighten, unnerve, and touch readers' hearts…[*Boys in the Valley* is] a beautiful novel that should be—will likely be—remembered as one of the best of the young decade."

—*Cemetery Dance Online*

"[Fracassi] brings a depth of understanding to his monsters, human and otherwise."

—*The Guardian*

"Old-school horror."

—**Stephen King**

"*Sarafina* is the literary equivalent of a cannonball that'll leave you bruised, bloody, and broken. A dark and unsettling novel that uses spiritual mythology, and the war America fought against itself, as the backdrop for a story that will twist your stomach and shred your nerves."

—Tyler Jones, author of *Night of the Long Knives*

"Philip Fracassi's *Sarafina* is a shape-shifting fever dream: part historical epic, part coming of age—but its horrors are one-hundred-proof: pure, potent, and wholly terrifying."

—Nick Cutter, author of *Little Heaven*

"A dark and delirious journey into the unraveling of a mind, *Gothic* is the accursed 21st century bastard child of the 70s horror boom and John Carpenter's *In the Mouth of Madness*. Deadly, compelling, and pulls no punches."

—Brian Evenson, author of *Last Days*

"[*Boys in the Valley*'s] prose is precise, the terror's exquisite, and Fracassi's got his hand on the chisel going into your chest."

—Stephen Graham Jones, New York Times bestselling author of *My Heart Is a Chainsaw*

"*Gothic* is the literary equivalent of the abyss gazing right back at you from the hellish depths of its pages. Don't lean in too close, lest you fall into this nightmarish novel and never find your way out again."

—Clay McLeod Chapman, author of *Ghost Eaters*

SARAFINA

ALSO BY PHILIP FRACASSI

NOVELS
The Autumn Springs Retirement Home Massacre
The Third Rule of Time Travel
Boys in the Valley
Gothic
A Child Alone with Strangers
Don't Let Them Get You Down
The Egotist

STORY COLLECTIONS
No One Is Safe!
Beneath a Pale Sky
Behold the Void

NOVELLAS
Commodore
Shiloh
Sacculina

FOR CHILDREN
The Boy with the Blue Rose Heart

POEMS
Tomorrow's Gone

HORROR

SARAFINA

Copyright © 2026 by Philip Fracassi
Cover by Joel Amat Güell
Interior by Naomi Falk
ISBN: 9781968043049 (paperback)

CLASH Books
Troy, NY
clashbooks.com
Distributed by Consortium
All rights reserved.

This is a work of fiction. Unless otherwise indicated, all the names, characters, businesses, places, events, and incidents in this book are either the product of the author's imagination or used in a fictitious manner. Any resemblance to actual persons, living or dead, or actual events is purely coincidental.

No part of this book may be reproduced in any form or by any electronic or mechanical means, including information storage and retrieval systems, without written permission from the author, except for the use of brief quotations in a book review.

This work's Library of Congress number can be requested from the publisher.

SARAFINA
Philip Fracassi

INTRODUCTION

It's interesting to see an author discover the aesthetic that suits them best. If you read a writer through their career, you'll see how they often try different approaches, stylistic or tonal gambits as they hunt towards what defines them—or at least what works during that epoch of their personal growth and history.

I'm thinking of writers such as Dan Simmons and Robert R. McCammon. Writers whose early work was passionate and raw and brilliant in its way, but perhaps hadn't found that place it would later slip into where a kind of alchemy was achieved and the gears began to mesh true. Those two writers, to me, are indicative of a restless creative spirit, moving from horror to sci-fi to crime fiction to historical fiction, their authorial voices shifting and mutating in astonishing ways while their core obsessions remained almost fixedly static throughout each new iteration.

It is both a joy and a revelation to see a writer hit his or her stride. Or what you as a reader prefigure to be that, anyhow. That place where their skills as a wordsmith and world-builder meet with their persistent fascinations and produce a run of really interesting works.

I first read Philip Fracassi a few years ago. I was sent a copy of his novel, *Boys in the Valley*. I read it in a few days, enrapt. As one does when one enjoys a novel which is not a debut, I sought out some of Philip's older work. In it I saw the same talent, the same obsessions, a lot of the same thematic concerns—yet perhaps not yet on the scale that was made apparent in *Boys*. Kind of like a musician who'd been given a cello or grand piano and was testing his skills against the might of that enormous instrument. The notes rang true, yes, and often with a furious precision. But like early Simmons and McCammon, there were subtle refinements to come as Fracassi saw what his instrument could achieve, dialled it in, and began to embark on larger and more complex orchestrations.

Which brings us to Sarafina. Reading it (with great delight, the occasional enjoyable revulsion, and frequently with horrified amazement) I had that same sense of a writer finding his groove. The historical setting feels authentic, those small and meaningful details anchoring a reader in that specific time and place—the leitmotifs of demonic forces, fallen angels, and religious malfeasance—the strong and fully-fleshed if not always likeable characters—all of it feels of a piece with *Boys*, carrying forward the strengths of that fine book and adding to it.

In *Sarafina*, we find Philip Fracassi continuing into this new phase of his career. His Imperial phase, let's call it. That place where, if a writer is diligent and driven and just a bit lucky, they're able to harness their writerly talent to their thematic drivers and create a run of memorable works.

Who can say where the road will take Fracassi next? I can only say that I'm excited to follow him, wherever it may lead.

Yours,
Nick Cutter

"O you who fly in darkened rooms,
Be off with you this instant, this instant—"
—*Syrian incantation (7th Century)*

"Thou shalt not suffer a witch to live."
—*Exodus 22:18*

PART ONE: PILGRIMS

I

APRIL 7, 1862
SHILOH

This is Hell.

Less than a year ago I was sixteen years old and my worst fear was my father's hand, a leather belt wrapped twice around the knuckles. Now I stare at a landscape blown apart by hate and mortar, drenched in blood and the flesh of countless men.

Ellie, please help me.

Our line advances, disheveled uniforms soaked through. The march from Corinth was two days of heavy rain. My socks—what remains of them—were hung from a branch overnight while we prepared for the latest attack on Grant's men, but the wool holds moisture and my feet burn and itch as I move forward with my line. Colonel Forrest screams from his horse, his voice lost amid a barrage of cannon from the Federal gunboats lining the Tennessee River. I've been separated from my assigned brigade under Brigadier General Ruggles, whose battery had been heroes only a day prior, capturing over a thousand Yankee soldiers. Now, under Forrest, who seems mad and vicious and—quite frankly—careless, we march with a speed and negligence that leaves us open to all forms of counterattack.

All around me, men fall.

Standing as a clean target atop a rise near a burnt-out peach farm, I pause to scan the breadth of the battlefield. The ground ripples like water as thousands of men march toward Union lines, the clouds of rifle smoke conjoining with the ever-present mist hanging over the land; the staggered batteries and their incessant cannon fire are a froth atop a breaking wave. The unceasing artillery blows apart great patches of earth. Screams of triumph and pain rise in chorus, deafening as the weaponry.

My brothers and I constitute three men of the Army of Mississippi. Three of thirty thousand sent to break Grant's forces at Pittsburgh Landing. I've never seen so many people in one place, nor so much death. When I scan the vista, I feel as if every man of the South has come to Shiloh to fight this battle, so unreal to me are the sheer numbers. For two days, victory seemed assured. The men sang, spoke excitedly of pushing the Federal Army into the Tennessee River. But then Johnston was shot, blood filled his boot, and by the time they laid him beneath a tree he was gone. Beauregard was given command just as reinforcements arrived to stiffen the Union defense.

Now, after two days of horror, the men no longer sing. They say that all is lost. That we've pushed too far for a possible retreat.

That we've been thrown into a hornet's nest. That Beauregard's cries of a counterattack are a death knell. Meanwhile, the naval boats don't stop firing. They don't ever stop, and men are blasted—again and again—into great blossoms of torn flesh everywhere I look. Hundreds. Thousands. On both sides.

I say this is Hell because it's the truth of what I see. Blood pools in fields like ponds, overflowing with limbs. The unceasing artillery is deafening thunder and the very air reeks of brimstone. Great swaths of earth have caught fire and are ablaze. Trees burn like angelic sentinels passing judgment.

Marching over the ridge I draw to a halt, raise my rifle, and fire at the distant line of blue. I reload. Across misshapen terrain I meet eyes with an enemy soldier, his own eyes wide above a wooly beard. I wonder what he thinks of my clean face, my thin frame awash in frayed grays, as I make to murder him and those he loves. He likely thinks me a child who has lost his way but needs to die all the same. I don't disagree; I'm convinced my short life has been chosen as a sacrifice for this war.

I fire my weapon and he disappears behind the cloud of my rifle shot. I reload, search for another target, but in the surrounding chaos my mind loses clarity—my feet walk, my rifle aims—

but my thoughts are sluggish. There are but two things I know clearly.

I will soon be dead.

I must find my brothers.

The earth beneath me erupts.

A blinding white light lifts me off the ground and sends me flying backward. Hot blood hits my face, and a fist of meat that was once the man walking ten paces ahead slaps against my cheek and slides past my ear to the ground. My breath is snatched away by the impact and when I try, heaving, to suck in a breath I inhale nothing but hot smoke that burns my throat like fire. My ears ring so loudly that—for the first time in two days—I can't hear cannon fire. My vision warps, tunnels, but remains good enough to see a detached arm resting to my left, the dirty hand clutched to a broken rifle.

It's my bad luck to have stepped into target range of the naval ships, which now seem to have coordinated on my exact position. Worse luck for the man whose back I followed toward the Union line, a stranger with whom I now share an intimate connection, his blood sprayed over my uniform, my face, bits of his flesh greasing my long hair as I gain my feet. I force myself to gather my bearings as piles of earth blast upward in great, sky-darkening sprays everywhere I look and showers of dirt and stone rain down on my head and shoulders. The detonations leave holes deep enough for graves.

The desperation to live—to see my brothers one last time and escape this nightmare, to perhaps make my way home and see my sister and feel her warm embrace—motivates me to push through the veils of horror, the rollicking tumult of the battle, and find shelter. I turn my back on the Union soldiers firing their rifles and face the hundreds of Confederate men in a line running toward them on either side of me. I spot the mad Colonel Forrest, red-faced and bellowing orders. Suddenly, all the things related to duty and honor that have grown inside of me dry up and crumble to dust, blow away like the shifting gray smoke clouding the battlefield.

And I run.

I'm not three steps when another blast hits me, punching me with a wall of hot air and I'm knocked clean off my feet. I waste no time searching myself for injury and, finding none, begin to crawl like an animal, scrambling on hands and knees away from the massive concussions of enemy fire. The smoke has gotten so thick I can see only shadows of soldiers sprinting past, toward the war, more ghosts than men. I get to my feet and run up a small hillock ending at the lip of a natural gulley. Without thought I throw myself over the edge, let my body go loose as I hit bottom, wincing as I collide with dirt and stubborn rocks. I roll toward a thin stream stained red with blood then push away from the water, curl myself into a fetal position beneath a stone overhang that I pray hides me from eyes as well as bullets.

I begin sobbing because I don't have enough sense left in myself not to.

I don't care if they think me a coward. I'm seventeen years old and I don't want to die.

Ellie, I love you and I miss you. Please save me.

I flatten myself against the earth, will my body to be swallowed by the dirt as the non-stop barrage of artillery from the Union batteries and metal-clad gunboats continues, shuddering the ground beneath me, pummeling the land hard enough to shake Heaven itself, cause the angels in the clouds above to cry out in despair and make God bleed from his eyes and ears.

I lie for what seems an eternity beneath that ridge as rifles and small arms fire at will, cannons roar, and the earth is beaten, as if mountain-sized giants had left the pages of fairy tales and were pounding their fists against the Tennessee soil in some mad rage against this evil world.

I shut my eyes tight and cover my head with my arms, the blood-soaked Confederate cloth sticky against my flesh, and wait for the end.

"Ethan! Ethan, God damn you!"

I open my eyes. Two men stare at me, wide-eyed; scraggly beards thick as moss cover their cheeks, mouths, chins. They lie prone in the dirt beside me, rifles laid flat.

My brothers.

"Christ, boy, we thought you were dead," Archie says, bent teeth flashing amidst his filthy red facial hair. He punches me in the shoulder—too hard—and I wince.

Mason stares at me with those intense, pale blue eyes, scrutinizing my head and body. Looking for injuries. "Can you walk?"

"I'm fine," I say, and feel a swell of joy in my chest at the sight of them. Both of them. Both alive. "Scared," I add, feeling no shame at the confession.

Mason nods. "Beauregard is either stupid or crazy. Perhaps both. Grant's got the whole damn Ohio army landing in support, and more coming. We're badly outnumbered. This battle is over."

Part of me knows this. I'd heard enough from the other soldiers who'd whispered similar things, but I don't have a mind for strategies of war. Back home I'm not even trusted to run Father's tobacco shop. Out here I'm asked to murder, day and night, and know I'll never forget my first kill in the heat of battle.

When we made our initial thrust into Grant's camps, catching the bastards by surprise, I'd been running and screaming like a demon—we all were, thousands of us—and I gloried seeing those bluecoats panic amidst all the chaos and death, retreating as fast as their legs could carry them, leaving spoils and prisoners behind like offerings. Somehow I found myself alone amidst a group of tents when a Union soldier burst from the mouth of one of those tents, holding his rifle like a spear, bayonet pointed at my gut. By instinct alone I swung my weapon and knocked the deadly point away, but the bluecoat threw his weight into me and we both went hard to the ground. I looked into his eyes for a brief moment and saw terror. He was only a few years older than myself, screaming in my face, primed to kill.

But I had an advantage.

In addition to the bayonet attached to my rifle, I keep a second tucked into my right boot (the boots being the only nice things I own, stripped off a dead Yankee colonel that Mason had found floating down the Cumberland River after the devastating loss of Fort Donelson. Luckily for me they'd been too small for my oldest brother, who is taller and broader than me by three inches and fifty pounds, and too small for Archie, who—although skinny as barbed wire—has feet so big he was wearing father's hand-me-down shoes at the age of twelve). It was into this dead colonel's boot I reached, sliding the bayonet free while the Yankee slid strong hands over my throat.

I punched it once into his side, saw his eyes widen in shock. His hands loosened, trembling, from my neck, and I cursed into his dying face as I plunged the steel into him again, this time into his guts. I twisted, pulled free, and thrust it into him again, and again. I pushed him off me, knelt beside his pale, shaking body—those murderous hands now grappling at the blood spilling from his stomach—and drove the bayonet into his heart, then his neck. I thanked God for preserving me even as I felt awash with the evil of my deed. Hands shaking, I wiped my weapon clean on his blue pants and returned it to my boot. From that moment on, I thought of that bayonet as a good luck charm and go nowhere without it stuck firm to my calf.

"What do we do?" I ask, looking into Mason's pale eyes, cold as a frozen windowpane, for guidance.

He spits and scowls, turns to Archie, who simply grins like the fool he often is. A mad, dangerous fool. When Mason looks back at me, his face is determined, his mind set. His eyes, however, are full of apology.

"We run," he says.

Archie drops his face into the dirt and laughs as explosions rumble across the sky and the firing of a thousand rifles crackle through the air, like dead wood popping on a campfire the size of Hell.

"Okay," I say, and whisper a prayer of thanks into folded hands. "Let's run."

2

As the afternoon wears on, it becomes apparent that the battle is lost and that Beauregard is set for another counterattack—despite immeasurable deaths and casualties—against an ever-increasing Yankee army building along the river.

The three of us head southwest, aiming for the hospital at Fallen Timbers. There's so much chaos no one spares us a glance. Entire brigades are already signaling retreat. Even so, we walk steadily, careful not to draw undue attention from a colonel or any of the regiments pushing toward Pittsburgh Landing and certain death. We stay to the trees as best able, and the further we walk the easier that becomes, since fewer of them are burning as we move beyond the range of Union artillery.

"We'll take the Corinth Road," Mason says, eyes studying the face of every soldier we pass, as if daring them to question our direction. "Anyone asks, we've been ordered to fortify the hospital. That the Yanks are surging and some of us are falling back to protect the wounded."

It's not an unfair assumption, and both Archie and I nod our assent. While the stacked regiments continue pushing east, there are several wounded being carried—by arm or by stretcher—back toward the hospital. It's only a few miles to Fallen Timbers, and we can regroup there, decide next steps.

"I don't feel bad about it," Archie says, and spits in the dirt. "We had the sons of bitches good as dead when Johnston got it. We never shoulda let up."

Archie's voice is deep and gravelly, and has always been hard to understand. I don't recall the event, since I'm nearly eight years his junior, but as a boy he'd been cursed with a disease called diphtheria that nearly killed him. Mason told me about it once when I asked why Archie talked the way he did; told me our brother was near strangled to death. Said it was some kind of poison in the blood, that he was lucky to have survived.

What was unknown, however, was whether Archie's grinding voice was the result of the disease itself or our father's frantic attempts at clearing his airways, which he did by repeatedly driving the shaft of a silver serving spoon down the boy's throat.

Whatever the case, his words always sound as if they've been scraped from his tongue with a rusty hatchet. Most people can't understand him the first time they hear him speak—if ever—but Mason, Ellie, and I have grown familiar with it and have little trouble in the deciphering.

"No reason to feel anything," Mason says, walking faster now than he'd done since we all joined the army six months ago.

The idea to join the 20th Regiment had been Mason's. Ellie had protested me going with them, having just turned seventeen, and young for a soldier. But Father served in the Mexican-American War and would hear none of her compassion on my behalf. He was proud of his boys going to fight for the great state of Mississippi, to "protect the morals of the South" against Lincoln's hordes. At first, we were excited. We marched to Virginia well-stocked and champing at the bit for some action. Men spoke of seeing the elephant, a real battle, speaking in rushed, excited tones, as if it would all be some sort of adventure.

Most of those happy-go-lucky men were killed or captured shortly thereafter, at the battle of Fort Donelson. My brothers and I were lucky as rabbits in a clover patch to sneak out of that one, and me with new boots. After regrouping, a bunch of us were sent to join Bragg's ten thousand in Corinth. A few weeks later we were at Shiloh, sprinting out of the trees like men possessed, howling like demons toward Union camps, thinking we'd win the damn war with one charge.

And now, after getting us into this, it's our eldest brother making the decisions once more. Only this time it's to get out of the war. To stay alive. I don't know what he'll tell Jeremiah—if we ever make it home, that is—but it'll be his mess to explain. He's the only one of us Father has any respect for. Not just because he's the oldest—having lived an entire decade before I'd even taken a breath—but because he's the only one of us as mean, if not meaner, than the old man himself.

Sure, Archie has his moments. But Archie ain't so much mean as he is cruel. If there was a disagreement, Mason (who is big as an ox and twice as strong) would invite a man to a fight before beating him to Hell and back. Archie's the type to say nothing to an insult, but a week later you'd feel steel sliding into your back on a dark night, and it'd be my brother grinning down at you as you bled out, his crooked teeth and grating, sandpaper laughter the last thing you'd see and hear on this earth.

I'm nothing like my brothers. I'm tall, but weak. Skinny as a pole, as Mason likes to say, teasing me about it all my years. I think my lack of temper has a lot to do with my twin sister, Ellie. Growing up, she wouldn't let me get mean, or cruel. Kept me on a moral path, I suppose. She's a good person with a big heart, and my love for her is boundless. Our whole lives we've been inseparable, and even now, with hundreds of miles between us, it's as if I can feel her heart beating next to mine, her hand squeezing my fingers tight, tugging at them—at me—to come home.

Lord knows I'm trying.

"We'll leave the road before Fallen Timbers," Mason says. "Don't need any questions from the officers at the hospital. We'll cut southwest, pick up the Natchez Trace from a distance, then make our way toward the big river. See if we can steal a boat or, hell, a canoe if we have to. Make our way back to Natchez on the Mississippi. We'll need to stay clear of roads, of stands and towns. Men like us, they'll wonder why we ain't fighting."

"What'll they do?" I know the answer but need to hear my brother say it, need to know it's certain and not just my being afraid.

"Shoot us, of course," Archie says, then chuckles. "We're deserters now, boy."

"Yeah," Mason mutters. "We're under Bragg. He's merciless with deserters. If we're caught we'll be dragged back, made an example of."

He looks at me with a frown. I notice how dirty he is. His overgrown black beard is matted with mud, or blood, I don't know which; the hair under his tilted cap is caked to his sweaty neck like a shadow. The whites of his eyes are bloodshot, red as lit furnaces, his lips chapped and bleeding. "I'm sorry, little brother," he says, then looks to Archie, who gives a nod, then looks to the dirt.

"Won't let nothing happen, Ethan," Archie grumbles. "We'll keep you safe."

"I know," I say, and adjust the rifle slung over my shoulder, and am reassured by the pressure of my lucky bayonet hiding in a dead man's boot as we tromp forward—criminals, cowards, deserters—toward home.

3

It's about six miles to the field hospital. As we walk, we come across fewer and fewer soldiers. There's a ridge ahead and if memory serves the hospital is just over the other side. Perhaps a half mile. I'm beginning to wonder when it would be wise to change course into the fields, and away from the road, when a lone figure appears on the ridge, close enough to be hit with a well-thrown stone.

"That's a lieutenant," Archie mumbles, face tilted down but his gaze ahead, watchful.

"Damn," Mason replies. "Keep your eyes forward, nod and show your palms but don't make a show of it."

I tense as the man comes closer. I try to appear relaxed, as if what we're doing and where we're going are perfectly legitimate. Following orders. But the lieutenant is scrutinizing the three of us—a deep frown creases his face above a trimmed beard; his hands balled like fists where they extend from a clean frock. He looks brand new, as if he'd been dropped down into this place from Heaven above, eager and fresh and unblemished.

Before we can decide whether to salute his moderate rank or continue on our way, he comes to an abrupt halt, eyes wide and glaring beneath his forage cap. I note that one of his hands is settled on the hilt of his saber.

"Stop!" he snaps, and we do.

I swallow hard, do my best not to look nervous. I glance toward my brothers. Mason looks bored. Archie smiles broadly, scratches at his rust-red beard. Both looks are unsettling, because I know what danger simmers beneath those masks.

The lieutenant stomps within a couple feet, glares at each of us individually; anger flares his nostrils, wide brown eyes bulging. "Where you headed?"

"We're to support the hospital," Mason drawls, that bored expression never leaving his face. "Retreat is imminent. Sir," he adds, and gives a dogged salute.

"That's bull," he says, spit flying. "Ordered by whom?" The hand on his saber tightens, the knuckles white as giant pearls.

Archie slides the Springfield rifle off his shoulder, sets the stock into the dirt, leans on it. That and the knife at his belt are the only weapons he brings into battle. Mason carries a rifle and a Colt revolver, both brought from home. I have an army-issued musket, one with no rear sight, but decent enough in a pinch. "Captain Stanford, sir," Archie says, grinning.

"Why you three? Why not the regiment?" He gives me a hard look, as if sensing the weak link among us. "Well, soldier? Answer."

"Sir," I stammer, looking to my brothers for aid but finding only mute expressions. "We're...we're brothers, sir."

I don't know why I say it—but it's the first thing that comes to mind by way of explanation. To my surprise, the lieutenant nods and his features soften, as if my reasoning makes some sort of sense in this senseless war. For a moment I hold hope he'll move on, continue with the business of killing men. I turn and look behind, waiting for more soldiers to appear, perhaps distract him into bothering someone else. But there's no one.

"You don't look like brothers," the lieutenant says, suspicion growing once more.

Admittedly, it's true. For reasons unexplainable, the Belle children are rather unique in design. Mason is dark-haired, built like a fortress. Archie is wiry, with brown eyes so dark they appear black, and copper hair, which takes after our mother.

As for me, I'm made up of bits left over. Dull brown hair, muddy eyes, and protrusions of bone where muscle should be. My twin, Ellie, is blonde as a new day's sun with skin pale as milk, dark blue eyes big as lakes. She's pretty, but not delicate. Strong in her own way—stronger than me by a longshot. Mason treats her like a child, protective to a fault, and Archie like a pet, a strange breed he doesn't fully comprehend but takes cares of nonetheless, as much as he's able to care for anything. Since Ellie came into womanhood, more than one overzealous man had made the mistake of being discourteous to our sister, only to be left broken and bloodied when tracked down by my older brothers, babbling apologies while picking their teeth out of the dirt.

For a moment, no one says a word. What is there to say? Archie kicks at the road like an impatient horse. Finally, Mason speaks up. "May we go, sir?"

"No, you may not," the lieutenant says, long and languid, like he's drawing a line in the sand. "I think you three better walk on with me. I wish to speak with Captain Stanford."

"Sir," Mason says. "We're a stone's throw from the hospital. It's four or five miles back. We were told to report, and we're reporting." Something in the air changes—tightens—and Mason's voice darkens. "I think you better move aside and let us follow our orders."

There's a heartbeat of stalemate as Mason and the officer lock eyes, then the scrape of metal as the lieutenant takes a half-step back and draws his saber. He points it, of all places, at my chest. "Turn around and march. That's an order."

Mason's eyes widen momentarily as he looks at me, then the sword. Archie chuckles and throws his musket over his shoulder once more, saluting formally. "Yes, sir," he says.

I open my mouth to speak—to say what, I have no idea—when a gunshot cleaves the air. I stare at the smoking Colt in Mason's steady hand, then at the lieutenant.

A black, bleeding hole has replaced his left eye. His mouth hangs open, the jaw working as if he were chewing great mouthfuls of death. A cloud of red powder floats in the air behind his head. His saber clatters to the packed dirt and he follows, dropping first to his knees, then facedown into the road.

I look ahead and behind, but there is no one within sight. A minor miracle.

I suppose I should be shocked, or appalled. But after everything I've seen these last few months there ain't much that can surprise me anymore. What's a single gunshot when you've heard nothing but constant artillery fire for nearly three straight days? What's one more dead man when you've been wading through fields of gored flesh, watching men die by the dozens in glorious battle? Though young, I've come to see life for the fragile thing it truly is, learned it can be taken away—like a slap to the face—from anyone with the will to do so.

Still, he was one of our own. An officer. Possibly a neighbor we'd never had the circumstance of meeting. And the killing wasn't done to defend the South from tyranny. It was just...done. As I stare at the body of a fellow soldier facedown in the dirt, I note the trembling in my hands, feel the fear—thick and dark as molasses—that floods my veins. My stomach gurgles and bile reaches for my throat, but I swallow it down. I realize our path is now set.

There is no turning back.

As I fret, Mason nonchalantly tucks away his gun. Archie hunkers down and pulls the fresh gray cap off the bloody head. He tosses his own kepi to the ground, puts on the lieutenant's. He mutters something indecipherable, nothing more than a low growl, then grabs both shoulders of the officer's frock and drags him toward the trees.

I turn to Mason, shaking.

We're dead men, I think.

And if not dead, then damned.

My brother winks at me. "I think it's time we get off the road."

4

As we tromp through dense forest, heading southwest from Falling Timbers toward Corinth, we give the main road a wide berth so as to avoid soldiers. The sky, through the heavy canopy of cloud above, grows dusty peach. The late-spring Tennessee air cools my exposed skin. Mason has been quiet since we dumped the officer's body, grumbling about the lack of rations the man had been carrying in the pouch strapped to his hip. Some tobacco (which we already have in decent supply and will do little to fill our stomachs or soothe our throats), enough hardtack to feed the three of us for a day, maybe two, some chicory root, and a mouthful of salt pork. Archie had taken the lieutenant's canteen and offered me the man's frock as it was too slight for either of my brothers, but I declined. As it pertained to clothes stripped from corpses, I was wearing enough as it was. Besides, the guilt of what we'd done gnawed at my guts like a swarm of flies. I preferred to keep my sin in the shadows, and wearing that coat would have been wearing my shame for all to see. Let the Devil have it to flaunt in Hell, a cape for me to put on when I meet him there.

Ellie, what will you think of me when I confess? What will you think of us? Because of course I'll tell you all of it—the truth of the war, of what I've done, of what our brothers have done. A small part of me thinks that, perhaps—from your seat by the fire while reading passages of Psalms to our father—you already know. When I fell into a pool of men's blood, did you absently wipe your hands on your skirts? When I was knocked onto my back by artillery, did you close your eyes and complain of a headache? When I killed that man with my blade, did you feel darkness swirling inside you? Did you say a prayer for my soul as I watched the light leave his eyes?

Have you always known my worst deeds? I wonder.

Thickening shadows grow around the base of the trees surrounding us. I glance upward, searching for the sun, but it's hidden by arching branches, tucked behind a curtain of wind- rustled leaves. It will be dark soon and we'll camp. We've taken only one break, for a share of food and a swallow of rust-flavored water from our canteens. Creeks abound, so water won't be an issue as we continue our trek, but food will become a problem in a day or two, which means hunting with guns or traps—or both—and prolonging our march home as we stop to kill whatever game infests these woods and meadows.

My nerves are on edge thinking about the Natchez Trace, that sunken road reaching north from our Mississippi home through Alabama and Tennessee, all the way to Nashville. Lying less than a mile to our east, it will be busy with merchants, soldiers, and slavers. Since the war's inception, stands have cropped up at regular intervals, and many folks who gather in those places accept gossip as much as currency. If just one person were to spot us, and know us for the deserters we are, the information would travel north and south along the road like wildfire in a summer drought. And then soldiers—the Home Guard—will come for us, and no place will be safe. Not even our home. Mason says we've over three hundred miles to march, none of it easy. I don't know how I'll stand the fear of being captured for the days and weeks to come, but I've learned to live with fear during the war and have grown used to it riding my shoulder like a demon.

"We'll have to watch for campfires," Mason says as we hike through brush and duff. "Keep an eye out for Chickasaw and Choctaw settlements, plus there's bandits in these woods, hiding, same as us. I don't want to stray near any of the little towns unless we go under cover of night to steal from a cornfield or an orchard."

"That's a better way to get shot than the army," Archie mutters, his voice a low rumble that well suits the dying day.

"True enough," Mason says. "And no beds for us, not for a while. No whiskey or sugar. But we're alive, boys. We'll stay alive."

The plan for the day is to make it as close to the Mississippi border as possible. Mason is itchy to get out of Tennessee, and I can't blame him. Archie is subdued about strategy and is content to walk in whatever direction Mason points a finger. I follow them both because it's what I've done my whole life, and because I have no other choice in the matter.

"Figure we can try for twenty miles a day, that'll get us into Mississippi sometime tomorrow, say another week or so until we get near Jackson."

"Even through forest?" I say, not wanting to debate his optimism but knowing it won't help us to be unrealistic, not with food in short supply. "Through swamps?"

Mason looks at me hard for a moment, and I try to meet his eye, though not in a challenging way. Archie mutters something under his breath, and my oldest brother nods, swats at one of the ten thousand mosquitos working hard to drain our blood. "Fair enough, Ethan," he says, albeit grudgingly. "Regardless, it's Jackson we'll aim for, then I figure we cut west toward the Big Black River, maybe get lucky and steal a boat, follow that to Vicksburg."

"Then we hop on a ferry and paddle home," Archie says with a chuckle. Mason shoots an angry glare at him, but I know he'd never act on it. I think even Mason, big and strong as he is, would want nothing to do with Archie in a scrap.

"We'll see," Mason says glumly. "I'm trying is all."

"Yup," Archie says, and pats him on the back.

I stare at my two big brothers. I find reassurance in their presence and am caught off guard by a strong wash of emotion. Archie notices me staring and gives me a crooked smile, black eyes studying me so intently that it makes me anxious. "What?"

Instead of replying, his smile broadens and he shoves me hard. I trip, fall to a knee, come up with a handful of dirt and throw it at him, laughing. His eyes go wide in comic shock and then we're on the ground, wrestling away what's left of our strength. Mason takes advantage of the delay to roll a cigarette, and by the time we tire out he's leaning against a tree, blowing smoke into the blushing sky.

Archie gets up, holds out a hand and helps me to my feet, then ruffles my hair like I'm ten years old again, instead of a man who's been to war. Who's killed.

He takes a moment to roll his own cigarette, lights it, and offers it to me. I take a puff, cough, and hand it back. My head goes light; white spots edge my vision. The two of them watch me close. Mason shakes his head but does so with a smirk. After a moment, we're all chuckling at ourselves, at the situation, as if we've just unearthed a hard-won treasure chest and found it full of sand instead of gold.

In this moment, it seems I've underestimated the importance of the officer's tobacco and—as sweat chills the flesh beneath my thin coat—I find myself wishing I'd taken the dead bastard's frock after all.

5

I'm startled awake by the crack of a rifle shot. I watch, blurry-eyed, as Archie runs away through heavy groundcover. I sit up to get my bearings and see Mason kneeling by a small cooking fire. His eyes flick to me then back to the kindling he's feeding into the flames.

"Morning," he says. "There's a creek twenty or so paces that way." He points at an impatient army of loblolly pine. The shadows clinging to their narrow trunks make me think of leeches. "You should bathe. You've got blood on you."

I shiver. Only now that I'm awake do I realize how cold I am.

The air is chilled and misty, the sky above hard and gray as slate.

Three days of walking has got me filthy, but the idea of squatting in cold creek water makes me pull my frayed collar tight to my neck. It's all I can do to keep my teeth from chattering.

"Sit by the fire," Mason mutters, then stands to greet Archie as he returns, holding the scrawniest goddamn squirrel I've ever laid eyes on by its mangy tail.

"What are you gonna do with that?" I say, hunkering down by the small fire, palms flat against the heat. "Suck the marrow from its bones?"

Archie kicks at me without venom and I swat his filthy shoe away, focus on getting warm. Mason takes what I assume is our breakfast and studies it close. Its head dangles by a red thread and I imagine that's where he shot it. "I'm just kidding, Arch. That's good shooting." I say this only because saliva is squirting the back of my throat and I'm sick to death of dry bread and jerky so tough you've got to work it in your mouth for an hour before it's soft enough to bite through.

"Thanks. I guess you can have some," he rasps, snickering.

"I'll clean it. You want to see what else is out there?" Mason jerks his knife free from its leather. "But Ethan's not too far off, something fatter would be nice."

"I'll see if I can track me a plump pig, or maybe a nice deer for you all," Archie mutters, but turns back to the dense trees, pushes through the green shrub and disappears.

"Perhaps a rabbit?" I call after him, silently hoping he actually does run across a whitetail deer. Maybe a whole family of them.

"Go wash," Mason orders, peeling the skin over the squirrel's carcass like a sock from a bloody foot. "But keep your clothes dry, we don't have time to hang laundry."

I stand, feeling more awake after some time by the fire. More human. "Whereabouts you suppose we are?"

"West of Corinth."

"Corinth? We've been walking three whole days." I hate the petulance in my voice but am unable to mask it. "Corinth is only twenty miles."

"We've been going southwest, not south, Ethan," Mason says with irritating calm as he cuts strings of meat from the worthless carcass, stabbing them onto a sharpened twig to hang over the fire. "I'd say we've covered close to thirty miles, and through rough terrain. We're doing fine, little brother. We'll be floating home on the big river before you know it."

I nod and turn in the direction Mason pointed earlier, toward the supposed creek, in time to see three men step out from behind the trees.

"Mason," I say evenly, my eyes not leaving the strangers.

All three are armed. Two hold rifles, the third a Remington revolver, all pointed at me and my brother. The guns waver between the two of us, as if uncertain who they'd like to kill first.

The man in front—the one holding the revolver—wears a canvas duster and a beat-to-hell slouch hat cocked over mangy long hair. He's tall, heavy, and almost as broad as Mason. The other two appear younger. One wears a white linen shirt, no coat, and stained britches; the other wears a wool suit, the coat buttoned over ratty long underwear. I note the exposed ankles and wrists and can't help but imagine the corpse he skinned it from.

"Nice fire," the man in the duster says, his grin full of brown teeth.

They aren't army, which I suppose is a blessing. Bandits, I figure. Thieves. Ones who work along the trace, stealing what they can, killing anyone dumb enough to wander too far from the inns and stands along the road.

Like us.

Mason steps forward, slowly, to stand next to me. I notice his Colt tucked into the small of his back, the large hunting knife still clutched—and still bloody—in one hand. "We've got nothing," he says calmly. "If it's not perfectly obvious, we're soldiers. There's nothing to steal or take. Not here. Not from us."

One of the other men waves his free hand languidly, as if bored with the whole enterprise. "You got weapons, so we'll take those. And Thomas over here," he points to the third man, "will fit nicely into those boots the boy's wearing."

The supposed leader, by virtue of being the tallest and meanest looking of the three, nods in accord. "That's right. Throw the knife, your field muskets, and whatever the hell else the army gave you into a pile, over here." He points to the ground, the .44 never wavering. "We'll take it and be on our way. Leave you with your lives."

The third man grins wildly, and I can't help notice one of his legs shaking, as if so overeager to kill that he quite literally can't be still. "Yeah yeah," he says, voice pitched into a high screech that would take varnish off wood. "Since you served and all, it's the least we can do."

Mason turns his head and looks at me, those icy blue eyes unflinching diamonds amidst a landscape of sunburnt skin and thick black beard. He talks low, but not in a whisper. "When you feel ready," he says, slow and steady, "take the Colt and shoot the one on your right."

"What the hell you say?" the lead man asks, and takes a step forward.

But my eyes don't leave my brother's. I stare deep into them, thinking about the variables of our situation, and then suddenly I understand. Slow that I am, it takes a few seconds.

I nod. "The one on the right."

"Hey, what…" the third man starts to say in that high-pitched squeal, before his words are cut off by the air-splitting crack of a rifle.

There's a puff of smoke from the brush to our far left and the lead man's face bends then blows outward. Bones and teeth and blood shoot from his mouth like a sneeze, but sideways. I twist to grip the handle of the Colt stuck into Mason's back, pull it free, and find my mark with ease. The army was hell on earth, but after a few months you could shoot a mosquito off a log from ten paces. You either learned to aim or you died. Not a lot of mystery to it.

I'd learned.

I pull the trigger and watch with numb fascination as the dirty white shirt covering my target's chest blossoms like a firewheel in summertime.

A heartbeat later, Mason roars like a bear and charges at the last man standing. The bandit points his musket at my brother and I cry out, but the coward never even pulls the trigger. He drops the gun and raises his hands, screaming like a red-tailed hawk for mercy, eyes wide as saucers. Mason plows into him, blade first.

They hit the ground in a pile and I turn away as Mason stabs at the man's chest. When I look back, he's running the edge across the bandit's throat and I do my best to ignore the sound of the bastard drowning in his own blood. A clamor I'm familiar with.

Archie steps out of the brush. He looks at me, as if to be sure I'm not dead, then walks absently toward the two downed bandits. He kicks them each a few times to be sure they're no longer a threat, then walks to the fire.

Mason is still astride his victim as Archie pulls a smoking stick from the flames, a charred worm of squirrel meat stuck to it like tar. He pulls it free, blows on it, then pops it into his mouth, chewing with contentment.

6

Ellie, do you believe in fate?

Three men walk into a camp, guns drawn, prepared to murder.

Three men strike them down, and God fills their cups.

Is that not provenance? Is that not an answer to prayer? I think it is.

I think that, perhaps, we are not the damned. We are avenging angels sent from the Lord—our muskets swords of fire, our journey home a Pilgrim's Progress.

Mason claims the canvas duster and the Remington, but we leave the bandit's muskets where they lay. He strips the bloodied shirt from the man I'd killed and tosses it to me. "Wash out that blood and wear it."

Archie takes the suit, grumbling about the holes in the chest. I study my brothers, Archie in the dark suit (it fits him better than the bandit), Mason in the long duster. If I squint, I can see them as roughened civilians—farmers or cowboys, abstainers from Kentucky or Missouri avoiding the war. I doubt my linen shirt will have a similar effect, but it's one more layer of warmth in the early mornings, so I don't complain.

Staring at the pale skin of the three dead men—pressed to the earth like the exposed roots of a river-swollen tupelo tree—makes me queasy and sparks a kind of pity in my heart. "We gonna bury them?"

Mason and Archie look at me in surprise. Mason ignores me altogether, but Archie walks over and puts a hand on my shoulder. "Are you a cruel man, Ethan?" His deep, grating voice gives the question an ominous quality, one drenched with guilt.

"No," I say, thinking it an honest reply. "I don't think so."

Archie points to the bodies. "Those men will feed the creatures of the woods," he says. "When their flesh is picked clean, then the bugs and worms will come. In time, whatever remains will sink into the soil, nourishing the trees and vegetation. Those bodies are gifts to the forest." He leans close. "Offerings."

I frown. "Bugs and trees will eat well enough if they're buried."

Archie leans in, black eyes settling on mine. "And the carcasses of this people shall be meat for the fowls of the Heaven, and for the beasts of the earth," he recites. "Book of Jeremiah." Then he pats me once on the shoulder and walks away.

After gathering our meager belongings—and me doing my best to scrub blood from the linen shirt—we track through the woods to find the bandit's camp. One of the men had been sleeping on a gum blanket, which Archie dutifully rolls up, ties, and straps to his back. There's half a bottle of whiskey, a pouch with real coffee, small tins of sugar and salt, a fresh sack of hominy, and tobacco. "Looks like these boys were over on the trace recently," Mason says, transferring the goods to his own pouch.

"Not much in the way of treasure," I say, wondering if Mason will serve up some of the homily before we begin walking.

"The treasure was in the coat." Mason pulls a leather pouch from a pocket of the duster, loosens the drawstring and dumps a variety of coins into his opposite palm. "Not much, but enough for some food if we come across a settlement."

Archie examines the folds and pockets of his new dark suit. I note he's also swapped his kepi for the bandit's slouch hat, which fits him well, but gives the overall appearance of a man assembled from the spare parts of other men.

"Any coin in your pockets?" I say, teasing, and he scowls in response, cocks his new hat in a ridiculous fashion, and tromps off after Mason.

As always, I follow.

For days we march through near impossible terrain, sleep on uneven ground like exposed animals, fight off insects and every manner of weather.

We've run out of everything.

We're all hungry and badly bug-bit. The lice we've brought from the battlefield are a constant companion inside our shirts and pants. Archie jokes he has to move fast, upon waking in the morning, to catch his cap from being carried away by the inhabitants.

Mason figures we've passed Pontotoc and are close to Houlka, a town I've never heard of. He says we're still a long way from Big Black, which we'll use as a guide to cut west toward the Mississippi. Traveling the river valley will be smoother than the dense forest and muddy swamp we've been slogging through, and with access to water we'll be able to catch fish and bathe. Mason says to save what ammunition remains in case of emergency, and by that he means soldiers or thieves, not rabbits or squirrels. Not *food*. I normally wouldn't disagree but for the weakness in my limbs and the lightness in my head. I've never been so hungry.

It's been a week since we deserted.

That night, we go to sleep miserable and exhausted. "Mason?" My voice is so weak I hardly recognize it.

He grunts from atop the gum blanket, which we've been rotating each night between us, as if a layer of rubber does a lick of good to slow our degenerating bodies.

"We gonna die out here?"

Mason doesn't answer. Archie, back flat against an oak, arms folded across his chest, coughs roughly, and it crosses my mind that he's fallen ill. Brain teeming with worry, I fall asleep.

Some hours later I'm awakened by heavy rain. There's mud in my mouth. An insect crawls past one of my eyelids. I swat it away, sit up, and spit.

I'd been dreaming of a house in the woods.

It had a door the color of honey. Smoke spun skyward from a stone chimney. I smelled biscuits and bacon on the air. When I stepped closer, the door swung inward and a woman stepped onto the porch.

I started to call her name, thinking it my sister…when I woke.

Now that sensory-rich dream sticks in my chest like a bullet, where it plagues me with hate and desire—for all the things I want, and all the things I cannot have.

The three of us huddle beneath a magnolia, barren of flowers. Mason tries to cast the blanket between two low branches, but it does so little as to be almost comical. I'd laugh if I wasn't fighting back tears and fear.

He looks at us with sunken, worried eyes, then shakes his head. "That's it, then."

I don't ask what he means because I already know, and it fills my sore heart with hope.

Finally, we have no choice.

We must seek out civilization.

7

After two more days walking in the rain, and for the first time since we deserted the Confederate Army and began this trek home, Archie and Mason are fighting. Not swinging fists or drawing knives, thank God, but they seem none too pleased with each other.

The rain has slowed, but not stopped. We walk a ways in the dark of predawn, but every ten paces feels like the ten paces before it—same dense trees, same muddy ground—and the general thinking is that we're lost. Without the sun (now almost continuously hidden by the heavy gray clouds), it's difficult to know which direction we're headed. But even with the sun as a guide we're not always certain. The forest is closely packed and increasingly claustrophobic. For miles on end we march beneath an opaque canopy of leaves; the twisted, arched arms of fat oaks reaching out for travelers such as ourselves. In my boredom I fantasize about being grabbed by those branches and torn apart, or sucked into the wide mouth of an old trunk and chomped to bloody ribbons by roughened bark teeth.

Despite my dark fantasies I now rest against one of those oaks, catching my breath and studying my hands while my brothers argue.

Archie wants to make hard west, away from the trace, hoping we'll come to railroad tracks for the Mississippi Central we can follow to a stand or an inn. Mason is resistant to the idea, wanting to continue south (assuming that's the direction we're heading) for the Big Black.

Personally, I'm with Archie. I don't know how much longer I can go without real food, and we've eaten through everything but a palmful of hominy and a moldy chunk of hardtack. Hell, even the tobacco is running low, despite the rain keeping my brothers from even attempting to roll a cigarette.

"If we find the tracks we can head into Coffeeville and steal some supplies," Archie says, his roughened voice barely decipherable amidst the pattering sheet of rainfall.

"We've passed Coffeeville by now," Mason replies, but doesn't sound all that convinced. "Anyway, the railroad is used for nothing but transport of soldiers and supplies. We'd be walking straight into a hangman's noose. If we keep south, we'll hit the river near French Camp. No way we're more than two or three days—"

"We'll be dead in three days," Archie growls.

Mason studies the ground at this thought. He looks insubstantial in the dim predawn, his soaked duster a fat shadow among the brush. I decide to speak up, maybe distract the two of them from each other for a moment. "Are we near anything at all?" I ask, trying not to sound as frightened as I feel. "Do we even know where we are? I mean, really?"

Mason looks at me, pale eyes somehow finding light in the misty gray, shining preternaturally bright. "We ain't lost," he says, then points in a direction that feels random, and I swallow the surge of fear that comes with that thought. "We keep heading south, we hit the river. We follow that ugly brown bastard southwest and we'll be in Vicksburg before you know it. Then we're home free."

Archie scoffs, shakes his head. "You're pointing north."

Mason puffs out his cheeks, turns murderous eyes toward Archie. If those two weren't so thoroughly exhausted it would have come to blows by now. "It's fucking figurative!" he roars, and Archie lifts his hands and backs away, not wanting to push too far. Mason is a dangerous man, and although he loves us with all his heart, he has a temper that can cut like a saw, and murder isn't a thing foreign to him.

After a few tense moments, Mason blows out a breath. "Listen boys, I know what I'm about," he says, then shakes his head. "But I know we're all hungry, and vexed as devils on a Sunday, but our direction is true." He pauses, gives me a sympathetic look, all his rage melted away by the cold rain. "Let's put it to a vote. I say we keep south for the river. Archie says we go west toward the railroad tracks. Ethan, you decide."

I swallow hard, unsure how to respond, or why my older brothers suddenly think me fit to say anything one way or another. Not to mention that the wrong choice could mean death. I start to say I want nothing to do with a decision, but both men are looking at me now, clearly expecting me to act demurely, to settle back into my role as pet instead of equal. Instead, I straighten my spine and consider. "I think," I start, clearing my throat. "I think the rail line has more chance of settlements. We need shelter, food, supplies."

Mason's eyes stay on me, but Archie is nodding.

We're damned, regardless.

"I vote we head west."

Archie points my way, but glares at Mason. "Good to know someone in this family's got a fucking brain in their head."

Mason holds my increasingly sheepish gaze another moment, then nods and looks away. I can almost feel the weight of his disappointment on my shoulders, but I'm frankly too tired to care. I just want to eat. I want a roof and a fire, and a man's got to watch out for himself now and then, even if it means upsetting someone you love.

"West it is," Mason says. He studies his surroundings a moment, as if making sure he has all the pieces of himself we've knocked asunder, then begins walking in what I pray is a westerly direction.

Archie smiles at me, shrugs, and follows.

Turns out Archie and I are right, though not in a way we figured.

While rain continues to fall, we trudge through brush and mud, guessing wildly at direction like a broken compass. After a bit, we circumvent a small lake and find a crop of black tupelo trees. Seeing the berries—despite their being out of season and sour as Cherokee corn soup—brings a small yelp from Archie, who all but runs toward them, pulling wildly at the unripe fruit.

"You're gonna get sick," Mason drawls, as if he doesn't care one way or the other.

Archie sticks a few of the little black-gum beads in his mouth, chews once, makes a face like he'd sucked on a lemon, and spits what remains into the brush. Mason and I laugh, but I'd be lying if I said I'm not tempted to try one, just to taste something other than sweat and rainwater, but eating berries out of season can do more harm than good, even if you're starving like we are. Getting the flux or vomiting our guts out isn't gonna help the situation.

"Damn it," Archie says, grinning like a mad dog, bent teeth littered with berry skin.

We continue on, shoulders slouched, stomachs caving inward, feet blistered, heads itchy, clothes filthier than they'd ever been while serving in the war. Every step feels less like a march toward freedom and more like a trudge toward death.

When we reach the far side of the lake, however, we hear a miracle.

The distinct chug of a train, steaming its way along the Central Rail, likely headed toward Corinth with a bellyful of fresh supplies for the army we'd abandoned. We all stop and stare wide-eyed at each other, as if making sure what we're hearing is real and not a fantasy. Then—moving fast as we can given our sorry state—we scamper our way toward the tracks.

We find them a half-hour later, the train now long gone, nothing but a puff of coal smoke in the distance.

"Hot damn!" Archie exclaims. He points south, and I don't know if I've ever seen my brother more excited. "Straight down these tracks we'll find a settlement, then figure from there," he says, all but jumping out of his boots.

Mason nods and, without a word, starts walking that direction, keeping to one side of the metal rails. "Keep to the edge. We hear another train coming, don't think, just hide," he says, and while it's an obvious command, I think it makes him feel better to regain control, to be in charge once more. As the rain slows to a drizzle Archie and I oblige, more than happy to give up the mantle of responsibility for our fates.

"Sir, yes sir!" Archie rasps, and chuckles as he walks a rail like a tightrope.

About a mile later, we find something different than what we'd hoped for.

An old Choctaw Indian stands in the bushes. He watches us, gripping a gnarled walking stick. Bright blue cloth is wrapped at his torso, a maroon headdress atop his head holds a spill of black hair, and leather leggings lead to dark bare feet. When we stop and stare back at him, the old man simply raises a hand, curls his fingers, and beckons us to follow. Then he disappears into the foliage on the opposite side of the tracks like a specter, as if he'd never been there at all.

Without a word or pause for discussion, Mason strides across the tracks and heads for the point in the heavy brush where the man had vanished. Archie and I exchange a look.

It seems we've indeed discovered something that may save our lives.

Not a settlement, but a tribe.

8

We spend the morning with a group of traveling Choctaw. We're happy for the respite from walking and over the damned moon for some actual food, meager as it is. Regardless, it's enough to abate the sharp pains in my belly and give me a charge of renewed energy and some welcome clear-headedness.

We're further south than we'd thought; information Mason allows himself to repeat ad nauseum in his gruff *I told you so* manner. According to the woman who handed us wooden bowls partially filled with steaming black beans, the town of Carrollton is less than a day's march. We're so close that Archie mumbles through mouthfuls how he's surprised we didn't come across a group of Gandy Dancers aligning the rails.

The Choctaw camp is sparse, less than a dozen of them in the group, but there's a lean-to we can sit under, the ground beneath blessedly dry, and after days of nothing we're eating the most delicious beans I've ever had. Through common words and hand gestures we come to understand that the Choctaw are also making their way west. Most of the women in the group wear traditional dresses of their heritage, while most of the men are dressed in button shirts and trousers, boots, and wide-brimmed hats. One older man wears a top hat and a bright red coat that gives him the air of a chief.

Generally speaking, the Choctaw have been scattered widely since well before the war. Some of the women married white men and now operate inns or stands along the trace, or in towns along the Mississippi River. Over the last few decades, most of the tribes have been forced off their land by Jefferson and moved west, across the river and into Oklahoma. The ones who remain are proud and resourceful. They know how to barter and hunt, how to work the land and raise livestock better than most.

The small band we've come across are indifferent to us now that they realize we have little to offer. Other than a curious little girl, none of them give us the time of day, seemingly occupied with moving on. Before we've finished our meager meals, half the group have gathered their things and walked ahead.

Mason hands over half the coins from the bandit's purse to a young man in a wool suit and dusty bowler hat. He wears a wide leather gun belt, complete with a well-cared-for revolver, and accepts the coins with a nod. A young woman, one with a serious disposition, speaks to us in fragmented English about the distance to Carrollton. She warns us with impressive insight that many soldiers—and, even worse, members of the Home Guard—often travel the railroad and gather at depots along the way. We nod our thanks to her.

As I run my finger across the bottom of my bowl, sticking whatever dark juice I find into my mouth, Archie whispers into my ear. "Where's the one that brung us?"

I lower the bowl and look around the makeshift camp, note those still packing their things. A few of the faces stare back at us, their solemn expressions unreadable, but I don't see the old man with the blue shirt and red headdress. I shrug. "Probably moved on with the others."

"He's been gone since we arrived," Archie hisses, and I note Mason giving us a hard look, brow furrowed.

Before we can discuss it further there are voices from the nearby trees, and the old man in question appears. He glances at us, then talks animatedly to those remaining, who hurriedly begin to pick up their babies, baskets, and blankets, their meager supplies. I look at the young girl, who suddenly looks unsure of herself.

She rises from her knees and starts to turn away, but I grab her thin arm, twist it until she looks at me. "What's he saying?"

She pulls her arm free and runs. The man in the bowler—the one who took our money—steps forward and puts a hand on the grip of his revolver, but doesn't pull it free. The six or seven Indians left in camp, mostly women, have finished packing their things and begin, one by one, to disappear into the surrounding trees. Cussing, Mason tosses his bowl and crawls from under the lean-to, me and Archie on his heels.

"What is it?" Mason says to the man with the revolver, who now holds the hand of the little girl, most likely his daughter. I figure one of the others was his wife—just a family trying to get by without a home, with no one to protect them but themselves.

He says something to his daughter, gestures toward us. The girl nods.

They are the only ones who remain. They look at us with pity.

"Men are coming," she says. "You should run."

Then she and her father turn away and vanish into the heavy brush.

9

I can't say I blame him.

Given the state of things with his family, it didn't appear they were doing a whole lot better than we were, and while I have no idea what kind of money the Home Guard is offering for deserters, it's probably a hell of a lot more than the measly coins we handed over for a bowl of beans. I imagine the old timer knew what he was looking at the second he spotted our withered carcasses walking those tracks. Hell, for all I know he was camped by those tracks for a reason, trying to raise some money to get his people where they need to go, and here we come along like fat rabbits, munching on a carrot surrounded by a wire snare.

I like to think the little girl tried to warn us, but I mistook the urgency in her eyes for nerves. Then that man with the bowler, holding her hand, the other resting twitchy on the butt of his gun, telling her what was coming, giving her a chance to clear her conscience, perhaps. Maybe it doesn't sit well on their people, turning army men over for court-martial or, more likely, a firing squad, but like I said: I can't blame them. A man's got to take care of his own. Morality doesn't feed children or buy clothes. Our government has taken everything from their people and they've got to take back what they can, when they can. I doubt the old man will have trouble sleeping at night, and a small part of me wishes them well.

The rest of me slings curses at their backs. Because we are surely dead men.

After the girl suggested we flee, my brothers and I took it literally; grabbed our guns and packs, and ran the one direction we knew to be safe. West.

Away from the tracks.

We run fifty yards through heavy brush and careless forest before we break into a meadow, where we stop and gather our breath.

As one, we look back at the wall of trees, a tangle of leafy green painted in sun-dabbled shadow. I see no pursuit, no Home Guard in their faux Confederate uniforms, carrying rifles and metal cuffs. "Let's keep moving," Mason says, Colt gripped in one hand. I debate unslinging my rifle and packing it, but we're nearly out of ammunition. Besides, as I study the tree line, I see no pursuers to shoot.

"That old man sold us out," Archie says, breathing heavy.

"Yeah." Mason spits, eyes the shadows. "Bad luck."

"I don't see nothing—" I say, scanning the heavy foliage. "Wait."

I spot movement within the waist-high brush, about ten yards into the trees. I squint, wondering if it's man or beast, when I hear the familiar *crack* of a rifle, clock a puff of smoke.

Archie grunts and falls backward. Mason raises his revolver, aims at the dissipating smoke, and fires three shots. A man screams from his hiding place, another yells out a name. Terrified, I turn to see Archie lying on the ground, one hand on his gut, the other reaching toward Mason. "Get me the fuck up!"

Mason yanks Archie to his feet then looks at me, wild-eyed.

"Run, goddammit!"

I turn and sprint across the damnable open meadow toward more broad forest just ahead. If we can make it to those far trees, we have a chance.

A loud shout comes from behind us and I don't need to look back to know men are in pursuit. A rifle shot cracks the air and I wait for a punch of pain to crash into my spine, my leg, or my head—my mind enveloped in a bright white flash as a bullet blows my skull into pieces. But I feel nothing, so I keep running.

An eternity later we hit the trees. The sunlight melts to shadow and I duck beneath a thick branch, tuck behind the rough trunk of an oak and look back toward the meadow.

Mason and Archie, running for their lives, are just a few feet from the tree line, and Archie's moving well enough that I begin to hope he's not too badly injured. Across the meadow a half-dozen men are coming hell-bent toward us, and I don't hesitate—now that I know my brothers are behind me—to keep going.

The forest here is quiet and dark—my heavy breaths, stomping feet, and thumping heart are the only sounds I hear as I twist beneath branches and jump over a cluster of red buckeye. I run through shadows until the trees spread themselves. The sun bleaches the sky overhead and suddenly I'm in a brilliant green world that feels like a patch of Heaven, one I would stop and rest in were I not weeping tears of panic and terror, praying to God for escape from these earthbound demons on our heels. I come to a slope and climb, not caring about the twine-like shrub branches ripping at my hands, clutching at me with ferocious hunger. I crest the rise, panting. Before me is a fallen, rotting cypress. I leap atop it, clamber over, and am shocked when my boots hit cold water. My chest burns with exertion, my stomach a hard knot of pain.

I turn and see overflow from a nearby river filling the land for a hundred yards in every direction. "Shit," I mutter, then look back over the top of the dead tree, wait for my brothers to appear. Beneath my splayed hands, pine beetles scramble for cover among trenches of bark, and a small part of me thinks to eat one. There's a ruckus in the brush and I spot Mason and Archie loping over the ridge.

"Here!" I yell, and wave a hand. "It's flooded."

Mason climbs over the fallen trunk with a grunt, Archie right behind. I note the patch of blood on the shirt beneath his suit coat.

"You alright?" I ask as he plops into the water next to me.

"Fucker ruined my new coat," he mutters, and storms into the resting water without a thought. Mason grips my arm so hard I wince.

"Go with him. Get him through this shit then keep going straight."

He sets the revolver on the tree, unslings his Springfield and begins digging into his cartridge box for whatever's left of powder and ball. He glances at me wide-eyed, as if stunned at my existence. "Are you deaf, Ethan? Go!"

I nod and plow through the cold, shallow water until I catch up with Archie. I'm knee deep in the overflow and my boots are sucking into the mud, but not enough to pull them from my legs.

I grip Archie's bicep and he seems grateful; his breathing is harsh and irregular, his face pale and sharp, as if all the blood in his body has already leaked out of him through that wound, leaving nothing but bones and flesh.

We're almost to dry land—and I'm practically carrying my brother now—when I hear gunshots. A man cries out in pain, then screams cusses and prayers. "He's killed me!" the bastard yells, and all I can think as I pull my boot from the water is: *Good. I hope you burn in Hell.*

I continue pressing forward, but Archie feels more and more like dead weight with each progressive step. I put his arm around my neck, mine around his waist, and pull him out of the water and into the trees. His fingers dig into my shoulder like claws, as if holding on for dear life. We hit a ditch hidden by detritus and tumble down into mud, my brother screaming in pain as we land in a heap of limbs and guns and stolen clothes.

"Stay here a minute," I pant, and crawl up the side of the ditch to scan the surroundings. I hear voices, so I do what I should have done at the get-go and shrug off my rifle, trained fingers automatically digging into my cartridge box for ammo. I feel around and count three bullets. I pack the rifle with powder, place a cap, and load one. Then I lay flat and aim at the bushes beyond the overflow.

After a few minutes straining for targets, I spot Mason high-legging it through the water like his britches are on fire. I lower the gun and lift a hand. He spots me, makes it through the last of the overflow, and climbs into the ditch beside me. His duster and pants are soaked and I figure that wet coat must weigh a hundred pounds. He's sweating profusely, but still holds a gun in each hand.

"I bought us some time, but we have to keep going," he says, panting for breath. "I got two of 'em. Maybe three. I dunno…but they'll keep coming. Whoever's left." He rams his revolver into the saturated holster, slings the rifle over a shoulder. "It's personal now, with them."

"What about Arch?" I turn to where I'd left him, sprawled at the bottom of the ditch, and am surprised to see him standing upright, one red-snaked hand clutching his bleeding gut.

"I'm fine, but I lost my damn rifle," he says, and spits. "Let's get on."

Mason nods, climbs up the opposite side of the trench, and we follow him through this new, unknown land toward the blood-red sun of late afternoon, as if that ball of fire has been our destination all along and we just need to reach it without dying and all will be well.

10

When night finally falls we collapse to the dirt, not bothering to roll out the gum blanket or even tuck a coat beneath our heads. Archie leans back against a fat hickory, his breathing steady and shallow, his face ghostly in a shimmer of moonlight.

I think Archie is going to die, Ellie. I think that ball is swirling around his guts right now, tearing him up inside, turning his blood to poison and there's not a damned thing we can do about it. If you were here, you'd fuss and go to your garden for herbs, break out the mortar and pestle that used to be our mother's and create some remedy that would fix him, that would cure him. That would save him. Is this why we ran, Ellie? I thought we were avenging angels but we're not. No. We're the hunted. We're the scourge to be vanquished; we are the flames that need dousing—judgment for the things we've done, for the criminality of our collective cowardice. We took the wide gate, the broad path, and we are destroyed.

"I'll keep watch," Mason grunts, sliding the rifle off his shoulder to hold it in both hands. "Sleep for a few hours, Ethan, then we'll switch."

"Okay," I say, and am swallowed by darkness before I hear his reply.

When Mason wakes me it's full night and the air is cool, the forest surrounding us placid, seemingly free of menace and foul men. "All clear," he grumbles. "Wake me at first light."

I sit up, turn to look at Archie. The gum blanket is draped over his legs and he's still breathing. At some point, after I fell into sleep,

Mason tied a strip of dirty cloth around Archie's middle and now the blood there doesn't flow so fierce. Or at least not as evident.

Mason follows my gaze, pats me on the shoulder. "He'll be okay. He's the meanest man I ever met. Your rifle loaded?"

I nod. He points in a direction I assume is easterly. "Keep an eye there. They might try to sneak up on us, cut our throats while we sleep, bounty or no bounty."

"I will," I say, and push myself to my feet. "Get some rest."

I find a nearby tree I can hide behind, hold my rifle at the ready, scan the nearby wood—darkened as it is—for movement. I won't sit. If I can help it, I won't even lean on the tree for support. I don't trust myself not to doze off, dog-tired as I am.

It won't be because of me that my family is murdered. It won't be because of me.

No men come for us in the night.

After hours of standing in the cold dark, my feet and hands have turned numb, the muscles in my legs knotted and aching.

Finally, the new day creeps in.

The only hint of dawn is a lightening in the air around us, the sunlight draping the leaves, sliding from black to green. The dirt at my feet gains texture, the sprigs of wild grass take shape. I think about the sun rising over the Mississippi River—that stunning horizon of burnt orange rubbing against a sky so blue and bright and clear it's like a painting. I imagine a rippling of scattered peach clouds, spectators to the event, the whole tableaux an artist's rendition of impossible beauty.

I step over to Mason and shake him gently. He stirs and wakes. "Anything?"

I shake my head. "Sun's up."

It's harder to wake Archie, who is white as cotton. At first, I mistake him for dead. In my panic I shake him harder than necessary and he jerks awake, wincing in pain. "Damn you, Ethan," he mumbles, and I apologize, but am relieved he's still breathing. Mason lifts a flap of the bandit's coat and studies the wound, which looks the same as yesterday.

"Can you walk?"

"One way to find out," he says, raising a hand. "Help me the fuck up."

We get him to his feet and he leans a hand against the tree, sucking deep breaths. He complains some, then announces he has to piss and staggers off. I consider offering to help but decide against it, partially due to not wanting to hurt Archie's pride, partially to my own embarrassment. Besides, no man wants to be helped relieving himself—if we can't do that on our own, well hell, we can't do nothing at all.

There's a meager debate about building a fire for coffee, but we're all too worried about the Home Guard catching up to us, so we strike camp—such as it is—and continue west.

At this point I'm not sure Mason even knows the right path.

"I think we've gone too far west to try for the Big Black. If we head south we'll run into more cities and, most likely, more trouble. We stay west and it's a lot of wilderness. We can try to find a boat and float down the Yazoo, or we cross it and find ourselves dealing with a lot of swampland before we hit the Mississippi. Not to mention we're being hunted, and seeing as how I killed at least two of those boys, they're not apt to let up anytime soon."

We decide to try our luck westward, then make further decisions on our course once we reach the Yazoo. Luckily, we can all swim and crossing the river shouldn't be a concern, but with Archie's wound nothing is certain. Hungry and stressed, bone-weary, we continue our trek, secretly hoping for a miracle. Or barring that, some good goddamn luck.

The only thing we have going for us is the land. While it's wet and sticky with spring mud in most places—and the trees are thick and the brush can clutch at your boots—the terrain itself is flat as a dinner table far as the eye can see, which makes for easy walking so long as you don't mind bugs landing on your face or the occasional thorn of a honey locust stabbing your shoulder like a Union dagger.

When morning breaks full, the clouds drop through the trees and settle over the ground. A wet, chill wind creeps through the woods like the last plague of Moses, a malevolent thing seeking to stop the hearts of first-borns. After another hour, the mist thickens and the cold settles on me like a second skin. Archie has been reduced to an awkward shuffle and it's the sound of his movements I follow—a shifting, uneven disruption of leaves and brush that sound more animal than human—rather than the actual sight of him, given that he's vanished into the surrounding fog along with Mason; along with any sense of direction we might have once had.

"You back there, boy?" Mason barks from ahead, and I smile knowing someone in this world cares about me.

"Yes," I say. "Archie's making so much noise a blind man could stay in line."

Archie coughs a laugh, then mumbles a curse in my direction.

Slide-step, slide-step, slide-step.

I keep my eyes cast downward, watching for upturned roots or ankle-twisting pits in the earth. I've rarely been in cover this dense and it slowly begins to unnerve me. As my unease grows, the trees don't seem to be trees at all anymore, but the ghosts of men lost in the war, dark shadows closing in around us with clawed, reaching arms.

And then—from one moment to the next—the dream becomes a nightmare. The trees move with us, inching closer. I slow my step, stare wide-eyed at the shadows taking form in the mist, and realize how very stupid we've been.

"Guards!" I scream, and then they're on us.

II

I spin inside a cloud. A man rushes toward me.

Were this one year ago and I no more than a skinny 16-year-old kid, working as a delivery boy for his father's tobacco shop, I would have yelped in terror and run away from the red-faced, grown man lunging at me, teeth bared, knife raised in one fist.

But I am not that boy. I've been in battle. I've been to war. I've killed men and seen men killed. I've buried soldiers who, an hour previous, I'd sat with by a fire and talked of everyday things. I held a man's arms, screaming and bucking, as a surgeon sawed through the bone of his thigh, then pushed the dead meat off the table like a rotten cut from a butcher's block.

Still, I am afraid. For myself, for my brothers.

Ellie, I'm coming home.

I lower the point of my rifle, still loaded from the night's watch, and fire into the man's chest. His legs come up from under him as his upper body snaps backward like a dog who'd run out of leash. I drop my rifle to the ground, slip the bayonet from my boot, and crouch so as not to be an easy target. In front of me I hear screams and sounds of struggle. Two shots bark in the morning air and I pray it's the sound of Mason's Colt, or perhaps the Remington he'd taken off the bandit. If he gave the revolver to Archie for safekeeping, I don't recall the transaction.

Still in a crouch, I hobble forward, bayonet poised. I come upon four men. Archie on his back, hands gripping the wrists of a Home Guard soldier who straddles him, pushing a knife toward his throat. Another member of the guard lies prone in the dirt, facedown and still.

I crawl toward Archie and—quick as death—drive the bayonet into the side of the attacker's neck, then yank it free. Blood shoots like a geyser and the fight flows out of him just as fast. I shove the body off my brother, put my hands on Archie's chest.

"You okay?"

He nods and his eyes shift to his left. "Help Mason," he says, and pushes the Remington into my hands. I guess he'd been given it after all.

I take aim, not at the man wrestling on the ground with my oldest brother, but at the boy standing at the edge of the arena, his rifle aimed at the tumbling, grunting pile of limbs and gnashing teeth. I hesitate only a moment, taken off guard by his youth. Perhaps that's me standing there, sixteen and green as fresh hay.

"Boy!" I yell.

He turns his rifle toward me, his face a mask of fear.

I fire the Remington into his chest and he stumbles back, drops the rifle, and writhes like a newborn calf in the dirt.

The man tangled with Mason looks at me as if he's the one who caught the bullet, all shock and despair. "No!" he screams. He leaves my brother to scramble toward the boy. He crawls atop him, covers the young man's face with his hands and wails. "Jeremy! No, not my boy!" he wails, calling out to God above as his son goes still beneath him.

Mason pulls the Colt free from his belt, gets to his feet, and steps casually toward the crying man. He puts the gun to the back of his head. I wait for the crack, the puff of smoke, the spray of blood.

"How many more out there?" he asks, calm and steady.

The man raises his hands, now bathed in blood and surrender. He doesn't move from his knees. "Just us. But there's more coming," he says, talking hurriedly. "One of the men you killed, he's from a rich family, the father owns three plantations all through the Delta. They're already forming a troop to hunt you down. Me and these men, and my boy here, we've been tracking you since the Indian gave you up outside Carrollton."

The man turns his head slowly, arms still raised, palms stretched. He looks at me with a hate I'll never forget. Then he looks at Archie and shows a feverish grin, tightened by grief. "Your friend is wounded. Y'all are easier to track than a six-legged bull."

"That ain't my friend," Mason says, his tone iron. "That's my brother."

"And he'll be dead soon." The man's hair is wild and strewn with twigs and leaves. His grin stretches wider. He tilts his eyes up to Mason, eyes the barrel of the Colt like it's a long-lost friend. Mason lets him get to his feet and they face each other like the last two men on earth. "You'll *all* be dead soon. There's a dozen men coming to claim a bounty on your heads. A sack of gold Eagles for each of ya. Dead or alive." He giggles, like it's all a grand joke, and I figure his mind has broken. "No court-martial for you three. You're dead men. You've got nowhere to run, nowhere to—"

Mason fires the Colt into the man's mouth. I clock the bullet leave the back of his neck and punch into a nearby tree. He falls to his side, clutching his face, gagging and choking. Mason tucks the gun into his belt, walks over to Archie and helps him to his feet. I hand him the Remington and he nods, tucks it away.

After a few minutes, the man finally dies lying next to his son, whose glassy eyes stare at the heavens. Mason knocks the dirt off his hat, crams it onto his head. "They're coming and we gotta move." He gives Archie a pained glare, then shakes his head.

As if knowing how futile it all is.

12

We evade the guard for two days and two nights, taking only snatches of sleep—never more than an hour—so that one of us is always awake to keep watch.

Within hours of leaving behind the men we killed, the rain started up again, as if punishing us, its arrival both a blessing and a curse—it covers our tracks from those hunting us, but makes our travels such a misery I can hardly comprehend its equal.

Archie slows us to a death march. The fact he's still standing—with a bullet in his side and a steady leak of blood—is a testament to his stubbornness and willpower. But the body has its own say in such things and it's obvious that his is breaking down. I don't think he'll live much longer if we keep going this way, but if the guard catches us we'll die for sure. The choices are so grim that, for the first time since leaving Shiloh, I long for the battlefield.

Things come to a head at the soft edges of swampland so vast it may as well be an ocean, given how spent we are. The idea of circumnavigating the swamp seems impossible. We'd have a better chance of taking to the air and flying across it.

In other words, we are trapped.

"We'll have to go through," Mason says, stating the obvious.

I stare at the vast acreage of dull water before us and groan.

The rain-dimpled surface is a mossy, mangy carpet of green, broken in places by jagged stumps, tree root protrusions, and the occasional toppled trunk—all convenient resting spots for reptiles, bugs, and gators. Towers of bald cypress are staggered drunkenly throughout—their wide bases sunken, long trunks stretched skyward a hundred feet or more, reaching toward the clouds like sentinels—daring us to try and pass.

I turn from the swamp to study my brothers. Since we've been on the run, we've all lost a small part of who we are; some elemental piece I can't define. As bad as things were in the army, we still appeared as a version of ourselves. Haggard and tired, but recognizable. But now, as I look at them, I realize they've become strangers.

Mason, in his duster, uncropped beard and sallow cheeks, is a poor reflection of the boy I idolized growing up, the man I knew in recent years. His piercing blue eyes are wild, the spirit behind them, once cunning and stalwart, now broken and searching. There's madness there that paralyzes me with doubt, if not outright fear.

As for Archie, he's no more than a walking corpse. It hurts me to think such a thing, but these are the words that come to mind when I look at him: *that's a dead man*. His skin, always pale, has become nearly translucent. His vicious black eyes are now watery and sunken, dark smudges inside deep sockets like smears of coal dust. One hand never leaves the wound, and I know he's trying his best not to bleed out. He can't stand straight anymore, but instead hunches like a crone, pushing his body past the point of its endurance.

And now, when Mason looks at me—for some form of agreement, or assurance, I suspect—I wonder who he sees standing before him. Who have I become? What pain-forged creature am I? A scraggly, bone-thin child wearing a dead man's clothes. A walking scarecrow wearing the stretched face of his long-lost brother.

"Can Archie make it?" I shrink back when Archie's head jerks up, those dark eyes boring into me with an anger so acute it feels like physical pain.

"I speak for me!" he roars, his gravel voice, amplified by anger, sounds like a boulder being ground to shards in God's fist.

Mason gives Archie a long look, and I know he's judging for himself whether our injured sibling can make the crossing. Besides the water, which runs deep due to the heavy rainfall, there are alligators, snakes, and other vermin we'll need to be watchful of if we want to make it across alive. The other danger, as with any swamp, is the softness of the ground beneath. The mud could eat a man whole.

Of course, if we make it, the odds of being hunted down dwindles to almost nothing, and our numerous threats of death will be narrowed to only one possibility.

The swamp.

It is a strange thing to take comfort in.

One by one we wade into the cold water, keeping in a line close enough that we can assist the other if we get stuck, or attacked by some predator beneath the surface. As the water rises to my chest and my boots sink into the muck hidden below, I say a prayer that this is as deep and treacherous as it will get. While praying, I reach out and clench the tail of Archie's coat beneath the water, find reassurance in being tethered to something other than God's will.

"I'm sorry if I offended you, Arch," I say to the back of his head.

There's a momentary pause, then he turns slightly. "Shut up, Ethan."

I smile at the rebuke, feeling forgiven, and grip his coat tight.

As we push through the thick layer of algae resting atop the water, tiny bugs jump and skitter onto my shoulders, neck, and face. I fight the urge to slap at a buzzing in my ear, the tickling in my nose as something climbs inside. Deep as we are there's no way to salvage what's left of our ammunition and provisions. The guns and rifles will need to be cleaned, dried, and oiled before they'll be of use again. Once we clear the water, we'll be helpless to kill anything that requires more than the edge of a blade, or the point of the bayonet in my boot. I can't help but wonder how we'll possibly survive going forward.

Halfway through, we steer toward a rise of earth cresting above the waterline surrounding the buttressed base of a bald cypress. The Spanish moss clinging to its arms is a dull gray instead of the vibrant green I've seen in summertime, as if this whole swamp is something from the afterlife, a purgatorial stopping place between this world and the next. It reeks of death.

"Let's stop a minute," Mason says. "My legs are rubber."

We weave between jagged cypress knees to reach a mound of

mud and have a rest; our bodies submerged from the chest down. I dig my fingers into the mud and shift my legs beneath the water until I find a sturdy root to set my boots on, relieved at having something solid beneath my feet, even temporarily.

"I've lost a damn shoe," Archie mumbles, his face bowed so low the tip of his nose grazes the gray water.

I try not to think what the water is doing to his open wound. I learned early the dangers of ingesting algae from a swamp. When nine years old, I went hunting with our father through a similar swamp outside Natchez. He'd beaten me to the ground when I dipped a finger into bright green water and sucked it clean. Screamed at me about poison entering my blood and stopping my heart. I don't know if what he said was true, but I know some of it is close to the mark based on what I'd seen happen to men in the war, and I bet that bullet hole in Archie's flesh is getting its fill of whatever diseases live in the swamp, turning it foul.

As we catch our breath, I take the moment of respite to scan the surrounding swamp. On the surface, a few feet away, I spot something long and black, it squiggles an 'S' through the algae and I pray it's just a water snake and not a cottonmouth; be it chance or fate, I've yet to see the cresting arrow of an alligator's head, but with the rain it'd be hard to see. I can only hope.

After a few minutes Mason shoves off. Silently, we follow, and I make sure to keep Archie in front of me in case he falters. The idea of him sliding into the water, his lifeless body settling into the rotten earth below, is too much for me to bear. I'll carry him if need be, or drag him to land. Alive or dead, I won't leave his body to feed the swamp, despite his philosophy on such things.

Pushing forward, we find a little luck. The land begins to rise.

The water lowers to my belly, then hips. I feel a tingle of hope we might yet get through this. After another twenty steps the surface algae is at my thighs, and up ahead the water skirts a shoreline of dark mud. Beyond that is hard land, then forest. Mason looks back at us, the beginnings of a smile on his lips. "Almost through."

I nod but keep my attention on Archie. Despite the lowering water level—now at my ankles—the walking grows more difficult, the muck sucking down my entire foot with each step. When my leg sinks to the knee, I grow worried.

"Soft bottom," I say, trying to keep my voice steady.

"Damn it," Mason yells, then twists around. "Hold there," he says, and Archie and I stop walking, cold mud pressing at our legs.

I lean around Archie to get a clear look at Mason, who stands a few feet ahead.

He's hip deep in mud.

And sinking.

"Mason?"

When he turns to us again, there's something in his eyes so foreign that at first I don't recognize it—something worse than uncertainty, than panic.

Fear.

"I...I, uh—" he mutters, shifting around as if trying to find a foothold, or a handhold. But there are no trees nearby, no roots or cypress knees to grab onto. The rain picks up again and the swamp vibrates with drops of water, as if it's something come alive.

"Stop moving around, goddammit," Archie yells, then takes a step backward, away from the pool of quicksand Mason has waded into. He turns to face me, and I fight the horror of how corpse-like he appears, how skeletal. "Ethan, you can move better than me. Go find a loose branch. We gotta pull him out of there."

"Right," I say, and scan our surroundings. There are no obvious answers. No floating poles or coils of rope. I shrug the rifle off my shoulder, realize it's not nearly long enough, and wade back into the deeper water, then parallel to the shore, study the areas near the cypress trees, hoping for some luck.

I'm about ten feet out when I see a stick jabbing clear of the water. I make my way to it, grab its slick hide. In my haste I let go my rifle, which sinks into the brown water, and get two hands on the long, crooked stick. I leverage it forward—its base pressed against a rock or log beneath the surface—and push, straining, until a vibration near my feet tells me the branch has broken clean of the root down below. I pull it free to study it. It's longer than my rifle, but not by much. I hold it aloft.

"How's this?" I yell, then gasp in horror.

Mason is sunk to his armpits.

"Oh, shit," I mumble, and begin wading back toward my brothers.

I push shoreward, beyond the point where Mason's head and arms protrude from the mud like a bobbing apple in a barrel of scum. Mason stares at me with a kind of childish wonder, as if surprised at how dangerous the whole damned world turned out to be.

I come at him from the side opposite Archie, where the mud is slippery but firm, and hold the stick toward him. I inch my boots forward; the muck grows softer, the water rises back up to my knees, and I am wary not to become trapped. Archie, meanwhile, is circumventing the hidden pit, wisely following the path he'd seen me take moments ago.

"Can you reach?" I say, straining to get the branch—no longer than a few feet in length—near my brother's hands, which now lay flat along the surface.

Mason shakes his head. Mud touches his lips. "I'm going under," he says.

"No you ain't," I snap, and shuffle another foot forward, lifting and dropping the stick. It's close now.

The water's at my waist when I feel a tug at the back of my belt, and I know it's Archie holding onto me with whatever's left of his strength. "Go on, I got you," he says softly, and I let myself sink to the knees, praying my legs don't continue downward.

"Grab it, you ass!" I yell, and Mason sets his mouth in a hard line.

I figure he's got one good lunge and then he'll slip away forever. He hollers and throws his arms forward. The lower half of his face disappears as fingertips fumble at the mossy branch. I can only see his eyes and realize he must be holding his breath as his hands scramble like spiders for a grip.

Suddenly, they clench tight, and hold.

"Okay, real slow." I begin to pull. "Archie, take me back."

With surprising strength, Archie pulls at my belt. I lift one boot free of the sucking earth and walk it backward. Mason continues to hang on. I take another step back and then his face is free. Another step, and his shoulders emerge. He blows mud off his lips, sucks in a gulp of air.

"I got you," I say, and continue pulling.

We continue in this way for what feels like hours, but inch by inch we yank my brother clear. He doesn't so much climb out of the muck as slide from it like a newborn baby. When he reaches the point where I'd initially been standing, he lets go the stick, shakes out his arms, and takes a big step forward. I let the stick drop and float away, panting with the effort of getting him free.

All of us on firm enough ground, Mason removes the duster and sinks it in the knee-deep water. "Too heavy," he says, washing the mud free. Archie and I stand patiently on the shoreline, waiting 'til he's good and ready.

I ignore the soft whimpering he makes as he washes the coat, the deep, ragged breaths as he scoops water to wipe mud from his beard and face.

When he finally walks over to us, face dripping with swamp water and tears, he wraps his big, sodden arms around our necks and the three of us stand for a minute, heads together, drenched and tired beyond measure, but somehow alive. Still alive.

13

I don't know how long I sleep but when I wake up its dark, and my brothers are still out cold. I stand up slowly, muscles achy and stiff, and walk off to a tree to relieve myself. The night is filled by the burps of frogs and chatter of insects who inhabit the swamp. Looking at the spot where we finally collapsed—only a few yards from the waterline—I consider us fortunate that an alligator didn't stalk out of the shallows, clamp down on an ankle and drag one of us, screaming, back into the cold water.

I don't want to wake the others, not yet. I check on Archie to make sure he's breathing, which he is, and say a prayer of thanks. Mason's duster is strewn on the dirt like a shed skin. I pick it up, notice it's relatively dry, and lay it over Archie.

No longer tired enough to rest, despite the weariness that comes from not having eaten a proper meal in two weeks, I decide to wander a bit, see if I can find some kindling and tinder to start a fire. Mason lost both his guns in the mud, along with his pack, cartridge box, and boots, which leaves us without weapons. Maybe we can figure a way to snare a rabbit, though I doubt many inhabit the woods this close to the fetid water. Too many predators.

I stare into the night sky. The trees are spread thin here at the fringe of the forest, their crooked branches still bare of leaves after the long winter. The sky is densely laden with stars, and the moon is so full and bright it looks too heavy for the plum-colored canopy, as if it might tear free from the strings which hold it and tumble down onto earth, break apart in giant chunks of curdled green cheese.

My mouth waters viciously at the thought of food, and I turn my focus away from the sky to study the ground, start to search for anything dry; anything that will burn.

I put some distance between me and my sleeping brothers, but

I'm not worried. I can smell the rank water of the swamp, and the moon is bright enough that the path back is clear.

Here, in the dark, I think of you, Ellie. I wonder how you're doing at home with Father. If you're still knitting socks for soldiers. Still reading by the fireplace in the evenings. If I close my eyes, I can almost picture you, happy and healthy, worried about me, about Mason and Archie. Don't fret, sister, we'll be home soon. Although I admit we are quite lost. And hungry, and tired. Our minds aren't sharp, and Archie...well, Archie needs help. A surgeon to take out that bullet. To give him medicine and sew his wound. He needs a bed, and food, and clean water. We all do. I miss you more when I think on all the things I don't have, all the things I so desperately need. Since being chased, we've been driven like cattle to an unfamiliar land. Have we moved north, or west? Are we closer to the great river, or farther away than ever? Is this the furthest point from home, Ellie? Have I found myself on the very edge of the world? If I have, don't let me fall. Bring me home, sister. Show me—

I stop...and listen. From up ahead I hear the soft burble of a creek. I hold still for a moment, pinpointing its direction before walking excitedly forward, desperate for clean water to drink, eager to wash the mud and scum from my clothes and body. After a couple minutes I come to a wall of buckthorn tall as a house. The creek gurgles on the other side and I scan for an opening, but in the dark it's near impossible. Finally, the temptation is too great. Instead of searching for a gap I throw myself into the brush, tear through tangles of branches dense as honeysuckle with my bare hands until I push through.

And there, no more than twenty feet away, is the creek.

I laugh at the sight of it, at the way the water sparkles with moonlight. It's wide but appears shallow. I notice crags of wood jutting from the surface to split the gurgling water. I take a few steps closer, already feeling that cold water on my skin, in my mouth.

And then I stop.

Across the creek—standing casually in the short grass, one hand resting against the bark-crusted hip of a white-haired peach tree—is a child. A small boy. He appears to be nine, or possibly ten, years of age. There's a little forage cap on his head, and he's wrapped in a blue coat that goes to his knees, closed tight down the front with large brass buttons, beneath which he wears white britches and black boots.

He's just...standing there. Staring at me.

I'm so confused by his appearance that I find myself staring numbly back, my feet temporarily unable to carry me one way or another. I have no weapon, my clothes are rags, and I'm filthy from top to bottom. I try to see myself as he must see me—a strange creature from the woods. Something feral, likely dangerous.

But he doesn't seem frightened, or nervous. He seems...curious.

And then he does the oddest thing I could have possibly imagined.

He waves at me.

14

ELLIE

I'm no damn coward.

But here I sit by the fire, sewing the knee of my father's trousers, listening to two old men bicker about the war and God and money. Ten pounds of horseshit, if you ask me. Meanwhile, Ethan and the other two are off getting shot at, likely dying. And in my heart, I know I should be there with them. A woman can shoot a damn rifle good as any man; my mother saw to that for me, anyway. Taught me how to hunt, and skin game, and prepare a meal from what I'd carried in. The boys liked to laugh about it, seeing me bloody and tussled. They stopped laughing when they smelled my stew, though. Yes, they surely did.

Listening to my father and the priest—old Father McKee, our long-time reverend in these parts—talk about action while they sit around a table drinking wine is one of the most pig-ass backwards things I could just about imagine. I swear, if I have to hear—

"Ellie? You almost done there? The reverend would like some supper, and I wouldn't mind it, neither."

"Yes, Daddy."

There's hardly enough to go around with the soldiers taking all our provisions for the war, and now I got to feed the pastor? I hope those men like biscuits and gravy, because that and beans is all we have until Father goes to the market and the butcher. Luckily for us, tobacco is the one thing folks still spend money on, even during a war, so we're doing better than most. But Father is stingy, perhaps rightly so…who knows how long this cursed squabble will continue. Better to save up. Of course, if the Yankees sweep south, we could end up in the street, watching our home burn. Or worse, if what I hear those Yankee soldiers do to innocent women is true. God help us if it is.

I put down the trousers and head for the kitchen to start supper. I feel Father McKee watching me so I give him a smile. He's an uncle, of sorts, and was friendly with Mother before she passed, so he must be a good man if she let him into our home. Although, I've heard stories about his past. Dark things he was part of before coming to Natchez.

"You look more like your mother every day," he says. "And I think you have her intellect, as well. She was quite the reader, your mother."

"Thank you, Father," I say to the priest, and feel the warmth of pride in my chest hearing such things about Mother, who I loved with my whole heart. She's not talked about much in this home, not by my brothers, and not by my daddy, who acts as if all us kids showed up at his door one evening and moved in; an inconvenience he couldn't drive away.

After serving the two men, I sit to join them for supper. Hoping to get off the subject of the war, I try to pick up the topic of my mother with the reverend.

"I know I was little at the time, but I remember you and Mama on many nights, sitting by the fire with your noses in giant books. I was always curious what you were reading and discussing, but Mama said I'd have to wait until I was older to understand."

My father scoffs. "Fairy tales."

McKee smiles indulgently, but gives my father a look that quiets him. Then he turns to me. "I wish your mama had seen you grow, you and your brothers," he says. "Mainly we discussed the Bible. There's a wealth of information inside those pages if one chooses to read more deeply. It's not all parables and psalms."

"Oh, I know that," I say, and it's the truth. "Before she died, Mother used to speak about parts of the Bible that were hidden from most folks. Parts that weren't—" I think back to that conversation, scrunching my face in an effort to remember. Then I snap my fingers. "Canon! That isn't canon."

"Correct," McKee says, smiling proudly. "Perhaps one day we can have similar discussions as your mother and I once did."

"You gonna poison her mind, too?" Father says, eyes bright and hard, a line of gravy stemming from his lower lip.

"Jeremiah, there's nothing wrong with being well-informed," McKee says, a hint of iron in his voice. "Where I come from—"

He pauses, and the room goes quiet for a moment, as if the priest's intensity has stilled time itself.

Then he smiles warmly, and I'm disappointed he won't finish the thought. Instead, he pats my hand and leans toward me. "Do you know your Shakespeare, Ellie?"

I shake my head, embarrassed. "I know Mama had his plays, but I haven't read them."

He nods, then sits back. When he speaks, it's in a baritone I find thrilling, like he's an actor in a play. He even holds out one hand theatrically, and I nearly laugh at my father's scowl of disapproval. "'There are more things in Heaven and Earth, Horatio, than are dreamt of in your philosophy.'" He winks at me. "*Hamlet*. I forget which scene...but I'm sure it's in your mother's books."

"I'm trying to eat," my father says rudely. "And we have more pressing matters to discuss."

McKee sighs, but turns his attention back to my daddy, and on they go with their talk of the war and the future of the world.

As I continue to eat, and ignore their ridiculous patter, I think on what McKee told me and, even more so, *why* he told me. *There are more things in Heaven and Earth...*

I chew my gravy-soaked biscuit and think of Ethan. I want to read *Hamlet*, and when he gets home, I'll tell him everything that happened, and learn the secret behind those words, which I hold in my mind like a key, waiting to turn a lock I haven't yet found.

PART TWO: THE FARM

15

By the time I make it back to my brothers I'm shaking, sweating, breathing in ragged gulps of early morning air. I'd been running so fast I almost passed right by them, and if it weren't the skirt of the swamp stopping me, I might have done just that. I'm surprised they're still asleep despite the lightening sky, the slow-creeping approach of dawn. I drop to my knees beside Mason and put a hand on his shoulder.

"Mason," I say, and gently push him over so his face is turned skyward and out of the dirt. Crumbs from dead leaves stick to his beard and hair, and his clothes are crusty with dried mud. "Mason, wake up." I pat his shoulder, his chest, grab his hand between mine and squeeze. "Mason!"

His eyes snap open and he glares at me as if I'm a stranger—an invader stealing him from the warm bliss of unconsciousness. I pull my hands away, wipe them on my pants.

"Ethan?" He rubs his face with dirty fingers, gets to an elbow, hocks and spits.

"You're not gonna believe it." I'm barely able to contain my excitement, not wanting to alarm him too soon after waking. "I found—"

He holds up a hand and I close my mouth. I wait as he gets to his knees, takes a deep breath, then rises to his feet, stretching his back. I stand along with him, all but dancing like a fool in my eagerness to tell him about the boy.

About what I'd found.

He studies Archie a moment to make sure he's breathing, then turns his eyes back to me. He looks so bone-weary that I want to hug him. To *fix* him. Seeing him like this, so weak, so beaten, makes me wonder how much longer we could have gone. Would it have been days or hours before one of us collapsed and could not rise again?

I hope we won't have to find out.

"Alright, Ethan," he says, eyeing me warily, as if I've gone mad. "What's going on?"

"Over there." I point in the direction of the creek. "Not far, maybe a quarter mile, there's a creek. I went there, just a bit ago. I wanted to wash myself, get a drink."

He nods, waits patiently as I babble like a gossiping schoolboy.

"I saw a child, Mason. A little boy. He waved at me, and I spoke with him. He lives just up that way. He said there's a house there in the woods. A *house*. I tried to ask him more but he turned and ran, and instead of chasing him I came back here, to get you and Arch. Maybe they can help us? They gotta have food, right? And medicine for Archie? Maybe—"

Mason holds up a hand again, cutting off my words. I take a breath, let it out.

"We gotta try," I say, frustrated with his lack of response. Of excitement.

Mason nods, worries his fingers through his beard, looks at the ground in thought.

"He was dressed nice, Mason. The boy. He was clean, had a nice coat and boots. He looked well-fed, like he's been living in comfort."

"No one lives out here, Ethan," he says, shaking his head. "It's impossible. This is—" He looks around at the trees, the rough land. "This is wilderness, little brother. This is *nowhere*."

"That may be," I say. "But Archie's dying, and we're starving. We've lost everything. We can't hunt, and anything we'd find on a bush is out of season, likely poison."

Behind us, Archie groans. His lumpy shape shuffles beneath the duster as he rolls over. His breathing is shallow and dry.

For the first time in my life, I put my hands on my oldest brother's shoulders and look him square in the face, lock on those ice-blue eyes as an equal. For a moment, he seems annoyed, but then he watches me curiously, as if wondering from where this grown man emerged.

"We don't have a choice," I say. "We're dead if we don't try."
Mason thinks a moment, blows out a breath, then nods. "Alright, then."

It takes us longer than we'd like to get Archie up and onto his feet, but it's not until I see him walk that I realize how spot-on I am about our options, or lack thereof. We'll be lucky if he can make it to the creek, much less the Mississippi River. Much less home.

Having no supplies to gather other than our mud-caked guns, we simply move forward, step by step. Mason leads and Archie shuffles slowly behind him, arms curled around himself, eyes on the ground. As we walk, the trees around us begin to lighten, the pale cypress trunks lose their shadows, the spattered leaves turn from black to cool green. I look back to see the sun rising, ever so slowly, the purple drape of night pushed away by a clear blue forming to the east. Above, the clouds are stained pink, like dyed cotton.

The mist at our feet thickens, and the forest, I realize, has grown quiet. All the sounds of nature—birds and critters, the creak of wind-pushed branches—are dampened, as if my ears have been plugged with wax. With my next step, however, there's a soft *pop* and the world of sound opens up—the woods alive once more—and then I hear it, plain as a mother's lullaby.

The creek.

"Mason!"

"I can hear," he says, but walks faster. Even Archie raises his chin, steps more quickly to keep up, invigorated by what may lie ahead. By hope.

We reach the wall of Buckthorn and I make out the indention of my passage. I rush forward, past Mason, and touch the impacted brush, run my fingertips over the freshly broken branches. I turn and smile at my brothers. "Through here."

A few moments (and a handful of colorful cusses) later, we're through the brush and into the clearing. Ahead is the creek, no wider than the length of two men, a clean straight bed, as if cut into the earth with a trowel. We stumble across the short grass toward the water. I drop to my knees beside it and lower my face into its cold, swirling current. I gulp mouthfuls of water, take a deep breath, and cup more handfuls over my head, rub dirt from the back of my neck. I turn and see Mason doing the same, all but laughing in relief. Beside him, Archie has walked in up to his knees. Slowly, one hand on a mossy stone, he lowers himself down until his lower half is submerged and I imagine the soft current carrying away the bad blood, cleansing him like some magical elixir from a fairy tale. When his eyes find mine watching him, I can almost believe the impossible—that it's helping. Some of his color has returned and there's a smile on his lips. Soon, he's scooping water into his mouth, rinsing his beard, pouring it over his mangy head.

Refreshed and clearer of mind, I'm eager to get my bearings. Looking toward the south, I notice the creek continues in a straight line—almost impossibly so—before disappearing into ground mist. To the north, I see the same. I study the opposite side of the creek and note the greenness of the grass along the shore; the lush, heart-shaped kudzu covering the trunks of wide, undefinable trees further back. The unexplored land beyond is tantalizing, but something about it worries me for reasons I can't define. It feels like sitting at the edge of salvation, and then discovering a surprising wariness to proceed.

It's a response one might have standing at the gates of Heaven, staring in awe at the majesty waiting for you just ahead, if you could only pass through those pearly, golden gates...and the hesitation one might feel at doing so; at leaving life, the world as we know it, our families and friends...leaving it all behind for some form of eternal bliss. Waiting to be accepted into a perfect world, a world seeping with honey-thick joy, is a moment during which one should feel pure, unfiltered happiness.

But I've often wondered about that. In my mind, the idea of paradise is both wonderful *and* terrifying. Who really wants an eternity of wandering through clouds? How long could one stand it before wishing to die? Before longing for the humanity they left behind, for the pain and suffering and heartache that makes moments of joy so much sweeter, or the pleasant tiredness at the end of a hard day's work? The comforting sense of peace that follows tears.

Studying the lush, green land on the other side of the water, I wonder if it's a similar sort of paradise: a creek instead of pearly gates, the haven within the promise of Heaven nestled in the middle of deep Mississippi woods.

How had Mason put it?

This is nowhere.

Before I can ruminate further, Mason is splashing through the creek, pointing to something on the far side. There's a strength in his step I haven't seen since we left the battlefield.

"Pears!" he yells, his voice so richly mingled with the splashing water it seems to be the creek itself talking instead of my brother. I watch as he climbs up the other side, heading toward a nearby cluster of trees I missed previously. My eyes follow his direction, and then I see them.

Pear trees.

From the looks of the fruit, ripened ones.

Misgivings are stripped from my mind as I bound into the frothing creek, my fears washed away like sins from a baptism. I stumble, laughing, through the water, which rises no higher than my waist. I have no fear of being pulled down, or slipping on a mossy stone, or tripping on a dead, jagged log jutting from the bed. I feel *safe*.

I step out of the water on the other side and inhale deeply. The air is fresh and carries a fragrance of jasmine mingled with ripened fruit. I realize I'm standing almost exactly where I'd seen the child and stare up at the tree. Fat pears hang in bunches and despite my eyes, part of me can't believe it.

It's only April and these pears should be buds, not fully ripened fruit.

They shouldn't be here.

Hungry as I am, it's impossible to worry about such things, so I jump and grab a fat green pear from the tip of a branch, releasing a shower of small white flowers to flutter down onto my hair and shoulders. I bite into the fruit and the eruption of juices against my tongue is the greatest sensation of my life.

I finish, core and all, then pull down two others. I walk over to Archie, who is just now emerging from the water, and hand him one. He bites into it, stares at me with stunned, dark eyes, then laughs.

He keeps laughing as he eats the entire pear, juice streaming into his beard where it mixes with tears flowing down his cheeks.

A moment later, Mason is pushing his way through knee-deep brush. There's a pear clamped in his mouth, covering his smile, but his blue eyes glitter with joy. In folded arms he holds half-a-dozen more, which he drops onto the ground at our feet.

Together we kneel and, like jackals surrounding a fresh kill, we eat.

16

Archie is biting into his third pear when he begins to cough.

He drops the fruit onto the grass, winces, and clutches his side. A low groan comes from deep inside him, his teeth bared in pain.

"Hey Arch—" I start, but hold my thought when his body convulses, as if punched by an unseen foe, and he begins to hack, wet and deep. We can only watch in revulsion as blood sprays from his mouth, coating his lips and dusting the remaining pears strewn upon the ground with a red mist.

"Jesus Christ," Mason says, and slides over to Archie, puts an arm over his shoulders. "You're gonna be alright, Arch. You're gonna be fine."

Archie wipes his mouth, raises his face. His eyes are unfocused, as if studying something in the distance only he can see. Then he crumples onto the grass, unmoving.

Mason drops low, puts an ear to his chest.

"Is he—"

Mason shakes his head. "Not yet. There's a heartbeat." He gazes toward the trees, then turns to me sharply. "Where's this house?"

I stand, energized by the food but also sickened, whether from watching my brother cough up his insides or the sugary fruit, I can't say. I do my best to focus, to recall what I saw last night. Looking toward the trees, I nod in what I think to be the right direction.

"The boy pointed that way."

"Fine, now help me," Mason says, and begins to pull Archie from the ground.

I grab one of Archie's lifeless arms and we lift him to his feet. He moans beneath his breath—*still alive*—but his eyes are closed; if we let him go he'd drop like a sack of meat and bones. Thankfully the food has renewed some of my strength—just enough to carry him—which I doubt I would've been able to do even an hour ago, despite his having lost so much weight.

We walk forward steadily. I glance down as I feel a tugging with each step and notice Archie isn't even attempting to walk; his toes drag along the ground and I have the sinking feeling we're holding a corpse between us.

As we move deeper into the trees, I'm surprised how firm the ground is. Despite the last few days of rain—only stopping late yesterday—the dirt is free of puddles or the slime of mud. There's no trail, no obvious direction, but I lead us by feel. As long as we are moving away from the creek in a relatively straight line, I'm confident we'll find what we're looking for.

I twist around to see if the water is still within sight, and it is, if just barely. The morning mist is burning off but it's still hard to make out any definition of the land beyond that strip of water, now blanketed by a thin haze. It's as if the world we left behind is devoid of color, that what lies beyond the creek is one of those new tintypes some soldiers have posed for—a sepia-stained reflection of reality—instead of reality itself.

We walk a half-mile or so. The land is thankfully flat, the trees scattered, the groundcover light. The day is warming and I'm grateful there's no rain despite the sting of sweat running down my chest and back. Mason and I both pant heavily, and neither of us has spoken a word, nor have we taken the time to study our brother, to see if his heart is still beating, or if there's breath coming from between his blood-splattered lips.

I'm about to ask for a break—my legs ache and tremble with the exertion—when the trees come to an end, and a vast meadow stretches out before us.

Without saying a word, we both stop walking.

The meadow glows with morning sun. There are wildflowers and trimmed fruit trees. There's a vast yellow field to the left, and a small pond to the far right, its surface broken by the green pads of water lilies. Like everything else here, they flower out of season, bursting with whites and pinks. The pond murmurs with the guttural croaks of frogs, the splash of unseen fish. The meadow itself has an odd swell to it, the land rising gently as it continues away from us, the grass growing wilder and taller, like the slope of a balding man's head. Knee-high switchgrass sways gently, rhythmically—almost hypnotically—as the clearing continues toward its centerpiece, the very thing we've come searching for.

The house.

It's constructed like a log cabin but is twice the size of any I've seen. It has a tall gabled roof; two matching dormers protrude from the mossy shingles like eyes, suggesting a second story. A kudzu-covered stone chimney protrudes up the left side, leaking white smoke, as if the fire in its belly is active and well stoked. The house has a wraparound porch and four windows facing out the front. From the size of the place, I'd guess it has multiple rooms, and I'm curious how far back the structure goes. There must be pens somewhere because I can make out the snort and shuffle of hogs, the occasional blat of a penned goat.

Not just a house, but a farm. My mouth salivates at the thought of fresh bread, of *meat*.

The home's condition makes me think it's been recently built; the log boards are even as piano keys, the porch columns straight as deacons on Sunday. The front door of the cabin, I notice, is partly open. As if expecting us. A warm orange light fills the gap of the open door as well as the lower windows—softly flickering like firelight, or a wind-blown lantern.

But it's not the house and its welcoming light, nor the beauty of the meadow, which halts us in our tracks.

It's the dogs.

One lies on the porch, big as a bear. Another sits at the side of the house, watching us, and a third is sprawled in the switchgrass, apparently asleep, at least until we came along. Now it's rolled onto it belly, ears up and alert, black eyes boring into our weak, bleeding bodies.

When the one on the porch lifts its massive head, I initially mistake it for a man wrapped in a fur coat and leggings. When it stands to full height, I hold my breath. It's easily the biggest dog I've ever seen.

"I count three," I whisper, as if debating how to counter the coming attack.

"Ethan," Mason says quietly, his body rigid, pale face set like stone. I look over to see a fourth one sitting a few feet away from his leg. It's a giant thing with scraggly gray fur and a long snout. When it sees me turn my head, it bares its teeth, and a low growl rumbles from deep in its chest. Its tongue slips between long canines and a line of drool slides from its mouth, draws a silver line to the earth.

"Shit," I breathe, and have to stifle a yell when I look back toward the others.

They're all standing now, including the one readying to tear Mason's leg off. Trying to consider what kind of danger we're in, I attempt to recognize the breeds, but nothing comes to me. The one on the porch is black, shaggy, and must weigh over a hundred pounds. The other two are similar to our snarling friend: short gray fur, big heads, oddly tall with arched backs. The one closest to me takes a step closer, and I clench for an attack. Thankfully, it's not grinning at me like the one near Mason, but there's something in the eyes I don't care for, like it's trying to decide whether it's worth the effort to rip my throat out.

"That's enough."

Her voice cuts through the air and all heads turn toward it, man and beast alike.

Standing on the porch is a woman. Her arms are folded across her chest, as if vexed. She wears a blue shirt and matching skirt. There's a bone-colored apron tied around her waist, a dark knit shawl over her shoulders. Her raven hair is tied back loosely, and her face has an olive complexion, like a Spaniard. She's young, and shockingly beautiful.

In these dark, miserable woods, she appears like a mirage.

At her casual command, the dog next to Mason puts its teeth away and whines. I expect the dogs to run to her, as one would to a master, but instead they simply...disappear. The two closest to us run into the trees, and the one beside the house vanishes before I can register its path of departure.

The only one who remains is the big black beast on the porch. He stands beside the woman, panting, and she rests a hand on its giant head. Scratches.

"He dead?" she says, nodding in our direction. It takes me a moment to realize she's asking about Archie, who I'd nearly forgotten about in the shock of the meadow and its canine guardians.

"No ma'am," Mason says clearly. "But he needs help, if you'd offer it."

She studies us from the porch another moment, and even from a distance I think I can see a smile touch her lips. There's a flicker in her eyes I find simultaneously alluring and unsettling. "You best bring him inside then," she says with a sigh, as if resigned to it all, then turns and walks through the door.

Mason and I exchange a look, and perhaps we're both thinking the same thing: that there's something very odd about this place, and this woman. Out of place, one might say. Like finding a donkey on a rowboat, or a chest of gold in the outhouse.

Regardless of our unspoken suspicions, we walk toward the house slowly, wary for more surprises, for things hidden in the high grass.

When we reach the porch, the giant black dog is gone. We get Archie up the solid steps and I give an involuntary jerk of surprise to see the little boy standing in the doorway, staring at all three of us with something akin to annoyance, and more than a hint of mistrust. His black hair is spilled like ink atop his head. He has a small mouth and black button eyes.

"Hey there, fella," I say, trying to remember how one smiles. "Remember me?"

The boy is about to reply when the woman's voice cuts him off from inside the house, speaking words I can't make out. He twists to look at her, then back to us. His suspicion—if that's what it was—is gone; replaced by boredom, perhaps. Or barring that, a sort of melancholy. Regardless, he pushes the door open wide with a shake of his head, as if one of us is making a huge mistake, then steps back to let us through.

17

"Put him there."

The woman gestures to a long table covered with a cream-colored oilskin tablecloth with four chairs set around it and a bowl of fresh fruit at its center. I look around the home's interior for a place more suitable to lay my bleeding brother.

The main room is large and clean. A massive stone fireplace is set into a tidy kitchen at the far end, a cooking pot over its flames.

The kitchen area also consists of an iron stove, sturdy shelves filled with pots, bowls, and pitchers, a worn butcher's block, and a countertop lined with tins of what I assume to be spices, flour, coffee, and such. Black pans of all sizes hang from nails along the wall, and there's an open pantry stocked with more varieties of food fixings and herbs than I've ever seen in my life. Past the table to the right, the room extends into a large sitting area. There are doused oil-lamp sconces on the walls, a small potbelly stove in one corner, and two small end tables set beside decorative chairs. A large bookcase bursts with variously decorated volumes, and beside that is a staircase leading to a second floor, possibly a loft.

I note three doors along the back wall, leading to what I assume are bedrooms or storage rooms. There's a window above the potbelly in the sitting area, and I'd suggest laying him on the floor if it wasn't for the ornate, deep-red rug splayed across the floorboards, warming the room.

"He's bleeding, ma'am," I say. "Your table—"

"I need him elevated if I'm to help him," she says coolly, and I shiver a little at her voice, which is stern, but also musical. It's been a long time since I've heard the voice of a woman and I'd nearly forgotten how beautiful it can be, especially when you've been surrounded by nothing but spitting, coughing, screaming, rough-collared men for half a year. "And don't mind the cloth, or the table. Blood can be cleaned, but a corpse must be buried."

I look at her and am taken aback that she's staring straight at me. Her hazel eyes are large and somehow luminous, as if backlit with gold, and I swear she's wearing makeup, although why one would bother out here with no one to see you is a mystery. But she's painted black beneath her eyes and deep red on her lips, which are full and—odd as it seems—still curved in a strange smile, as if our plight was somehow amusing. Perhaps dying men arriving at your doorstep is a pleasant distraction from the boredom of living out here all alone, with only a boy and a handful of dogs the size of carriage horses to pass the time with.

Of course, I'm making more than one assumption.

A husband could be nearby, hunting, or working the crops.

Or at war.

She locks eyes with me a heartbeat longer, then points to the table. I can't help noticing the length of her nails, or the fact they're painted a glistening shade of black I've never seen on a woman before. "The table," she says, repeating the command, but more softly this time, as if we need to be coaxed into it.

"Ethan, just lay him down," Mason grumbles—sounding annoyed, tired, and impatient.

We carry Archie to the table as the woman moves the fruit to the counter, then slides two of the wooden chairs out of the way, giving us a clear path. We set his behind on the edge first, then carefully lean him back. Mason lifts his legs, unlaces and removes his filthy, ragged boots.

"Titus, heat some water," she says, and the boy—whose existence I'd near forgotten about—hustles out the front door, I assume to a nearby well, or a barrel full of rainwater. She turns her attention back to us as we stand, somewhat dumbly, at Archie's side. I spare a look at his face—his eyes are closed, his lips oddly gray in the thicket of his red beard. For all I know he died before we came through the door, and I now have neither the interest nor the willpower to discover otherwise. The woman, however, pushes past me and lays a hand on his chest. I watch as it rises, as if to meet the pressure of her. A slow exhale parts his lips. She studies his face closely, puts a hand on his brow, gently smooths back his mangy hair.

I'd be lying if I said I wasn't envious of that touch. It near takes my breath away.

"Gentlemen, I'll need your help removing his coat and shirt. Such as it is," she mutters, plucking at the frayed, blood-soaked fabric beneath the stolen suit coat.

Mason and I exchange a glance then move toward Archie's head. We lift him to a sitting position and I almost holler in joyous relief when he groans under his breath. By God, there's life in him yet. The three of us do an awkward dance getting the coat off, one arm at a time, before our host drops it unceremoniously to the floor. We follow with the shirt, which is more like pulling away rags than an article of clothing. As we're laying him back down, bare-chested, the boy returns holding a large bucket. He manages to duck-walk it over to the fire, then pours it into the large cookpot. When he's done, the woman gestures toward the floor.

"Take these clothes out to the burn pile," she says, and the boy moves quickly to obey.

"Those are his only clothes," Mason says, but the woman only *tsks* at him.

"No offense, but these clothes are crawling, as I'm sure yours are." She looks up from the wound in Archie's side, then to each one of us with pity, along with a hint of revulsion. "But first things first. There's a bullet inside him that will poison his blood. I need to get it out and that will cause him a lot of pain. I'll need you to hold him steady while I work it free."

Mason and I nod at once, this not being a type of surgery we're foreign to.

"You," she says, looking pointedly at Mason. "In the pantry you'll find a few bottles of whiskey, bring one for your man here. He'll need it before I start to cut."

Mason's eyes widen only momentarily—whether he's surprised at being ordered around by a strange woman or that said woman has bottles of whiskey in her pantry, I can't say—but he moves with urgency to retrieve the liquor.

"And you," she says. "There's a stack of cloths on that shelf behind you. We'll need all of them before we're done."

I mumble a "yes ma'am" and turn, pull a neat stack of folded hand towels off a wooden shelf hung over the counter. I make to hand them to her but she shakes her head. "Hold onto them for now."

Mason returns with a stoppered bottle of brown liquid and I lick my lips in response. The woman notices and gives a little laugh—that sound of music again that hurts my heart. "None for you boys. Not yet anyway. The way you both look—and by that I mean malnourished and exhausted—you'd likely pass out halfway through the job. But give some to your friend. He may need help getting it down."

I cradle Archie's head, raising it just enough so he can swallow from the bottle Mason holds to his lips. He coughs hard, coating Mason's hands, the bottle, and anything else within range in a bloody spray of saliva and liquor. Then he swallows, greedily, as Mason tilts the bottle higher.

"That'll do, I think," the woman says quietly. "We don't want him hungover on top of everything else."

"Oh, Archie can take a drink, ma'am," I say, gently setting his head back onto the table.

Despite our host's orders, Mason pulls his own swig from the bottle, not bothering to ask permission. My stomach roils uncomfortably as I see a curling backwash of blood mix in with the brown liquor when he finishes.

She gives him a hard look, but then turns her attention to me. "You and me, then," she whispers, and smiles, revealing a white, even row of teeth. "What's your friend's name?"

"He's my brother," I say, and glance toward Mason. "We're all brothers."

The woman's eyes widen for a moment, then she nods, as if something she was wondering about finally clicked into place. "I see."

"This one's Archie," I say, resting my hand on his bared shoulder. "That's Mason, and I'm Ethan."

"It's good manners to give a name when entering a stranger's home," she says, but does so mildly, rather than as a rebuke. "Circumstances being what they are, a delay is forgivable."

I don't fully comprehend her tone, something between serious and playful that unsettles me. I don't know if I feel chastised, teased, or warned. So I say nothing, just lower my eyes and focus on Archie, who seems to have drifted off, or near to it, a small smile playing on his lips.

"The boy over there is Titus," she says, nodding toward the child, who still stands by the fire, readying the hot water.

"We met last night, by the creek," I say. "He invited us, I guess." I don't know why I feel the need to justify ourselves—our plight seems obvious enough—but I mention it anyway, a comment borne from instinct rather than thought.

"Yes, I'm aware," she says. "It's how I knew to keep an eye out. It's why you're alive."

I shake my head. "Ma'am?"

But our host ignores me and straightens, chin held high. "My name is Sarafina," she says, and that name—that *word*—echoes through my head like a sad, sweet melody; gently squeezes my heart like a poem, a hymn, or a prayer.

Sarafina.

"Thank you for this," Mason says, breaking the enchantment, my senses once more consumed by the smell of sweat, the spill of blood.

Sarafina walks to the counter, takes matches and a candle from a shelf, then pulls a drawer and removes a long, thin knife. "Don't thank me yet," she says, lighting the fat candle and moving the blade over its flame.

"What are you doing?" I ask.

"Cleaning the blade."

Mason and I glance at each other a moment, and he gives an imperceptible shrug.

"Regardless, we're grateful," Mason says, blue eyes bright and intense, likely ignited by the whiskey.

Done warming the knife, Sarafina rests a hand near the bloody, black hole in Archie's gut, poises the knife tip over it, then slides it inside, gently incising an inch of his flesh, widening the wound. Archie doesn't flinch or react in any way.

"Don't mention it," she says, and slips one of her black fingernails into the cut, the flesh around it now smeared with fresh gore. "When I'm done with Archie here, I'll get you boys straightened up as well."

A sudden squirt of blood shoots from Archie's insides, striping her blue cotton top and hitting her face. I hold out a cloth, but she only shakes her head, then tilts her eyes up to look at me.

I'm stunned to silence to see her smiling; strong white teeth contrasting with the red of Archie's blood running a thin line down her cheek.

"And then you'll feel right at home."

18

After much worrying with her fingers, Sarafina finally locates the bullet lodged in Archie's gut and is able to remove it. Once done with the surgery, she creates a poultice using hot water along with some herbs from her shelves, then packs it over the wound. Archie, though conscious enough to moan and twitch, stays otherwise quiet during the entire procedure.

"Ain't you gonna stitch him up?" Mason asks, his voice slurred, his tone belligerent.

"Later," Sarafina says dismissively. "That poultice will help with the healing, but the wound should stay open for now."

Mason scoffs. "All due respect, we've been in war, ma'am. If you don't stitch that wound you made, he'll bleed out."

"You don't—" she begins, but Mason cuts her off.

"Stitch him," he snaps, and for a moment they stare at each other. Finally, Sarafina shrugs, shakes her head. "As you wish." She points a bloody finger toward me. "Ethan, hold a clean cloth to the wound, press down gently until I come back."

I nod and press the sole remaining clean cloth to Archie's stomach. We'd already gone through all the ones I'd taken from the shelf, most of them drenched in blood and discarded to the floor. About five minutes into the procedure, Sarafina gave up any pretense of decorum and simply used the bone-white apron around her waist as a surgery smock, constantly wiping her hands on it so they didn't get too slick for her to pluck the bullet from his innards.

I do what I'm told and press the small cloth against the wound. I don't know how much blood Archie's lost these last couple days—or during the surgery—but it's a lot more than a human is supposed to, I think, and still live.

And yet, he breathes; his stomach rising and falling beneath my pressed palms.

When Sarafina returns, she's already threading a needle from a spool, one likely used to darn socks and hem the boy's trousers.

She gives me a quick look I find hard to read and I wonder if she'd hoped for me to come to her defense against my brother's wishes. As she leans over Archie, her long hair comes loose and, covered in blood like she is, the combined effect somehow dulls the magic of her existence—turns her more human...more common. More of this world.

I'm not sure which version of her I prefer.

"Okay, Ethan," she says quietly, and I pull away the cloth.

Deftly, and with precise movements, she sews the flesh. After a moment she speaks quietly—candid, but not without sympathy.

"I don't know how much good removing the bullet will do at this point. If the blood's poisoned, it will be a challenge for him to survive."

"What do you mean, poisoned? What poison?" Mason asks.

Sarafina continues without answering, as if he hadn't even spoken. "I also think the bullet may have damaged an organ. The liver." She looks up at us, momentarily pausing her stitching job. "I'm no doctor, of course, but I do have a knowledge of the human body. It's something I've studied over the years."

"What does that mean?" I ask. "If the liver got hit?"

She purses her lips. "Maybe nothing. Maybe everything. Only time will tell. There's an herbal tea I'll make that will expedite his recovery. Otherwise, he needs rest, and proper food." She snaps the thread, sighs, and looks at us with searching eyes. "You all do. And I'm willing to help you, to let you rest here, in my home. But if you do, there are things I'll ask. And if you stay, you must comply. For the good of myself, and of Titus, of course."

I look to Mason, but his eyes don't leave Sarafina. There's something in the intensity of that gaze that worries me. I can't tell if he's angry, worried, or something else altogether.

"What do you want us to do?" I ask, hoping to break the connection between them—a connection, I sense, that's brewing like a storm.

She sighs wearily, wipes her hands on her ruined apron, and looks at the mess we've made of her clean, tidy home. "For one, we need to get him into a bed so he can rest. I have a room the three of you can use, I'll just need to move some things out of there first. I can give you clean blankets and pillows for bedding. But before we do that—and please know that I mean no offense—you'll all need to bathe. And, well...shave."

"No worries there, ma'am," I say, rubbing the stubble of my chin. "This is a week's growth, if you can believe it."

She laughs a little—that music again—then once more offers a pitying expression. "Shave your beards, yes, but also your heads. Down to the scalp. I have shears, lye soap, a straight razor and a strop, if needed."

"Would that razor be your husband's, then?" Mason plucks the whiskey bottle from the table, the glass now covered in dry, sticky blood, the contents tinted dark. He spins one of the dining chairs Sarafina had moved aside and sits in it heavily, takes a long pull from the bottle.

"Mason, don't be rude," I say evenly, not wanting to provoke him but feeling a protectiveness for this beautiful woman, her child, and her home. "That ain't our business."

"Oh, I don't mind," Sarafina says, dipping her hands into the water-filled bucket on the floor, the one she'd been dousing filthy rags in while fixing up Archie. "Yes, it's my husband's. As are the clothes I'll give you after we burn what you're wearing. And before you ask—he's alive and well, thank you. And no—he's not here. He's fighting in that damned war, of course, like all the other fools."

I say nothing to that but can't help looking down in shame at the idea of being in a man's home who is off fighting the very same war I ran away from. Mason, however, just grins, takes another swig of the bloody whiskey, and glares at the woman like he's the Devil come for her soul. I want to shake him and tell him to be civil, but when he gets mean like this there's nothing to do but let it run its course. He and Archie are both built that way—mean streaks a mile long and rattlesnake tempers.

"You think us dirty?" Mason asks.

I look to see if Sarafina is nervous, but she appears unfazed by Mason's attitude. If anything, I think she might be amused.

Which would be a mistake.

"Yes...but that's not the reason. It's the lice, Mason. The bugs infesting your clothes and hair. There's no treating it. So I'm asking you to burn the clothes, shave off your hair, and clean your bodies if you want to remain as guests in my home. If not," she says, gently plucking the filthy bottle from his fingers and setting it neatly on the butcher's block behind her, "you're welcome to sleep outside with my dogs."

The room goes very still. Tension fills the air like smoke. For a full minute, the only sound I hear is Archie's shallow breathing, and I'm about to say something placating when Mason stands abruptly, runs filthy fingers through his beard, and smiles. When he speaks, it's with a conciliatory tone, the same one he'd use after being chastised by our sister—sincere, but in a way that comes off as magnanimous rather than humbled.

"Ma'am, you've taken us in when others would have turned us away. You've cared for my brother, perhaps saved his life. We have stained your floors with our mud and our blood. My brothers and I accept your hospitality and will do whatever you ask during our stay, to your satisfaction."

Sarafina cocks her head at the speech, then laughs pleasantly. "You're quite the character, if you don't mind my saying."

Mason, reveling in a drunken glut of charm, bows gracefully.

I let out a held breath, grateful that the knot of tension has loosened, and that we'll be safe for a while. I don't suspect the Home Guard will find us here, and if they do, well, I have a feeling Sarafina might have something to say about it. We're her guests now, after all, and she doesn't strike me as a woman who takes kindly toward someone threatening a person in her care, or living under her roof.

It's a mental note I tuck away for my own remembrance.

19

Sitting atop a slippery rock—waist-deep in cold water and naked as a baby while my brother shears the hair from my head—was not a situation I foresaw myself being in just a few days ago. But here we are.

True to her word, Sarafina provided us with shears and razor, soap and towels. She gave each of us a studious, and somewhat uncomfortable, look-over before disappearing up the stairs of her home, to what I assume is her bedroom. She came back holding two sets of folded clothes—trousers, shirts, socks, and long underwear—and handed each of us a pile. I was both grateful and, frankly, excited to clean myself thoroughly and put on my new duds. She handed me a heavy bar of soap that smelled like flowers, and gave Mason the shears, a strop, and the straight razor.

"She wasn't lying," Mason says from behind me. "You got an entire village crawling around up here."

"Well, cut it all off then," I say, embarrassed but too tired to care. "Get me to stubble and then I'll soap the bastards out."

As Mason slices away thick clumps of my hair, I watch as it floats downstream, past my knees. Brown curls of my past, washing away.

As I stare at the clippings riding atop the burbling creek, however, I grow perplexed. The hair isn't running downstream like I'd expect. Instead, it bustles around in place, bullied by curled lips of water, tossed this way and that...but not floating *away*. I try to find reason in this but can't figure it. It's as if the creek doesn't flow up or down, north or south.

It's as if the creek is flowing in both directions at once.

As if it was, quite impossibly, flowing into itself.

Before I can gnaw on it further, Mason smacks the back of my head and I'm surprised to feel skin on skin, just now noticing—

broken from my reverie of the creek's mysteries—that I can feel the sun on my pate, the cool breeze on my scalp.

"All right, that's good as it's gonna get. Soap it up then dunk yourself, get all those critters off so you don't give our lovely host and her strapping young boy a bout of Typhus. I won't have her boiling our nice new clothes every day."

I half-swim, half-crawl to the shore and grab the bar of soap, begin to violently scrub it onto my newly sheared scalp, under my arms, down to my privates. It feels glorious to be washed, and I can't recall the last time I was free of bugs or the sour stink of myself.

My only wish right now is that Archie were here with us, laughing and splashing in the creek, scrubbing his body clean. Sarafina said she would take care of him, and I assume she'll bathe him as best she can with sponge and bucket, likely shear his hair while he sleeps. I smile thinking of him waking up to a beautiful woman shaving away his beard.

He'd probably think he'd died and gone to Heaven.

For all I know, maybe we have. Maybe we're lying face down in the mud beside that fetid swamp, our bodies rotting away, picked at by carrion and the creatures of the forest. I think of Archie's scripture: *And the carcasses of this people shall be meat for the fowls of the heaven, and for the beasts of the earth.* Or, perhaps even now, our bodies are roped to the backs of mules led by sour-faced men taking our corpses to the city for their bounties.

"Ethan, quit daydreaming and get over here to cut my damn hair, I'm shriveled as a raisin in this fucking creek, and I'm hungry."

I dunk myself once more beneath the water, feel the currents flow against my skin in seemingly every direction. The creek bottom is thick with small pebbles, the water unclouded and translucent. As I rub the last of the soap from my scalp, a small trout rushes past. I twist my body, look up at the sky through the creek's surface.

The sun shimmers overhead. The thick silence overwhelms my senses, and my bare skin tingles down to my toes. I feel more than clean.

I feel holy.

After we leave the creek, clean and bug-free, we use the white linen bath towels Sarafina gave us, along with the clothes, to dry off. The warm sun feels good on my skin after the cold water, but I quickly put on the long underwear, socks, dark trousers, and cream-colored cotton shirt. The clothes are well-made, thick and warm. I feel civilized for the first time in months. Suddenly, the world feels full of opportunity and hope, rather than death, fear, and despair. It's hard to believe only a couple days prior we were being hunted through the woods, a whisker away from dying, time and time again.

The war feels like a distant memory. Our escape like a nightmare.

Fully dressed, I'm surprised how well the clothes fit me. I'm skinny in the best of times (lanky, some would say), and taller than average. It makes me wonder what Sarafina's husband must look like. Does he share the dark hair and small black eyes of Titus, carried on a frame eerily similar to my own?

I try to conjure an image of the man and fail.

It's only when I turn to see Mason that any poorly constructed ideas of Sarafina's husband fall apart. Curiosity is replaced with confusion, along with another feeling, one that hovers very close to fear.

Mason, a couple inches shorter than me, but broader in the chest, arms, and legs—a body so unlike mine that Ellie would sometimes jokingly refer to us as the Bull and the Scarecrow—is also fully dressed. His own clothes, like mine, fit him perfectly.

We stare at each other a moment and, given the inquisitive look in his eyes, I know we both share a similar suspicion: that these clothes do not belong to Sarafina's husband.

They don't even belong to the same man.

20

Upon our return to the house, we're surprised how different it is than when we left it, no more than an hour ago. The oilskin tablecloth has been replaced, the floors cleaned of blood and mud. The bowl of fresh fruit is back on the table and the smell of cooking stew fills the air, mingled with the warm, sweet scent of baking bread.

Sarafina stirs the large black pot over the fire, and Titus sits at the table, reading a book.

Archie is nowhere to be seen.

When Sarafina sees us, she smiles broadly, pushes a loose hair out or her face and puts her hands on her hips. She also looks renewed. Her face is clean, her hair pulled back neatly. She's changed into a slim-fitting lavender dress, and a new apron is tied around her waist. "Well look at you two," she says. "All cleaned up and looking almost human."

Mason runs a hand over his sheared scalp, his beardless face. There are cuts on his head, along his jawline, and a rather nasty one on his neck, from the razor. I'm fortunate it was easier for me to shave the soft fuzz on my cheeks and chin, but I still struggle getting used to the feel of every small draft electrifying the nerves of my face and head.

"Clean, and bald as babies," Mason grumbles, then looks longingly toward the oven.

"Rolls and stew will be ready in a bit, in the meantime there's apples and pears in the bowl there. I'm sure you're starving. By the gaunt looks of you, I'd say you haven't had a proper meal in weeks. We'll fix that. Get you nice and fat again."

Mason chuckles. "More like months," he says, and plucks an apple from the bowl.

"There's water in the pitcher on the counter, cups on the shelf," she says, and goes back to her stirring.

I watch as she plucks herbs, or seasoning, from small pouches stitched into her apron and tosses them into the pot, which smells of beef.

"You have a lot of meat stored?" I ask, wondering if this woman and small boy will have enough reserves to feed the likes of us for more than a day or two.

"There's a large cellar bursting with all my salted beef and pork, butter, milk, and preserves. We have more than enough," she says, as if reading my thoughts. "After dinner, or perhaps tomorrow when you're more rested, you two able bodies could help with some chores, if you wish."

"Happy to," Mason says between mouthfuls of apple. He glances down at the book the child is quietly reading, scoffs, and stalks out to the porch.

"Ma'am?" I ask. "Where's our brother?"

"Ethan, you may use my name. You might be young but I'm certainly not old," she says, and winks at me. "And your brother is resting in the spare room. I pulled the crates out of there and set up bedding for three. It'll be cozy with three grown men, but I'm sure you've had it worse, am I right?"

"Yes," I say. "Thank you."

Sarafina waves me off, tosses more herbs from her pockets into the boiling stew.

"Sorry, which room?" I stare dumbly at the three doors leading deeper into the cabin.

"The middle one," she says, pointing with a wooden spoon. "That far one is Titus's room. And the door by the kitchen leads to the rear yard, and the cellar." She nods toward the stairs. "The stairs go to my room which—not meaning to be rude, of course—is off limits to guests."

I nod, look at the stairs. "You mean you and your husband's room," I say.

Sarafina doesn't look up, nor seem in any way bothered by my comment. "That's what I mean," she says. "You should go see your brother, Ethan. The sick one, I mean. Not the boar pacing my porch."

I turn toward the door she indicated and notice the boy staring at me, one hand on the flat pages of his open book, the other curled into a loose fist atop the table. His cap is removed and his black hair is mussed. I meet his gaze for a moment, then go check on my brother.

The room is much larger than I'd anticipated.

Sarafina has laid out thick blankets in three places along the walls, each with a pillow at their head. There's a washing stand with a porcelain basin and a small, wood-framed mirror nailed into the wall above. As furniture goes, there's a stool in one corner and a couple of trunks I assume hold additional bedding or linens. A curtained window faces out from the rear of the house, beneath which lies Archie.

I hardly recognize him.

Like me and Mason, he's been thoroughly shaved—head, cheeks, and chin. Unlike Mason, he has no nicks or cuts to show where the razor caught flesh, and I assume he has Sarafina's steady hand to thank for that. I notice that he's also been washed. The caked dirt under his eyes has been wiped away, his bared neck and shoulders are clean. The rest of him is covered in a thick quilt, his body wrapped up like a hairless, man-sized insect inside a floral-patterned cocoon. His eyes are closed, his breathing slow and steady, causing a slight rise and settling of his chest. That movement is the only thing to keep one from mistaking him for a corpse awaiting burial.

I pluck the stool from the corner, set it beside him and sit. Looking down on this thin, pale creature, it's hard for me to discern how it's the same person as my sly, violent, rough-throated brother. As if sensing me, he opens his eyes—brown and deep, filled with that intelligent cunning they've always harbored—and I smile at how it transforms him back into Archie, into the man I grew up with and love so dearly.

"Hey, son," I say quietly. "You look like a bleached tick."

He stares at me. "Then I must be looking in a mirror," he says, his voice scratchy and quiet, like it comes not from his throat but a hole in the earth beneath him, one lined with rocks and roots, and endlessly deep.

"You want some water?" I ask, noticing a filled cup that Sarafina left beside him.

He shakes his head, pulls a hand from beneath the quilt and rubs at his smooth jaw. "When I came to, I was lying on a stone table, naked as the day I was born. The woman had a bucket and sponge and was scrubbing every inch of me." His eyes shift to the window above and the light reflects in his eyes as he grins. "She even cleaned my balls."

"Worse ways to be woken, I suppose," I say with a laugh, trying not to feel a stab of jealousy at his being hand-washed by our host. "Luckily you're not one for modesty."

"No sir," he says, then coughs hard enough that he winces at the pain of it. "Anyway, I passed out again, because when I came to, I was here, staring at your ugly face."

I nod and smile, but deep down I'm wondering how she got him in here the way she did, him being a grown man, and injured at that. And Archie must be truly scrambled given his talk of having been on a stone table, as there's no such thing here that I've seen.

"She should have waited for me and Mason to move you," I say, feeling a rush of anger mingled with shame—anger that she could have hurt him by moving his body on her own, shame for not being more thankful she'd taken care of him so well. "Not sure how she did so much in so little time, but maybe we were away longer than I supposed."

I tell Archie how we'd gone to the creek and bathed, shaved ourselves. I mention the clothes on my back, how odd it is that her husband's clothes fit both me and Mason so well.

Before we can ruminate more on it, I see the focus fading in Archie's eyes; his eyelids flutter like butterfly wings and I rest a hand on his shoulder. "Get some rest, Arch. When you wake up we'll get some food in you, and you'll feel right as rain. Then we can all get home."

Archie nods and his face turns away from me. His eyelids close and a breath escapes his lips, a sigh of contentment. Of peace. "Hell, I might just stay on," he mumbles, then says no more as he falls back into a deep sleep.

21

The cabin is warm and quiet, heavy with the scents of stew and baked rolls. The porch windows, shaded by the easement, show a late afternoon rich with sunshine. Light dances on the tips of wind-blown sawgrass, ignites the distant trees that surround the homestead like a castle wall, and washes over the meadow which, in turn, surrounds the house like a moat.

It's strange to feel so protected when the large cabin, and the smoke it must send up for miles, lies here for anyone to wander upon, such as we have. And yet I don't worry about seeing Home Guards stride through the trees, guns at the ready. There's a feeling of security, of protection, that has no grounding in reason. Perhaps it's the dogs, or the fact the cabin is buried amidst so much wilderness. Perhaps it's something else. Something beyond my ability to comprehend. Or perhaps I've grown weary of contentment.

Regardless, as the fire crackles and the afternoon glows, we eat our meals.

And by God, it's heavenly.

There are pitchers of cool milk from the icebox, soft butter for the rolls—still warm from the oven—and a thick brown stew filled with hearty bites of potatoes, carrots, onions, and beef. It is easily the best food I have ever tasted—whether that's the result of getting by for months with just hardtack, cold beef, and raw vegetables, or simply because it's well prepared—I don't know and don't care. I only know I want seconds and pray Sarafina won't think it rude of me for asking.

While we eat, I watch Mason from the corner of one eye, listen to him tell the same tired old jokes he's told in bars time and again, getting laughs from the workers at the docks, the men smoking in the street, from the mean-looking women who'd sit on his lap late at night while I stood nearby, hands in pockets, trying to act like I belonged.

To my surprise, Sarafina laughs at his jokes the same way those women would. It surprises me because she seems smarter than that. Much smarter. Independent and self-assured; self-aware. I find myself glancing at her face, trying to decide if she's sincere or mocking. Hell, perhaps she's just being polite.

I reach for a roll and catch Titus staring at me from across the table, his beady black eyes locked on mine, shameless and unafraid. His mouth is a hard line, his jaw clenched. I don't see his hands, but I imagine them balled into fists beneath the tablecloth. He hasn't eaten his stew, and I point at his bowl with my spoon.

"If you don't want yours, I'd certainly be obliged."

Sarafina, seated at the end of the table like a matriarch (Mason edged close enough to the corner they could be holding hands) lets her laughter die out. For the first time in our brief acquaintance, she seems upset. Perhaps even angry.

"Titus? You don't like the stew?"

Titus shifts that penetrating gaze away from me and toward his mother. There's a brief battle of wills, the kind of thing that takes place every day in households across the country between stubborn children and their parents, and then the boy—wordlessly—sticks a spoon into his bowl, lifts a mouthful of brown liquid to his mouth, and eats it.

"Better," she says, then turns her attention to me. "Ethan, how's yours?"

"Delicious, Sarafina, thank you," I say, flushed with embarrassment at how pleased I am for her attention. "You think I should bring some to Archie?"

"In a minute," she says, smiling and studying me with those large doe eyes, her silken black hair falling over the side of her face like a raven's wing. "I'd like to know more about you boys, and what brought you to my doorstep."

Mason and I exchange a glance, and I know better than to speak.

She looks at each of us in turn, seemingly amused at our reticence. She puts a hand on Mason's sleeve. "Tell you what? How about I guess, and you tell me if I'm right?"

She removes her hand, settles back into her chair, nibbles casually on a buttered roll. "All three of you were in the war. Fighting a horrible battle somewhere against the Union." She takes a bigger bite from the roll, chews. She's studying my face, which I lower in case my expression gives anything away, or accidentally confirms her ideas. "Three brothers," she says, shaking her head. "All fighting against progress."

"Fighting for the South, you mean," Mason grumbles, and he also sits back, folds his arms defensively.

"For the South, of course," she says, but does so playfully, as if it's nonsense. A joke. "So, you three brothers decide to leave this war and head home. I'm assuming somewhere south, given that there's nothing north but more fighting. Plus, going north means more soldiers, more chances of being captured and dragged back to the battlefield."

"Natchez," I say, and do my best to ignore Mason's angry glare. "Our family's in Natchez."

"Natchez," she says slowly, as if it's the first time she's heard the word.

"How far...excuse my asking, but how far do you figure we are from there?" I ask. "I mean, to be honest, we're a little unsure where we've landed. See, we were being chased—"

"Ethan," Mason says quietly, and I stop talking.

Sarafina looks at me curiously, as if I'd said something profound, or philosophical. I scrape the bowl with my spoon and lick it clean.

"Here."

I look up as Titus pushes his own, still mostly full, bowl toward me. I glance from him to Sarafina, to be sure, then pull it close and begin eating the boy's meal. I'm somewhat ashamed of myself for doing it, but I'm so hungry I could eat ten bowls if they were offered.

"A growing boy, on the cusp of becoming a man," Sarafina says, and I wonder if she's speaking of me or her son, but don't ask her to clarify.

"And what of you, Sarafina?" Mason's voice cuts into the discussion like a butcher's knife, removing any polite discretion like gristle. "How long have you lived here? You and the boy?"

"Titus, go to the pantry and bring the tobacco and pipe for our guest," she says, and waits until he comes back a few moments later, setting a pouch and a wooden pipe on the table. Sarafina pulls a tin of matches from one of her seemingly never-ending pockets and sets it down next to the tobacco.

Mason wastes no time in filling the pipe and lighting it. When he sets the match down on the tablecloth, its head burns a black dot into the oilskin.

"Time is an unusual thing," Sarafina says quietly, eyes downcast. "Have you ever noticed how it shrinks and stretches depending on the moment? Or, in some cases, within the events surrounding us? This war, for example, has slowed time considerably, don't you think? Days move slower. Almost sluggishly. As if history is being written in such detail that the actions of men must be drawn-out for posterity, so not a single death will be missed, a single malicious act forgotten. Other times," she continues, tone brightening, "it's as if the days simply fly right by, like the flipping pages of a book blown by a hard wind. Out here, in our little paradise, it feels as if time doesn't exist at all. As if it's neither needed nor wanted. And out there," she says, looking toward the windows, "the years roll on, heedless of our existence."

Mason blows out smoke, rubs a hand over the short hairs of his scalp. "I'm not sure I understand, but then again, I'm not the brains of the family, as you've likely gathered. That one," he points at me with the pipe, "he's the smart one. Him and his sister."

Sarafina's gaze on me intensifies. Her eyes widen, questioning, and deep as mountain pools. "Sister?"

I nod. "My twin, Ellie."

"I see," she says, and looks confused, or caught off guard. As if we've confounded her in some way.

"That said," Mason continues, and I hear the hardening of his voice. "I know when a person has avoided the answer to a question. In my experience, smart people like to talk in circles rather than straight lines. I'm more the straight line type."

"I sense that," she says distractedly, then abruptly stands and gathers up the emptied bowls. "Ethan," she says, turning toward the stove and setting the dishes into a large pan, foaming with hot water and lye soap, "would you like to take Archie some broth? That might be best to start with, so he won't have to chew the meat."

"Yes, of course." I slurp what remains of the cooling stew, then stand, holding my empty bowl. "We can use mine. Less to wash."

"Titus," she orders, and small hands snatch the bowl from my fingers. Titus walks it over to the pot, begins ladling the broth.

I didn't even see him get out of his chair.

"I look forward to chatting more with you gentlemen, but we have chores to do before the sun sets, and I'm sure you're tired from your journey. You're both welcome to explore the grounds. There are pens in the back of the house for pigs, plus we have goats and two cows in the small barn. You'll also see the chicken coop, where you might find a fresh egg or two."

Mason stands, pipe in hand. He pockets the tobacco and the tin of matches. "Think I will take a stroll around, while there's daylight to see with. Ethan?"

"I'm gonna feed Archie," I say, accepting the bowl of broth from little Titus, who hands it up to me like an offering.

"Wait a moment." Sarafina walks over holding a small tin container, like one might use for spices, or snuff. She twists it open, pulls out a pinch of dried, crumbled herbs, and sprinkles it into the broth. "It'll help with the pain," she says, then places her fingertips on the back of my hand.

I do my best to ignore the tingle of her touch, the way it crawls up my arm as she smiles at me, eyes dancing. "Make sure he eats all of it."

22

When I wake the next day, I feel more whole—more *alive*—than I've felt since the day I walked out the front door of our house on my way to fight for the Confederacy. I feel renewed strength, thanks to the food and the good night's sleep. How nice to wake up and see a roof above my head. To not pick bugs out of my mouth, or wipe dirty, sodden leaves off my face. My skin isn't chilled, my clothes not heavy with moisture. The itching in my scalp is gone, along with the knowledge that mites aren't laying eggs in my clothes, on my skin; that I don't have to pull ticks out of my legs.

For a few minutes I simply lie here, quietly smiling. Content.

A groan comes from the other side of the room. I turn onto my side to see Archie. He's doing his best to sit up, using the wall as leverage.

I look toward the bedding where Mason had slept last night and find it empty.

"You want help?" I throw off my blankets, rub sleep from my eyes.

"I want off this damn floor," Archie growls, and while he still looks sickly and out-of-sorts, like a man assembled with spare parts, I take it as a good sign that he's impatient to get up, that he has the energy and willpower to fight through his injury.

Archie makes it to a sitting position, his bare torso slumped beneath the window, his bare head hung low, as if too heavy to support. "What I really want," he says, breathing heavy, "are some goddamn clothes."

I laugh, forgetting he's been naked under those blankets for a full day, and pull on my trousers and boots, eager to help him. "Let me get something from Sarafina," I say, quickly buttoning my shirt over clean long underwear.

At the mention of her name, he looks at me, his hairless face weathered, his cheeks hollow. But he smiles wide, showing off all those crooked teeth, and his eyes crinkle with an eager joy. "You do that, little brother," he says, his gravel voice made even worse by injury and exhaustion. "And maybe a biscuit and some milk, if you'd be so kind."

"Of course," I say, and hustle for the door. There's an excitement in my heart at starting this new day here, at this new place, this safe haven from the weary weeks we've spent running and fighting, our bodies starving. I want to eat fresh food, drink cold milk and hot coffee. I want to sit in a warm kitchen and help with what needs helping.

Oh, Ellie, to feel human again is divine!

When I enter the kitchen, I'm surprised to find Mason at the table with a rifle.

He has it laid out in parts, cleaning it piece by piece with a tin of oil and a grease rag. A steaming cup of coffee sits among the detritus of the disassembled rifle, and it saddens me that it's not one of ours, which are all lost, given away to the Choctaw or taken by the swamp. Thinking back on all that running—the fear and the panic—embarrasses me, so I push it away. My mother used to say that dwelling on mistakes of the past is a fool's errand, and the present needs attention if you don't want things repeating.

I note Sarafina standing in the kitchen, arms folded, studying Mason with a dubious expression. She notes my entrance, however, and offers a warm smile. "Ethan," she says. "Good morning."

"Morning," I say, and note how pretty she looks in the pale light coming through the front windows. Today she's wearing a cornflower blue dress and a wide, white ribbon ties back her hair. But her boots are muddy, as if she'd been out doing chores while the rest of us slept. Well...while *I* slept, anyway. "Whose gun?"

Mason looks up at me, takes a sip of coffee. "Sarafina's, of course. Needed a good cleaning, but it's a pretty thing."

I feel a wave of envy—and, truth be told, annoyance—at Mason's appearance. Dark stubble already covers his head, cheeks, and chin. Whereas I look like a wet, hairless mongoose washed up on the banks of the Mississippi, and compared to Archie, the shadow of the man he once was, Mason looks downright handsome. I dare say the clean shave suits him. Makes his blue eyes somehow brighter, his stone jaw more prominent. The only negative, if you were to qualify it as such, is that it also makes him look meaner—his hard edges no longer hidden behind a beard, his natural scowl more prominent, as if he's been forced to appear as his true self in this version of paradise, a role akin to a vengeful angel, or a trespassing demon.

Sarafina sets a second cup of coffee on the table, slides a plate of steaming biscuits beside it. "It's the only gun I have, I'm afraid. I hope you men don't mind sharing."

I spot Titus across the room, sitting neatly in a stuffed chair, a book on his lap. I'm beginning to wonder if the boy ever does anything except read, but as he doesn't look strong enough for much else, I suppose the way of the scholar is a natural fit. "Morning, Titus," I say, but he doesn't bother to acknowledge me. Admittedly, were I in his shoes, dealing with three strange men invading my home, I might have a similar disposition.

I sit across from Mason and take a sip of the coffee—which is hot and strong, without even a hint of chicory—and grab a biscuit off the plate, restraining myself from shoving the entire thing into my mouth. As I swallow a lump of buttery dough and take a second sip, a pang of guilt twists my stomach. "Hey, brother, I should mention that Archie's up. He's hungry, and a little ornery."

Mason laughs. "Good."

Sarafina sweeps by me toward our room. "I'll bring him coffee and something to wear. You finish your biscuit," she says. "There's eggs and sausage coming."

I can't help grinning at our good fortune. Mason sees me and shakes his head, but I know he's thinking it as well.

How lucky we are to have found Sarafina.

I think about the words Archie mumbled to me before passing out.

I might just stay on.

Of course, Sarafina's husband will likely toss us out on our ears once he returns, which is fine with me. At some point I'd love to see Ellie again. Be *home* again. But there's no urgency to move on, not when we're finally—

"Hello!"

A man's voice hollers from outside.

I freeze with my hand halfway toward the plate of biscuits. I stare at Mason, wide-eyed with fear. His eyes narrow a moment, then he quickly begins to reassemble the rifle.

We're gonna need it.

23

"Hello, I say!" the man hollers again, his invasive voice crossing the meadow to reach the front door of Sarafina's home, our temporary sanctuary.

I stand from the table and step backward, toward the bedroom door. I'm careful to stay clear of the windows but, from where I am, I can peer through them while remaining hidden. I make out two men standing at the tree line, both wearing gray.

Both holding rifles.

"Home guard," Mason says, rising from the table with the newly cleaned rifle. He keeps close to the wall, tucked between windows.

I'm about to suggest we hide when Sarafina strides confidently toward the door. I note—with no small amount of alarm—that she means to open it.

"Sarafina!" I say, then chide myself for sounding aggressive. "Ma'am," I say, softer. "Those men—"

"Those men...what?" She turns her head to study me, a quizzical expression on her features. I find myself at a loss with how to describe the danger.

They're hunting us.

They'll kill us.

Sarafina looks from me to Mason, who only scowls back at her. Finally, she sighs and folds her arms the way I've seen her do a few times since our arrival—something she does when she's restraining herself, I think. And isn't it funny how quickly you get to know some people? As if they aren't strangers at all, but friends or family from a past life.

"Gentlemen, I only need to know one thing from you," she says, and her eyes harden in a way that gives me pause. I swallow when they land on me. "Are they welcome?"

Holding her gaze as best I'm able, I shake my head slowly.

She raises one eyebrow. "They mean you harm?"

Mason scoffs, squeezing the empty rifle as if it will do him any good. "And then some," he says. "I need ammunition for this."

"In time," she says, then waves a hand dismissively, and pulls open the door.

Mason curses and I scuttle toward the kitchen. I doubt these men would view me as much more than a young boy given how much weight I've lost, my sheared scalp and clean clothes. But I stay in the shadows, watch through the open door as Sarafina steps onto the porch, hands on hips, and stares down the two men of the guard.

One of the men is older, maybe in his forties. He's broad as a bull and vicious looking, despite showing his jackal's grin to our hostess. The other—shorter and younger than the larger man—hangs back a bit, but seems no less dangerous. I note the Colt in his belt in addition to the rifle, and I pray it doesn't come to a gunfight. They both wear Confederate gray, the makeshift uniform of the guards who like to call themselves army, even if the only men they ever shoot are from their own side.

The big one takes off his hat, slaps the dust off against a thigh.

"Hello there, young lady," he says, still grinning. "I'm Confederate Army Captain Tom Finnegan of the Mississippi Home Guard This here is my lieutenant. If I may ask, is the man of the house available?"

"He's north with the rest of you fools," she says, and crosses her arms. "I suppose I'll have to do."

The short one laughs and the big one loses most of his smile. His tone becomes less conciliatory, and I take him for a man who doesn't like to be mocked, or even looked at wrong. "We're looking for three men," he says, his voice hardened. "We know they come this way. Deserters, all of them." He spits into the grass. Symbolic, I suppose, of what he thinks of those who'd run from the war.

"Tell me, Captain Tom Finnegan, how do you know they came this way?" Sarafina says coolly. "Do you even know where you are? What part of the land you've stepped upon?"

The two men look at each other, obviously confused by the line of questioning. When the smaller one speaks, his voice is warbly and high-pitched, like a broken whistle. "We in Mississippi, ma'am," he yells proudly, and even Mason, I note, cracks a smile at that.

"We tracked them 'cross the swamp," the self-proclaimed captain says, and I see a cloud of confusion pass over his face, as if he himself is wondering just how they'd gotten here. "Then, we heard the creek, and—"

"There's a bounty on their heads," the lieutenant chirps, stepping forward so aggressively the older man holds out an arm to keep him back. "They're killers! They killed my brother, and a rich man's son."

"A rich man's son, you say. Well, that's a real shame, isn't it?" Sarafina says, and this time her mocking is plain, and worry begins to gnaw at my guts. She's unarmed, unprotected. These men won't kill her, at least I don't think so, but they won't take kindly to her if she riles them up.

I crouch near the counter, watching and waiting. I rest a hand at the cuff of my boot, caress the end of the bayonet secured there. It's all I have, but it'll have to do.

Captain Finnegan takes a couple steps forward, deeper into the tall grass of the surrounding meadow. His face has darkened with anger, and I ready myself for a fight.

"Enough talk, young lady. We're coming in there, and if you're harboring deserters, we'll be forced to deal with you as well, such as the law allows." He grins again, but there's no kindness left in it. It's a predator's grin—a hyena before he rips into prey. "We'll take what we want," he says, and the shorter man chuckles at this.

"Will you now?" Sarafina lowers her arms and turns her head to the side. Her features are shadowed beneath the easement, creating a silhouette I see plainly against the bright light of the sunlit day beyond. Her lips move quickly, silently, as if she were whispering a fervent prayer that only she and God could hear.

The men continue to move closer, then stop in their tracks when a loud, arching howl carries across the meadow, as if borne on a light wind, the same wind that now rustles the tips of the tall sawgrass. Another howl comes, and then another, like a chambered echo of despair, the sound of the dead baying in the depths of Hell.

I take a step to the right in time to see Sarafina's giant dogs approach the two men from all sides. I count three heads. Now four.

Surrounding them.

I'm reminded of a picture Ellie once showed me in a schoolbook about the African continent; an illustration of lions hunting a cluster of zebra, the tops of their brown bodies floating through the tall, dry grass of the plains, half-hidden, preparing to pounce.

Even from a distance, I see the fear on the men's faces as those big bastards begin to growl and bare teeth. No longer worried about being seen, I step into the light of the open door, stand a few feet behind Sarafina, who doesn't move, doesn't speak. She just stares ahead, watching.

"Call these fucking dogs off!" the big man screams, terror in his voice. He points his rifle at one of the grays—the one with the big head, long legs, and arched back, its growling face now a full mesh of teeth. "I'll shoot the damn thing!" he roars.

The shorter man has dropped his rifle and pulled the revolver, which makes me wonder if the rifles are even loaded. If they've come through the swamp like they said, their powder is most likely wet, and the guns worthless.

"You gonna run them off?" I say quietly to Sarafina's slight, shadowed form, her back straight and tense, fists clenched at her sides.

She turns to look at me, and I see something in her eyes that raises the hairs on the back of my neck, pinches at my bladder to release itself.

"You mistake my nature, Ethan," she says. Then—her eyes still on mine—she releases her clenched fists, fingers splayed wide, as if letting go of something she'd been holding tight.

There's a scream and a gunshot. I hold my breath as the dogs, as one, leap at the men.

The lieutenant disappears beneath two of the hairy beasts,

and though there's more than twenty feet between us I hear his wet cries for mercy, the sounds of ripping clothes and tearing flesh beneath voracious, angry snarls.

The captain manages to keep his feet as one dog rips into his calf with massive jaws, while another—standing on two legs—snaps and growls at his face, his throat. The big man shouts furiously at it, but then those shouts are muffed as the dog's teeth clamp onto the bottom half of his face, tearing away lips and flesh before going back for more. The captain shrieks and stumbles backward, arms flailing, his face a mask of blood, lipless teeth shining in the sun. He takes a wild swing with the butt of his rifle at the black dog latched onto his calf, but the beast only shakes its head more savagely, half the man's leg clenched in its jaws. It is a mercy of sorts when the gray one, still on hind legs, finds the fleshy throat and chomps into it. Only then do the captain's legs give out as he tumbles into the sawgrass and disappears beneath the savage, guttural sounds of Sarafina's hounds, as if he'd never been.

24

Mason and I stand on the porch in silent contemplation, staring at the black and gray humps moving through the tall grass, tracking the arched backs as they feast on the flesh of men.

Sarafina also watches, her expression one of boredom, a contrast to my own feelings of shock and horror. Titus has moved outside as well; he sits in a rocking chair a few feet away, a closed book in his hands, the chair barely moving beneath his weight. His small feet dangle inches above the porch boards. He looks more interested than his mother, and it gives me some relief to see a glint of fear in his eyes, a stoic expression of dismay on his cherubic face. Unlike Sarafina, he seems to recognize the degree of violence in what has occurred.

It's Mason who finally breaks the silence. "You'd let them dine on men?"

Sarafina's eyes widen, but there's the hint of a smile on her lips. "Do you find it unseemly?" she asks. I feel a chill at the memory of her blazing eyes, the powerful thrust of her fingers.

You mistake my nature.

"Very," Mason says, setting the rifle against the wall.

"I see," she replies, but there's an anger in that smile now. "Should I return to baking you biscuits instead? I saved your lives."

Mason nods, recognizing this. "Agreed, and now will you call them off? Ethan and I will take care of the bodies. If you have a shovel, we'll bury them in the woods."

She studies Mason for a moment, as if debating, then walks briskly down the steps and into the sunlight. "Enough," she says, and all four heads rise above the swaying, sunlit grass, the dogs all wide eyes and bloody muzzles. It would be comical if it weren't so gruesome.

She flicks a hand and the dogs lope away, two of the grays nipping at each other playfully as they run into the trees. The large black, tongue lolling, comes toward us, but with another twitch of her hand he changes direction, disappears around the side of the house.

"Tools are in the shed out back," she says as she walks past us, back into the cabin. "Bury them where they lay."

The door closes behind her.

There's a pull at my cuff and I look down to see Titus staring up at me. "I'll show you," he says, and steps off the porch.

Without a word between us, we follow.

With Titus's guidance we find the shed easy enough, the short walk allowing me to finally see the full extent of Sarafina's domain.

The structure goes back further than I'd anticipated, which makes sense given the size of the room she prepared for us. From the back, however, the house also appears taller, broader. The porch wraps around the side but stops at the rear, where I note the window of our room, and a door—the one off the kitchen—leading from the house. At least, I *assume* it's the one leading from the kitchen...but there's something about the size and shape that throws me off, makes it hard for me to rationalize what I've seen of the inside and what I'm seeing now. It's as if there's more to it than I'd imagined, or that there's something off about the construction I can't quite put my finger on. It's almost as if the space we've been given access to—the kitchen and sitting room, our bedroom—is but a portion of the entire building, where I'd been thinking of it as nearly the whole.

In addition to the house, the property contains a large tool shed, a low-slung barn with an attached pigsty, a fenced-in area for goats, and a good-sized chicken coop. Just past the goats is an old well—a thigh-high circle of stones covered in kudzu, the rocks themselves gray as charcoal, as if they'd been sitting there for a century. I stride over to it, wondering why there's no winch or well head, no bucket for carrying water. I look past the circle of stones, down toward the water below, but make out nothing but darkness. Part of me wonders if there's water down there at all.

"It's dry," the boy says, and I jump, nervously stepping away from the well's maw, something about it making me decidedly uncomfortable.

I study the rest of the area behind the house, note the fenced crops and golden field to my left, and realize this entire place is a farm unto itself, the air alive with the sounds of animals moaning, bleating, clucking, or snorting as we pass through it. It makes no sense why I hadn't heard all this ruckus from my bedroom, sitting just a few feet away, and I shake my head at the wonder of it.

"The house is very quiet," Titus says, as if reading my thoughts.

The explanation is a vague one, but I accept it greedily, as if I need all of this to make sense.

This farm in the middle of nowhere.

Sarafina.

The dogs, and what they'd done to those men.

"Here," Titus says, and opens the double doors to the shed.

The inside is clean and tidy. The floor is packed dirt and the tools hanging along the walls include axes and hatchets, a pickaxe, some hammers. A large workbench, topped with an unlit lantern, is lined with jars of plant parts—herbs, perhaps—and other things I don't recognize. Roots. Mushrooms. Seeds.

"Shovels are there," Titus says, and points to a wall hung with multiple shovels and spades of various sizes. "I'd help you," he says, studying his hands reflectively. "But I'm too small. Too weak."

We stare at the boy for a moment, unsure how to respond, and then Mason plucks two shovels off the wall, tosses one at me. "It's okay, kid," he says. "You'll get there."

Titus says nothing to this, but simply walks out of the shed, seemingly embarrassed, or as if we'd somehow upset him.

A few minutes later, Mason and I approach the spot where we'd last seen the men. I keep a wary eye out for the dogs, but see no sign of them.

"There." Mason points with the shovel.

I note the patch where the brown grass has turned red. There's a tramped-down arc in the field of sawgrass like a bloody wound. As we get closer, I steel myself to see death.

I'm not disappointed.

The bodies are torn apart to such an extent I can't rightly say which pieces belong to which man, the gore as bad as any battlefield. I've seen men blown apart by grape and other artillery, and it is much like what I'm seeing now: intestines thrown across the ground like coils of black rope, deep puddles of blood that your heel would disappear into, chunks of unidentifiable meat.

Their faces are no better. Skin chewed away to reveal masks of bone and gristle.

Flies already blanket the corpses, and it's a wonder no other animals have come from the nearby trees to feast on the fresh, warm game.

"We bury them together I suppose," Mason says, wiping his mouth with a sleeve.

I nod and kick an armless, detached hand back toward the rest of the mess, as if wanting to keep it from crawling away.

"Guns?" I ask.

Mason sighs, thinks on it. "Yeah, I suppose. Those are good rifles, and the Colt looks new, don't it?"

"It's shiny all right. Maybe that rich man gave it to him. An advance on the bounty."

Mason chuckles a little and begins to dig. "Maybe," he says, grunting as he turns over a pile of rich, dark soil beneath the grass. "By God, those dogs did a number on these two."

I begin to shovel as well and, while I work, think about our own arrival, just over a day ago. How the dogs had come at us. How Sarafina had kept them at bay, sent them scurrying. I imagine the results if she'd decided *not* to show us mercy. To help us. If she'd decided instead to let her dogs have a good meal. I think back on her words when I told her about my meeting with Titus, how he'd invited us.

It's why you're alive.

"Moving forward, think I'll keep clear of those hounds," I say, already working up a sweat on my back, arms, and legs. The sun above is warm and watching.

After we dig five or so feet, we scrape the bodies into the hole, set aside the guns for cleaning. I consider taking the slouch hat—it looks to be about my size—but am suddenly wary of wearing a dead man's clothes, and instead hand it out to Mason, who shakes his head.

I turn around and see Titus watching us from the porch, half in shade, half in sun, due to the growing day, and hold it up. "You want it? A real soldier's hat."

He looks at the hat, then at me, then rocks back in the chair he's sitting in, like an old man with his pipe at the end of a long day. "I got all I want," he says, his thin voice carrying through the meadow like a reedy birdsong.

"Fine," I say, and toss it into the hole to be buried along with the rest of it.

25

The next few days are peaceful.

Once we'd buried the Home Guard soldiers who'd come to claim us, things became relatively docile, giving us all time to recuperate. After a few days of solid meals and shelter, I feel my body returning to me; there is meat on my bones and a clear-headedness I hadn't realized I'd lost. When I look in the small mirror pegged to the wall of our bedroom, I no longer see black circles under my eyes. My cheeks aren't the hollow caverns they were upon our arrival. My ribs, which had been so prominent that even Mason had pushed second helpings on me at the dinner table, are beginning to sink once more into the newfound fat of my torso.

Archie has been making progress and now joins us for meals, if not chores. He walks as far as the porch, where he sits most of the day watching the trees and counting the birds that attack the feeder hanging from the easement, the one Sarafina fills with fresh seed every other morning. Titus will sometimes sit on the boards at his feet and read from whatever book he's pulled from the shelves. Arch hasn't put on as much weight as I'd like—certainly not as much as me and Mason—but he's eating and moving around, so I take it as a positive sign, and pray he's on the mend.

Sarafina, after the incident with the dogs, has been nothing but charming and maternal. She seems happy to have us broken, wayward men to dote on and care for. Even little Titus has shed some of his earlier anxiety about our presence, seeming to enjoy the change of pace; being around men he can relate to, perhaps, more than his mother. I like to imagine there's a trust growing between he and the Belle brothers, and part of me realizes he must miss his father very much. It could be our being here fills a small void in his heart.

We've seen no more members of the Home Guard and are satisfied the men who'd tracked us were the last of them. Anyone else would have found us by now, or lost any remnants of a trail. As far as I can foretell, we're safe.

The only thing that worries me, if I'm being honest, is Mason.

After burying what remained of our would-be captors, Mason and I spent the evening thoroughly cleaning the rifles they'd left behind. We appropriated the ammunition from their pouches before scraping their remains into the earth, pleased to have found a full cartridge box for the rifles and a good handful of .44 caliber bullets for the Colt. After the cleaning, Sarafina suggested Mason and I have another bath in the creek while she washed our earth-smudged shirts and trousers.

It's upon our return—wearing nothing but the linen towels she'd given us before our departure—that things start to go sideways.

When we enter the house, Archie sits at the kitchen table, wearing a loose-fitting shirt and pants, thick socks on his feet and a wool cap covering his shaved head. He and Sarafina drink tea and chat unabashedly about who knows what. Personally, I'm just pleased to see him upright and animated, a far cry from the walking corpse I've been trailing behind for the last week or so.

"Fresh clothes are laid out on your bedding," she says as we enter, then laughs at whatever story Archie is whispering to her. Naked as I am, I'm too embarrassed to do anything other than hustle toward the bedroom, eager to be clothed and warm after another bout of soaping myself in the icy water.

But Mason pauses, hand clutching the towel wrapped around his hip, and glares at the two of them, a sparking flint in his eyes I don't care for.

"Mason, let's get dressed," I say, but he ignores me, that hard gaze shifting between Archie and Sarafina, his expression accusatory. I know the crux of whatever stormy thoughts are brewing behind that stare, and I worry anew about how things will go from here on out. Despite my relative youth, I know something of jealousy, and how it can cause a man to act in a way unnatural to his typical disposition. With a man as mean as my oldest brother, that way can quickly become dangerous, if not deadly.

"He telling you the story of how he got that boulder-rumbling voice of his?" Mason asks Sarafina, leaning casually against a wall, as if he weren't nearly buck-naked, putting on a smile like a mask. "How our daddy scraped his throat to shreds with a spoon when we were kids?"

"How awful," Sarafina says, putting a hand over Archie's and squeezing. I groan internally at the lightning flash in Mason's eyes at that touch, the way Archie's lips twitch upward, his own eyes dropping to their hands in a sort of wonder.

Mason's smile—fraud that it was—dissolves to a frown. "Why don't you tell this lovely woman about the time Father McKee caught you masturbating to the Bible?" Mason says. He looks to Sarafina, grins like a jackal. "Son of a bitch was caught drinking the church wine, so the preacher sticks him in his offce. When the old man comes back to deliver a lecture, little Archie is going at himself over a Bible picture."

I'm not sure what Mason's hoping to achieve by telling the story—one I'd heard countless times over the years. Archie isn't one to get embarrassed, and I have the feeling Sarafina isn't easily shocked. Turns out I'm right, as she only smiles devilishly, then squeezes Archie's hand even more tightly.

If I didn't know any better, I'd think she was more aroused than disgusted.

She looks to Archie, wide-eyed with humor. "What was the image?"

Archie laughs. "It was a beautiful, half-naked angel," he says quietly, with a sort of wistful reminiscence. "She was holding a great sword of fire, and I'd never seen a woman's legs so long, or so exposed," he continues. "Got the better of me, it did."

Sarafina bursts out laughing, and Mason's face goes dark as the storm clouds behind his eyes take over his features. "Couple of perverts, the both of ya," he mumbles, and knocks into my shoulder passing me by. I leave Archie and our host giggling and go on to get dressed, praying the situation doesn't escalate further. As comfortable as it is being under a roof, I now imagine that our days here are numbered. Which is for the best, I think. My brothers have, somewhat surprisingly, never fought over a woman before. Never even been at odds, as far as I know. I shudder to think of the two of them—vicious and mean as they can be—squaring off over a married woman in the middle of a great expanse of nowhere.

    I'd hate to think what they might do to each other.

    Or to her.

26

After getting dressed I decide to take one of the rifles, see what kind of game is in the woods surrounding the house, thinking I can perhaps bag some quail or woodcock. If I'm lucky, a whitetail deer. If I'm unlucky, a squirrel. When I was growing up, we had an old redbone named Jasper that could sniff out a rabbit burrow like he'd been given a map, but I doubt Sarafina's hounds will do me much good to take along—they're too big and ungainly to help catch a coon or a rabbit. Not to mention I wouldn't trust one of them not to rip my own throat out, given the chance. Those big maneaters scare me, and if I see one trailing me through the trees, I'll be more apt to shoot it than scratch its neck.

I'm halfway out the door when Sarafina turns from the countertop, where she's been chopping carrots. She catches my eye, then nods toward the wall beside the door. "See if it fits," she says, then goes back to her work.

On a peg hangs an old brown slouch hat, and I'm not surprised, when I put it atop the stubble of my head, to find it rests neatly at my brow.

"Until your hair grows back," she says to the diced carrots, and doesn't bother turning at my uncomfortable "thank you" before I pull open the door and step outside.

Wanting to see parts of the land I haven't yet explored, I decide to head out behind the farm rather than the now-familiar trail leading to the large creek we came through initially. As I circle the building, I spot Mason by the barn chopping wood. Rather than engage him, I go past quietly as I can and slip into the field of tall pines that starts just past the pens. The ground is level, dry and fertile, carpeted with spongy duff and green, ankle-deep wiregrass.

The trees—mainly scrub and longleaf pine—are spread out and budding with fresh needle clusters, saturated from all the heavy spring rain. I don't fear getting lost as there's plenty of daylight spilling through and I can see clearly for a quarter mile in near every direction. In fact, it's so sparse I doubt I'll find any game worth hunting, but I keep walking as the day is pleasantly warm and the pine scent on the air relaxes my mind, steers my thoughts away from the anxieties and horrors of the last few weeks.

I walk straight-on for quarter a mile or so, keeping an ear out for any whistling that might lead to quail, but for the most part enjoy the leisure of being alone, well-fed and safe. I look up and note the location of the sun, wanting to keep myself oriented for my return. I look to my right and note that the woods thicken and the land rises gently. I head toward the rise, curious about the rock outcropping at the crest and wanting a better look at the dark cluster of white oak surrounding the rocks, their twisting branches hung with Spanish moss like overgrown beards. I figure I'll hunt for acorns to pass the time, or see if there's a lake or pond nearby to use as an alternate watering hole to the small pond near the house and the cold, brittle creek.

Clouds pass beneath the sun; the day turns dim and gray. As I walk, the green underfoot becomes a bed of dry, brown detritus that turns into rock-strewn soil as it leads toward the crest. When I'm partway up the hillock, heading for the outcropping of beige rock that I figure must be sandstone, I hear the scream of a child.

Titus.

I run toward the sound but the ground below my boots has turned to chipped stone and dust. I slip, fall hard to a knee, then hear the boy talking. Begging. I gain my feet and scamper up to the outcropping, brush aside a shroud of moss and there I see Titus, holding a damned book of all things, backed up beneath an overhang of earth and stone. Part of my brain tells me this must be some secret place of his, some tiny domain I've stumbled onto.

His eyes shift to me and I see the naked fear on his face. When they shift away, my gaze follows, and I spot the large mountain lion slinking closer toward him—head bowed, powerful shoulders hunched, teeth bared.

Any second it will pounce and tear the boy limb from limb.

Quiet as I can, I shrug the rifle strap off my shoulder, let it fall against my forearm while I raise the gun. I say a prayer of thanks that I had the foresight to load Sarafina's rifle before heading into the woods, unsure when I might spot a scurrying rabbit, or see the flapping wings of a blackneck pheasant. I take aim at the lion, who crouches low, belly touching earth.

"Here!" I yell, and the lion's head twitches to face me, its large brown eyes blazing with hunger and fury. Its jaws stretch to show a mouth full of sharp teeth, the growl from its throat deep and threatening as its ears flatten against the skull. It takes a few small steps toward me, and I jerk back like a scared child when a jagged scream rips from the animal's throat.

Then it leaps.

I fire the gun and the top of the cat's head turns into a spray of bloody mist, a red cloud hovering in the air like a swarm of gnats. The creature lands awkwardly—with nothing but gory pulp where its eyes and ears used to be—takes one last drunken step sideways, then crumples to the ground.

I'm breathing heavy; adrenaline hits my veins, my heart hammers in my chest. I lower the rifle and blow out a held breath. I look over at Titus, expecting to see him crying, or shaking with fear. Instead, he looks...hell, he looks *angry*.

The boy takes three large strides toward the dead cat and kicks its chest. Then he kicks it again and again until I move in, put a hand on his shoulder, gently pull him away. "Easy," I say, unsure how to react to this outburst. He knocks my hand away and drops to his knees.

"You're okay, kid," I say, trying to comfort him as best I can.

"Thanks to you," he says, but it's not said in a grateful way, but bitterly, as if he resents me saving his life. He turns his back to me, stares off toward the dense forest. My ears ring from the rifle shot, but I swear I hear a creek or a stream burbling nearby.

"I suppose," I say uncertainly.

I kneel down and give the cougar's misshapen head a little shake, just to make sure.

Titus sighs heavily, stares down at the animal with resignation; his fury quieted, I suppose, by pity. "It shouldn't be here," he says.

I look at him and chuckle. "I don't know about that," I say. "This is the wilderness, and the cat has as much ownership of it as we do."

I run a hand along the smooth fur of the lion, feel the cooling heat of its body, the cords of its muscle. An amazing creature. I strap the rifle back over my shoulder and debate the best way to lift the beast onto my back.

Titus shakes his head, looks off again, as if solving a puzzle. "No, I mean it shouldn't be *here*." Then he adds, more quietly: "Predators don't cross the creek."

Before I can ask what he means, he turns toward the overhang where I'd found him, plucks a couple books off the ground, holds them tight to his chest. He starts to walk down the ridge, then stops and looks back at me, his small black eyes intense as a Sunday pastor. "Thank you for saving my life," he says. "I suppose I'm in your debt."

"It's okay," I say, and awkwardly hoist the heavy lion over one shoulder, its long sleek body still warm and heavier than I'd imagined. I hoist it higher, toward my neck, and feel the cat's loose head knock against my back, most likely bloodying my new clothes.

"You got it? I'm sorry I can't help."

"I got it," I say.

He stares at me, those black eyes searching, as if looking for sin. "Well, come on, then," he says, and begins walking down the stony slope. When he speaks again, the words are thrown over his shoulder and, for reasons I can't fathom, they chill my heart.

"It's time we had a talk."

27

I follow Titus down the slope—through the dense, thick-trunked oaks—until we reach the spongy green wiregrass and the tall narrow spread of pine. The boy keeps looking back at me, as if to make sure I'm following, but hasn't yet spoken.

Finally, he pauses. I catch up, panting and sweaty, the heavy cougar over my shoulder, the rifle strap chafing my skin beneath its weight. He stares up at me and I stare back, dumbly, waiting for whatever it is he needs to tell me, if anything. I decide to break the silence, hoping it might unjam whatever he's working out inside that black-haired skull of his.

"This all your property?" I ask, making conversation, but also genuinely curious.

Titus looks around, then nods. "As far as the creek," he says.

"You mean the one we crossed? The one where you and I first saw each other?"

He smiles, and I notice how white and strong his teeth are, how it changes his whole face into something, I don't know...astute. "You scared me," he says.

"Well, I'm sorry about that. I thought maybe you were a hallucination." I shrug. "I was starved, tired—"

Titus nods, looks into the distance. "And you looked like a ghost," he says. "I normally would never be out so late, but I'd decided to pick pears that night, for no good reason at all, and there you were—standing across the creek, staring at me like a spirit." He squints against the light pouring through the trees. "I thought, there's a ghost, and he's trapped between Heaven and Hell. That's how you looked, Ethan. You were so thin and pale in the moonlight, like a hard wind could have blown you away. That's why I waved. I wanted to see if you'd wave back."

"And here I thought you were being friendly. Well, I'm no ghost.

And this isn't purgatory far as I know," I say, growing weary. "And this cat ain't getting any lighter, so what you say we walk while we talk."

"No, not purgatory," he says, but obliges me and continues walking in the direction of the farm. I'm working up a good sweat now, the day warm on the parts of me the mountain lion doesn't cover like a hundred-pound cape, my flesh even hotter where it does.

"You miss your daddy?" I ask, itchy to get the boy speaking again, curious about the way he looked at me back at the rocks, like there was something he wanted to tell me. Something I'd be interested in hearing. Or hell, maybe he's just a dumb kid with a nose stuck in books and a flighty imagination.

At first, he doesn't respond, and I'm about to give up trying when he points off to the right. "The creek runs all around us," he says. "Like a moat around a castle."

I look off in the direction he points. "All around? I don't understand you."

"All around," he says again, as if that explains things.

I laugh, searching ahead for signs of the house. "This isn't an island, Titus," I say, breathing heavy. "And it's no castle, either. There's no drawbridge, no king or queen or wizards…no moat. You got your head in the clouds, boy."

Suddenly, he quits walking and grabs my cuff, slows me to a stop alongside him. He stares up at me, hand clutched to my sleeve. "If you cross the creek," he says, "then you're free. You can go home. You can go anywhere." His beady eyes are locked on mine, and his tone is urgent, but whispered, as if he's worried about being overheard.

"Uh-huh," I say. The kid is talking nonsense, and for the first time since I've met him I wonder if he's simple; whether he's even reading the books he always carries around or just staring at the pages, studying the shapes of the letters like a painter might study a bowl of fruit, or a landscape. "That makes sense, I suppose," I say, not wanting to hurt his feelings by making fun of him, or being dismissive. "Thanks for the tip."

He lets me go and starts moving again, but now he's turned around so he's walking backwards, studying me in earnest, and I look at those eyes of his and wonder how I could have ever thought him simple. There's an inquisitiveness there, a searching that feels like fingers crawling up my spine, working their way into my head, pulling apart my thoughts as if my brain were nothing more than balled string.

"If you cross the creek, you can leave," he repeats, enunciating slowly, as if suddenly I'm the dullard. He's watching me close, as if gauging for some kind of reaction. "You can go home, Ethan. I'm telling you this because you saved my life, understand?"

I shake my head. "Titus, I don't understand a goddamn thing. I know quite well that I can walk through that vein of water on your land and get myself home. I mean, I appreciate it, but it ain't like you're revealing some big mystery."

"Just remember what I said," he says. "Your brothers, they're not good men, are they?"

"Tree," I say, pointing numbly, and he turns his head in time to dance around it, then continues walking backward. Strange kid. "The world isn't good, Titus. And we live in it, don't we? So, by definition, I guess you're right, we're not good men."

"Your brothers have done bad things."

"So have I. I killed men in the war. Ain't proud of it."

"True, but you have a good heart, I think. But your brothers... they're evil," he says, as if daring me to contradict him. "Aren't they?"

I look at him a moment, muscles aching, back strained with the weight of the cat, wondering what the hell he's up to with this. "Not sure how you'd even know such a thing, even if it were true."

"Sarafina knows," he says, then turns abruptly around, begins walking faster.

"Oh yeah, how's that?"

"Remember what I said," he yells over his shoulder, then begins to run away from me like I'd whooped his bottom with a stick on fire.

"Hey!"

But he's far off now, sprinting through trees toward home, which I can now make out in the distance.

About ten feet ahead of me something shifts, and I see it's one of Sarafina's dogs—the shaggy black one the size of a bear—lying in the grass. Its giant head is turned toward me. I stop in my tracks, sweating with the realization that I'm carrying fresh, freely-bleeding meat. With a sour twist in my guts, I recall the way her hounds tore those men apart like paper.

"Hey there," I say, praying the thing isn't smelling the fear coming off me in waves, or the cougar's blood leaking down my back. "Good boy."

The dog stares at me a moment longer, then stands, stretches its back like any dumb old dog would do, and trots away, dark tongue lolling. I wait until it disappears through the thinning trees before I let out a shaky breath and continue.

As I pass the mashed grass where the hound had been lying, a surge of bile rises in the back of my throat, hot and acidic.

Nestled in the grass is a bone the size of a man's thigh. Red, wet meat sticks to parts of it, fresh and well-gnawed, and brown marrow is exposed where it had been chewed to splinter. I don't know which of the Home Guard bastards it once belonged to, and I don't want to know.

All I do know is that I feel watched.

And part of me—a very logical part—knows that if I were to bend down and take that bone away, I'd be a dead man. Then it would be *my* bones those hounds from Hell would feast upon in the shade of the tall pine trees.

Mine and my brothers, evil men all.

28

I get back to the house, pushing through a hot stitch of pain in my gut, and am disappointed at not seeing Mason by the barn. I look for Sarafina, but she's neither in the large garden or among the crops she has fenced off toward the south, growing anything that can survive the perennial heat of summer.

Figuring they must be inside, I decide to make an entrance and walk around to the front of the house, wearing the cougar like a caveman's trophy. I climb the porch and all but kick the door inward, a stupid grin on my sweaty face. "Dinner's on!" I yell like an idiot, waiting to hear squeals and laughter, but am met with silence instead.

Sarafina and Mason are seated at the dining table, hands clenched together, both looking at me with wide, desperate eyes.

Titus is nowhere to be seen.

I stare at them, at their enclosed hands. My grin fades. "Hey."

Sarafina, at least, has the decency to pull her fingers from Mason's. She stands, walks over to me and gazes into my eyes a moment with a strange look—something between a warning and an apology—before giving her attention to the creature burning the muscles of my back and shoulder. "Titus told me, but I almost couldn't believe it." She puts a gentle hand on my chest, palm flat on my sweat-soaked shirt, and I try not to shiver at the thrill of it. "Are you okay?"

"I'm fine," I say. "What's going on here?" I don't mean the intimacy, though that certainly caught me off guard. I'm referring to the looks on their faces—both of them are damn morose. "Who died?" I say, meaning it as a joke, but no one laughs, or so much as smiles for that matter.

"Archie's sick," Mason says. He stands abruptly and is at my side in three strides, pulling the wretched animal from my back. I almost sigh with the ecstasy of having that hot, dead weight off of me.

"Sick how?" I remove the rifle, set it against the wall. "Yesterday he was sitting at the table telling stories." I look at each of them in turn, feel panic swelling in my chest. "He was on the mend," I insist.

Sarafina shakes her head. "I'll do what I can, but the wound is infected. If it was his leg, or an arm—"

I look after Mason as he steps past me onto the porch. "Gangrene?"

Mason drops the cougar in the grass, kneels down and pokes a finger at its snarled teeth. "Maybe," he says, running a hand along the cat's fur. "Probably. But he doesn't look good. The skin near the wound is bright red, and there's pus coming out of there—" He stands, hands on his hips. "I don't know what to do. It's in his damn belly, Ethan. Can't cut it out. Can't saw it off."

"Where is he?" I say, as if there were a world of options.

"Sleeping," Sarafina says from behind me, having followed us onto the porch. "I gave him some tea that will slow the poison, but there's a limit to what I can do."

I want to shout at them both, to scream at them as if they caused this, as if it's their fault. For holding hands like they were a couple and not strangers. As if she weren't married and he not an evil, murderous bastard like Titus said. Acting like lovebirds when they should have been fixing Archie, making him better...

Hell with it all.

I turn and stomp back through the house, into the bedroom.

The stink hits me first, and I'm taken back to the field hospitals where wounded men had lay dying, surgeons hacking off limbs by the dozen, nurses tossing arms and legs out the back of the tent into a newly dug ditch, where they'd sit in a pile with the rest of the severed pieces.

I walk over to Archie and sit, cross-legged, next to his blankets. I put my hand on his forehead and wince at the heat of his skin, the fever running through him. I figure we should take him to the water, soak him in that icy creek for...

His hand reaches out and clutches my knee, squeezes the fabric there with a strength I wouldn't have thought him capable of. I put a hand over his, trying my best not to look at the exposed wound, the beet-red flesh surrounding it, or the milky yellow pus that leaks from the stitches, slides across his sunken belly.

"Hey, Arch."

Archie opens bloodshot eyes. They rove for a moment, then slide over and find me. There's spittle at the corners of his mouth, and though he looks like a day-old cadaver and smells like dead meat, his voice is surprisingly strong and steady. I have no problem understanding his words or the sentiment behind them.

"I love her," he says, his shaved head nothing more than a skull wrapped in tight skin, his cunning eyes wide with hate and fear. "I love her, Ethan."

I squeeze his hand, unsure what to say to such a thing.

Unsure how I feel about his saying it.

"If he takes her from me," he says, that deep, grating voice low and ominous as thunder, "I'll kill him."

"Take it easy, Archie," I say, hating the tickle of cold tears running down my cheeks. "Just take it easy."

His fingers squeeze mine so tight it's a wonder my bones aren't cracking. With an obvious effort, he lifts his head from the damp blanket, sunken eyes boring into me as if Death himself was standing over my shoulder, scythe at the ready.

He spits the words like a curse.

"I'll fucking kill him."

After a few minutes, I get him to relax, and soon his eyes are closed, his breathing regular, if shallow.

As I look down at my dying brother, troubled thoughts brew in my head. I think how lucky we are to have found this oasis— this miracle dropped into the wilderness of an endless, untamed forest—but I have trouble coming to terms with our supposed good fortune.

For reasons I can't explain, I want to move on from this place, from the beautiful woman and her odd little boy, from the seeming perfection of it all. I want Archie to heal so we can continue west, toward the Mississippi, and ride the mighty back of the brown river homeward.

I miss you, Ellie, and I miss the everyday normalcy we had before the war. Before this damned journey through Hell.

I know I should feel fortunate; I should be thankful, relieved that we've been kept from certain starvation, from being hunted, from the fear of what new trouble might be lying in wait just ahead.

I should feel like we've been saved.

Instead, I feel like we've been trapped. Three black flies stuck fast in a sticky web, a fat long-legged spider—its multitude of shining black eyes watching from the shadows—poised to strike out and gobble us up, drink us down, leave nothing but the husks of the men we once were.

Or perhaps *we* are the spiders, and it's Sarafina, and her child, who are the doomed flies.

I think of the way Mason looked at her; the hungry wolf behind his blue eyes, and I worry what he's capable of. As much as I love him, I don't trust his morality when it comes to being stranded with a beautiful, helpless woman.

Ellie, if you were here you could talk to him. Reason with him. Remind him of the good in his heart. Remind me of my own. Keep us turning from prey into predators.

Spiders in a house of flies.

I leave Archie to his rest. I wonder why death has lodged itself so stubbornly into my imagination. I can only hope it's due to the savagery of the recent past, and not a dark foreboding of what's to come.

There's danger here.

I just don't know if it's coming from this place...or from us.

29

Shortly after dinner I decide to go to bed. My body is still recovering from months of abuse, lack of food, and exhaustion. The long walk into the woods, and the long walk back carrying the cougar, has done me in. I'll need a lot more rest before I'm back to how I was before marching off to war. The question now is whether to rest here, at a stranger's home in the middle of nowhere, or back in Natchez with my sister and father; surrounded by familiar walls and trappings, in a town I grew up in with people who know my name, who care about me. If I could somehow transport all three of us back to Natchez, back to where we belong, I would do so at the drop of a hat. This place, I feel, is a sea of poison. And we're drowning in it.

Archie hasn't moved since the afternoon, when he declared his love for our host. At dinner, Sarafina took a bowl of broth into him while the rest of us ate at the table, sunken in a heavy silence filled with unspoken questions. I wanted to ask Mason about Sarafina, and whether he had intentions with a married woman (or, at best, a widow). I want to ask Titus about his cryptic advice regarding the creek, and his statement about my brothers being filled with evil.

Instead, we talked about the lion. Titus tells Mason how I saved his life, which gets a grunt from my oldest brother and not much else. He and I spent a good part of the late afternoon and early evening dressing the beast, and now its guts are in the pigsty, its meat in salt, and its skin stretched and drying in the barn. I tell Titus we could fashion him an entirely new suit from the hide, but that only gets me another grunt—this time from the boy—which causes me to give up on socializing for the evening.

When I finally climb into my blankets, stomach comfortably full of stew, it's only a matter of moments before I fall asleep. I try to ignore the rasping breaths from the other side of the room, the smell of rot in the air. I think on what Titus told me that afternoon, how he compared the creek to a moat, as if surrounding a castle; a defense to help keep out any unwanted souls.

Or, I suppose, to help keep them in.

I wake in the dark.

A dream...a horrible dream. My siblings, all four of us, were burning in the flames of Hell. Ellie was staring at me through the fire, eyes wide with terror and pain, screaming. Her skin had melted to the bone and she'd become a shrieking skeleton, reaching for me with flesh-eaten fingers, and then—like a miracle—she'd be whole again, eyes wide in momentary wonder before she'd begin to shriek once more, her skin dripping into the fire. It happened again, and again; seemingly countless times—an eternity. An endless cycle of pain.

My brothers were there as well, both of them tearing at their charred flesh, pulling it off like rags, their insides falling into the flames. Then, like Ellie, they'd regenerate, become whole, before it all started anew—the burning, the pain, the horror.

I became sickly aware of my own body—also burning—drenched in liquid flame, heard my own ragged cries of pain and terror, my throat raw with them as I stared, wide-eyed, at an entire lake—a shoreless ocean of hellfire—filled with souls.

Countless sinners tortured for eternity.

Now, in the cool dark of reality, my heart beats too fast, my breaths come in quick, shallow gulps. I'm covered in sweat despite the chilled night. Dusty moonlight slants through the room's sole window, and beneath it I make out the slumped, ragged form of Archie, his throat scraping out one shallow breath after another.

I sit up, trembling in the cold room, and look toward Mason's bedding.

He's not there.

I throw aside my blanket, pull pants on over my long underwear, and walk quietly to the bedroom door, not wanting to wake Archie. I open it—slowly—step into the main room of the house, then close the door gently behind me. My mouth is parched and, knowing that Sarafina keeps a pitcher of water on the table, I walk in that direction carefully, fighting to see where I'm going in the total dark of this lost house in the wilderness.

I find the pitcher and drink straight from it, not worrying about a cup at this time of night. The water is cool and soothing, and the last remnants of the dream—the feeling of my flesh burning—dissipate and float away, as if the water were a magical elixir.

"Can't sleep?"

I nearly drop the pitcher in surprise and turn toward the voice.

On the stairs which lead to the upper floor, I see a slim shadow.

Sarafina.

"Bad dream." I set the pitcher down, wipe my mouth with the back of my sleeve. "Is he up there?" I ask brazenly. Rudely. I don't care, I need to know. "With you?"

Her shadow moves soundlessly down the steps, then crosses the room toward me. When she finally steps into a slant of blue moonlight, I see her more clearly.

Her black hair is loose over her shoulders. She's barefoot, and wears a common shift dress. There's a black knit shawl pulled over her shoulders and chest. Her small pale hands, clenched together beneath her breasts, hold it tight to her body. Her face is angelic in the soft light, her full lips curled into that gentle smirk she so often carries, her shining eyes dark as bottomless black oceans. She comes closer, so close I can I feel her heat in the air. Standing only inches from me, it's obvious how much shorter she is, her chin rising no higher than my chest, forcing her to look up to meet my eyes. But when she does, I'm the one who feels intimidated, who feels small. Like the child I am.

"Yes," she says, and speaks it in such a way that I know—without either of us needing to say it—that the conversation, as it pertains to Mason, is over. Then she smiles brightly, as if all has been forgiven and forgotten, with no one saying a word.

"I'm glad you're awake," she says, and takes my hand in one of hers, her fingers intertwining with my own. "Will you walk with me?"

I swallow hard, put all my willpower into not taking a step back, away from the heat of her. "A walk?" I ask, like a true imbecile. "You mean outside?"

She nods, eyes dancing.

"Come on," she says, and—still holding my hand—pulls me toward the front door.

"There's someone I want you to meet."

30

There's been no rain since our arrival, and when I step onto the cool grass in bare feet, the ground is dry and comforting. Sarafina lets go my hand and walks toward the fenced-in crops at the north end of the farm. I follow, feeling awkward and gangly as I study the tinted luminescence of her slim, bare calves, her doll-like feet. We walk past the crop fence and gardens, then up a small rise I hadn't yet explored. At the top is a beautiful view of a barley field, turned gray by weak moonlight. Fat spikes sway in a light breeze, the stalks ripe for harvest. At first, there seems no end to the field, but from atop the crest I make out a straight, silver line in the distance. A narrow creek.

Perhaps the boy was right.

"Come on." She tugs playfully at my sleeve, then presses into the tall barley stems.

I follow, nearly chuckling at the thought that I always seem to be *following* someone. At home, when I was a child, I'd follow Ellie wherever she went to such a mad degree that when my father asked her of my whereabouts, he'd say: *Where's that shadow of yours?*

I don't think he meant it kindly.

For the last year, I feel like I've been following my brothers. Following orders. Marching blindly behind men, toward the killing fields.

Even today I followed Titus like a dog on a leash, the dead lion hard and hot against my neck. And now, Sarafina, through the barley field, trying to keep up with her as she strides briskly through the lake of brown stems, the loosened spores of barley dust tickling my nose.

Finally, we burst through the field and into a small clearing, a near perfect circle of thick grass and scattered leaves. Oddly, the ground is moist here, as if rain had fallen on this spot and no other. In the center of the clearing is an imposing, gnarled tree that I can't immediately categorize. Some sort of white oak, I'd guess, but it's stunted in height, its branches intertwining like ivy in places, its trunk broad and dark. I study the leaves, which are not unlike the flat hands of a maple tree, but the region is all wrong, as is the tree itself.

Sarafina walks toward the hulking, twisted thing, lets her shawl slip from her shoulders and fall recklessly to the ground. On instinct, I bend over and pick it up. It's warm and smells like jasmine. I'm mindful to hold it gently.

In nothing but her form-fitting, milk-shade shift, Sarafina is nymph-like and stunning. Her olive-toned neck and arms bared, her black hair flowing like silk down her back. The moon—a horizontal, slung crescent—bares a devil's grin in the black sky, where it rests amid a vast sea of countless stars, casting just enough light to show me the curves of Sarafina's naked body beneath the thin fabric. To my shame, I feel myself growing aroused and hastily lower the knit shawl to my waist, hiding the area where I press against the cloth of my trousers.

She bends low, near the base of the tree, temporarily lost in its heavy shadow, and plucks at the ground with her fingers.

"What are you doing?"

"Wait," she says, then strides quickly, gracefully, over to me without an ounce of shame or self-awareness of how exposed she is. Were she standing here naked I doubt it would have given her a moment's pause.

That image, of course, only worsens my condition, so I cough lightly and focus on what she holds out in the flat, open palm of her hand.

Thin brown stems with pointed domes at their tops.

Mushrooms.

"Eat one...then we can talk," she says, a quiet command.

I pluck a curved stem from her palm, hold it aloft between pinched fingers, study it in the blue light of the moon. It's domed head bows at the tip of a moist, flaccid stem, and by some miracle of mockery my own hardness is likewise drawn away.

As if knowing what I'm thinking—and what my body is struggling with—Sarafina laughs. "Are you going to eat it or stare at it until dawn?" she says, then plucks up the other stem lying in her palm and pops it neatly into her mouth. She closes her eyes as she chews it, apparently in some ecstasy of flavor, although I don't foresee the raw, slick mushroom being very tasty. Regardless, my pride and foolishness are the lesser of no one, and I follow her example and eat the fungus.

I chew once and grimace at the bitter squirt from the earthy, flaky thing as my teeth grind it to bits. I hurriedly swallow it all down, not wanting to prolong the experience. I reflexively want to spit, but manners win out and I let the taste linger on my tongue. After a few seconds, I find I don't mind it too much.

"Now, let's sit." She takes my hand once more, as if we were lovers instead of war-torn strangers. "Over there, where we can see the sky without Novah blocking our view."

"Novah?" I ask, letting her lead me back toward the edge of the small clearing. The low wall of swaying barley waves at me to come closer, and the spikes lift and turn my way, as if watching my approach with eager, manic glee.

"The tree's name," she says. "Because there was a time when it was new to this world, and now it rests here, with me, staring at the stars."

"I see," I say, not seeing at all.

Sarafina pulls the shawl from my hands, lays it on the ground. She spreads it out like a small blanket, which she in turn lies down upon, her back to the earth, her face toward the heavens. Her shift is low-cut above her breasts, and I feel sick with desire. "Lie down next to me, Ethan. There are things I wish to say."

I sit beside her and find myself mildly disoriented. There's a strange tilt to the world, as if I were on a boat instead of firm ground, and a sprout of nausea takes root in my guts. I take a few deep breaths, focus my vision on the barley. Slowly, I become spellbound by the swaying of stems, the inverted black ocean above. My eyelids feel heavy and, given the hour, it's not a surprise that I begin nodding off, head bobbing between my bent knees.

Before sleep can take hold, the palm of her hand settles on my back, rubs in slow, gentle circles over my spine. "Lie down."

I agree with the voice, the sweet melody of the words, and settle back onto the cool, moist ground. I stretch my long legs, steady my breathing. I roll my head to the side and am surprised to see Sarafina's face only inches from my own, studying me, her eyes so wide and dark I feel like I could crawl inside them, curl up in the warmth of her beauty like an unborn child. It would be wonderful.

"How old are you, Ethan?" she asks, her breath warm on my lips.

I think about lying, but that doesn't feel right, not with her gaze fixed on me the way it is. It's not a face I can lie to. "Seventeen."

Sarafina *tsks* and turns her face skyward. "Just a child," she says, almost sadly. "And they make you fight. They make you kill."

"I'm no child," I say, full of foolish pride, despite knowing it to be true.

"Of course not," she agrees, placating me. "You're wise beyond your years, Ethan. And you've been to war, which has forced you into adulthood."

I tilt closer, take a deep breath of her fragrant hair, then sigh and turn away, stare up at that devil's grin of a moon. "It was my decision," I say. "My brothers were going off to fight. Our father, he was also a soldier. Years ago. He's a big believer in fighting— and dying, if necessary—for the things you believe in."

"And what things does your father believe in?"

I think a moment, unsure how to respond. "The South, I guess. Tradition."

"Not love?" she says, her tone serious. "Not family?"

"I don't think my father's big on either of those things, not in the way you mean."

Sarafina says nothing, but I sense her waiting.

"You have to understand, my mother died when I was very young. I've been told he was different before…before that happened. But now? He's a hard man, my father." I pause, thinking carefully about my next words, debating the honesty of them, and realizing—perhaps for the first time—that it's the truth. "If I hadn't gone to war with my brothers, he would have been disappointed."

"Disappointed," she says, and the anger in her tone is evident. "But not disappointed to see his sons die? To send a child to fight a war over slaves and cotton?"

"It's more than that," I say defensively, but am unsure how to justify the statement, so say nothing further.

Sarafina sighs heavily, and her warm hand slips into mine. My mouth tastes sour from the mushroom, but my stomach has settled. As I stare up at the stars, they seem to vibrate; those pure, blazing white sparks take on hints of color—red, green, yellow. They dance to music I can just barely hear at the edge of my perception. Something deep and sonorous that thrums from behind the canopy of night, emitting from beyond the stars, a source hidden from human eyes.

"I hear music."

Sarafina squeezes my hand gently. "The heavens are a glorious thing. You cannot fathom the expanse, the incredible sights, of what's out there. The planets, the galaxies, the eternal cosmos. There are layers to our reality, Ethan. Layers that, if pulled away, would drive you to madness at the glory of it all. There are things in this universe that go beyond what you read in your Bible, what you hear from philosophers and scientists. You think of Heaven and Hell as being above and below, but they're right next to us. If I didn't think it would kill you, I would show you. I would open your eyes to the true reality of what surrounds this world."

I grunt a response, but honestly have little idea what she's going on about and, frankly, I'm too distracted by the prancing stars to pay much attention; they're creating rainbow streaks of color across the plum-colored sky—colors I can't name, because I don't think

I've ever seen them before. I hold her hand tight because part of me feels like I'm being lifted away, pulled toward the night sky, and I want to stay here, on Earth, on the ground beside this woman, lying beneath the gnarled tree she calls Novah. I want to hear the swishing song of the barley field and, suddenly, I know why Mason wants to stay, why Archie has fallen in love with this stranger; would be willing to kill his own brother if it came to it.

I don't doubt Archie's words, nor his intent. I do, however, doubt his ability to act on such a thing, because it's obvious to anyone with eyes that he's beyond recovery, that he'll soon be dead. Perhaps we'll bury him here, beneath this tree, so he can watch the sky, eternally asleep, his spirit soothed by the hushed whispers of the wind-blown stalks in the field, the trembling flat leaves of the tree.

"Ethan, you still with me?"

"Yes," I say, but my voice sounds strange to my ears, as if I'm speaking with a multitude of mouths, rather than one. "I'm just watching the stars."

"I brought you here to thank you," Sarafina says. "You saved Titus's life, and because of that I owe you a debt."

I shake my head, enjoying the feel of grass against my stubble-haired skull. "You're welcome," I say, and absently wonder if those glittering stars will ever fall to the earth in giant streaks of color, explode like dynamite. Wouldn't that be something?

Sarafina rolls over, rises to an elbow, puts a hand on my chest... then moves it to my cheek. She turns my face toward her and she's so close to me that I feel her breath, the warmth of her body pressed against my side. She leans in and kisses me, lightly, on the lips. Not a passionate kiss—not the kiss of a lover, or so I would suppose. But something else. Something heavy with meaning. A message.

When she moves her face away, the sky above her is streaked with color, and now it's her wide eyes that hold the stars—millions of them going on and on forever.

An entire universe inside her.

"This is my way of thanking you. Are you listening?"

"Yes," I say, but the word is only a murmur, barely passing my lips.

"I want you to leave here, Ethan," she says, her voice echoing and distant. "I will give you everything you need to get home safely. Clothes, food, and weapons. I will show you a map in the sky that you can use at night, that will point the way toward your sister, your father. I'm doing this to pay my debt, do you understand?"

"Leave?" I feel something deep inside myself grow thorns, then wrap around my heart.

I release her hand, gently push her away from me—so I can think clearly—and force myself to a sitting position. I rub my eyes in an effort to stop the way the world around me rotates, as if years were flowing by instead of seconds.

"I can't leave," I say, fumbling for the right words. "I can't leave my brothers."

Sarafina sits up as well, tucks her knees beneath her. "Your brothers are going to stay here, Ethan. You know that by now, don't you? Archie will be dead soon. Possibly tomorrow, or perhaps the next day. As for Mason...he will stay on and live here, with me."

"He's only using you." I blurt the words out, not knowing if they're true or not, but needing to lash out, to hurt her if I can.

Instead, she laughs. "Why do you assume that I am the one being used?" she says, and there's a threat to her words I don't dare contradict.

"But your husband—" Then, suddenly, I realize what a fool I've been. "There is no husband."

She shakes her head. "No. I lied about that, I'm afraid. I have my reasons."

"Then why do you stay out here? Alone, in the middle of nowhere."

Sarafina smiles sadly. "Trust me when I say it's not my choice. I would give anything to see the world in which you live." She laughs, waves a hand at the horizon. "I want to see trains, and boats. Rivers, and oceans. I want to hear music and dance in a crowded hall. I'd like to see buildings taller than mountains, and machines that fly across the sky."

I don't know what to think about her ramblings, her storybook fantasies. My mind has been jarred askew and I can't think straight; my thoughts are muddled, rolling around my head like loose marbles, taunting me, refusing linear reason. I close my eyes, try to focus. "So why don't you leave, then?" I say, fighting the drift and pull of the dark behind my eyelids.

I open my eyes, clutch at her hand. "You could leave with me."

"I can't," she whispers, her eyes darting away, sparing me from the rejection I'd most certainly see there.

I nod, flushed with embarrassment and hurt. "So, you have no husband."

She shakes her head, picks at the grass.

"And Titus?" I ask, curious. "Is he your son?"

"Titus is a companion," she says slowly, measuring her words. "I care for him deeply, and I take care of him. And he's happy, don't you think?"

I tap the fabric at my chest. "And what of the clothes?"

Sarafina rolls her eyes, groans with annoyance. "Must everything with you be a question, Ethan Belle?" She looks up at the stars, as if seeking answers for my existence, then back at me. But her eyes have narrowed now; that small, contemptuous smile is back on her lips, and I know any moments of intimacy we shared—or may have thought of sharing—are forever lost.

"Ethan, you are a wonderful boy, inquisitive and polite and handsome. But you are also stubborn and...there is a darkness inside you. A poison that also lives inside your brothers. Mason overflows with it. He is consumed by it, which is why he must stay with me. I'm telling you this, Ethan, as a gift. I'm paying a debt. You must leave here. You must go home."

"Cross the creek..." I mutter, thinking of the words Titus shared with me.

"What?"

I clear my throat. "Titus said, if I cross the creek, I can go home."

Sarafina's expression darkens at my words, and for a moment I see a flicker of something behind the veil of her beauty, behind the mask she wears.

It is powerful, and frightening.

"When—" she begins, but then the mask returns and she nods to herself, as if realizing. Abruptly, she stands and holds out a hand toward me. I accept it, let her help me to my feet. She plucks her shawl from the ground, shakes it once, then wraps it around her shoulders, the black meeting her hair so the entire top of her becomes one with the night. Only her gleaming eyes give her away.

"What did he mean by that, Sarafina?" I take a step toward her. "Why are you both offering my freedom as if it's a gift?"

Sarafina wraps her arms around herself. "There's only so much I can explain."

"How about you try?"

She nods. "I will tell you what I can. And then it's up to you to decide your fate. After that," she says, her face buried in shadow, "there will be no turning back."

31

"There are five powers on this earth," she begins, holding her hands at her sides, palms flattened, parallel to the ground. "Air. Fire. Water. Earth." Then she pokes my chest gently, near my thorny, hardened heart. "Spirit."

"I don't—"

She points to the sky, but her eyes stay on mine. "Those powers combine into five points, like a star."

"I've never heard anything like that," I say, frustrated by her, by the situation, by the fact that I feel close to understanding something important, something that eludes me. Nothing in my vision will sit still, and the more I try to make sense of the things I see, the more fantastical they become—the whole world is liquid, and Sarafina an impossible being of light and darkness. I cling to her words and focus as best I'm able.

"The powers are binding, incredibly strong, and very dangerous," she continues. "But they can also be used for good. They can destroy, or protect. They can heal, or kill. These powers are all around us, Ethan. You are surrounded by them, and if you could only reach out and touch them, harness them, you could do anything, see anything...you could *be* anything."

In a daze, I watch as she lifts one open hand between our faces, twists and twirls her fingers. Light flows from her fingertips, then fire...then a swirl of darkness so rich I feel its pull like a physical force, and somehow I know that the hollowness she holds is a gateway, a secret path to all the things she'd spoken of earlier—a portal to parts of this world I cannot see, to places and things that would drive me mad.

I look away, rub furiously at my eyes, frustrated with my inability to comprehend what she's telling me, what she's showing me. "You talk plainly of magic, of mysticism," I say, suddenly angry. "But it's the Devil's work, Sarafina. You pull light from your fingers as if it's a trick, but to me it's like watching a small child play with fire."

"Is that right?" she says, seemingly amused, all the while holding that gateway like a charm. Her arrogance, and my ignorance, ignites that anger in my chest, and I slap at the hand, which she pulls back, out of my reach, her smile never faltering as the strange portal disappears.

"I *have* seen things." I point an accusatory finger at her curling, mocking smile. "I've seen men gutted with knives and shit themselves, then fall to the earth and bleed out, covered in their own filth as they scream for mercy, and receive none. I've seen men blasted to pieces by grape, or die gasping from a gunshot wound while begging for their mothers. I've listened to men pray to God in a surgical tent, held them down as the surgeon sawed through the bone of their leg. You talk of stars and air, of spirit and things unseen, you conjure parlor tricks and whisper grandly about powers, but I say that this earth is covered in filth and evil, and we must all wade through it, just like my brothers and I waded through that swamp to arrive here, this paradise, where you sit with your dogs and your strange child, alone and unloved. You look at me as if I'm a schoolboy and you some great teacher, but the truth is you know nothing of the world, of pain, or sacrifice. So spare me your show of magic, your great revelations of worlds within worlds that would drive me to madness." I step toward her and am surprised when she takes a step back, her smile erased. "The things that I have seen, and the things that I have done on this earth, have already broken my mind in ways you could not possibly fathom. So put away your fire, and never speak to me again as a child."

Sarafina drops her hand to her side, now devoid of light and illusion and, it would seem, love. Avoiding my eyes, she adjusts her shawl, lips moving silently in a way that reminds me of the day the dogs tore apart those men. Despite my bravado, I tense, wondering if something awful is about to happen to me.

"I've offended you, which was not my intention."

She begins to turn away, but I clutch her shoulder and twist her to face me, momentarily shocked at the expression of hate in her face, which does not soften until I pull back my hand, as if burned. "That's it? You're leaving?"

"I've said what I wanted to say," she says. "The rest is up to you."

"Then I have a proposal," I say. "You owe me this favor, this debt. You speak of powers—be they by the Devil or otherwise, I care not. But I'd ask you to heal my brother. Will you do that as payment of your debt?"

Sarafina shakes her head, but I plow forward, knowing there's a way. There must be a way.

"If I stay, will you save my brother's life?"

After a moment, she nods, albeit slightly. "He will be different," she says. "He won't be the brother you know...but yes, I can save him."

A surge of joy rushes through me, tingles every inch of skin. "Then save him. Use these powers you speak of. These magical, incredible worlds I cannot see. Pluck a miracle from them and give it to my brother."

She studies me a moment, eyes narrowed. Finally, she nods once more.

"We are agreed," she says, her face set and stony as a marble statue. "I'm sorry you have refused my offer, but you are a man who has killed, who knows the ways of the world and makes his own decisions."

"I am," I reply, but suddenly I'm unsure of anything, including my own desires, or decisions, and a part of me wonders if I've just made a huge mistake.

"An accord," she says briskly, and walks away.

Within moments, she's disappeared into the barley field, and I can see nothing but the shifting of the stems, the shadow of a path trailing away from me. Standing there, alone in the dark, I feel abandoned. As if this small clearing were a lifeboat, and all around me is an endless, storming sea. A lake of fire.

32

ELLIE

Our Lady of Sorrows.

It's bigger than a church should be, in my opinion. Although it's not yet finished—and likely to be in a half-built state indefinitely, given the resources going to the war effort—it's sprawling and grandiose, peaked and vaulted to signify the greatness of God. All I can think is how much money must be going into it. Money that could be going to those in need, or put in reserve for all the families who will be losing (or *have* lost) husbands and fathers.

Brothers.

Still, it's important to worship. Everyone needs someplace to pray. Or, at the least, meditate on the horrors of the world. Congregate with like-minded folks bursting with sorrow.

I step through the shadow of the massive belltower pointing to Heaven and continue around the side of the church, avoiding the pit and rubble of the unfinished structure, until I come to the black iron gate which leads to the cemetery.

Mother's grave is featureless and plain. A patch of dry grass with a stone cross bearing her name six feet above her cold forehead. I lay down a blanket and sit with her, as I like to do on the first Saturday of each month. Just to check in.

"No word from the boys," I say. "No soldier's letter telling us of their demise, which I suppose is a good thing. I'm sure Mason and Archie are fitting right in, but I worry about Ethan. He shouldn't be up there, fighting and killing. If you were here—"

I take a breath, let it out. No sense in getting riled up.

"You'll be glad to know Father is his usual grumpy self. Ever since he...well, ever since he had that doctor do what he did, he's been desperate to find me a husband. Guess he hopes to marry me off before I create another problem for him to solve. You know me, always making trouble. The other day he brought home a man twice my age, a tobacco farmer who sells to the shop. You should have seen Papa at dinner, all smiles and oiled hair…thinking he was a matchmaker to beat all."

I pluck at the grass, rub it between my fingers, watch the breeze take away the bits and pieces. I wipe a tear from my cheek and place my hand on the earth, wishing I could feel her one more time, hear her voice.

"Can you imagine?" I say quietly. "Me a homemaker for some old man? A tobacco farmer of all things? I mean, it's one thing to care for my father, I owe you that. But I'd rather be an old maid than have some ugly old farmer sticking himself into me every night."

I lie down flat on the ground, lengthwise above the grave, my body in symmetry with the corpse below. "I'd rather die," I say, whispering it into the grass.

On my way out of the churchyard I'm spotted by Father McKee, who offers to walk me home, which I accept.

I tell him about the tobacco farmer courting me, about my worry for my brothers. He listens just as well as Momma once did, quietly considering my words.

"You're getting older, Ellie," he says with a gentle sigh. "It's natural for you to consider marriage. You're not a little girl anymore, you're becoming a woman."

I scoff, then feel my face redden, but he says nothing in retort. "I just wish my father would realize—"

He looks over to me, one eyebrow raised.

"It's as if my father wants me to become a woman in all the ways I don't wish for, and none of the ways I do."

McKee nods, but keeps his thoughts to himself. As we near our house, he touches my elbow, brings us to a stop.

"I'll talk to your father, Ellie," he says. "About the suitors, I mean. I know you've had your hardships, but God has forgiven you, and you have a long, full life ahead. There's time to make those bigger decisions, and your past isn't...while it may be a scar on your soul, it doesn't define you. And doesn't define your future."

I nod, appreciating the words but knowing they're false. He doesn't know what the doctor did to me, to my body, how it cleansed me of the future joy of parenthood. How it's forever tainted my desire for men.

"Thank you, Father," I say lamely.

He smiles, and I'm glad he feels as if he's done some good, that he's helped me. I also notice that he's handsome when he smiles, and perhaps understand a bit more why my mother spent so much time with him.

"Were you visiting your mother?"

"Yes," I say. "I should come more often but—"

He shakes his head. "She lives on in your heart, not in the ground. I'm sure you think of her every day, and that's what matters."

I nod, watching the people walk by in their nice clothes, the dirt of the street seemingly repelled by their finery, by their wondrous lives. We have nearly a block to go, and I've no desire to walk in silence. McKee is a mysterious man to me. He's been close friends to both my parents, but in such different ways. And while Mother never spoke of his past, Father has hinted that the priest's history is slightly ominous, and I wonder about it now as we walk. I try to think of a polite way of asking without seeming rude, or unseemly.

"Father says you're from Ireland originally. I find the idea of Europe fascinating, but know I'll never travel there."

From the corner of my eye, I see him smile. "I've worked hard to subdue the accent. America is a young country, volatile. An infant awash in afterbirth, still screaming in confusion. I've no wish to confuse the members of my congregation, so I hide my past as best I'm able."

"Oh, I don't think anyone minds," I say, unsure of the truth of my words. We are all immigrants, really, perhaps a generation or two removed, but this deep in the South folks are more persnickety when it comes to family lineage. "If you don't mind my asking, how long have you been in America?"

The priest laughs. "A kind way of asking my age?"

"Oh, no—"

But he only waves a hand, nods to a passing parishioner. "I'm only joking, Ellie. I don't mind. Let's see...I left Ireland when I was thirty-five, and I'm fifty-seven now, so do the math and you have your answer."

"And were you always a priest? I hope you don't mind my prying."

"Not at all! I'm glad we have some time to chat." He goes quiet a moment, thinking. "Let's put it this way...I've always worked for the church. In some ways, you could say I'm retired now. I enjoy my quiet parish, my quiet life. I like reading and studying, learning more about this wonderful world God has created."

"Retired? But you're so busy."

McKee pauses, and I pause with him. He looks around, as if to see if there is anyone standing close by, perhaps listening. His eyes hold mine, as if he's trying to decide my merit.

Or my trustworthiness.

"Did your mother never discuss my past?"

I shake my head. "We were young when she died, but I know she enjoyed your company, and we were always fascinated with the books you two would pore over on evenings." I take a stab in the dark, curious as to his behavior. "Were you a soldier?"

He nods slowly, his eyes suddenly distant, as if living in a memory. "You could say that. But as I said, I was always with the church. The enemies I fought were not mortal men."

"I'm not sure I understand. I'm sorry."

His expression changes once more, and he's Father McKee again, smiling and charming and kind. "No need to apologize. I'll see if I can explain more clearly."

He begins walking again and I continue alongside him, wishing we had several more blocks to cover so I could find out more of his secretive past.

"Remember what I said to you before, about the Bible?"

"You mean how there are stories outside the canon?"

He nods. "Well, there are also things outside the everyday practices of a church, just as there are things outside the standard text of the Bible. There is much evil in the world, Ellie. Satan and his minions walk among us, twisting the hearts of men and women. Turning them to his will. Infesting them with his presence, and those of his minions. When I was younger, I was trained to defeat such infestations, to turn the evil away from mankind...to send it back to Hell."

I don't know how to respond to any of this, so I say nothing.

"We're here," he says after a few moments more, and I look up to see my house, which suddenly seems small. Insignificant. There are so many questions in my mind, so many things I'd like to ask.

I wish Ethan were here.

"I'll pray for your brothers," he says, and pats me on the arm as he turns away, making his way back to the church. "I'm sure they're alive and well."

"The Belle boys aren't easy to kill, that's for sure. It'll take more than a few Yankee bullets to cleanse the world of their like," I reply, injecting confidence in my voice I don't feel.

"They're strong, like their sister," he says with a smile. "They're survivors."

He waves a hand and continues away. I watch him for a few moments in frustration, wanting to call him back. But then he's gone, and I'm left—alone—to think on his words, my mind overflowing with thoughts of battles and death, demons and Hell.

Please survive, Ethan, I think, my fists clenched tight, sending the thought out like a prayer. *All three of you boys...just survive. No matter how you do it, no matter what it takes.*

No matter the cost.

PART THREE: THE ESCAPE

33

Archie is worse.

Much worse.

A few days after my strange nighttime meeting with Sarafina, things at the farm have become increasingly odd.

Archie has stopped eating entirely, and now only keeps down water and whatever concoction Sarafina began giving him the day after she promised to save his life—a sort of herbal tea, the ingredients of which she refuses to share.

It smells rancid.

But once she gets it down Archie's throat, he does relax and drift off, his pain subsiding for a few hours.

The other strange thing about it—other than the horrid smell and the black, oily sheen of the liquid—is that she refuses to administer the tea with either Mason or myself in the room. While we are handling chores, or even sitting at the kitchen table, she and Archie stay behind closed doors. She's been in there twice yesterday and twice today, once for as long as an hour, and when I press an ear against the door to try and hear what might be happening, I can only make out the sound of her mumbling voice, repeating some form of prayer in a language I've never heard.

Mason—who now sleeps every night on the upper floor and, during the day, is often outside working the crops—tells me to stop worrying so much. I suppose he's right, but he's also neatly twisted around Sarafina's little finger. He does whatever she asks—without question, without complaint.

Ellie, you'd hardly recognize his demeanor. I've never seen him so docile. I'd suggest he's been secretly neutered except for the fact I can hear them, up in her loft, fornicating for hours on end; her bed—I now painfully realize—being just above our heads when we sleep. At times it sounds like I'm sleeping beneath a barroom brawl.

It wouldn't be so unbearable if not for the fact that poor Archie must listen as well, lying there in his stinking sweat and fluids, likely dying, while the woman he claims to love is ten feet above, spreading her legs for our dear brother. Archie's anguished moans while Mason and Sarafina are—to be blunt—fucking a hole in the ceiling above us, are far worse than the sounds of physical pain he's been mewling since our arrival. Part of me hopes he survives—that Sarafina keeps her promise—and part of me hopes I wake up one morning to find him cold and still.

At this point, I think it would be a mercy.

As for Titus, he either doesn't notice or doesn't care. His mannerisms toward her—toward any of us—haven't changed since the moment we arrived, and though he's been warmer toward me since the incident with the mountain lion, I still wouldn't call us friends.

That goes double for Sarafina.

Yes, she smiles and flirts and cooks and cleans. She gives us clothes and nurses Archie as best she's able, but there's something deeper going on with her, something she only hinted at the other night, under the stars, by that hideous giant of a tree. She refuses to answer my questions about where she got our clothes, which leaves me wary. Taken together, this place is a series of benign mysteries that are easy, I suppose, to shrug away.

And yet...

I know, deep in my heart, that there's something else wrong here.

There's something about this house—and the land that surrounds it—that raises the hairs on the back of my neck. It's as if the cabin is a mirage, or *detached* somehow, from the world in which we live. In which society operates. While I don't feel we're in any danger, the benign mysteries of this place are piling up in a way that makes me wary. I lay my head down every night with more questions than I have answers.

For example, why is this young woman living out here all alone? There's no nearby town for supplies, no neighbors to help with issues that may come up from time-to-time. She lied about having a husband and has ordered—and numbly watched—the savage, horrific death of men without a hint of empathy or guilt. It's as if we're in a fairy tale of sorts, prisoners of a beautiful queen who rules with an iron fist.

In my mind, I keep replaying my strange conversation with Titus about moats and castles, his odd words about the creek. I mocked him at the time, insisting that we weren't on an island.

That we could leave at any time.

Now, I'm not so sure that's the truth.

And so, having spent over a week here as guests, I decide to wake early, take a gun, and do some exploring. It's been a long night. Archie reeks of rotting flesh, and he hasn't stopped moaning since I laid down yesterday evening, the sounds coming from his side of the room increasingly strange, as if his torn throat has worsened to the point that every noise he now makes is more animal than human. Lying near him in the dark, I all but beg for the sun to rise so I can get away from his ragged laments, his death stench.

The moment I look at the window and see the brightening sky, the distant red haze of the approaching sun, I waste no time in getting up to gather my things. I don't know what I expect to find out there on the outskirts of this land, but I know where to start.

If Titus thinks I should cross the creek, then that's exactly what I'll do.

34

The morning is bright and cool, early enough that the sun is still low, the shadows long.

I've loaded the rifle and have my bayonet in my boot. I put on the hat Sarafina gave me, unsure how long I'll be outside and knowing that, if the day heats up, I'll be happy to have it. On my way out the door Sarafina hands me a pouch stocked with apples and jerky that I quickly sling over my shoulder with a muted thanks. She nods and smiles that strange, knowing smile of hers, then watches me go without a word.

I step off the porch, debating on direction, and take a moment to inspect the sky. It's cornflower blue and cloudless, and I suddenly realize that it hasn't rained since our arrival. During our weeks on the run, it rained almost every day, but while with Sarafina it's been bone dry, comfortably sunny. Near perfect.

Just one more oddity added to the growing list in my head.

With no real plan in mind, I decide to start at the beginning, as it were, and head for the point of the creek where we first entered Sarafina's domain. That lone peach tree where Titus waved at me, the stretch of water where we shaved our heads and scrubbed the bugs, blood, and mud from our skin.

I follow the invisible path we've used a few times or more, and after a ten minute walk I find the creek easily. Across the dappled water is the large wall of Buckthorn; tall trees and woods darkening the land beyond. I know that if I were to cross the water and continue straight, I'd eventually reach the massive swamp where Mason was nearly smothered by the deep, sucking mud. Instead of crossing, I decide to follow the creek for a while and see where it leads. If I stray too far, it'll be simple enough to find my way back, and at least I won't have to worry about thirst.

I look both ways along the shoreline, which—as I'd noticed

previously—runs straight as a ruler north and south. I choose south.

The ground is flat and easy to traverse, and though the trees thicken as I move further from the homestead, there's plenty of dry shore between the woods and the water. I hear no strange sounds, see nothing out of the ordinary. The water trickles on, carelessly, to my right, brewing like a pot about to boil. I notice that the shorelines neither broaden nor narrow and, from what I can tell, the water maintains the same depth—just a few feet—as it did where we first crossed it.

Finally, after what I estimate to be about a half-mile, the creek bends.

Actually, it doesn't bend so much as *turn*.

Dramatically.

Sharp as the broken shaft of an arrow, the shoreline simply stops going one direction, then cuts hard to the left. I stop at the crux of the angle, looking back the way I'd come, then off to the left, where the water continues in a newly formed straight line.

I've never seen anything like it, and wonder if the creek is manmade. Perhaps it was dug out so the water would...*what?* There are no mills I've seen, no dams. And yet I'm standing at the apex of a triangle, which would indicate that the creek isn't natural, because water doesn't simply stop going one way, turn sharply, and begin running another.

I step closer to the shore to study the way the water moves, hoping to see some indication of a direction. I kneel, pluck grass, and toss it onto the surface. For a while I watch the small green blades dance and swirl, but they never drift one way or another. When I finally give up and turn east, eager to continue following the water's path, the broken grass still lies on the surface, spinning madly.

I walk another quarter mile, give or take, when I reach the next turn.

This time it shoots off to the right. Meanwhile, the forest to my left has grown darker, denser. The trees here appear much older than the ones I've seen closer to the farm. They're tall hardwood oaks and elms, the bases wide as two men shoulder to shoulder. Part of me wants to enter these woods; I have the feeling the game there will be plenty...but the creek confounds me, and for now I need to stay with it.

As I continue walking along, I keep waiting for it to branch off and run away to the north or east, but instead it seems to run almost parallel to the house, which I estimate is about a half mile from where I stand.

Across the water from here is flatland. A prairie. I would love to walk through it, stir up the insects, pick flowers for Sarafina's table, or find a burrow of rabbit for stew. I could just step into the water and cross. I could...

But I don't.

Besides, the morning is being burned away by a ripe afternoon sun, and I've a lot more to explore. I turn myself north, pull an apple from my sack, and continue along the mysterious shoreline, eager to make sense of things.

I walk the rest of the day, stopping only once to rest and eat more of the provisions Sarafina packed for me. I lie on my belly and cup cold water into my mouth from the creek, and feel tireless.

All together I've counted ten bends—ten hard turns— throughout the rest of my exploration. I make mental notes of the direction in which the shore angled, and by the time I return to the familiar part of the creek—the point where I started—the light is fading in the west, and the arching sky has turned a fiery pink blaze fading to purple in the east, where the escaping sun's reach is tenuous.

At no point did the creek terminate or runoff. At no point did it widen, or narrow, or bend in a natural way. There are no inlets or outlets, and it flows in no single direction. It is therefore a self-sustaining water source that somehow—the answer to which is far beyond my knowledge—runs into *itself*.

I wipe my forehead. My legs have grown weary, my stomach grumbles for a meal, and my feet groan for a rest. Time to head back.

As I enter the house, I say hello to Sarafina, who is busy in the kitchen. I remove my hat, set the rifle by the door, and return the leather satchel—now empty—to its owner.

"Just set it on the counter," she says, chopping at some vegetable or other, her back turned to me, as if my appearance has become commonplace, a routine she's grown not only used to but silently weary of, in the way well-worn shoes become molded to your feet, or the repetitive laughter of a sibling you live with day after day sounds like birdsong. The weariness of comfort.

Instead of going to my bedroom (the door is closed, and I have no immediate desire to smell Archie's decay nor hear his delirious moans and death rattles), I cross to where Titus sits on the couch by the window, a book on his lap and a lit lantern on the table to his side.

I sit next to him, then spare a quick glance at Sarafina across the room, who still has her back to me, humming a tune to herself I don't recognize. I gaze at the pages of the book open on the boy's lap and am surprised at the strangeness of the characters. It's not English, or any other language I'm familiar with. My curiosity temporarily overrides my anxiety.

"What's that you're reading?"

"Part of the Zohar," he says, eyes not leaving the pages.

"Never heard of it," I say, which is true. "What language is that?"

The boy turns his head toward me, a quizzical look on his face, one I take as mild rebuke, as if he's wondering just how uneducated and stupid a person could possibly be. "Aramaic," he says, all brittle hostility. Then, likely knowing the word means nothing to me, or simply noting the glazed expression in my eyes, he adds, "Ancient Hebrew."

"And you can read that?"

He nods, and his face transforms into one of childish pride. It suits him well. "Sarafina taught me."

"That's good," I say, and glance once more across the room to make sure we're not being watched. I lean close and lower my voice. "Titus, I need a favor. Do you by chance have paper and pencil?"

He looks at me, eyes widening in surprise for a mere second, before his expression settles back into the casual boredom he wears so well. He sets down his book and walks to a cabinet on the opposite wall, opens a drawer and pulls out a thin book, a stubby pencil. He comes back and hands them over.

"My journal," he says, seemingly not worried I might read whatever private thoughts he's written down within. "Use the blank pages at the back."

I nod, open the book to the last page. With the pencil, I make a point in the center of it, then draw a line from that point to another line, this one perpendicular.

The dot is the farm. The perpendicular line is the creek where I first met it this morning, and upon our initial arrival.

Carefully, I begin to trace the creek as I walked it, including each turn, approximating the distance between each as I remember it. At first, I'd paid scant attention to measurements, but by the halfway point of my walk I was counting my steps between each break. They were all, by and large, identical.

Titus watches me with great interest, his eyes moving from the rough sketch to my face, then back again. At one point I note that he also looks toward the kitchen, then subtly moves his body so he's standing between my work and his mother.

If that's what she is.

When finished, I sit back and stare hard at the image. I meet the small, dark eyes of the boy, and something passes between us. Some form of understanding—of what, I have no idea. An agreement between two ignorant conspirators.

On the page is a rough, somewhat uneven, sketch of what can only be described as a star.

The creek, as I've recreated it, is a pentagram, drawn into the earth by water.

At the very center of this star, represented by the dot I'd drawn upon beginning, is Sarafina's house.

It is completely surrounded by the unnatural shape of the creek.

"An island..." I mutter quietly, a thousand questions racing through my brain, itching my lips in a desire to be spoken aloud. I look up at Titus, desperately wanting to ask what the hell is going on here, but his eyes hold mine with a hard glare.

Then he slowly—almost imperceptibly—shakes his head.

Say no more.

After a moment, he gently reaches out with his small, pale hands, and takes the journal from my shaking fingers. He closes it, holds it tight to his chest.

"Titus—" I start, but he cuts me off.

"You should go check on your brother," he says. "The one who isn't seeding my mother."

I'm sickened by his words, but my mind is too fragmented, my emotions too flayed, to truly care. "Why?" I ask.

But think I already know the answer.

"Because he's about to die," the child says, then turns on his heel and walks away from me and into his room, leaving me with empty, upturned hands, desperately searching for answers to questions I don't even know how to ask.

35

"Mason!"

I cry out his name—not knowing what else to do—hoping he hears me and comes running.

I can't handle this alone.

I haven't seen Archie—truly *seen* him—since yesterday evening when I tucked into my blankets. And even then, he'd been cocooned in his own bedding, wrapped in the thick wool blankets Sarafina had given us, and covered with a large lavender quilt stitched with white roses. At the time I hadn't wanted to disturb him, so I left him alone (truth be told, I'd no desire to be any closer to the sour stink of his body rotting from the inside out).

But after speaking with Titus, I'd come into our room unsure what to expect, not knowing the state of things. How far along was the gangrene that'd been chewing up his guts, turning his skin black and brittle as burnt leaves? How much time did he have left?

I noticed right away that he'd kicked away the bedding, that he'd somehow found the strength to tear off his shirt—the fabric sopped with pus, sweat, and blood. I took a step toward him, thinking to cover him back up, find a way to clean the stains of piss and shit in the bedding beneath him...

And froze halfway across the room, my flesh crawling with repulsion and horror.

Archie was still sick—surely dying—but there was something else. Something much worse.

"Mason!" I yell again, praying the bastard hears me.

Archie stares in my direction, eyes wide and rolling in their sockets, chest pumping in rapid, shallow breaths like a runaway train. Outside the window, the bright day melts into a red curtain of dusk, and the sun turns to blood.

"Archie?"

I am afraid to step closer toward him...toward *it*.

Toward whatever my brother has become.

His scalp, cheeks, and chin are covered in thick black hair, as if he'd had a month's growth in the last twenty-four hours. He opens his mouth—as if to tell me something—and reveals a blackened tongue, black gums. I hear the soft *click click click* of what I assume are the last of his teeth tumbling out over his lips and tapping onto the hardwood floor (with the exception of one straggler tangled in the filth of his beard, white as a maggot). His ribs protrude grotesquely, all but punching through his skin, and his legs are abnormally bent—as if they'd been broken below the knees, then improperly healed. His stomach oozes with a steady flow of yellow pus, and the flesh around the wound is black-veined, pulsing with its own sinister heartbeat. He raises a bared arm—reaching a clawed hand toward me, as if seeking comfort, or help. Perhaps death.

Instead of moving closer, I take a step back, my disgust and fear and despair in this moment easily overpowering the love I feel for him.

When he finally speaks, the words are too guttural and shapeless for me to know what he wants, what he needs. "Archie, please..." I beg, tears dripping off my cheeks.

As his wild eyes plead and the puddle of filth beneath him grows, I step hesitantly forward, thinking that, at the very least, I can take his hand, try to bring some comfort. I take a deep breath to steady my nerves. This is my *brother*. I need to help him if I'm able.

Before I can go to him, however, I hear a distinct...*crackling* sound.

Archie's head jerks upward and he *screams*—mindless screams loud enough to shake the walls—as the bones in that reaching, pleading arm begin to break—*SNAP SNAP SNAP!* His fingers twist backward and his wrist cracks like a gunshot, then dangles from the end of his arm, the hand misshapen and clawed.

"Oh, God, please stop—" I say, and only then do I hear pounding feet on the porch, the front door thrown violently open. I turn and see Mason striding toward me, his face a dark cloud, his rough blue shirt sweat-stained and covered in dust and splinters, as if he'd been chopping wood or moving hay.

His anger twists into confusion, however, when he sees the look on my face—which I assume is a mask of horror. Not able to find the words, I simply point across the room.

"Jesus Christ!" he cries, staring at the twisted, screeching abomination on the floor. Braver than I, Mason runs across the room and kneels next to Archie. When he tries to take his hand, I hear more fingerbones snap like kindling beneath his grasp, causing Archie to howl in pure anguish, loud and frightful as a demon of Hell. Mason lets go the broken hand and raises his own hands into the air—not wanting to do anymore harm—his face pale and strained. He looks at me, eyes filled with fury.

"What the fuck is this?" he says, but I only shake my head, take another step back toward the open door, even now thinking of escape from this nightmare.

"I don't know," I say.

But then I recall Sarafina's words from the night in the field, the night she promised to save his life.

He will be different... He won't be the brother you know...

"I think he's changing," I mumble, knowing it to be the truth.

I don't know how she's doing it, or what my brother will become, but I firmly believe that his body is turning into something else—and my God, it's happening right before our eyes.

"What the hell are you talking about, Ethan?" Mason stands, takes two strides toward me, hands clenched into threatening, white-knuckled fists. "He's sick. He needs help."

"I agree," I say, but I'm thinking something altogether different.

I'm thinking it's too late.

For a blessed moment the sound of screaming stops as Archie rolls onto his stomach, panting heavily, his back coated with a glossy slime of sweat. The rear of his pants is stained and foul, and his legs are bent so oddly that I doubt he could stand on his feet if held up to do so.

"Mason, we have to go," I say under my breath. I don't know

where Sarafina is, or if Titus is out of earshot, but I want this just between us. "All of us, we need to leave here."

Mason stares at me, brow furrowed, as if trying to comprehend what I'm saying while, a few feet away, our broken brother writhes in a fetal position on the floor, monstrous and obscene. For the first time in my life, my oldest brother looks lost, beaten.

After a few moments, however, his expression clears with sudden understanding, followed quickly by an expression of rage. "It's her," he says tightly. "She's the one doing this to him. It's some sort of... hell, I don't know. Witchcraft."

I begin to reply—perhaps share my findings about the creek, or tell him what Sarafina had said about letting me go. What she said about Mason *not* leaving, and how Archie would become something different than what he was.

Oh, God! How all her words become plain to me only now.

I want to sit him down and tell him about the strange conversations I've had with Titus, how he thinks this place is an island. Or, more likely, a prison.

But before I can say any of these things, Archie raises to all fours—hands and feet—his bony behind reaching toward the ceiling, back arched like a strained bow. He shakes his head as if confused.

He jerks his face toward me and I gasp.

The whites of his eyes are gone.

"Arch?"

I stare, wide-eyed and numb with shock, as his nose breaks with an air-splitting CRACK and his face distorts—then *extends*. A new, bristled nose pushes outward, the flesh above his mouth bulging, lengthening, until it becomes a deformed, fleshy snout. His cracked, blackened lips curl into a snarl and brand-new canines push through his gums, crest his lower lip. With a sharp series of concurrent sounds—not unlike the breaking of brittle kindling—the bones in his legs fracture, one by one. This time, instead of screaming, he only grunts and whines as his legs fold inward upon themselves. Long, blackened toenails scrape the floorboards.

There are fast, heavy footsteps behind me and I spin to see, through the house's open front door, the large black dog standing on the porch, teeth bared.

"Close that door!" Mason yells.

I sprint out of the bedroom and lunge for the front door, slamming it shut in the dog's growling face. Immediately the beast begins scratching and pounding at the outside of the door, howling as if in the throes of madness, desperate beyond measure to get inside.

"Get away!" I scream, terrified and overwhelmed with despair, wishing I could run from this place and never return.

Then, from the back of the house, I hear the others.

They're *all* howling now, the air filled with their elongated cries. I'm suddenly reminded of being in battle, surrounded by enemies who sense defeat, who smell blood.

Jesus Christ. They're all around us.

"Ethan! Dear Christ, Ethan!"

I check the latch is firmly in place, then run back into the bedroom to find Mason backed against a wall. He looks at me with an expression of such acute terror that I hardly recognize him.

The thing at his feet is the reason.

What was once Archie now paces in small circles, walking on the palms of broken arms, the feet of broken legs. His back is shaded by sprouted dark bristles and his pants have torn open at the seat. As if blinded, he throws his body against one wall and leans there, panting, his body emitting hundreds of small *clicks* and *clacks* as unseen, tiny bones continue to break and reform, as organs shift and move.

Slowly, he pushes off the wall and turns in a circle, as if getting used to this new, wretched state. He cocks his hairy head to look at Mason, then turns his deformed face to me.

"Archie, I'm so sorry," I say, my words no more than a whimper.

In response, my dear brother tilts back his shaggy mane—neck extended—to stare at the ceiling with black eyes.

And then he howls.

36

"I'll kill the bitch!" Mason pounds down the stairs from the loft, where he'd found no trace of Sarafina. He paces the floor like a caged tiger. I look to make sure Titus's door is still shut. Since there's no way he hasn't heard all the commotion, I assume he's hiding in there. I don't blame him.

"How is it possible?" I say, lost in my thoughts. I glance warily toward our bedroom, knowing that the thing that used to be Archie is lying down somewhere behind the closed door, still morphing into whatever he would become, assuming he survives. "How can she do such things?"

"Witchcraft!" Mason screams, pointing at me with a trembling fist. "Devilry!"

Could it be true? Is she so powerful?

"Mason, we should leave. We should go and fetch a doctor—"

He glares at me, eyes filled with ice blue death. "Never. Not until she pays for what she's done. Or hell...fixes him!"

Suddenly, the howling from outside stops. There are shuffling footsteps on the porch, followed by Sarafina's voice, shooing the black dog away. Or giving it further instruction. We both stare at the door. My nerves vibrate with tension.

She comes through the front door wearing a dark cloak with a hood. A woven ash basket is looped over one forearm, brimming with fruit and flowers. Beneath the hood, her face is almost luminescent in its beauty, and I wonder if it's the coloring of the cloak flattering her features, or some sort of spell she's cast upon us like a charm. She notes me standing by the dining table and smiles warmly, humming a tune, then turns and closes the door behind her.

It's only when she's turned back that she finally notices Mason at the far end of the room, staring at her with murderous rage. Instead of shrinking from his expression of pending violence, however, Sarafina only continues to hum her wispy little song, places her basket gently onto the countertop, and pushes the hood back from her head.

"I've been to the berry fields," she says, turning her back to us as she removes fruit and flowers from the basket, sets it all neatly on the countertop. "You'd be surprised how much of it is already ripening. I plan to make a pie."

Mason stomps across the room and I tense in anticipation of the ensuing violence, but he surprises me, stopping less than a foot away from her turned back. For her part, Sarafina doesn't so much as twitch, doesn't acknowledge him in any way. Instead, she cleans her fresh pickings and hums her song. Mason glances at me, and I shrug. Finally, his face red with restrained fury, he takes a step *away* from Sarafina, unclenches his fists, folds his arms tight across his chest. I don't know if it's restraint, or love, or something else; some form of manipulation I can't fathom.

"What did you do to Archie?" Mason says, his bearish, brutish size next to her small form makes me reflexively want to help her, stand up for her, despite knowing what she's done. I resist the urge and, instead, sit down at the dining table, waiting to discover what harm has been done to our brother, and how.

"Answer me!" he shouts, restraint fraying, and slams a hand against the countertop.

For the first time, I note the smallest hindrance of her movements.

I wonder if she's frightened of what's to come.

A door creaks open to my left, and I turn to see Titus standing just outside his room, watching us. He seems dazed, as if he's just woken from a nap.

Sarafina gives Mason a sidelong look. "I'd ask you not to take that tone with me in my house," she says, then continues to remove the contents of her basket, as if nothing happened.

Titus clears his throat and Sarafina turns around, facing the room. She spots the boy, smiles brightly. "Titus, I'm going to bake a pie," she says casually, and I can't help wondering if she's taunting us, as if this whole bizarre scene was her plan all along.

I stand from my seat at the table, readying myself for what's to come next.

Will my brother kill them both?

Or just her?

Before I can think on it further, Mason begins to laugh. A most terrible sound.

He walks to where I stand by the table, plucks the ceramic pitcher off the table, and takes a long drink.

I catch Titus's eye.

He winks at me.

Then he disappears back into his room, and closes the door softly behind him.

"Mason," I say, perhaps to stay his hand, to calm him.

To warn him.

Gripping the pitcher in one hand, he throws it with all his strength at Sarafina's head. The pitcher misses the back of her skull by inches, crashing against the wall above the counter, shards of pottery and a spray of water showering the kitchen.

Sarafina stops humming.

"You dare—" she says quietly, the words hissed like a serpent. She turns, slowly, and I find myself taking a step backward, my back pressed against the far wall.

But she only has eyes for Mason.

She takes a step toward him, hands at her sides, fingers curled into hooks, long black nails like talons. "You dare assault me in my own home?" Although Mason hasn't moved—momentarily, at least, standing his ground—the boiling rage on his face seems to falter. She takes another step, one long finger pointed at his chest. "You dare threaten me?"

"You deserve worse for what you've done to our brother," Mason says, straightening his spine to reinforce the fact he stands a foot taller than her.

Sarafina turns her head to face me, one eyebrow arched, as if waiting for me to say something, to step in. Perhaps to explain that I'd begged her to save Archie's life, no matter the cost. Instead, I only shake my head, force myself to breathe.

"You're killing him," I say, feeling courage bloom in my chest.

After all, what is she compared to us? A thin, small woman. Her little boy. The oddities of the house, and the land surrounding it, have tricked me into thinking that the world is full of great mysteries, that there are powers hidden from our eyes.

But I know firsthand what a ball shot from a rifle does to a body. I know that disease can fester in a wound, rot the flesh. I've seen hundreds of men die in unspeakable ways on the battlefield and in the medical tents.

Burned. Shot. Blown apart.

I've heard the screams of men while doctors dig hands into their guts, slice open their skin, hack off their limbs.

That's reality. That's the true horror—the true power—in the world, not this backwoods woman and her silver-tongued words, her herbs and mushrooms, her bizarre mannerisms.

Parlor tricks. Deceptions.

And now she's done us harm, like so many others have done, and it's her turn to fall in step with them. She will cure Archie, or she will die.

I reach behind me, Sarafina's gaze still fixed in my direction, and grip the loaded rifle I'd leaned against the wall earlier that day.

Her eyes flick from me to the gun, then she closes them, sighing heavily, as if disappointed. She whispers a prayer, but the only part of it I hear clearly—that even sounds like the English language—is the end, when she mutters three words:

"So be it."

Mason grabs her by the throat and slams her body against the countertop. I take a few steps toward them, musket primed and loaded, but pointed toward her feet. For now.

"Fix him," Mason growls. "Or I'll rip your fucking heart out."

"The dogs…" Her voice is weak, strained as it works to find its way past Mason's grip.

Mason turns his head and looks at me wearing a sick, murderous grin. He shakes his head, as if amused by the supposed threat. "Woman, those hounds can't help you here."

Despite his words my eyes glance toward the front door, making sure it's closed tight and latched. Thankfully, it is.

"Now," Mason continues evenly, as her face reddens above his grip. "You *will* help my brother, witch." He curls his right hand into a fist, readies it for the coming blow. "Or so help me God, you will be dead and buried before nightfall."

He moves in closer until their bodies are nearly pressed together against the countertop, then he unclenches his fist and moves his free hand roughly to her breast. I want to look away, my guts sickened by his action, but instead I watch, pushing away the burning shame rising in my chest. Instead of saying something to stop him, I only raise the point of the rifle in her direction. I aim for her heart.

"You think your body will save you?" he says, then removes the hand from her chest and slaps her across the face. Her head rocks to the side, but he keeps the other hand tight to her throat. "This is your last warning," he says, making that fist once again, and I know this time he's not bluffng, that he's going to beat her until she either helps Archie or not.

Either way, she's going to die.

Before he can say anything further, the window shutters slam shut, sealing out the meager light of the dying day.

The lanterns in the room dim.

Mason pauses, cocks his head. "The hell?"

"Hold on," I say, and then I'm at the front door, yanking on the handle.

It doesn't budge.

"Mason—" I begin, but Sarafina's voice stops me short.

To be more precise, her laughter.

When I spin back to look, it takes me a moment to understand what I'm seeing.

Mason is no longer standing over her, one hand on her throat, the other raised to strike. Now it's Sarafina who stands taller, as if she'd grown two feet in the blink of an eye.

Her black eyes have enlarged, impossibly wide in her pale face, and her toothy grin is more animal than human.

It's the grin of a predator.

"You threaten me?!" The words erupt from her like a command from God—her voice fills the room as if shouted from every corner. My ears ring so painfully that I drop the rifle to the floor, clamp my hands to the sides of my head, willing it to stop.

Through the painful, piercing ringing, I once again hear the howling of the dogs.

One of them howls from our bedroom.

Sarafina steps boldly toward Mason, who backs away, colliding into me before tripping over my gun. He stumbles to the floor as if gutshot.

Before he can regain his feet, or his anger, Sarafina's clenched fist tucks into a pouch of her dark cloak. She kneels, spreads her fingers wide to reveal a palm filled with gray powder, and blows it into Mason's face.

I stare down in horror as my brother's eyes water—tears spilling down his face in rivulets—and the whites fill with blood. He grips his throat as if choking, and begins to convulse.

"Stop!" I yell, not knowing if it's possible, not knowing if it's too late.

After a few heartbeats, Mason's body stops shaking and he lies still, as if petrified. Paralyzed. His wet, terrified eyes shift left to right in panic, but not even his lips tremor, nor his fingers twitch. Sarafina stands erect, already reaching once more into her small pocket.

I raise a hand defensively, backing away. "Wait—"

But she only smiles wider—impossibly wide—her teeth long and white and gleaming, her eyes bulbous and black as oil. "I told you to leave," she says, her voice ragged, deep. Inhuman. With a quick motion, she lifts her palm and blows the powder.

"Now no one is leaving."

The powder hits my face like a mass of stinging bees, tearing at my eyes, burning the insides of my nose and mouth. It tastes bitter, a dry mist of raw onion and putrid flesh—the dust of a decayed corpse taken straight from the grave.

Within seconds my body goes numb. My muscles stiffen, hard as iron. I try to speak but cannot move my mouth. My eyes water uncontrollably and I attempt to turn my body, thinking that I must run, must get out the front door, past the creek and all the way home, to my sister, and my life. But my legs refuse to answer my brain's desperate pleas. Instead, they seize as if made from stone and I fall like a tumbled statue onto my side. As if from a great distance, I feel my body jerk and spasm, my limbs pound mercilessly against the floorboards.

Then a strange warmth blooms in my chest, and despite my body's rejection of whatever it is she's put into me, my mind slows, my terrified thoughts retract. I feel a strong desire to simply close my eyes, and sleep.

Sarafina steps over Mason's body, taps him with a toe, then crosses over to look down on my own. Her face has returned to its normal, beatific state, and her smile is more sad than vicious. Pitying.

"I warned you," she says, her voice musical—and *human*—once more. "I told you that your brother would be different. That to save him, he would be changed. And now, Ethan, you will also be changed. Although not in the same way, I'm afraid."

She kneels next to me, gently strokes my face.

I'm surprised I can feel her touch despite my body being rigid as a fallen tree, limbs numb, my heartbeat slowed to a distant drum on a far shore.

"After all," she says, wiping a tear from my cheek with the tip of a finger before putting it into her mouth, drinking my fear. "One can never have too many pets."

37

I'm not able to turn my head to see what's happening, but I distinctly hear the creak of our bedroom door opening. "Well, you're coming along nicely," Sarafina says, and there's a bestial huffing, a loud grunt, and what sounds like crying. Or, more accurately, *whining*.

Archie.

"I'll be back soon," she says.

I shift my eyes to try and see what's happening around me as another door creaks open, this time from very close—but it's not a door to one of the rooms.

It's in the floor.

There's a *whump* and a gust of air as the door lands a few feet from my head, heavy enough to send a vibration through the boards beneath me. It must have been hidden, likely beneath one of her rugs, because I've been walking over these boards for a week and never saw a pull-ring or a seam of any kind.

I hear the brush sound of something heavy being dragged. If I shift my eyes fully to my right I can make out the top of Sarafina walking past, hunched over but easily pulling dead weight along the floor.

Mason.

There's a moment of quiet, then boots on stairs, leading down. I hear—almost *feel*—my brother's body being dragged along, his weight thumping on every step...

Until I hear no more, and am left in silence.

From behind me, there comes the soft padding of uncertain footsteps. I wonder if it's Titus, but the sound is wrong. Too heavy.

Whoever it is, they're not wearing shoes.

His shaggy head appears above my face, blocks my view of the ceiling.

Archie, on all fours, stares down at me, black tongue protruding from between thin lips. His eyes are wide and depthless, his nose bent and pressed unnaturally outward, stretching the skin of his face as a tentpole will stretch canvas. He lowers his head to my face and sniffs my cheek, my eye, my forehead. He whimpers.

"That's enough, Archie." Sarafina's sharp voice. "Back to your room."

Archie gives me one last look, and I'd like to think there's a longing there, a sorrow. Perhaps even a goodbye. Then he swings his head away and pads back to the room, crawling on all fours like a madman. Like an animal.

Now it's Sarafina's face that fills my view, smiling and beautiful, as a true devil would be.

"Come, Ethan," she says, and I feel her hand in my own, lifting, then pulling. My body slides across the floor like a sack of grain, and if she struggles with my weight there is no sign of it. I glide easily, as if being pulled by a horse. "It's time to show you the rest of my home."

My head drops lower, sinking below the floorboards as I'm pulled, through the opening, into a cold, damp dark. A hidden world.

"I don't believe you've seen my cellar."

38

My eyes shift frantically left to right—desperate to see what's coming, where she's taking me. I feel the stairs rub against my spine as she pulls me down, and down. After what seems an eternity, we meet a dirt floor. Staring upward, I'm shocked at how far away the warm light of the house is. Twenty steps? Thirty?

This isn't a cellar, it's a dungeon.

"Most of my work is done down here," she says genially as she drags me through the damp darkness, dirt feeding into the collar of my shirt. "I find the dark more conducive, and down below like this I'm more tuned-in to the great spirit of this Earth, and all she provides."

As the square of light high above is about to disappear from view—the light which has become a symbol of the world above, a world I have left behind, perhaps forever—there's a new source of light that allows me to see that the walls here are not dirt, but rock. As if we are inside a vast cavern.

I can't help thinking that the house perched above is nothing more than a decoy. A hunter's trap.

"Almost there now."

I'm pulled into a vaulted chamber. Cold blue rock surrounds me on all sides, and I glimpse a flicker of torchlight from somewhere; sconces set into the walls, perhaps.

Sarafina drops my arm, then stands over my prone body, hands on hips, staring down at me with a grin on her shadowed face, dark eyes glittering with the reflection of torchlight. "You're heavier than you look," she says. Then she crouches low, drives her hands into my armpits, and raises me—easily as one lifts a newborn baby—to a sitting position, my back pressed firmly against stone.

"In time, you'll be able to move your fingers, and your toes," she says, walking toward the far side of the chamber, where I see my brother. "Perhaps even move your head side-to-side, but it'll be at least a day, maybe two. I'm sorry."

Though I listen to her words, nearly all of my attention is fixated on the room.

There are massive shelves lining most of the walls, each filled with bowls and bottles, tied bundles of flowers, or herbs, and wicker baskets overflowing with detritus I can't identify. There are two long tables in my view, both covered in massive leather tomes, scattered candles, knives of every shape and size, and at least three sets of mortar and pestle.

At the center of the chamber is Mason.

He is not sitting—back upright against a wall—like I am. He's laid out on a stone table in the middle of the room. A beam of sunlight hits him from somewhere above, giving his flesh a strange, almost ethereal glow. If I could look up, I imagine I'd see a hole in the cavern's ceiling, creating a shaft of light that would slide across the chamber's floor during the day, marking the sun's path from east to west.

Despite Mason being paralyzed, Sarafina has cuffed his wrists to bindings set into the stone table. Above his body an oil lamp hovers, hung from a frayed rope. Near the lamp, a large black hook dangles from a heavy chain that continues upward before disappearing into shadows. I recall an illustrated page from an old Bible I saw as a child, the Apostle Paul chained inside a Roman prison, and it comes to mind now as I see my brother, helpless as I've ever seen him...

Oh, God, what's to become of us?

Sarafina walks to a long wooden table adjacent to the edge of my vision and picks up a long, shining blade. She returns to my brother, points it at his midsection.

I want to scream. I want to cry out for her to *stop this*, to leave him be. To let us leave here in peace. I want to beg for mercy.

Instead, I watch helplessly, silently, as she pushes the knife into his side.

Relief washes through me when I realize it's not torn flesh she stabs into, but only his shirt being cut away, then pulled off entirely.

She looks over at me, drops the useless fabric onto the dirt floor. "Don't worry, Ethan. I'm not going to kill him. Well...not yet," she says with a smile. "After all, he is the father of my child."

She puts a hand on her stomach and I feel a wash of revulsion at her claim, impossible though it is. Even if Mason had impregnated her, it's not possible she'd know so soon, not for certain. I happen to know some things about women, about their cycles and how they're interrupted by a pregnancy. When we were kids, my sister would delight in telling me about women's bodies, sharing her own newfound knowledge told to her from our mother.

The witch couldn't know.

"It's true, I'm afraid," she says, as if reading my thoughts. She lets out a heavy sigh, tosses the knife onto a nearby table, where it clatters. "A necessary evil."

I hear a new set of footsteps and shift my eyes to the left as Titus emerges from the shadows, his black hair and eyes clinging to the darkness he passed through to arrive here—a massive underground chamber that hosts only three outlets (that I'm able to see), as if we are sitting at the center of a network of caves deep beneath the earth. A stretched web we are stuck in like flies...

And Sarafina the spider after all.

"Titus," Sarafina says by way of welcome, her tone neither pleased nor angry.

The boy looks at me, then Mason. He pulls a stool from beneath one of the far tables and sits. Seemingly bored of the bizarre goings-on, he turns his back to the room and inspects the oddities spread about the table before him, begins plucking at them with the natural curiosity of a child.

When my eyes shift back to Sarafina, she's closed half the distance between us and is crouched on the dirt floor, her hooded robe wrapped tightly around her, her pale face ghastly and intent. I shudder and feel a pinch in my bladder that I refuse to release.

"Remember when you asked about Titus, Ethan? Always with the questions, you are...well, allow me to give you some answers."

She points a finger at me. "The clothes you wear? It comes from other men, such as you. You, and your brothers. Men who stumbled upon me by accident, by chance. But they're all gone now," she says, turning to look at Titus, who only grimaces in return. "But I am no monster, Ethan. I am not...what was it your brother called me? A witch?" She laughs, puts a finger to her chin as she stares at me. "You men and your labels—"

Then she scurries toward me on all fours, climbs my frozen legs and sits on my lap, places her hands on my shoulders, her wide dark eyes boring into my own.

A predator preparing to eat its prey.

"You wanted to know about Titus, did you not?"

She lifts her chin, speaks loudly enough for the boy to hear. "Would you like to tell the story, my sweet? Or shall I?"

Titus has found a book that absorbs him and doesn't bother to look up when addressed. Instead, he says, "As you will, mother."

Sarafina laughs, holds my face between her cool hands. "I told you to leave," she says, for what feels the millionth time. "But now I'm glad you stayed." She pokes me in the chest, and I feel the sharp point of her fingernail through the thin cloth. "I know what Mason is. The darkness that stirs inside him like smoke. And I know what Archie is. A devious, but loyal, jackal. One I look forward to having in my lap, where I do believe he'll find some happiness, don't you?

"But you, Ethan…" she says, her voice so low I can barely make out the words despite being mere inches away from her lips. "You're hidden from me. At first, I thought you an innocent, and I was going to spare you. But now—"

She grins in a way that makes me feel as if my mind, already cracked, will soon shatter.

She leans closer—so we are cheek to cheek—and whispers into my ear.

"I think you might be the worst of the bunch."

Sarafina lifts herself off me and walks briskly across the cavern floor, standing by my brother once more. She plucks up the knife.

"Do you know what a child needs most?" she says, looking at me with a mock innocence that chills my heart.

"Their father."

Without another word she sticks the tip of the knife into Mason's side and slowly slices downward. Blood spills over the edge of the table, into the dirt below. From my angle on the floor, I can clearly see the part of his body she cuts into—how deep, how long.

Mason's head is turned toward me, and I watch in horror as his eyes flutter, then roll to whites. I pray he's passed out from the pain, but there's no way to know for sure...he couldn't cry out if he wanted to. But dear God, he must feel *everything*.

Sarafina folds back a layer of skin, then continues cutting, going deeper into his body. "Titus, darling," she says casually, "come hold the lamp for me."

Titus sets down the book with reluctance, takes the lamp from the table and walks it over to my brother. He holds it as high and close as he's able, but not so close that he's within range of the spilling blood.

"I want a small slice of the kidney," Sarafina mutters, and pushes her fingers into the gaping cut. "Just a taste."

If I could convince my body to move, I'd be vomiting into my lap at the sight of my brother being carved up alive—awake and fully aware. Instead, though my stomach boils, my muscles refuse to act, even so much as twitch, as I watch the butchery.

Finally, after several minutes and many colorful curses, Sarafina looks toward me, her smile wide and triumphant. Her black dress hides the spray of blood, but it speckles her face, and her hands wear red gloves. Between two fingers she holds what looks like a cooked anchovy.

"Success," she says brightly.

Then she tosses the kidney slice into her mouth and chews greedily.

After she swallows, she turns back toward one of the wooden tables, drops the knife, and picks up a needle and thread tossed among the detritus.

"Don't worry," she says, then winks at me. "I'm very good at this."

I watch her smooth hands begin to work the needle on Mason's flesh, as if darning a suit coat. He's lost so much blood that I wonder if he's still alive. A puddle has formed on the ground beneath the steady *drip drip drip* coming off the table's ledge.

"I harvest many things, Ethan," she says as she works, Titus dutifully holding the lamp at her side. "Herbs, flowers, roots…parts of animals and insects…and sometimes, for special occasions… humans."

I look on, helplessly, as she works the stitching. I'm relieved when the flow of blood falters, then stops. I try to ignore the stark white color of Mason's skin and pray he's still breathing.

"Titus darling, why don't you entertain our guest while I finish my work?"

"I don't want to," Titus says, shuffing his feet, seemingly eager to be back on the stool, reading whatever book he had his nose into.

"Oh, Titus," she says, with a hint of exasperation. "My sweet little boy."

She turns from her work, fixes me once more with that dark gaze, that skin-curdling smile. I notice her chin is covered in gore, and the sun's reflection off Mason's pale flesh reveals the spray of blood on her dress, like sparkling red diamonds.

She's covered in it.

"Would you believe me," she says, watching me intently, as if curious to see how I'll react, "if I told you that young Titus here—this small child—is actually older than you and your brothers combined? I must insist he tell you all about it. You will, won't you, Titus?"

My eyes shift to the boy. A grimace creases his cherubic face.

His eyes move from her, then to me, as if debating.

Finally, he nods.

"Wonderful!"

Titus sets down the lantern, gets his stool, and drags it across the room toward me. Sarafina watches him, a maternal expression of love on her face, then glares wildly at me with laughing, malicious eyes.

"You'll enjoy his story, Ethan. Despite his impish appearance, he'd shame the Devil," she says, grinning like a madwoman.

I can almost smell the copper tang of Mason's blood on her red-stained teeth.

"He's the most evil man I've ever known."

39

Titus sits on the stool by my feet. Behind him, Sarafina hums as she works over Mason's body. The ray of sun from high above has slanted since I was dragged down here. Since Sarafina began cutting. It no longer illuminates Mason, but a patch of stone just past him, leaving the two of them in a gloomy haze, lit only by the sconces and overhanging oil lamp, swaying lazily, caught by some subtle breeze from one of the surrounding caves.

With the brief passage of time, I find myself able to control my eyelids, if nothing else. Gratefully, I squeeze my eyes shut against the sting of chilled sweat running off my forehead. I pray to God to free me from this hellish place, and amidst my prayer I command my mind to move my fingers, my toes, to give me my body back.

I've never been so afraid.

"You'll find most of this diffcult to believe," Titus says, and I open my eyes at the sound of his thin voice. He sits there, hands on knees, coat buttoned to the chin, looking like a toy soldier. "But I was born in 1745, which would make me...well, over a hundred years old, I guess. I'm not strong at math," he says, and shrugs carelessly. "It's hard to recollect the years, given that I've been here, with Sarafina, for a decade or more."

"Titus dear," she says, her voice carrying easily from across the stone chamber. She does not look up from her work. "You've been with me much longer than that. Since the turn of the century. 1805, to be exact."

Titus's eyes go comically wide, and he looks even younger, even more like a child, and he's right about one thing: I don't believe it. I don't believe any of this. I'm dreaming, and soon I'll be awake, and my brothers and I will leave this place and return home, and all will be as it was.

"I suppose she would know. Honestly, I haven't been keeping track. Every day here blurs into the other...and besides, look at me. Ten years old. Always ten years old..." he says, voice drifting, as if even he has trouble coming to terms with such an impossibility. "Before coming here, I was a grown man, of course." He looks at me hard, as if daring me to contradict this supposed fact. As if I have the means to disagree with anything.

He scoots his stool a few inches closer, his dark, narrowed eyes shining like black diamonds.

"I was also a thief," he says. "And a murderer."

He pats my leg and repulsion courses through me. "Much like you, I had a brother once. He and I, we were born in Tennessee, but our parents were immigrants. Came over from Belfast. But that didn't stop my brother and I from taking up arms during the war, back in '75. Given that our heritage was European, we sided with the British."

The boy smiles sadly; his eyes grow distant. "A mistake, of course. But hell, we thought they had the pats outgunned, that they knew more about such things as warfare. In the end, it didn't matter what side we chose, because we went our own way." Titus offers a sly wink, and for a moment—for the blink of an eye—I can almost see the man behind the child's mask. It's there and gone, like a quick-moving cloud blown across the sun. "But was I evil?" He shrugs, little legs kicking the air. A bored schoolboy. "I can't really say. It's hard to remember all the bits and pieces now. When I changed...when she changed me...it was more than just my body. It was, to some extent, my mind. I *am* a boy again, Ethan. Healthy and fresh, free of aches and pains, free of hate and all the sour things the world puts in your mouth. Nowadays, I read, I walk. It's restful. Heavenly."

Titus stops kicking, his hands ball up into fists, and he looks down at the dirt floor, away from me. "No...maybe not evil. But I was most certainly *bad*," he says quietly, as if ashamed. "Before I came here, my brother and I tore through the country like madmen.

There was no law, you understand? No one to stop us, to catch us, or hunt us down. At first, we stole from travelers. Money, food, jewelry, guns.

"The first one we killed was self-defense, if you can believe it. A man tried to stab my brother, so we took care of him. Then his family. After we'd killed once, the rest became easy. From then on, when we'd rob folks, we'd murder 'em, then leave their bodies for the animals. My brother, he—" Titus sighs, and when he looks at me there are tears on his cheeks. "We raped women. We murdered children. At one point, I'm not sure how or why, only that the Devil himself had us by the necks, we began to make ornaments of the bodies."

Titus, the small, frail boy I'd befriended, says these things with distant eyes, and it's impossible for me to connect his sinister words with the innocent child who speaks them.

"We'd cut off their limbs and hang them from trees," he says. "Chop off the heads and set them on stones, or spikes, and we'd laugh...mock those poor souls as we counted their money, pocketed their goods. For a brief time, we were pirates on the Ohio River. We joined up with a band of terrible men who'd invite pioneers to the shore with promises of goods and trade. Once they were safely ashore, we'd pounce. One of the women...a young girl...I kept for a wife. Murdered her family and took her for my own. Forced her to give me children.

"My brother, he killed one of my babies. Couldn't stand it crying, so one night he ripped it from my wife's arms and crushed its head against a tree." He shrugs, barely noticeable in the heavy blue coat. "By then I'd had enough, and I killed him. I tore his body open and stuffed it with rocks while my wife cried and cried. In the end, I sold her and my other child, a baby girl, to a band of Cherokee.

"More years went by, and the century turned, and years later I rode with a group of men along the Natchez Trace, raping and killing and thieving at will. But the war was ending by then and the British were sailing home. Soldiers who'd been off fighting started to return, and soon there was law in the land. I meandered around for some years, and finally joined a band of crooks that ran into some of those new lawmen. I was hunted down, along with the others. They shot me in the head as I ran." Titus points a small, thin finger to the side of his head, rubs it gently, as if recalling the wound. "Grazed me here.

"For a few days I stumbled through forest and brush, running... always running...I was a wanted man, of course." He flashes a toothy smile at me. "Quite the bounty on my bleeding head." Then the smile fades, and his eyes grow distant once more.

"There was a posse on my trail and they weren't going to stop. Not ever. So, I decided to return to a spot where my brother and I had buried some loot—gold and jewelry, enough to buy me passage upriver, to the north. If I survived. But when I found that clearing, a few miles east of the Trace, near the Tennessee border, it had become...something else. Something I couldn't fathom. There were women living there in tents, and they'd—" Titus swallows, wipes beads of sweat from his brow. Past him, I notice that Sarafina has finished with my brother and is now paying attention. Watching us. Listening.

"They were witches. A few of the men in my band, they'd had a similar thought as me, and had returned for the treasure we'd buried. By the time I arrived, however, they were dead. They were hung from the trees and the witches danced, Ethan. They danced beneath the dangling legs of murderers and thieves, danced by torchlight and by the light of the hideous gray moon. Some were unclothed, others wore masks. Some sang. I hid in the bushes and I watched, wondering if they would leave, if I could still get to that gold.

"And then, one of them called out to me. She told me to 'come,' to 'join them.' And they all laughed and I pissed myself, Ethan. I've never been so scared in my life. I felt that Hell itself had bubbled up through the crust to take me, to pull me down into the lake of fire, and these women were there to assist, to make sure I didn't get away. Not again."

Titus sighs. "I ran. I ran for what seemed like years. A short time later, another posse caught up to me, just west of the Mississippi, where there were no towns, just the Indian nations and a few pioneers. They refused to let me go."

Titus slides off the stool, crosses his arms, scuffs his shoe into the dirt. "I don't blame them. They nearly killed me then, but tied me up instead, put me on a horse. I threw myself into a river as we crossed and escaped for what would be the last time. I blacked out at some point... I'd lost so much blood. When I woke, I was lying in the mud beside the river, my body wedged between rocks and bramble like a piece of driftwood. It was a miracle I hadn't drowned. From there, hands still bound, I half-walked, half-crawled inland. I didn't know where I was—I only knew that I needed food, that my wounds would kill me if they weren't treated.

"Much like yourself, I was days...maybe hours from death. I came to a creek and I drank. And when I looked up, I saw a large cabin in the distance. A farmhouse in the middle of the forest. I crossed the creek, and I never left."

Titus turns and looks at Sarafina, and although I can't see his face, it must be a kind expression because she smiles in return, the blood on her hands, face, and arms dried to the color of mud. She nods once, as if prodding him to finish.

He turns back to me, puts his hands in his pockets, and paces. "I think Sarafina collects evil," he says. "Others have found their way here. Some were killed, like those Home Guard. Some stayed."

He looks at me now, meets my eye.

"You've seen the dogs. You've seen your brother."

I can't nod, can't speak, but he seems to take my blinking for acknowledgment. "Bad men all. And me? I guess I'm special. I became a companion. A *human* companion."

"Someone to talk to," Sarafina says, smiling, as if the story of their coming together was a thing to touch hearts instead of blacken them. "A friend."

Titus laughs. A child's laugh, and I can't reconcile that high pitched, innocent laughter with the things he's told me. I don't try.

"It helped that I was sterile," he says, then looks at me once more. "Unlike your brother over there."

I don't know what he means, what any of this means. All I know is I must escape this place. Escape, and save my brothers if I can.

I don't belong here.

I am not evil.

40

"You think us monsters."

I open my eyes, and while I have no recollection of closing them, I assume I've slept because the ray of daylight is gone, the chamber doused in near complete darkness. I say "near" because there is a lit lantern hovering a few feet away, a young boy holding it aloft, watching me.

Titus takes a step closer, his small face lit by the flicker of flame, his black button eyes an amalgam of innocence and murder. Now that I know what he is. The things he's done.

In some ways, he's a reflection. But that's something I've no wish to think about.

"We are not the devils you think we are," he says. Then his eyes shift away, as if considering. "At least, she's not."

He kneels next to me, holds the lamp to my face. He's close enough that I can make out flecks of gold in his dark eyes, beads of moisture on his lips, the redness of his cheeks. White mist pools between us, our collective breath chilled by the air. "She's no witch, Ethan. And she's no demon. She's...something else." He looks at me quizzically for a moment, as if debating my merit. "You've read the Bible, of course. A good boy like you goes to church, studies the scripture." He pokes my shoulder gently. "But not all of it, I don't think. If you can find it, read the Book of Enoch. You will find answers there. Or perhaps more questions. Or perhaps comfort. Assuming you make it out of here, of course."

Titus stands, stares down at me, his small face reflecting the wavering flame in the dark. "You've heard my story, and you can judge me if you wish. But what I am, what I was, doesn't matter. Not anymore. What's happening to your brothers doesn't matter, either, because there's nothing to be done. But there's still time for you, Ethan. Still time to escape. I wished it for you once, as did

Sarafina, but you were stubborn. Loyal to a fault. Now look at you."

Slumped against the cold wall, it takes all my effort to keep my eyes pointed forward. My head has sunken onto my chest, as if my neck were broken, my spine gristle. I wish I could speak! If only I could stand and fight!

Instead, I drool, and wait. And listen.

Titus looks over his shoulder, then back at me.

"It's time for you to flee," he says, then reaches into his pocket and pulls out a clump of grass, or weeds. Broken flowers. "This is a mixture of belladonna, eleuthero, and rue. Too much of it would kill you. But I think I have the quantities correct."

Titus sets down the lantern and hustles to a nearby worktable, pulls down a mortar and pestle. He puts the herbs into the bowl and begins to grind them. At the edge of the lamplight, I can see flickers of Mason's pale body lying on the stone slab. Motionless by death or by magic, I know not. I turn my focus back to the boy, willing him to do—whatever he is doing—faster.

After a few minutes, he brings a stone bowl.

"Normally this would be brewed into a tea," he says. "But I don't think there's time for that, do you?" He looks into the bowl, considering, then pours some of the powder into the opposing palm. "I think that's right," he says, looking dubious. "Anyway, like I said. No time."

He steps toward me, rests the tip of the mortar against my lips, then takes it away.

"Sorry, we need to get you straightened."

He sets the bowl down, grips my head and moves it to an upright position. Then—as best he's able—he tilts my face back to look upward. He pulls my jaw open.

"Good," he says. "Here we go, then."

I feel the cool lip of the bowl, followed by a rush of powder on my tongue. It fills my mouth, my throat, and I gag.

"Swallow!" he says, dropping the bowl, which cracks sharply against the stone, then grips my jaw between two small hands.

After a few seconds, my body's reflexes take over and, rather than choking on the powder, my throat moves most of the gooey, bitter mess down into my stomach.

"Here, a bit a water to get it all down."

The smell of leather, then a moist pouch is put to my lips. Water pours out, cool and delicious, and washes the rest of the thick paste down. My body convulses, my mouth lunging for the pouch as I swallow, swallow...

Almost immediately, my hands and feet begin to tingle, painfully so. A second later, I pull in a breath—on my own power—and let it out. I blink my eyes, then slowly lift my head, the muscles in my neck sluggish but responsive. Although my neck is tight and tingling like mad, I'm able to move my head. I look down at my limp arms and legs and will them to obey. At first, there's nothing, but as the potion in my belly begins to work, I find myself able to wiggle my fingers, my toes.

"That's it, Ethan. That's it. Slowly now," Titus says, watching me.

I look at him and nod, feeling a wave of relief at the realization that control is coming back.

"If your heart doesn't stop, I'd say I did it right," he says, and his tone wavers between humor and concern to such an extent that I consciously slow my efforts, terrified that if I move too much, or too quickly, I'll burst my poisoned heart.

After a few minutes of my body and brain reconnecting, I can freely move my arms and legs. I reach out and grip Titus's hand, ignoring the wide-eyed look of fear that leaps onto his face. "I'm not going to hurt you," I mumble, as if I'd just been born into this body, learning how to work the tongue, jaw, and lips for the first time. "Help me up."

Titus nods and pulls on my hand, giving me the leverage to stand. My legs wobble a moment, and I lean back against the wall, breathing heavily. My heart pounds frighteningly loud in my chest, and I try to calm myself.

I'm hungry, and weak, and tired. I've been sitting in this underground chamber for at least a day; my body would be feeble and stiff even if I hadn't been poisoned.

"Water?" I manage, and Titus hands me the skin. I lift it to my mouth, relishing the strength in my arms to do so, and drink it nearly dry. I feel better. Stronger. More myself.

The boy has saved me.

"You need to go, Ethan," he says. "Now. While you can. You can leave through that cave over there." He points to a black circle in a far wall. "That will take you to the rocks where you found me that day, when you saved my life. If you can make it there, you'll be outside, and you can run for the creek. If you cross the creek, you're free. Remember?"

I nod. I remember.

"Mason—" I say, wishing there were more water in the skin. My throat feels like sandpaper, my mouth coated with glue. "You need to give the powder to Mason."

Titus begins to answer when there's a loud *clank* from the darkness. We both freeze, stare blindly in the direction of the sound.

"Oh no..." he whispers, and the blatant fear in his voice sends a chill through me.

I stare into the deep subterranean night that surrounds our lamplit halo. A small hand grips mine and I look down.

"Take it."

Titus pushes the lantern's handle into my palm, then points once more toward that black hole across the chamber. "That way. To the rocks. Escape, and live."

I take two weakened steps, fall to a knee, then stand once more. I stagger toward my brother, who lies naked and bloody on the stone. I hoist up the lamp.

His eyes are open wide, showing whites.

Save me!

"Titus!" I beg.

But he's already backing away, into the shadows.

"I've done what I can. You must leave now. Run away, and don't ever come back."

Then he disappears into the gloom, leaving me to stare helplessly at my brother's motionless body, his side gored as if run by a bull.

A voice carries from the darkness.

"Titus?" the voice says, sounding almost curious.

Almost playful.

As if a game were about to begin.

"Sweet Titus," Sarafina says, her voice slick and deadly as a serpent's tongue. "What have you done?"

I lean down and kiss my brother on the head, stare one last time into his wild, desperate eyes. "I'm sorry," I say.

And then I run.

41

I stagger, leadfooted, through the narrow cave, cocooned inside the circle of golden light coming from the lantern—nothing but darkness behind and ahead.

Anticipating an exit, I wait to feel a cool night breeze on my skin, but so far feel nothing but the same stagnant air; the earthy stink of the cave. My heart thumps in my chest and I say a prayer that Titus's concoction doesn't kill me in this horrible place. Despite the cold I'm dripping with sweat, but pleased to feel that my muscles are regaining their flexibility and strength.

The ground, unfortunately, is hazardous, especially in the murky light. There are jagged edges of rocks and sloped stones grasping at my feet, hoping to pull me down, smash open my skull. But I'm watchful of where I step, thankful for the lantern; the carved rock walls and ceiling encircle me like a band of gold as I move forward, forward.

"Ethan?"

Her voice slips through the air to reach me. I know she's distant, likely back in the cavern where my brother lies, wondering which way I've run. I hope she doesn't know about Titus's secret exit, his hideaway in the rocks.

Or perhaps she's following even now, preparing to throw some new magic into my face that will paralyze me, or kill me. Turn me into a child. A dog.

Or worse.

"Ethhhhaaaaannn...I see your light. Where are you going, Ethan? There's nowhere to run. This is my domain, child. These caves stretch far and wide, but eventually you'll return to me. Shall I wait?" she says, her voice sounding louder, closer. "Or shall I chase?"

I stop, spin around, my breath coming in loud, harsh gulps. I raise the lantern, as if it could somehow let me see her in the distance, through the impenetrable dark. But of course, beyond the light's reach, there is nothing but a wall of black. I lower the lantern, wincing at a sharp pain in my chest. I put a hand to my heart, will it to slow, but my breathing is too fast. My clothes are soaked through with sweat; beads of it stream down my temples, neck, and back.

I'm too visible, and she could be anywhere.

I know what I must do, but hesitate. I glance ahead, hoping there are no pitfalls, that I'll be able to feel my way along, using the walls as a guide.

I pray that Titus was right. That he hasn't killed me.

I turn out the lamp.

"Ahhh—" she says. "You welcome the dark? Then it's a game."

I kneel, blind and helpless. I set the lantern's base softly upon the ground, do my best not to panic.

I can hear her moving. Closer now. Closer.

"If it's a game you wish to play, then I will play. Go on, Ethan. You run—"

When her voice comes again, it's not from some far-off point.

It's from just behind my ear.

"And I'll chase."

I cry out and leap to my feet, spin wildly toward her voice, the lantern clutched in my hand. The bulk of the heavy thing connects with something—a head, or a shoulder—and the glass smashes. There's a soft grunt and I let go the handle and push out with both hands. I find flesh and thrust her away, hard as I can, toward the wall. She grunts once more, as if injured, or at least momentarily stunned.

I don't hesitate. I turn and reach out my left hand so my fingers brush bumpy stone, and I begin to run—blindly—through the dark.

I've gone no more than twenty steps when I hear laughter from behind. But it doesn't sound like the woman I've heard these past days. It sounds like someone else.

Like *something* else.

I run faster and then—from one step to the next—I feel it.

A breeze.

I speed up, my fingertips flying along the bumpy stone wall. And then, just ahead, I see a patch of blue among the heavy black—a blue the color of sky just before dawn.

Escape!

I pull my hand from the wall and sprint toward the light. My muscles have warmed, my strength returned. I run toward that small patch of blue freedom with desperation, my heart and lungs set to burst, as it grows larger...larger...

The laughter behind me has stopped, now replaced with a new sound—a sound loud enough to hear over my thumping heart and gasping breaths.

It's a sound I can't quite place, like the flapping of sails in a twisting wind.

It sounds...

It sounds like wings.

Ten steps later the ground rises sharply, and within moments I reach the crevice in the cave's wall. It's barely wide enough for a small boy—or, in a lucky twist of fate, a skinny young man. I thrust my arms up and through, relishing the feel of early morning air on my skin, the mild warmth of the rising sun.

But I need to climb.

Panic surging, I grip the hole's edge, raise my foot, seeking a step or ledge. I scrape the toe of my boot once, twice, along the rocks, but there's nothing. There must be a foothold! I'm twice the height of Titus, and if the boy was able to...

There!

My toe settles on a narrow ridge, and I hoist myself up.

Before I put my head through the opening, I turn back, one last time.

"Oh, God—"

Something large scurries toward me through the tunnel. It half runs, half flies along the floor, then up one wall—without losing speed—and onto the ceiling. I can almost make out its face as it nears the daylight—see its bulging yellow eyes, its stretched, toothy grin.

With a scream, I push through the hole, not giving myself time to consider what I've seen, what sort of creature pursues me.

Not a witch...something else.

I grunt and claw as my hands dig into wet, weedy grass. Quick as I can, I lift my lower body through the hole and onto solid ground. Seconds later, there's a loud *thump*. A flurry of limbs scramble at the crevice and I fall onto my back, away from the thing, and begin sliding myself backward along the ground, out of its reach.

I wait for it to burst into the daylight. But instead, with a shriek of rage, it vanishes back into the cave.

I realize, suddenly, why it doesn't follow.

The creature can't fit.

It can't get through.

The demon—monster, animal, whatever it is that Sarafina has become—seems to realize the same thing I do, and the thrashing stops.

I wait, listening in horror to its heavy, muffled breaths...

And then it's gone.

I get to my feet and begin searching for a clear direction in which to run, toward what would be the nearest point in the star-shaped creek. Recalling my prior visit to this rocky outcropping, I locate the direction of the farm, and know that the straightest, shortest path to potential freedom is the exact opposite direction. I leap down from the rocks and onto level grass, already at a sprint.

The sun is still settled below the horizon of treetops to the east, but the rose glow that precedes the break of day swells like a chorus, turning the clouds above a dusty pink and the sky a blue the color of a clean lake. I'm surrounded by white oaks, their shaggy arms dripping with Spanish moss wishing to hold me here a few moments longer while Sarafina—in whatever form she currently takes—comes for me.

But I have my bearings, and I know it's a straight path to the water.

I just need time.

Running fast as I'm able, I pass through the cluster of oaks and into a broad, wide pasture of skinny longleaf pines. There's a morning mist covering the ground and I pray I don't step into a gopher hole or twist my ankle on a root or rock as I race toward the water.

The ground is spongy but level as I pump my legs harder, willing myself to go faster.

I'm so focused on low-hanging branches, or tripping on something beneath the mist, that I don't see the dog until it's too late.

The beast barrels into me with the strength and mass of a full-grown man. My breath is punched from my lungs and I crash into the earth, the massive weight of the beast landing atop me. It growls and snarls; hot, rank breath wets my face—there's a *SNAP* as its jaws clamp shut inches from my throat. Instinctively, I turn my body while pushing the shaggy hound away from me as we roll, using its own weight against it.

I scramble to my knees, and reach for my boot.

In the blink of an eye the massive dog twists up and off the ground, once more standing on four feet, its jaws wide and snarling. It's one of the gray ones. The head big as a man's, its legs long and strong. Foaming drool drips from its mouth, disappears into the ground mist. Wide, blank eyes stare at me as it sinks into a crouch, readying itself to pounce, to tear me apart like it did the Home Guard. Slowly—my eyes never leaving the dog's own—I get to my feet, sink into a crouch of my own. I spread my arms for balance, and wait for it to come.

The dog snaps its jaws once, twice, then barks furiously.

"Come on then," I mutter.

And then it leaps.

My left hand comes up toward its jaw, miraculously clenches the mat of dirty fur beneath it. I let myself fall back, taking the hound with me—keeping those blazing devil's eyes, those white fangs—away from my flesh a few moments longer.

With my right hand I bring up the freed bayonet and sink it into the beast's chest.

Still gripping a lock of fur beneath its jaw, I allow the weight of the hound to fall atop me and use all my strength to push the long, wide blade deeper, aiming for the fucking thing's heart.

It snarls and snaps a few more times, my clamped hand keeping those deadly teeth away as I let the blade do its work, twisting now, desperate to damage its insides. Searching for organs, for lungs, I work the bayonet like a butter churn until, finally, a low whine comes from the dog's throat, its jaws slacken, its breath slows, and the weight on top of me is still.

I roll it off, slide the bayonet free, and watch its stomach move a few last times, until it finally slows...then stops.

Watching it die, my bayonet dripping with its blood, I know I'm lucky to have survived, but I also know there are three more of the damned things, and if this one knew where to find me, the others must as well.

No more time.

I get to my feet, stick the blood-drenched bayonet back into my boot and limp forward, toward the water. My knee revolts, delivering a jolt of pain with each step. I must have twisted it in the fight, and it's difficult to put much weight on it. But I hear the creek now, the ever-running water, and I push on through tall trees as the sun rises behind me, lighting my path with patches of gold, the trees pointing toward freedom with long shadows, as if guiding me home.

There's a rustle high and to my left. I turn my head toward the sound as I run. It takes me a moment, but then I see it, way up in the sparsely leafed treetops, leaping from tree to tree in chase, no more than twenty yards behind me...and gaining fast.

Sarafina.

I curse and focus my eyes forward.

I don't slow down. I don't look back.

The creek is just ahead. Twenty paces, no more.

In my peripheral vision I note a blur of black movement as the thing flies parallel to me, tracking me, springing between the trees, all flapping wings and long, extended limbs.

I can almost hear it laughing as the creek grows larger.

Ten paces away.

My knee is stiffening badly, and the bayonet blade rubs harshly against my leg, tearing into skin. The grip is turned the wrong way and it cuts into me again and again as my feet pound the earth—matching my racing heart, my harsh breaths—as I force myself to move faster.

A tree limb snaps—loud as a gunshot—and I hear a heavy branch land just behind me, close enough that I feel the breeze of its passing on the back of my neck.

She's above me now.

I extend my strides, the creek just a few feet away.

I don't run into it.

I dive.

Water slams against my face, fresh and cold. I tuck my legs and let my body sink beneath the surface, curled into a fetal position, desperate to make sure no part of me is visible above the waterline.

Will it be enough?

Is the creek itself safe? Or past the creek? Is the creature entering the water right now, grinning a mouthful of long teeth, reaching for me with clawed fingers?

The thought is enough to spur me forward. I open my eyes beneath the water, find a handhold on a smooth stone, and pull myself toward the other side, not wanting to break the surface, pure instinct telling me to stay *down*, to stay hidden until I reach the far shore.

The water churns around me but I move forward, half-swimming, half-crawling my way until the bottom begins to rise. I reach out a hand and it breaks free of the water, clutches tall grass. The other side.

I rise up—head clearing the surface—and wait for hard, sharp claws to dig into my cheeks, for the sound of flapping wings above my head.

But as I crawl from the water...there is nothing.

Nothing but the soft sound of a forest facing the dawn of a new day, and my breathing, and that's all. Wet and ragged, pressed against the earth, I look back.

And see her.

She stands a few feet from the opposite shoreline; taller and broader than any man or woman I've ever seen, her body sinewy and black as night. Behind her, giant wings flap open and closed, wings smeared with a multitude of colors, glinting like oil in the sun.

Her eyes are hooded and golden, but her face...is still somehow *her*.

Somehow human.

This is no animal, no storybook monster. Despite there being a delicacy to the features, there's an unfathomable power in its bearing, a deadly cunning in its eyes.

She is the personification of death itself.

As she studies me, she lowers into a crouch, as if contemplating her next move. The wings extend—fully and breathtakingly wide—then retract.

She does not speak, or make any sound at all.

She just...watches.

Moving slowly, not taking my eyes off her, I pull myself back from the water on elbows, digging into the mud with my heels, until I'm well clear of the shore.

The air seems to shift—to *change*—and the world around me comes alive with new sounds. The eerie silence fills with birds chirping in the trees, the rattle of wood as they work the bark with hard beaks. I hear the rustle of small creatures moving through the undergrowth, the hum of insects attracted to my sweat, my blood.

The sun is higher than it was only a moment ago, the day somehow brighter, warmer. The air moist and alive, thick with the sweet smell of sap.

I get to my feet, turn my head to study this new world—the *real* world—the one which exists outside of Sarafina's domain, her...

The word springs into my mind, and the moment it does I know it's right.

Her *prison*.

When I look back toward her—part of me wanting to see her one last time, to try and understand what she is—she's gone.

The creek, also, is gone.

The skinny longleaf pines I ran through during my escape have been replaced by dense sweetgum, their blooming crimson leaves like red clouds against a deep blue sky. To my right is a rise where a tepid waterfall spits over the edge into a bowl-shaped hollow, then trickles forward to meet a brown stream that runs—naturally—in one direction, carrying off snapped twigs and fallen leaves.

I watch the waterfall for a few moments, waiting for my shattered mind to reassemble into coherence, for my aching heart to slow its thumping drumbeats.

Finally, I take a hitching step forward, then another—in which direction I do not consider, nor care—then I collapse to my knees, and I weep.

I cry for myself and for my brothers; for the terrors of the night, for the horrors I've seen.

I do not consider returning to the farm.

I do not consider vengeance.

I think only one thing, over and over again.

I'm alive.

I'm alive.

I'm alive.

Some minutes later, I'm able to gather my wits and come to terms with this new world.

I use the sun to figure the way west, and begin walking.

Toward the great Mississippi River.

Toward home.

INTERLUDE

Ellie

Christmas Day, 1852, was the happiest day of my life.

Ethan and I are seven years old. My mother, Francine, is alive and well. My father is a vibrant hero, a former soldier who speaks of great battles, who happily strides through the house like a welcome storm, roaring about God and Satan and Sin as if they are the pillars of our very existence, all his morality lessons ending in black and white: Heaven or damnation. It didn't matter if the sin was lying about a broken window or murdering an orphan in cold blood.

Heaven, or damnation.

Golden gates and eternal bliss, surrounded by angels and songs, or a lake of burning fire that would melt your flesh, burst your eyeballs in their sockets, and turn your bones to ash.

Then do it all over and over again. For eternity.

Depending on the day, Hell took on different forms. Mostly it was the lake of fire, eternal torture of the flesh. Other days, damnation was a black abyss through which you would forever fall—blind and screaming for salvation—through a bottomless pit.

Even as a child, staring at him wide-eyed, bursting with a strange mix of trepidation and exhilaration, I remember it was the "abyss version" of Hell that consumed me, the impossible vision I dreamed of on so many nights. Every now and then I'd wake up, terribly frightened after having had a nightmare about it, and I'd whisper my dark vision to Ethan, who always laid next to me in our shared bed.

"It doesn't seem *too* terrible," I'd say, giving it serious thought, wondering if, when it came to damnation, we might be given some sort of choice. Perhaps, if I could hold audience with the giant, white-haired figure of God Himself, I could beg for my preferred version of damnation while angels stood guard behind me, flaming swords held aloft, the open pit between us a one-way ticket to Hell.

That hole was the real horror.

In my imagination, the hole was a void staining the surface of pure white clouds which constituted Heaven's floor (or so we were led to believe in Sunday School).

A void I'd be cast into, never to return.

When I got truly frightened, I'd grip his warm hand in mine, stare wide-eyed at the dark. "We need to pray, Ethan. We need to pray every day so we can be together in Heaven."

One night, during one of our late-night chats, he meant to shock me.

"Heaven sounds boring," he said, trying to sound confident, but I knew he was nervous about the blaspheme. "What do we do with all that time? Just sing and sit around?"

"Don't say such things," I scolded, then squeezed his hand tight. "I can't wait for Heaven. I'm going to have a harp, and play with the angels, and fly."

"I'm going to live in a house made of gold," he replied, and so it would go.

Ethan

On that fateful Christmas Day—which turned out to be the last one we'd spend with our mother and, in many ways, the father we loved—Ellie and I woke at dawn, excited to sit beneath the decorated tree, the sweet anticipation of wrapped gifts set beneath our tongues like candy.

Sitting in the cold house—the tree's decorations muted in the dim, early-morning sunlight, absorbing its rich pine scent—we guessed at what our presents might be, knowing we wouldn't be allowed to open them until later that day, until after church and supper. Mother came into the room while we sat there—our fingers and toes near frozen, our cheeks and noses bright red, our smiles uncaring for such trivial things. She scolded us playfully, pulled a blanket from a chest and dropped it into our laps while she lit a fire. She told us to stay put, that she had a treat for us.

We did, and together, huddled and shivering under that blanket, we moved as close to the fireplace as we dared, our wrapped packages put back beneath the tree with great care, as if they might shatter if mishandled. A few minutes later, Mother returned holding two mugs of hot chocolate, something we'd had only once or twice before.

"Be careful, it's hot. Don't spill," she said, and kneeled down on the floor next to us, pulling her sweater tight around her shoulders, smiling while we sipped the chocolate and made grateful sounds, like two suckling pigs rooting at their mother's teats for the first time.

Father was the next awake, and although we'd long finished our chocolate, we still sat by the fire, wanting to prolong the moment. He wished us Merry Christmas and then told us to get dressed for church. Mason and Archie stomped in as we headed to our room, neither one saying a word as they went to the kitchen for biscuits and coffee.

I like to think that Archie ruffed my hair as he went by, but that might be my invention, overly eager to make the day, the memory, more magical.

Later that evening, we finally opened our presents.

Ellie received a yellow dress that my mother made with fabric she'd said was "imported," the word itself seeming expensive and delicate. Ellie treasured it. That I can recall, she wore it every Sunday until she grew out of it. By then she'd started to make dresses of her own.

I was given a novel called *The Pioneers* by James Fenimore Cooper. It was a two-volume set and the first book I'd ever owned. My mother was enamored with stories, with reading books and telling tall tales to us children. When I was very small, she would often praise my imagination, tell me that I'd be a great novelist one day, like Melville or Dickens. "A natural storyteller," she'd say.

My father scoffed at this notion, chastising Mother for filling our heads with mysteries and lies when the world was built on facts, and God...which is why I think my second gift was from him.

It was a new Bible; my name engraved on the leather cover. Inside, my father had dashed a brief, almost illegible note, one that ended in *Merry Christmas*.

In the years that followed I read both books. I enjoyed the adventure featuring the great frontiersman, Natty Bumppo, who was brave, and good, and tragic. I eventually read the next book in the series but, as I grew older, found myself more interested in the Bible. During my teenage years I read from Genesis to Revelations more times than I can count, and it was the beginning of a great fervor in me, an unsettling of the soul I found both euphoric and terrifying.

I carried my Christmas Bible with me the day I went to war, stuffed into my pack, a sort of talisman to keep me safe. Or so I'd thought at the time.

I lost it the first month, along with most of my other personal possessions. It burned along with many men at Fort Sumter, where I learned quickly about death, and where I traded the innocence of childhood for a pair of leather boots stolen from a river-swollen corpse.

A couple short months after that Christmas morning, Mother died of tuberculosis.

She never saw spring.

To that point, it was the saddest day of my life.

At least, until the war.

Ellie

Father changed, immediately and dramatically, following her untimely death. He stopped smiling, was harder on us. Beat me and my brothers often and well. My brothers also changed. As teenagers, they became sullen and defeated, their previous happiness buried deep by tragedy and violence, the surprising and immediate loss of love. As they grew—especially the older boys—their gazes became as hard as Father's.

I did what I could to protect Ethan, but watched helplessly as Mason and Archie drifted further toward darkness, their very souls transforming before my eyes, from wild but good-natured boys, into ruffians that caused trouble wherever they went. My older brothers grew strong and savvy, until my father lost control of them completely. Not that he minded. As much as he spoke of God, of Heaven and righteousness, the reality was that he had been corrupted by his own despair. He'd turned monstrous, and my two older brothers were his monstrous offspring. I think the three of them got along better during those years than they ever had.

At times, I wondered if Father was proud when he heard whispers about their deeds, as if those dark rumors fed his own need for revenge on the world. If I'm speaking honestly, I think that if it hadn't been for the war, my brothers would have found another way to murder.

Assuming they hadn't already.

As for Ethan, he became quieter after Mother's death. He lost his smile, his childish joy. My father beat him severely for every conceived slight, as if ashamed at his weakness—his goodness—when compared to Mason and Archie.

He'd only whipped me once, but it was the most terrifying moment of my life, and I was sure in the instant that he would kill me. Ethan tried to intervene, of course, but he was just a skinny child— we both were—and besides, there was no stopping him that day.

If the older boys had been home...perhaps. But they rarely were in those days.

Father kicked in our bedroom door, dragged me off my bed by a bare ankle, and strapped me mercilessly with a leather belt, beating me with it until my nightgown was torn to ribbons, my naked, bloody body streaked with savage welts. I was so ashamed and tried, and failed, to cover myself while fending off the belt. The entire time he kept screaming that I was a whore, and a slut. At one point he called me the Devil's cunt.

You see, I'd been caught kissing a boy. We were both thirteen years old at the time.

Samuel Bartlett had been his name. Sam, as I knew him.

He disappeared a few weeks later. His body never found. Some folks in town blamed Mason and Archie, accused them of unspeakable things. My father defended them vigorously and with a strong dose of that righteous fury he had honed like a sword, until folks spoke no more of it. At least not where my father could hear.

I cried for weeks after Samuel's vanishing. Cried for the pain I was in, at my shame.

Ethan and I had grown into separate beds by then, but we still shared a room, and one night I whispered my belief that Father knew what had been done to Samuel. Had maybe even blessed it. Ethan listened and didn't argue, but told me to be wary of ever saying such things aloud, that it would only make my life that much harder.

I did not disagree.

In fact, with the clarity of hindsight, I'd take it one step further:

I think it was my father's idea all along, my brothers his eager henchmen.

I think they murdered him. And while I love Mason, and Archie, with all my heart, whenever I think of them hurting that sweet boy, I hate them.

Sam's body was never found, and foul play was never discovered. But I knew better, and the burning in my vengeful heart knew better.

After all, little boys don't simply disappear.

Ethan

When we were sixteen years old, a darkness fell upon our house—a darkness so malevolent, so complete, that it smothered whatever life had been left inside.

Ellie had become pregnant.

When my father found out, I knew there would be no forgiveness, no quarter given.

This time, there was no beating. No screaming.

What happened, in many ways, was far, far worse.

Her pregnancy was the first secret my twin sister ever kept from me, and it wasn't until she was slowly, methodically, packing her small suitcase that she finally confided the truth.

Or some of it, at least.

Our father was taking her away. When she returned, she would no longer be with child.

She would *never* again be with child.

If she lived, that was.

After a time, Ellie did come back, and it was immediately apparent that whatever remained of the sister I had grown up with had been torn out of her. She was older, somehow. Much older than I, despite our identical age. She rarely spoke, and moved into a room of her own—the low-ceilinged loft where our mother's things were stored, along with trunks and crates my parents had brought with them when moving to Natchez from Virginia, where they had both been raised.

She never told me, or anyone else, who the father was, for obvious reasons.

I assume she didn't want another boy to disappear.

If there was any sort of small blessing that came from the awful ordeal, it was that my father—as far as I ever knew—never again raised a hand to her. In time, once she'd recovered, Ellie filled the role which had been vacated by our mother's death and my father's inadequacies, taking over the household duties of cooking and cleaning, darning the elbows and heels of clothes for all the men who now surrounded her, who relied on her.

Less than a year later the war broke out. My father, a Virginian in both birth and rigid spirit, became a stalwart supporter of the South. That his three sons would go and fight for the Confederacy was never a question, and certainly not a discussion.

On the day Mason, Archie, and I walked away from home, I was happy for what felt like the first time in years. I was desperate to be away—away from my tyrant father, my morose sister. Away from that place filled with hopelessness and despair.

It was to be an adventure for me and my brothers. We'd become closer as I grew older, taller, more masculine. Became something closer in body and spirit to one of them. And, in turn, they took me under their collective wing and taught me to fight, to shoot, to use a knife.

When we left home that day, I opened the door a boy, but stepped into the street a man—my childhood forgotten and forgiven, my future brimming with poisonous deeds, doused in regret.

And now, all this time and suffering gone by, I walk westward, toward home once more. My brothers left behind—dying, dead, or hideously transformed by some witchcraft I can't begin to understand or explain. As I turn my back on them, I feel my newfound manhood has been torn away from me like a coat that was too big, one I wasn't meant to wear in the first place.

As I walk through the forest, I'm filled with shame, and hate. I don't know what waits for me in the days and weeks ahead, I only know what I've left behind: my pride, for one; my self-respect, and my best friends—the flesh of my flesh, and blood of my blood.

My brothers.

It isn't until I've been walking for two days and nights that I come across a river to follow south. Soon, I reach a settlement called Black Hawk, named after a dead Choctaw chief. I agree to work for a day, and no one is overly suspicious given my non-army issued clothes, my close-cropped hair, and my youth. I sleep in a shed near an active grist mill, the owner giving me a blanket, food, and nothing else.

The second day in Black Hawk I walk past a post office. There's a man on its stoop reading a newspaper spilling ink with talk of war. I slow my passage to study its front page, curious about the date.

Today is May 7, 1862.

One month since my brothers and I ran from the war.

Later, I inform the miller I'd be moving on, and ask if he knows the easiest path to the Mississippi River, where I hope to find passage south.

He tells me of an old trade route that will avoid major towns but keep me from getting lost, or swallowed by the wild. As he lays out the directions, I don't question why he assumes it advantageous for me to travel with as little notice as possible. Perhaps it's the haunted look I now carry in my eyes, a buried terror mixed with the shame of where I've been, and the things I've left behind.

I'm no more than three days' walk from the big river, he says.

I thank him for the information, truly grateful. I sleep restlessly that night, eager to be on my way come the first light of dawn.

God willing, Ellie, I'll be home in a week.

I only pray that home is there waiting for me.

I long to sit with you by the fire.

PART FOUR: THE RIVER

42

The trade route the miller spoke of—a lightly beaten trail from the outskirts of Black Hawk to a port along the river—is as easy to follow as he'd led me to believe. Equipped with a thin blanket (he gave me the one I'd slept on for two nights), a full skin of water, and a pouch packed with dried beef and hard tack, the walk to the Mississippi seems a holiday compared to the nightmarish conditions in which my brothers and I traversed the road from Shiloh to Carrollton and, ultimately, Sarafina's farm.

It helps, of course, not to be hunted by murderous members of the Home Guard. It also helps that I had a full week of recovery, and had been well-fed and sheltered while staying in the house. My flesh no longer crawls with vermin, my clothes are relatively clean, and it hasn't rained a single drop since the day I fled across the creek, escaping Sarafina's mysterious domain by the skin of my teeth.

At night I camp beneath the stars on dry ground, and during the day I walk the marked trail, allowing me to make good time to the river, reaching it on the evening of the third day, just as the miller said I would.

I don't know the name of the small port town that resides on the river's shore, but I skirt the settlement regardless, hands in pockets—just a young man on a stroll. Once I'm confident there's no immediate threat, I allow myself to walk to the banks of the great river.

The Mississippi is grand as I remember, a mile wide and stretched the breadth of this bitter nation that is on fire with war; and yet the river is a paradox, simultaneously serene and almighty. A benevolent god to be harvested, to provide, to carry men and women to new lands, new homes. To bring fortune and commerce along its current wherever men settle along the banks, from which towns blossom like flowering branches off an ageless tree.

I study the water for a few minutes, wishing my brothers were standing beside me.

I turn my attention south, toward the port town. The newly built buildings are primarily single-story log structures—housing and storage for workers, merchants, and goods. A large steamboat rests at the deepest end of the dock; there are multiple fishing boats tied to its pillars. I spot at least one dinghy pulled up onto the mud, just this side of the platform.

It won't be hard to steal one in the night.

I take a sip of water from my skin, then turn back toward the trees, away from the small port and its humanity. I've no place there. When it grows dark, I'll return—unseen and unheard—and claim one of those boats for my own.

Until then, I slip into the trees, welcome their shade on a warm day, and search for a place to hide, to rest; to ready myself for the last part of my pilgrimage.

Under a full moon, I return to the docks.

The steamboat is gone, the shoreline empty.

I walk along the riverbank, wary of any noises from the small settlement up on the rise. There are no lights on the dock—no lanterns, no watchmen. Now that it's night, there are even more boats tied to the dock's pillar, resting in the shallow lapping waters of the Mississippi.

I come to the first one—a twelve-foot dinghy with oars resting on the rails, locked into iron rings. There's a canvas thrown across the vessel, which stinks of fish but seems solid enough to take one man downriver. I untie the boat, push the canvas back from the bow. I walk it into the water until I'm knee-deep, then climb in and settle onto the bench. I grip the oar handles, dip the blades into the water, and slowly—quietly—row away from the dock.

The night is cold, still, and dimly lit, the fat moon dreary and cloud drenched. I keep rowing until the dock is the size of a fingernail, then a shadow along the riverbank, then gone altogether. I think it's best if I row through the night, putting as much distance as I can between that settlement and myself. The river will be busy during the daylight hours, ships heading north and south with war supplies and soldiers. I'll be small, insignificant, to anyone spotting me from a ship like that. Just another local fisherman. But better to be cautious.

I am so close now. So close.

I row for an hour before I begin to tire. I decide to let the river's southward flow take me along for a while, and I rest the dripping oars upon the boat's rails. I turn around on my bench and tug at the rest of the canvas tarp, bunched up toward the rear, with the intent of throwing it overboard. As I yank it forward, clearing the rudder, I'm shocked to see two wide eyes staring back at me from beneath the small seat at the stern.

My heart lurches in my chest as thoughts of the winged creature fill my mind, and for a brief second that's exactly what I see—Sarafina in her monstrous form, wings wrapped around black limbs; golden, goat-slit eyes and fanged mouth fill my vision...

I rip the bayonet free from my boot and point it toward the specter.

"No! Please—"

Small hands push their palms toward me and, as my vision clears, my imagination falters, and rising fear turns into trembling relief.

It's just a boy.

A little boy curled into the stern, likely sleeping beneath the canvas to keep warm, waiting for another day of work.

"You scared me pretty good," I say, lowering the point of my weapon. "Is this your boat?"

The boy shakes his head, still hiding, tucked below the small bench, as if keeping his limbs close to his torso will protect him. He's dressed in loose, soiled clothes, and is barefoot.

"I just work it," he says.

I nod, wondering what to do with him. "Well, sit up. I'm not going to hurt you."

Slowly, he uncoils, then slides cautiously into a seated position by the rudder, arms over knees, unsure of himself. Scared.

"Can you swim?"

The boy shakes his head again.

"Well, if you can't swim, I suppose I can't throw you overboard." I look toward the near shore, a quarter mile away, give or take. A hard swim for anyone in these currents. "I'll drop you off in the morning, you can walk back," I say, pointing north, toward the dock from which I'd stolen the boat. "Until then, you're gonna row. You row, I'll take the rudder."

The boy's wide eyes hood slightly, and I wonder if he's debating my worth as a physical opponent. "You stole the boat," he says.

"Very astute, kid. Now, are you gonna row, or are you gonna swim?" I raise the tip of my bayonet, let the metal soak in some of the meager moonlight.

The boy looks from me to the blade, then back to me. "I'm gonna row."

We beach just before dawn, and I estimate it's twenty miles to the dock we'd left from, although we've passed several since. Thankfully, all are under Confederate control. I spotted dozens of supply ships moving north and south, but at least I didn't have to worry about any Union gunboats.

During the night, I asked the boy if the battles had been hot along the river. "They control the river to the north, and to the south, but not here," he'd said. "All this still belongs to Confederacy." He looked at me then, thin arms languidly pulling the heavy oars along with the current. "But not for long, mister," he said. "They say Vicksburg will fall next. Then the whole river belongs to Lincoln."

"I doubt it," I say weakly, my defiance withered by the fact he was probably right, that Vicksburg would fall. I'd seen those gunboats close up, firing artillery from their black iron carapaces, and they'd terrified me. We'd watched them from a distance at Shiloh, along the Tennessee, and they'd torn the earth in half beneath our feet.

After turning the boy loose, I travel another hour downriver before finding a crag of rocks and broken trees to tuck into. I tie the boat to a bent, mossy pine, wrap myself in the stinking tarp, and sleep.

That night, I pass Vicksburg. I keep as far to the east side of the river as possible in order to avoid the many ships gathered outside the hill city, the town rising above the river like Olympus, a beacon of the South. Even in the dark it seems an impenetrable fortress. I'd heard of, but not yet seen, the grand new courthouse built at the city's crest—the new structure is watchful and awe-inspiring, even from the distance. I stare at that shining courthouse, and that great city—even now, well past sundown—bustling with activity and light, until the river pushes me well past, the flow of the Mississippi desperate as I am to keep moving, ever onward, toward home.

I sleep through another day.

The night is warm, and I'm grateful for it as I push the boat out onto the river, shimmering moonglow spread over the surface like strings of silver, the north star at my back as the current plucks at the boat and turns my bow south.

I get the boat good and deep into the belly of the wide river and let myself be carried. I need to be watchful. I have no idea how far I am from Natchez. I don't recognize this territory.

An hour into the journey I glide past a cluster of Confederate steamers and our own ironclad gunboats, all of them pushing north. I see soldiers standing on the deck of the steamers, their boats pushing them against the current toward battle, toward death.

I wave and imagine myself a ghost in the night to their eyes; a dead fisherman haunting the old wide river, eager to devour any souls who venture too close. One of them waves back, another sparks a light, smoking a cigarette, or a pipe. I lie back in the boat and watch the emerging stars blast across the midnight sky like heated shrapnel, burning the dark canopy.

I think of the night I shared with Sarafina beside the tree she called Novah. How we spoke of the stars and the mysteries they held, of what lay beyond. After that night, I'd often dream of her moonlit face, her laughing smile, the depth of her knowledge, her candor and her free spirit. I realize now that I fell in love with her that night, something I haven't admitted to myself until this moment. Like my poor brothers, I'd fallen for her completely. Fool that I am.

The boat rocking beneath me, the stars pouring into the sky overhead, I search for answers to what I'd seen, what I'd experienced. I search for answers as to what she truly is.

Demon. Witch. Shapeshifter. Angel.

You men and your labels.

I watch the stars float by high above, and wish, deep in my heart, that I could tear her apart and bury her deep.

I think how I would love to watch her die.

43

I beach just outside Natchez, push the boat into the current, and come up by the Under the Hill Saloon and onto Main Street, heading toward home.

It's near dawn, and the fishing boat I'd stolen rocks clumsily atop the river, untethered, floating toward New Orleans, or perhaps the great sea, where it will live out its days with a clean back, free from the burden of man. The air is chilly in the early morning, the sun casting pale yellow upon the surfaces of our town, pastel and plain, the muted tones and soundless streets making the entire town seem purgatorial.

I walk through the center of downtown, past shuttered shops and empty walks. I see my father's tobacco shop on my left.

As a child it had always felt so *grand*. The large men at the counter, smoking and barking at my father, who laughed and barked in return. The barreled stores of sweet tobacco saturating the air with a rich, heavy aroma that made my head spin. In those days it seemed my father ruled over an empire of men—men who needed his stores of leaf, his wit and charm, his cigars and cigarettes and tins.

I look at it now and it's a sad, feeble place. The sign—JEREMIAH BELLE, TOBACCONIST—is weathered and beaten as the town, as this broken nation. A wooden Indian is perched beside the door, a native of this soil now hawking cigars. The big man's hand is raised, as if swearing an oath. Or, perhaps, he's waving.

I don't wave back.

A couple blocks later I pass Our Lady of Sorrows, a great Gothic cathedral that took root in our town a few years before I was born. Parts of the exterior—primarily an extension that would eventually house priests and missionaries—are still under construction (likely slowed by the war). But I know that Father McKee will be holding mass, like he's done since I was a boy, on Sunday morning in the nave, the only public part of the grand church, and the first portion fully completed.

I turn on Union Street, less than a block from my front door, feeling nervous.

Will I be welcome? Will Ellie be happy to see me?

What will my father think of his youngest son, bedraggled and dirty, skinny…brotherless. A deserter not only of the war, but of his own kin. A coward who ran instead of fought.

But there is no other option. I'm hungry, and I'm so, so tired. I long for a meal and a bed—my own bed—and to hold Ellie's hand and tell her of the things that have transpired since I last saw her. All the heartache and death. The strange farm where Sarafina trapped us like an insidious spider, used her sorcery to ensnare us. To destroy us.

As I approach the front porch, I pause. The house is smaller than I remember; smaller than in my daydreams while lying in a ditch, artillery storming around me, bullets flying overhead like hornets. It's a modest home with whitewashed siding, weathered green shutters, a porch big enough for two chairs and no more. I stare for a moment, wondering how that small building once housed all of us—my mother and father, me and Ellie, and especially my two older brothers, their personalities too big for such a small place. There is so much of the world inside of them; I find it hard to reckon it all fitting beneath that humble roof.

The house is dark, of course. I debate sleeping in the shed out back, waiting on any reunion until the morning, when my appearance won't seem so sinister. But the call of my room—of food and familiar shelter—is too great. I knock loudly on the door, loudly enough to rouse one, or both, of them. I dare not try to slip in quietly. My father would likely take me for an intruder and shoot me in the heart with the loaded rifle he keeps mounted above his bedroom door.

A few minutes pass, and I'm about to knock again when one of the road-facing windows begins to glow. A lantern, or a candle, has been lit. I hear voices—muffled argument.

Finally, the door jerks open and there stands my father. He wears long underwear and a beard that has grown wild. His hair is whiter than I remember, his stature smaller, his skin more aged. He looks at me, wild-eyed, the rifle held tightly in two hands, the muzzle pointed at my head.

"Ethan!"

Appearing from behind the old man is Ellie, wrapped in a blanket, unkempt blonde hair falling over half her face. Unlike Father, she looks exactly as I remember—young and beautiful, eyes sharp with intellect, lips set tight with underlying strength.

I can't help but smile, even with a rifle poised to shoot me dead—the muzzle of which, I notice, is unwavering, even after my identity has been made clear.

"Where're your brothers?" Jeremiah's eyes narrow, then dance to the left and right of me, and of course sees no one at my side. I swear his finger tightens on the trigger.

I sigh inwardly, feeling a mix of relief and bone-deep despair, knowing that my journey is far from over.

PART FIVE: HOME

44

The story I tell my father and sister the following morning is not the truth.

After fending off a barrage of questions, and with Ellie's coaxing, the old man allowed me to eat some leftover supper from the icebox and get some much-needed rest. My bed, to my dismay, had been stripped to nothing but a mattress, but my sister brought me a heavy quilt she'd made that past winter. I rolled into it like a caterpillar entering a chrysalis, hoping to emerge as something different, something better.

In a way, I do. I wake to the smell of bacon and biscuits, open my bedroom door to find the living room warm and brightly lit by the late morning sun pouring through the windows. My father smokes at the kitchen table while Ellie fusses at the stove. I sit heavily at the table, just across from him. I'm groggy and in need of a bath, but my sister brings me coffee and puts a plate of food on the table. I eat greedily.

After a few minutes, my father puts down the newspaper and stares at me. He looks more himself in the daylight, properly dressed and not rudely awoken from slumber—his back is straight, his hair neatly combed, his clothes pristine. This is the man I remember, for better or worse.

"Now you've had your rest," he says calmly, but in a tone I've heard before. That of repressed anger. "You've had your eggs," he continues, nodding to my plate of crumbs and yolk. "And your coffee." He leans forward, elbows on the table. "Now you'll tell me what happened." He pauses, taps one finger on the tabletop. "You'll tell me where my sons are."

Beside us, Ellie folds her arms and leans against the counter, apparently also eager to hear my story.

Having eaten breakfast too fast, I belch uncomfortably, wondering where to start, or even what to say. How much to tell them, how much to withhold.

"We were at Shiloh," I begin, and relay the details of our forced march, that glorious first day when we surprised Grant and nearly ran the Yankees into the Tennessee River. How it had seemed like a sure victory until cowardice prevailed and we were held back from that fateful, final blow, explaining that Johnston was killed and Beauregard put in charge. How, fatefully, a decision was made by Beauregard to halt at nightfall, allowing Union reserves to arrive hours later, fortifying their position. How we were routed the next day...

"I can read a paper," Father says, rapping the table with a knuckle. "Get to it."

I nod, spare a glance at Ellie, who looks horrified at hearing about my ordeal in battle—rightfully sickened, but also compassionate. Something I feel a deep need for just now. I clear my throat and continue, unable to meet my father's icy gaze. He has Mason's eyes.

"On the battle's third day, we were sent to the field hospital, the three of us, to fortify against Union attack," I say, sticking with the story we'd come up with on the Corinth Road. "But as we left the main field of engagement, a Union cavalry erupted from the trees. They'd somehow gotten past our defenses. It was chaos by then. We were *losing*, Father."

The old man says nothing, but I see his jaw working, the whites of his knuckles as they clench into fists. I take a breath and continue.

"Archie and Mason were killed. They...they fought bravely."

Father points a shaking finger at me, his eyes wide and wet. "How are they dead and you alive?"

I shrug, look at Ellie, then to the sunlit kitchen window. "I survived," I say.

"And how are you here?!" he roars, slamming a fist onto the table. I jump, nearly fall backward in my chair. Father stands, paces, runs his hands through his thin white hair. When he finally stops pacing, he turns on me, eyes blazing with hate. "Why are you home?" he asks, jaw clenched.

I look around the room for inspiration, unsure of the right thing to say. With an inward sigh of resignation, I settle on a version of the truth. I must confess, and bear the cost.

"I ran," I say quietly.

Ellie groans, but I keep my eyes downcast. I don't dare meet my father's gaze.

"I deserted. I didn't want to die, so I snuck away. I came home."

Father moves fast—three quick steps and he swings a fist at me, connecting awkwardly with my forehead. He rears back to swing again, but my hands shoot up defensively. Ellie screams.

"Like a thief in the night!" he bellows, and I glance up at his beet-red face, the wide whites of his intolerant eyes. "A coward! A child who would let his brothers die and then run away like a yellow-bellied, no-good bastard!"

I keep my arms raised. I don't cry, and I'm not afraid. I just don't want to be hit again. His rage is expected, but it means little to me. After the things I've done, the things I've seen, the horrors at the farm in the woods...this is the tantrum of a child. One that must be weathered and then navigated until normalcy returns.

He storms out of the room, spitting curses, and for a moment I wonder if he's going for his rifle. Distantly I consider what I would do if he were to come out of the adjacent room, gun aimed at my chest, and pull the trigger. I suppose I'd do nothing. I suppose I'd die.

When he does emerge from his room, however, he holds no rifle. His brown slouch hat rests atop his head, and he wears a thick wool jacket. He walks briskly, without a word, toward the front door and leaves, slamming it shut behind him. To the pub, I imagine. Or the priest.

After he disappears into the bright day, I let go a held breath and sit still for a moment, unsure what to do next.

"You need a bath," Ellie says gently. "I'll heat one for you."

I nod, numb and lost in thought, in butchered emotions.

So this is home, I think, and then sip my coffee, which has gone cold.

When Father returns that night, I'm sitting alone by the fire, Ellie having already gone to bed. I'd been studying his old war saber, mounted above the fireplace as if it were a trophy.

After he stormed out earlier, I'd had a bath and got dressed, feeling a wave of guilt at seeing my dresser brimming with clothes. And though it was a luxury putting on a familiar pair of pants and a clean shirt, I was depressed—and a bit shocked—at how baggy my clothes were. I don't know how much weight I'd lost, but knew it was severe enough that Ellie gasped while sitting on the tub as I got undressed.

"Your ribs," she'd said, when I peeled off the shirt given to me by Sarafina. Then she'd looked away, as if ashamed, and left me alone in the washroom with a bar of soap and a cloth.

Now, with a full belly of hot food, my own clothes on my back, and my feet tilted toward the fire in my childhood home—the place I knew better than any other, where I'd grown from a baby to a man—I finally feel, for the first time in forever, *safe*.

I'm sick to death about my brothers, of course, and there are moments I consider growing stronger and going back there, hunting down that creature in the woods and saving Mason. Possibly Archie as well. I have fantasies of holding a knife to the witch's throat and demanding she turn him back into what he was. Turning him human.

Then I think back on the day I escaped, how I'd spun around to face that demon and seen nothing—the creek, the farm, and Sarafina...little Titus...the hounds...my brothers...all of it *gone*. I don't know if I could retrace my steps to get back to that spot, but even if I could, what would I find?

Nothing, I think. Her whole world hidden by a dark magic I couldn't possibly understand, or hope to defeat.

My father walks up to me, stands silently next to the fire, stares into the flames.

When he finally speaks, he does not look at me.

"You're my son, Ethan. My blood." His tobacco-stained fingers twist at his beard. "And I've been down to Our Lady of Sorrows, praying on it with Father McKee, and I've decided." He shakes his head, sniffs loudly and rests a hand on the mantle, as if steadying himself for what he must do. "I will not have a coward living in my home. A deserter. Even worse, a man who left behind his own kin to rot on a battlefield."

Now, he does turn toward me, wide eyes flickering, a reflection of the flames. I wait patiently for his judgment to be over so I can sleep. "You can stay here three days," he says. "The same amount it took Jesus to rise from the grave. On Sunday, Ellie and I will go to church in the morning. When we come back, I want you gone, and I don't want to ever see you again."

I nod, rock back and forth in my mother's old chair.

"This is my home," I say quietly, without anger. "I was born here, and I'm your son."

I look up at him, then I stand. I'm a half-foot taller than the old man and—even in my weakened state—I'm twice as strong.

And infinitely more dangerous.

"I'll stay here as long as I see fit."

We lock eyes for a moment, and then I yawn, my body suddenly on the edge of exhaustion, my mind blurry with a need for rest. I walk away and leave him by the fire. I go to my room and shut the door.

As I fall into sleep, I think about a revenge that will never come.

45

After a few weeks at home, I begin to grow restless. Agitated.

My father has taken to ignoring me, which works out fine for both of us. I have nothing to say to the old man, and even if it causes Ellie to grumble beneath her breath and toss out cusses when she thinks us out of earshot, it's better than the alternative. Better to be called a "pigheaded bull" than listen to Jeremiah lecture me on bravery or hear about his fighting in the Mex-American War for the hundredth time.

Still, I can't hide at home forever, so I venture out one morning with the idea of finding work. Something to occupy my mind and my mostly recovered body with male camaraderie and good old-fashioned physical labor. I miss my brothers, and there is a void inside me I need to fill.

I start at Under the Hill, try to latch on with a fishing boat crew, or dock laborers loading cotton onto steamboats. Somewhat surprisingly—with the obvious shortage of manpower in the South—I'm given the cold shoulder from every harbor master and boat captain I come across.

Practically ignored.

Frustrated at the docks, I attempt to find work downtown. I walk in and out of dry goods and grocery stores, Tanner's drug store, and the two produce markets. I stop in at the butcher shop, the haberdashery, and even the post offce. I ask the baker if he needs an errand boy, the shoemaker if he needs a clerk. I could try some of the nearby plantations, of course, but with all the slaves the owners have on hand, I doubt they'll have any interest in paying for labor.

Finally, with the sun setting on a miserable day, I visit the small bookseller run by an old family friend, David Perry, who sold books to my mother once upon a time. To his credit, he at least hears me out, and has enough pity on me to let me know the truth of things.

I've been blacklisted.

It seems my father has been souring my name to everyone in town—to the folks at church, to his clients at the tobacco shop, in the pub when he drinks his whiskey and holds court with the other old men who feel that their longevity alone has gained them some sort of stewardship over the city's residents. He's told them all about me, and then some.

That I am a deserter. A coward. That he's disowned me. That I humiliated him and the city of Natchez. All of Mississippi, in fact.

That I'd abandoned my brothers on the battlefield. Left them for dead.

Left them behind.

Never mind that I personally know of at least three other men who'd run home, tail between their legs, sick of fighting. Hell, there are hundreds—*thousands*—of deserters across the South, if you believe what you read in the papers.

I don't know if it occurred to him or not, but the worst part of all his tongue-wagging is the very real possibility it might alert the Home Guard, or bring the Confederacy to our front door demanding I re-enlist. Thankfully, Natchez has been relatively free from military action, at least to this point of the war. For those who live here, the war was recently viewed as if from a distance, the city untouched and unscathed while great battles raged in the North.

But that all changed a few weeks ago, the day a Union vessel landed at our docks, only a few days after my own stolen fishing boat nosed the shore. The mayor handed Natchez over to Union control without a fight and, in turn, the Yanks (headed by a genial old bastard named Farragut) now use our port to move supplies up and down the river, turning Natchez into just another foothold as they take control of the Mississippi River, piece by piece.

Does my father pick up his rifle and fight? Does anyone?

Of course not. And yet I'm the coward. I'm the one who is shunned, who is damned.

Outside of having that massive sloop in our harbor to keep things civil, the city is of little import to the great military strategists of the Northern army, and as a younger man—not yet eighteen—I was left alone. No soldiers knocked on our door. No overzealous Home Guard chased me through the streets.

But my father, it seems, will see me in battle or hanged. And without a way to make money, I am quickly optionless. Stuck. Wedged into a crevice between stones, a shadowed place where there may well be a snake, coiled in the cool darkness along with me, waiting for the right time to strike.

46

To make things worse, I've begun to have nightmares.
Horrible ones.

Over the last few weeks I've woken a handful of times, screaming and clawing at my flesh. Poor Ellie came bursting into my room on more than one occasion to find me standing by the window, screaming my lungs out into the dark—just screaming and screaming.

Another time she found me naked and crawling on all fours, sobbing as I sniffed into corners and beneath my bed.

The last time, I was standing in the corner of the room, hunkered in shadow. I don't remember it, but Ellie told me the next day that I'd had a strange expression on my face, that my eyes had been wide open. That I'd watched her come in, grinning like a madman.

"Like a thief, or a murderer," she said, shuddering at the memory. "I called your name again and again but you just stood there, staring at me, smiling. If you'd had a weapon in your hand I would have called for Father."

"Lucky you didn't," I said, hoping to lighten things. "He'd love an excuse to shoot me."

Early on after my arrival, Ellie and I interacted as congenial strangers, as if I were a boarder instead of the brother she grew up with. After a few weeks, however, we fell into our old banter, our old comfort.

I didn't tell her any details of the nightmares that plagued my sleep—I could hardly remember most of them, being honest—but I also didn't want to frighten her.

Or, perhaps, didn't want to frighten myself.

In one dream, a dream I can only recall fragments of, I wake up under Novah—the old, gnarled tree in the fields by Sarafina's farm—lying flat on my back. The witch is there, as well, sitting in the grass, legs crossed, eyes closed. She smiles, then speaks my name.

"Ethan," she says slowly, quietly, as if in a trance.

It's nighttime, and the grass beneath my back and head feels brittle, the earth hard and rough. The air is bitter cold, and the sky is filled with so many stars I gasp at the sight of them—a bucket of silver dust poured onto black glass. There are colors as well, smoky tendrils of red, purple, and blue. I'd never seen anything like it.

"Galaxies," Sarafina says, as if knowing my thoughts in this strange dream world. "There are worlds beyond ours, Ethan. Worlds upon worlds. More than you can possibly comprehend."

"Yes," I say, feigning confidence. "So you've said."

She laughs and I feel a shameful pull of desire for her. Of love.

I sit up and cross my legs, matching her pose. I look around at the swaying barley. I ignore the heavens as best I'm able, somewhat sickened at the way the sky rotates, as if years were passing instead of seconds.

"That's right," she says, eyes still closed, that small smile on her lips. "I'd forgotten about our secret rendezvous."

"It wasn't a secret—"

"I thought you would kiss me that night. You wanted to, didn't you?"

I don't say anything. I consider standing and walking away from her, from this place, this dream.

"Would you like to kiss me now?" she says.

"Open your eyes," I say, but I don't know where the words come from, or why I say them. I don't want her to open her eyes. I want her eyes to stay closed.

"Open your eyes," I repeat, like a mantra.

Suddenly, there's a tremendous pressure on my shoulders, my chest. Something is holding me down, refusing to let me stand, to *escape*.

I can't move.

"I have such worlds to show you," she says. "I'll show you angels, and I'll show you demons. I'll show you things that will shatter your mind, Ethan. That will destroy your reason. Look at me, Ethan—"

She opens her eyes. They're yellow and slit down the middle, like the eyes of a goat. When she expands her smile, her teeth are long and pointed and too large for her mouth, white tips curling past her lips. Black wings unfurl from behind her.

"Look into my eyes."

God help me, I do.

I don't recall what happens next, but when I wake I'm standing at the window, staring up at the night sky, crying and babbling nonsense.

A different night, I dreamed of something else. Something from my past. Ellie hears me calling out in my sleep and wakes me. She asks what I'd dreamed about, and I tell her I don't remember.

But I do.

In the dream I was holding a fist-sized stone, covered in blood. I'm at the shoreline of the Mississippi, staring at a fallen, moss-covered log, floating away on the mighty river...

After a few months, things at home began to settle.

My father continued to speak to me only when necessary, and never in conversation, but I was able to get a job hauling crates of cotton three days a week. My father's words against me dulled in time; people eventually grew tired of holding a grudge against one of their own, especially given that more men were returning every day.

Deserters arrived by the dozens, making weak claims that they'd return once they settled some unspoken problem at home that demanded their attention. Of course, none of them ever did; all the empty promises nothing but convenient lies for folks to hold onto, as if there were as much honor in gesture as there was in action.

Before I knew it, the summer had passed us by, and the first colors of autumn were staining the trees in rustic earth tones of auburn and gold.

One afternoon, Ellie invites me for a walk along the river, a basket in her hand and a warm sweater over her dress. We find a clearing of dry grass and lay down a blanket. She unwraps bread and cheese for a picnic, and after a few minutes of eating (and glaring at the Union boats in the harbor as if they were jailers), she finally asks the question she's wanted to ask since the day I returned home.

"What happened, Ethan?" she says, and looks me in the eye. "What really happened to you, to our brothers?"

I know there's no point lying further. Not to Ellie. Not anymore.

While formulating a response, I stare out at those Union boats, chew a knot of crusty bread topped with sharp cheese. She offers me a flask and I raise an eyebrow. "Just for us," she says, and I take a long swallow of persimmon brandy. I wince and she laughs. "Don't say anything coarse, Ethan. Old Mr. Allison at the drugstore makes it himself, and I'd have to tell on you."

I nod, hand it back to her, and fold my hands in my lap.

"I'll tell you," I say. "But you won't believe a goddamned word of it."

Ellie watches me a moment, then takes a large swallow of brandy and smacks her lips. She turns her body to face me, like we'd do when we were kids, focused on a game of Jacks, or a trapped frog.

"Okay," she says quietly, and waits.

And so, I tell my sister everything, and leave nothing out.

Well. Almost nothing.

I leave out the fact that Mason and Sarafina were lovers, omitting her claims at being impregnated with his child. I don't know why I do it. I suppose it feels unnecessary, and would confuse the facts of what went on in that house. The horrors.

But I do recount the battle at Fort Donelson, and the story of the dead man's boots. I tell her about Shiloh, and deciding to run. Killing the lieutenant. The bandits. The Choctaws and the Home Guard. Mason's close call in the swamp.

I take a deep breath and tell her of the strange homestead we found in the deep woods.

Of Sarafina, and Titus. The hounds...

I tell her what happened to our brothers. Spells and witchcraft. Demonology. Archie transformed into a beast. Mason left for dead. The flying creature that chased me to the creek. My escape, and the trip home.

When I finish, the afternoon has grown closer to dusk, the sky over the great river is painted with pink clouds, the horizon swollen with a crimson sunset.

"Can I have some more of that brandy?" I ask, and Ellie hands me the flask without a word, her face expressionless. Finally, she takes my hand gently in her own, gives it a little shake until I look up at her. So pretty in the dying day, my twin. Her blonde hair glows with the sun's last testament, her blue eyes wide and filled with bravery and confidence, her jaw set firm as ivory. She is stronger than I, my sister. Stronger by far, and I relish the comfort of that.

"We can't leave them there," she says.

I nod, even though I disagree. Her response doesn't surprise me, given I've had the exact same one every day for near six months. But even now, her hand in mine, I know I can never go back.

"Ethan, they could still be alive," she says. "They can still be...hell, I don't know...fixed. Healed. We must go get them, don't you see that?"

"I know," I say, plucking a nearby blade of grass and twisting it to green mush in my fingers. "It's all I think about, Ellie. And that goddamn witch...she haunts my dreams. She taunts me. There's a connection there I don't know how to break, and I think she'll drive me mad if she can. And if she doesn't, I'll go mad anyway, from shame. The shame of leaving them behind. The old man is right, he was right all along, just not for the reasons he thinks." I look at her sharply. "You can't tell him any of this," I say. "He'll think me the Devil himself."

Ellie shakes her head. "Of course not. But I think there is someone who can help us, Ethan. A man who knows about witches and demons, of the preternatural world."

"It doesn't matter," I say, despite my curiosity. "I couldn't find her again if I was given a hand-drawn map. I told you, her entire world vanished the minute I crossed that creek. I don't see how it would be possible to get back."

"It's possible," she says, and looks toward the river, the blood of the cerise sunset smeared across her face like war paint. "We'll find them, and we'll save them. We'll kill that witch and burn her house to the ground, and then we'll spit in the goddamn ashes."

47

While I consider myself religious, I haven't found much use for the church.

Mother raised us Catholic, and Father is a deacon at Our Lady of Sorrows. Has been for as long as I can remember. Father McKee, who presides over the ever-growing cathedral, is considered a family friend and is often invited over for meals, more so while my mother was still alive, my father seemingly more comfortable socializing with the priest at the church itself, or the local pub, which McKee is known to frequent for a glass of wine or an occasional stout.

When my sister suggests that Father McKee is the man we need to speak with, I initially balk at the idea. For one, McKee is close with Jeremiah, and I don't want my father knowing the truth of my recent travails or the loss of my brothers. Secondly, although McKee is a kind man, he has always struck me as odd. He has wild, white hair atop his head, heavy eyebrows, and a face that makes me think of a hatchet, sharp and hard. One of his eyes is lazy and unsettling to look upon while he yells about damnation and sin and the labors and temptations of God-fearing men and women. It's as if he's looking at your soul with one eye and Heaven with the other, receiving messages from high above to relay to us sinners.

But Ellie is nothing if not persistent, and I know there's little chance of convincing her that the idea is a poor one. If I'm being honest, I've been longing to speak to someone about what I experienced out there in those woods, share the things I'd seen and heard, and have some reassurances I didn't imagine it all. Perhaps assuage some of the guilt gnawing at my gut since the day I ran away, saving myself, and damning my brothers.

So I agree to the visit with McKee, and the very next morning, while my father works at the shop, Ellie and I go to Our Lady of Sorrows to speak with the old preacher.

Part of me hopes he'll comfort me. Part of me hopes he'll inform me, and another part of me—one I don't dare examine for too long—hopes he'll help me find a way back; a clear, shining path toward revenge, if not salvation.

The rectory is attached to the main cathedral, and though the additional parish rooms are still being constructed, Father McKee's office is furnished and comfortable. Wearing full robes and collar, he sits behind a dark oak desk smiling brightly at Ellie, who chatters on with him about his last sermon, and how much it seemingly affected her. I don't roll my eyes, but I feel ridiculous being here, talking to this man about witches, shapeshifters, and murder. Even so, when the small talk is banished, he turns to me with kind eyes, and I begin to hope I'll find absolution here after all.

"Ethan," he says. "Before you tell me...what it is you're here to tell me, I want to first say how sorry I am. I owe you an apology, son."

I glance at Ellie, who offers a small nod. *Go on.*

"Apology, Father?"

"Yes. You've had a hard time since you've returned from the war. I know your father has been diffcult on you, and I hope you know that I've done my best to counsel him on being merciful, and supportive. It's a terrible thing for a boy your age to see such horrors, to be forced into battle, to kill others...and no one blames you for what happened to Archie and Mason. Tens of thousands have been killed, Ethan." He shakes his head, studies his hands, long fingers folded atop the desk. "Just awful."

"Thank you," I say. "And, well, I guess that's part of what I'm here to talk about."

His eyes widen, expectant. "Oh?"

I shift in the leather chair, feeling insignificant in this ornate office with its velvet window dressings, shining wood shelves, massive old books, and golden crosses. I feel as if I've stumbled into the annex of God Himself, wearing rags and soiled shoes, my heart dark and scarred and full of sin.

"Yes," I manage.

I lean forward, grip the edge of the ornate desk with both hands, steady myself for what's to come. "Father...have you heard of the Book of Enoch?"

A large, leatherbound book is splayed open upon a pedestal, one seemingly made for the sole purpose of holding ancient tomes the size of a suitcase and heavy as a sack of oats.

"Enoch is not part of the standardized Bible as you know it," he says, gently turning the thin, frail pages, some illuminated by colorful drawings, the words pressed in black ink.

For a second, I wonder if this was the very book Archie had once pleasured himself to as a boy—while staring at the illustration of a scantily-clad angel—and I have to stifle a mad giggle that tickles my throat. Ellie, who seems to know my every thought, gives me a hard look that douses my humor like a bucket of cold water tossed on a candleflame.

"Enoch," the priest continues, oblivious to my juvenile thoughts, "is part of what the church calls the apocrypha, books that may, or may not, be divine, but have been excluded from the primary canon. Genesis, Exodus, what have you."

Father McKee speaks in a way that doesn't make me feel judged, or ignorant, and I find myself growing more comfortable with the idea of telling him the truth of what happened in the woods. I also feel a pang of loss for not having come to church more often. Perhaps having this man's good nature in my life would have made things easier for me, softened the prickly relationship with my father.

Perhaps I could have been a better person.

"Here we are," he says, pointing to the book.

I note the chapter heading, etched in oversized letters: ENOCH.

"I was told," I begin slowly, being careful with my words, "that this book would help me understand some things that happened to me. That happened to me and my brothers. Things that no one, outside of Ellie that is, knows anything about."

McKee's eyes narrow. "Not even your father?"

I shake my head, eyes locked on his, beseeching that he appreciates the severity of my intention when I say, "Especially him."

The priest nods, then folds his arms within those heavy black robes. "Perhaps we should start with your story, Ethan, and then I can pull from Enoch what I think would be helpful." He chuckles, taps the pages of the book. "Trust me when I say there's a lot to dissect in these pages, and I think a good part of it might add more confusion, versus understanding."

I study the large book for a moment, growing ever more curious about what ancient stories live within those pages. Would it truly help me? Help my brothers? Or was this simply another way for evil to shake my faith? In God and in myself?

"Ethan?" Ellie says quietly.

"Could we possibly sit down?" I say. "It's a long story, Father."

He says that we can, and the three of us settle around a small table, the hard oak seats somehow more comfortable to me than the plush leather chairs by his desk.

"Just tell him exactly what you told me," Ellie says, noting my hesitation.

I take a deep breath and, over the next hour, tell the priest every detail, withholding nothing. Praying he will not think me mad.

48

Father McKee is silent for several moments.

I look to Ellie for guidance, or reassurance, but her eyes are fixed on the priest, as if willing him to believe me.

She needn't have worried.

When he finally speaks, it seems as if he's been drained, or terribly burdened. That carefree joviality—like the twinkle in an eye—has been burned away. Stomped out. As if he's aged ten years while we all sat around the small, polished table in the bowels of the great cathedral.

"Father?" I say, needing him to say something. Anything. I hope he doesn't think me a liar or, even worse, bring Jeremiah into it. I'd have to run away then, find a new life, a new town, a new home. My old man would tell everyone that his son saw witches and monsters. I'd be the laughingstock of Natchez.

"I believe you, Ethan."

Although I'm relieved to hear the words, it's Ellie who gives an audible sigh of relief.

"You'll have to excuse my indecision about what to say next," he says. "It's more delicate to me than it is to you."

"I don't understand."

"I believe you," he says, "because I've had similar experiences." McKee looks from me to Ellie with earnest eyes, as if weighing our wills, or judging our fortitude. "What I'm going to tell you can't leave this room. In the same way you'd like to keep your story from others, I would ask you the same courtesy."

"Of course, Father," Ellie says, and I nod along, intrigued.

"Good, good. Now," he says, some of the spark returning to his eyes, the years slipping away from him yet again, "there's something I need to show you. Something that will help you. But before we do that, let's talk about Enoch, and why this boy—"

"Titus," I offer.

"Yes, the man trapped in a boy's body," he says, and actually smiles, as if amused at the Devil's power. "Amazing. But yes, what he told you makes sense to me now, at least to a small degree. Let's start simple, eh? You both know the story of the great flood, of Noah and his ark."

Ellie and I nod like children in Sunday School, listening to the outlandish, exciting, and often terrifying stories of the Bible for the first time.

"Fine, fine. Now, part of Enoch tells of a time before the flood. It speaks of angels who came to earth, and in doing so became entranced by human women. Physically, that is," he adds awkwardly, then gains momentum as he continues the tale, losing himself in the story. "There were two hundred of these angels, and in the Book of Enoch they are referred to as The Watchers, also called *iyrin* in the ancient Hebrew. They were called such because they were supposed to be watching over our world, helping us, guiding us. Instead...they destroyed us. These angels—these *watchers*—altered their normal beastly shapes in order to appear human. Then...fornicated with the women."

McKee clears his throat, perhaps waiting for a childish gasp from me or my sister. Seeing no shock on our faces, he continues.

"Subsequently, many of those women gave birth to giants, called Nephilim, a hybrid of human women and the angels. For many years, the Nephilim ran rampant over the earth, feasting on the meat of man and beast alike, destroying homes and murdering men, women, and children to such a degree that mankind cried out to God. Cried out and said, 'Save us!'" The priest raises his arms and bellows, as if *he* were the one crying out to the heavens instead of these storybook men from Biblical times.

"Giants, father?" Ellie says, brow furrowed. "Like in fairy tales?"

Surprisingly, the priest nods, and laughs. "Now you see why the Book of Enoch was left out of the canon for those who study and worship. It's simply...well, it's too hard to believe. At least for those still finding their faith, that is."

"My mother told us once about Daniel slaying a dragon," I say, pulling the memory from my childhood. "She and my father argued about it—he claimed it was myth, while she insisted it was biblical."

McKee nods. "Your mother was quite the scholar. She could have told you all about Enoch and The Watchers, make no mistake. And yes, the story of the dragon is also apocryphal, but we need not get distracted."

Ellie leans forward. "And the flood?"

"Yes, well, these angels—and the human women they impregnated—were punished. The angels bound, the women lost to history, and the Nephilim all wiped out in the great flood."

"That's why God destroyed the earth?" Ellie says, a note of skepticism having crept into her tone. "To slay these giants?"

The priest nods, shrugs. "So says Enoch, anyway."

"Father, with respect, what does any of this have to do with Sarafina?" I say, but vague puzzle pieces are already forming in my mind, taking shape, coming together.

"I think what Titus was hinting at had to do with the relationships between the Watchers, and the women who bore their children."

Ellie begins to say something, but McKee holds up a hand. "Hold on, dear. I think this might be easier to explain if I just read it." The old priest stands, then walks back to the pedestal.

Intrigued, Ellie and I follow, looking on from either side of him as he flips the pages.

"Here," he says, and presses a fingertip to the center of a page. "Chapter eight, verse three. 'Semjaza taught the casting of spells, and root-cuttings, Armaros taught counter-spells, Barqijal taught astrology, Kokabel taught the constellations...'" McKee turns to me. "That's the study of the stars. Some believe the stars tell our future—which is nonsense, of course."

I say nothing, but recall the night of lying beneath those impossible star-blasted skies with Sarafina; her telling me about worlds upon worlds.

"According to this book," the priest continues, "the angels taught us many things. How to make and use weapons we'd never before seen, concepts of war, even how to enhance material beauty—a weapon in its own way," he says, allowing himself a small chuckle.

"And how does Sarafina fit into all this mythology?" I ask, but think I already know the connection. I've seen firsthand what she could do, the strange powers she used on my brothers.

"Witchcraft," he says bluntly, tapping the thick pages of the book. "This passage describes the very beginning of witchcraft. Sorcery! These demonic—yes, demonic, for what is a demon but a fallen angel—teachings were handed down to women over the centuries, harnessed and refined. Forbidden secrets on how to create remedies from roots and herbs, how to read the stars, to cast spells. These angels were shapeshifters, Ethan, which was yet *another* thing they taught the witches who roam the earth. I should know," he says, growing heated, his eyes alight, as if lit by fire. "I've hunted them myself!"

49

We walk down the center of the nave toward the altar. Night has crept in since we first arrived, and shadows arch across the chamber's high ceiling like black wings. The sounds of our footsteps tapping stone echo throughout the broad cathedral as we pass row upon row of long pews and marble statues with ornate gold trimmings. The west-facing windows are backlit by a strong moon, illuminating biblical imagery in jagged cuts of red, blue, and green. I notice the scene of Abraham fighting an angel, trying to thrust his dagger into the chest of his son, Isaac. The look on his white-bearded face is one of pure madness as the son lies placid, eyes closed. Sacrificial. Inevitable.

We come to a narrow wooden door just beyond the confessional. McKee removes a thick chain from around his neck, one that bears several keys, and unlocks the door. When he pulls it open, I'm surprised to see stone stairs leading downward. He pauses, pulls a tin of matches from his pocket and lights a sconce on the wall.

"Watch your step. The stairs are narrow, and steep."

He enters the stairwell, and we follow him down spiraling steps that lead far below the cathedral itself, into a heavy darkness.

"When the bishop decided to build Our Lady of Sorrows," he says as he descends, his voice muffled by the surrounding stone, "establishing a foothold of the Catholic Church here in the deep South, he knew it would be a place of great sanctity, a cornerstone of our outreach throughout the new territories as we expand God's word west of the river."

Eventually we reach the bottom to face a stunted corridor. McKee lights another sconce, then selects a second key from the chain, his robed figure barely visible in the dim light. A metal door stands before him, one that appears formidable as a bank vault, and I wonder how much more there is to the construction of Our Lady of

Sorrows, how many more secrets have been built below its public-facing structure.

For a moment, I think of the caverns beneath Sarafina's farm…

Then Father McKee unlocks the door and pushes inward. It glides silently into the dark beyond, and the priest replaces the chain around his neck.

"A moment," he says, and disappears into the room.

I turn to face Ellie, the sconce above backlighting her in such a way that her golden hair appears as a halo surrounding her shadowed features. "What is this?" I whisper, but she only shakes her head.

"There we are," McKee says, having returned. "Come in, come in."

I enter the room—now lit with candles, their soft orange glow rippling against brick walls and tall wooden shelves. As I move deeper into the narrow vault, I notice the array of objects on the shelves, strange shapes in the candlelight that spark no recognition, no familiarity.

Father McKee keeps walking until he reaches a rounded space at the end of the room. There's a large, sturdy worktable at its center, and a lantern set upon it which he now lights, chasing away the shadows and making the room less sinister.

"What are these things?" Ellie asks, reaching for a rounded, metal object on one shelf that reminds me of the grape we'd blast out of a cannon.

"Artifacts," he says, smiling. "Relics. A treasure trove of spiritual talismans the church has brought here for safekeeping.

"This is but a trifle of what resides to the east," he says, gently removing the ball from her hands and placing it, reverently, back on the shelf. "Some of it had been forgotten in old, overflowing storerooms. Some of it is my personal property, from the days when I was doing a different kind of work for the church." The old man winks at my sister, and I repress a shiver at the way it makes him seem like a different person. Someone with filth in the wrinkles of his hide. "Now, stay here a moment while I gather some things."

Ellie and I stand by the candlelit table while the priest shuffles along the shelves—picking up and putting down seemingly random objects—before finally settling on what he's looking for.

He returns to the table three times.

The first time he brings a square—but misshapen, as if beaten—iron plate, pierced with holes. It's bent and old and makes me think of armor, though I could easily hold it in one hand. Perhaps it could protect my heart, but no more.

The second time he sets down a kitchen knife, the blade no longer than my hand, the handle dark wood. There are symbols carved on the metal.

The final time he carries a leatherbound book, and a gold ring, the setting an intricately carved symbol.

When the objects are all laid out, he glances at Ellie before his eyes settle on me, and I sense a challenge in them. "If I help you, it's because you're going to do what is right. You will act as God's holy instrument. You will be brave and not waver, and will not be seduced by the Devil. If I help you," he continues solemnly, "you will go back. You will find this witch and her imp, and kill them. If you are not willing to do that, I'll pray for you both, and you can go about your lives. But I must know now, before we go further. Ethan Belle, will you go back? Will you finish what was started?"

I think of my brothers, of Archie's beastly, transformed face sniffing at my own, of Mason on a block of stone, carved like a pig; the witch smacking her lips after eating a slice of his kidney.

I think of something else. The one thing I kept from both Ellie and the priest.

After all, he's the father of my child.

Ellie puts her hand on my arm and squeezes. "You won't be going on your own," she says, as if concerned that my determination is wavering. "I'm with you every step of the way."

I turn to her, thinking of all the things I should say:

It's too dangerous.

I should do this alone.

I can't risk losing you as well.
But instead, I feel great relief, and smile at my brave twin sister. Then I nod at the priest.

"I'll go back," I say. "I'll finish it."

50

McKee lifts the leatherbound book, holds it forward like a shield against evil.

"The *Malleus Maleficarum*," he says, with no small amount of reverence. "Also known as 'The Hammer of Witches.' This book was written two hundred years ago by a great man, an inquisitor of the Holy Church who devoted his life to hunting and killing witches around the world, stamping out evil wherever it took root. His methods are tried and true, Ethan, and this book will teach you everything there is to know about how to identify a witch…and how to *deal* with them. If needed, torture them until they confess their mating with Satan."

He pauses, a sly grin creeping onto his face, and once again I feel as though I'm getting a glimpse of the man he used to be.

"And, of course, how to dispose of them. I'm giving you this book, Ethan. My personal copy, the very same one I've carried with me, and studied, for more than thirty years."

McKee hands me the book. The leather is worn and cracked, the pages thin and well-thumbed. "I can't accept this, Father."

"You can," he says, his usual gentle, gleeful eyes now hard as ice, his sharp features and wild hair no longer comical, but intimidating. I can see the killer inside of him. "And you will. Besides, I've memorized the entire thing front to back. I've no need for the printed paper anymore. If you study it the way I did, you will become a Holy Warrior in God's army."

"May I see it?" Ellie says.

I hand it to her and she begins scanning the pages, frowning.

The priest ignores her and continues to the next object, the one that looks like a scrap of ancient armor. The holes in the metal are random, as if it had been repeatedly shot at close range. He holds it up; the black metal seems molten in the flickering candlelight, as if the thing is alive.

"This is a *defixio*. Known to many in ancient times as a curse tablet. People would write curses on them and bury them—writing curses on neighbors, or hated family members, whomever. This one, however, is a variation of that. You see these markings?" He points to a series of faded scratches. The writing fills both sides of the thin metal, the hand thin and spidery. "This is no curse, but an invocation. I've used this particular object myself."

"What language is this?" I ask, not recognizing a single word.

He grins as he runs his fingertips over the text. "Much of what's written here is known as *voces mysticae*, which is a fancy way of saying that it's Latin, but the words are uncommon. It is the language of demons, you understand?"

I nod, not understanding at all, but begin to feel the press of this room and its bizarre objects, and suddenly wish to feel fresh air on my face.

"Using this tablet will enable you to find the witch. If you can return to the location where you last saw the creature, use the *defixio* and it will reveal your path. It will invoke the foul thing and erase the cursed spell which keeps its world hidden from the eyes of men."

The priest holds the plate near his face, his blue eye looking through one of the holes.

"*Daemon, quorum pars esto subjecto voluntati meae,*" he intones. "Say that phrase while using this tablet, and you will find your way back to its lair."

"Father," Ellie says abruptly, breaking the strange spell the priest is weaving over me with his trinkets and ancient words. "Are all witches women?"

I look over to Ellie, notice she has her finger pressed to one of the pages.

Father McKee shakes his head. "Bewitchery is not confined to women, child. There are other things their equal—wizards and sorcerers, for example. Or necromancers who commune with the dead. But witches *breed*, Elizabeth. They adjoin with demons and fill our world with wickedness like a dark plague. They must be burned out," he says grimly. "Like a tick in the thigh."

He thrusts the iron plate into my hands. It's lighter than I'd imagined, and I run my fingers over the carvings. I put it to my face, look through one of the holes at Father McKee, but see nothing but darkness.

"There are two more things I must share with you," McKee says, and I lower the beaten metal, hold it awkwardly as he continues.

"This ring is made of brass, and imprinted here," he points to a flat circle on the ring, black as a midnight pond, emblazoned with gold symbols, "is the seal of King Solomon. And these markings are the secret name of God Himself, sent to Solomon from Heaven in time of great need."

Ellie's eyes widen. "Something so ancient must be worth a fortune."

McKee smiles abashedly, gives a small shake of his fuzzy head. "I doubt this exact ring was worn by the great king, Ellie. It is but a mimic, styled off the original or, at the least, a facsimile, handed down over the years. Regardless, it is a powerful talisman."

I stare at the ring, fascinated. "What does it do?"

"Repels demons," he says, studying the carvings on the gold. "The wearer will be protected from the minions of Hell, even from Satan himself. No demon—such as Sarafina or her imp—will want to be anywhere near it, trust me on this."

I take the ring. When McKee turns around, I hand it to Ellie. "Put it on," I whisper.

She glances at the priest's turned back, then snatches it from my palm and slips it onto one of her slim fingers. We're both a little surprised at how perfectly it seems to fit.

"And finally, a weapon." McKee turns back to us holding a slim leather sheath. He picks up the knife he'd set down previously, tests its fit in the sheath, then nods approvingly. He removes the blade once more, holds it aloft so the light catches the metal. Both Ellie and I lean in close, squinting to study the strange symbols carved into the blade.

"A Witch Knife," he says. "More formally known as a *Trudenmesser*—or Trud knife—a 'trud' being synonymous with 'witch' in Austria, where this blade was crafted. It will protect the wielder against any Druden presence. These symbols here," he points to the black etchings along the metal, "are nine crescent moons and, just beneath them, nine crosses."

"Why nine?" Ellie asks, and I note the flutter of annoyance that passes across McKee's face, and try not to smile at my sister's innate curiosity.

"Three and nine are very powerful numbers. The number nine symbolizes the trinity of the Father, the Son, and the Holy Ghost—then tripled. What's known as a triple triad. The number three, of course, is also associated with many pagan gods, such as Diana, or Hekate. If you wield this knife, no witch will be able to touch you. If you swing it at her, she may flee. If you stab her...it may end her."

"What's that on the other side?" I ask, silently imagining thrusting the blade into Sarafina's chest, severing her black heart.

McKee flips the blade to show the backside, the metal catching the orange light of the candleflames. "This number is the year it was crafted. 1710. And here, these initials," he points to the blackened letters: **C.M.B.** "Caspar, Melchior, Balthasar. From the Bible. These are the wise men. The magi. The Germans considered them protectors from evil. They thought that if you stuck a *Trudenmesser* into a door, a witch could not pass through it, among other things."

The priest sheaths the blade and hands it to me.

"Now," he says, his tone turned grimly serious. He rests his hands on my shoulders, looks into my eyes. "I've done what I can, and it's time for you to do what must be done."

"I will," I say, then glance meaningfully at Ellie. "We will."

McKee smiles warmly, looks from me to Ellie. "Of course. Let's go to the nave, I want to baptize you both, and put a blessing upon you."

As we walk up the winding stairs, the old priest speaks over his shoulder.

"One other thing, this woman will have a devil's mark on her body. When you kill her, find it, and burn it off her skin. Then cut off her head and bury her."

He pauses, then turns to face us in the dark stairwell, his features lost in shadow.

From behind me, Ellie clutches my hand.

"That child you spoke of is an imp. A familiar. Part demon. A spawn of the Devil she likely feeds from a hidden teat. Kill him. Bury him with the witch. Cut off the teat."

I swallow hard, feel Ellie's fingers squeezing mine. "Will the knife work on the child as well?" I ask, the solidity of the leather sheath wedged beneath my belt warm as a sleeping animal, eager for use.

McKee shrugs, then continues walking up the steps. He waves an errant hand, as if swatting a fly.

"No need," he says. "Just shoot the damned thing."

51

Ellie and I agree to venture out by week's end.

After meeting with the priest, we plan what we'll need as far as food and supplies, then return home before Father is done at the shop. Ellie bakes some bread while I cull as much salted pork and beef from the cellar as we can carry.

In the evening, we eat dinner with our father in near silence—Ellie and I thinking of little but the journey ahead, Jeremiah still toughened by hate to belligerent silence, even after all these months. It's become so Ellie and I hardly pay him attention anymore. He's not much more than a ghost who lives in our home—fluttering in the shadows, resting by the fire, creaking the floorboards in the next room while you're falling off to sleep.

After dinner, I try to reason with him one last time. Knowing that the odds of my returning alive are slim, I feel it important to attempt a reckoning.

But he wants none of it.

When I ask him about his day at the shop, a topic he usually brightens at, he simply grunts and rocks in his chair, smokes his pipe. When I tell him I'd like to help him out with the business one day, he stands and walks to his bedroom, closes the door behind him. The click of the latch is like a period at the end of our sentence together, a story fully told.

The next day we shop for supplies. Given that it's January, it'll be cold on the trail, especially at night, so Ellie uses what little money she has to buy a proper coat and good boots. I buy two gum blankets, heavy wool blankets, a pup tent, a new backpack that will hold more than my old side pouch, and three thick pairs of socks.

Father spares us another awkward evening meal, staying out late at the pub while Ellie and I pack in our respective rooms, me calling out if she has *this thing* or *that thing*, her rolling food with wax paper and string. She even swipes a bottle of the old man's whiskey from the pantry, a pound of good coffee, a travel pot for heating water or stew, and enough tobacco to keep an army well supplied.

I laugh when I see the bounty laid out atop her bed.

"I hope we can walk under the burden of all this weight, Ellie," I say. "But good Lord, I'm happy to have it all. The way the boys and I traveled was downright barbaric in comparison."

"Our packs will lighten soon enough," she says, and I nod in sober agreement.

I consider how long the trip will take, try to work out some form of timeline. The river is our best way north, and the best chance of retracing my path, which Ellie and I have gone over ad nauseum on a crude map. The morning prior I spoke with a steamboat captain I haul cotton for, and he agreed to take us as far north as he's able, a point unknown given the growing Union presence along the river. He assured me it's fairly open for a few hundred miles, but we'll need to be wary of skirmishes. Still, his boat is a civilian vessel and will, hopefully, be left alone. It's the only chance we have, so it's a risk we'll have to take. The journey will be hard enough without trekking through a war. Given how things are warming up, it'll be a miracle if we even make it back to Black Hawk.

The night before our departure I sit at the table, working through the map, when Father eventually comes home. He's in no mood for talk, which is the norm, and I can see plainly that he's drunk. Regardless, I try.

"Busy at the pub?" I ask, and he grunts the way he does, takes off his hat and coat, kicks off his muddy shoes by the door. He walks past me without a word and I turn, a sudden desperation to be his son one last time.

"I'm sorry," I blurt out, annoyed at the tears wetting my face. "You're right. I was a coward, and I was afraid. I killed men, and saw men killed. If I could have saved my brothers, if I could have given my life to bring them home, I would have. Please stop hating me."

He stops at the door of his room, one hand on the handle, swaying a little on his feet. "I don't hate you," he says. "I don't even know who you are."

Then he pushes into the room, and shuts the door firmly behind him.

At six a.m. the next morning, my father leaves to open the shop. Ellie and I dress in our traveling clothes, strap on our packs.

She wears the ring given to us by the priest. I keep the symbol-carved knife in its sheath at my waist. The *Malleus Maleficarum*, which I've been reading exhaustively the last couple days, is in my pack, as is the strange tablet. The steamboat doesn't leave for an hour, but we hurry anyway, not wanting to risk it.

Once packed, I go into my father's bedroom, take the Springfield rifle off the pegs above his door. In a chest I find a cartridge box filled with pouches and bullets, and take it all.

As we're about to leave, Ellie asks me to take Father's saber from its decorative mount over the fireplace. I do, then hand it over. She removes her pack and coat.

"One moment," she says, and I wait while she also goes into Father's room, then returns with his old saber belt. She ties it tightly around her waist, slides the sword into the leather holster, then puts on her coat and pack once more.

I nod in approval, then look around the house one last time. I've been home for over eight months, and even though it's now 1863, it feels as if nothing has changed. The war is worse than ever, the winter is brittle—even for the South—and times have never been harder, nor more tumultuous.

"In it together," she says, and kisses me on the cheek. "Happy birthday, by the way."

"You too," I mumble, stunned at the realization. I'm sorry I forgot."

"Eighteen..." she says wistfully, then shakes her head, as if forever dismissing youth.

Something I'd done long ago.

PART SIX: THE OFFERING

52

The land is different in the winter than it was in May of last year. It was spring then; flowers in bloom, trees budding with leaves and fruit. Now, in the dead of January, nothing grows. Tree branches are begging arms reaching for gray sky and charcoal dust clouds.

The foliage underfoot is brittle and hard, rife with dandelion weeds, browned grass, moldy pinecones, and acorns wearing cracked hats.

It's been ten days since we left Natchez.

The river was touch and go. The steamer had been stopped twice by Union barricades, and once docked for a full day while a battle raged a few miles ahead at Vicksburg, which the bluecoats were desperately trying to seize. When finally allowed passage, we pressed hands to our ears as artillery fired on the city from the Union gunboats.

Eventually, our steamer—with its civilian passengers and civilian goods—made it back to the small settlement where I'd stolen the fishing boat. I was surprised to see the buildings deserted, and had to beg the captain to let us off at the lifeless dock. I thought about my young stowaway, then pushed the memory away. It wouldn't do me any good to reflect on it, or on what I'd done.

After scouring the buildings for supplies (they'd already been well-ravaged), we stayed the night in an abandoned cabin. I was worried about soldiers, Union *or* Confederate. There was no good scenario if we were found at that dead port. I nervously recalled the bandits we'd run into after leaving Shiloh, and Ellie told me I worried too much, which might have been true, but I loaded Jeremiah's rifle regardless, kept it on the floor between us while we slept.

Besides the rifle, and the witch knife the priest had given us, I had no weapon other than the bayonet in my boot, the same boots I'd worn into battle. Ellie had the saber and, knowing her, another blade hidden away somewhere. She was fiery, and had learned to take care of herself over the years, especially while her brothers had been off fighting.

That night and the ones that followed were devoid of drama, or undue hardship. We were but two small humans in the vast wilderness, the world all around us on fire…how could we possibly be of notice, or consequence?

We made our way inland using the mill owner's hunting trail, and on the seventh day reached Black Hawk. I found the miller, asked if we could pay for food and shelter once more, and though he obliged I didn't care for the way he watched Ellie. It was a hungry look, and one I'd seen many times before. Starting with Samuel Bartlett all those years ago, who she'd kissed, and who'd disappeared without a trace.

At times, in the dark of night, I'll think about Samuel, and the boy from the boat, and Sarafina, of course. And it will strike me how strange life is. Winding and winding are the trails of our lives, each turn unseen until the road bends when we least expect it—leading us somewhere new, somewhere unplanned for—and we won't know the destination until we arrive there. Fate controls our paths. God, I suppose, if He cares.

We humans are nothing but ever-traveling pilgrims, blindly seeking passage to something greater, more often finding something worse.

Now, settled for the night in the miller's shed, I have another nightmare. It's the first one I've had since we met with the priest, and I'd hoped Sarafina's power had lessened due to the artifacts.

It seems I either overestimated the priest, or underestimated the witch.

In the dream I'm sleeping in a bed, in a room I don't recognize. I'm woken by a knock at the door. I sit up and shout, "Who's there?"

Laugher comes from the hallway. A woman's laugh, and I know it to be Sarafina's.

"Aren't you going to let me in, Ethan? Isn't this what you want?

Come now, open the door, let me into your room."

My breath comes fast and heavy. I throw back the covers, drenched in sweat, my underclothes stick to my skin. A bar of light stretches beneath the door and I see the shadows of her feet. I hold my breath, praying she will go away.

"Have you seen yourself, Ethan?" she says, and I can almost visualize that damned smirk twisting her lips. "Have you seen your face?"

I blink and there's a lit lantern beside my bed. I get to my feet and pick it up. I catch a flicker to my left and turn to see a looking glass hung from a wall. I walk toward it, move my face close to the mirror, and hold up the flickering light.

I'm old, and disfigured. My face is lashed with gnarled red scars, my hair thin and gray, my beard scraggly, unkempt.

"Go away!" I shout, and hear laughter from outside the door. "Go away, damn you!" I'm hysterical, adrift in a maze of old age, my mind foggy and rife with disruptive thoughts.

"Ethan, come back to bed," a voice says from behind me.

Confused, I turn, holding my breath, and extend the lantern.

Ellie is in the bed. She's young and beautiful, and stares at me with a wicked smile I've never seen. She's sitting up, nude but for a sheet spilled across her hips, arms extended. "Come back, Ethan," she says. "Let's finish what we started."

From the door, the witch screams with laughter and I scream as well. I cry out—in shame, in horror—and throw the lantern at the bed, where it bursts, showering oil. I watch as flames catch the bedding and ignite—oh God the whole thing ignites—and then Ellie is also screaming, except it sounds like the shrieks of a great bird, shrieking and burning, black charred skin writhing as smoke fills the air and I drop to the floor on hands and knees, clutch madly at my chest, my heart, which feels as though it's caving inward.

I wake with Ellie shoving at my arm, telling me to wake up, to *please wake up*.

I do, and I'm panting. She throws herself over me protectively, hugs me tight.

"I'm here," she says. "I'm here with you and nothing will harm you."

My heart races, my breathing is ragged, my chest tight. Early morning sunlight bleeds through the boards of the freezing shed. I watch my breath frost in the air, the mist catching the sunlight of a new day, and I think, oddly, of Heaven.

I've brought us back to the place where I was—as best as I can recall—cast out.

Being honest, I'm surprised I was able to retrace my steps with such accuracy. But the landmarks are clear, and I'm fortunate for that, otherwise it would all look like wilderness.

The priest's knife is strapped to my belt, the bayonet in my boot. I take a moment to load the rifle, take a sip of water from my canteen. I note that Ellie has removed her long coat, rolled it up and packed it, our father's saber now clearly exposed on her hip. She wears wool pants and a thick flannel shirt over long underwear, heavy boots. A long, serrated hunting knife is in a sheath strapped to one thigh. Her blonde hair, dirty and tangled from hard travel, is tied back, her face firmly set and grim. I would not envy the one competing with her in such a state.

I note she's wearing the ring bearing the sacred sigil, and am thankful that she will be protected if we happen to separate.

"That waterfall," I say, pointing to a spot I'd noted when first spit from Sarafina's domain, just as Jonah was excised onto the shores of Nineveh. "That's where I last saw her."

Ellie looks toward the waterfall, then surveys the surrounding land.

"The sweetgum isn't fragrant like it was that day," I say, as if needing to convince myself this is indeed the correct spot. "It's been dried up by the cold, but this is the place, I know it."

Ellie nods and taps my near-depleted pack. "Use the tablet," she says. "The *defixio*."

"Yes, of course!" I shoulder off my pack, drop to my knees. I undo the ties, remove the food and blanket roll, and dig out the iron plate.

"Let's pray this works," I say, then lift the warped iron plate—with its strange words of invocation—up to my eye, and peer through one of the ragged holes.

I repeat the Latin phrase the priest had recited, the one I'd since memorized like a Bible verse. "*Daemon, quorum pars esto subjecto voluntati meae.*" I breathe the words in to the cold air, and then I wait.

At first, I see nothing but bright, white light. Something tickles in my ear, deep and resonant, as if a hummingbird were fluttering beside my head, its wings beating a continuous chord. Then the light filling my vision pushes outward, toward the fringes, and I see clearly through the center.

Sarafina's domain lies a few feet ahead.

The cursed creek bubbles only steps away, but my mind can't reason how it can exist at the same time and place as dry land, how we could have walked straight through it and never known—never seen—the water, or the farm that I know lies beyond.

"Take my hand," I mumble, and extend my free hand toward Ellie.

"Can you see it?"

"Yes! Now take my hand."

Ellie does, and our fingers intertwine. "Walk with me," I say, and step forward, toward the mysterious creek, the one that runs in no direction, that is shaped like a pentagram.

That cages the creature, Sarafina.

I step into the water, and I know by the gasp from Ellie that she has stepped into it with me. "Ethan!" she says, in obvious wonder.

"I know, just keep moving. I think I should use this until we're across. I don't know...it's just a feeling. Come on, quickly."

We wade into the creek, which never rises above our thighs, and I do my best to keep my focus on the land ahead—looking only through the tablet—until we step once more onto dry land. "Can you still see the creek? Look behind us."

Ellie laughs. "I can. Ethan, this can't be real."

I close my eyes for a moment, then slowly lower the iron tablet. I do not feel the ground shift beneath my feet, nor any change in the temperature or the smells in the air. I open my eyes, and my breath catches in my throat.

"Ethan, you're shaking."

"We're back," I say, and am filled with blinding terror.

I know, deep in my heart, we will never be allowed to leave.

Not again.

53

I tuck the metal tablet back into my pack and grip the rifle with both hands, making sure it's ready to fire and quickly reload if needed. Ellie has a hand on the hilt of Jeremiah's saber, but for now keeps it sheathed. We begin walking toward Sarafina's farm, but I angle us slightly west, in search of a certain rocky outcropping, and an entryway to the underground cavern.

I've no wish to knock on the front door.

An optimistic part of me hopes to find Mason still down there, unconscious but alive. If we get lucky, we could sneak him out, get him to safety, and then return for Archie.

Or whatever it is that Archie has become.

As we walk, Ellie tugs at my elbow. Her eyes are wide and frightened.

"What," I ask, keeping my voice low. "What's wrong?"

She glances to the left, and I turn—slowly—toward the trees.

It takes me a moment, but then I see it. A large black dog, pacing us from about fifty feet out. For now, it seems content to stay within the trees. It's not hiding—the trees aren't dense enough for that—so perhaps its intention is to appear less as a threat, and more as a warning. I continue searching the nearby trees, focusing on any movement, and quickly spot the two grays.

"Come on," I murmur, and we begin to walk faster.

The dogs keep pace.

"She knows we're here," Ellie says, eyes forward.

I nod in agreement. "Likely since we crossed the creek. It's on this side of that dividing line that most of her magic seems to work." I shrug. "I assume that's why she didn't chase me before—either she can't cross the water, or she'll be powerless if she does. Regardless, we're in her realm now."

"What are those dogs doing? Why don't they attack?" Ellie asks, sounding frightened for the first time since we started the journey.

I note, however, that her grip on the sword hilt has tightened.

"Herding us," I say, instinctively knowing it's the truth. "Making sure we don't turn around, run away."

"Are these the same ones you talked about? The ones who killed those men?"

"Yes," I say quickly, then point ahead when I see what I'm searching for. "Look, there's our way in."

The outcropping is obvious from this direction, and it's close enough that, if we needed to make a break for it, we could likely get there before the dogs got to us.

Likely.

"Let's hurry now."

We walk fast as we dare toward the outcropping, and I can already make out the shadow of the small opening.

"If she knows we're here, why would she let us enter the caves?"

"I don't know," I say, wondering the same. "Maybe she wants us alive. For now, at least."

Ellie says nothing to this as we climb toward the opening. We drop to our knees and hurriedly strip off our packs. I push mine through, then Ellie's. They land with soft thumps against the rock floor beyond. "You go first," I say, and Ellie doesn't hesitate to drop her legs into the opening. She turns onto her belly and slides down until only her head is visible. She looks up at me, a question on her lips...then freezes.

Her eyes are fixed on something high up, past my shoulder. "Ethan..."

I turn and look skyward. The trees here are leafless, dark and wicked against the slate of pale, gray sky.

Making it easy to spot the witch.

She's taken the form of the creature—a massive, winged beast with a hooked mouth and golden eyes, black pupils smeared at their center. Its feet are talons, thick with fur. Its wings expand once, as if in greeting, then fold flat against its back. Unlike birds, I notice, the beast has four wings instead of two, and there are limbs beneath, long and sinewy, I did not notice previously. They grip the nearby branches as it watches us.

Even from a distance, part of me recognizes the woman I'd come to love. Somehow—even in this monstrous form—I can almost make out the human beneath, frail and beautiful, clothed in a dress and cowl.

"Sarafina—"

Staring into that demon's face high above, I can tell she's smiling.

"Go," I say, and Ellie makes no argument, vanishing quickly into the crevice. I don't bother to look back again, but instead swing my legs into the opening and push my body through, into the dark.

When I land inside the cave, Ellie is already rummaging through her pack.

"What is it?"

"This will light our way," she says, and hands me a thick stub of wax. A candle. She finds the tin of matches, pulls one free. "Put your pack on."

I do as she says. Then she lights the candle as I hold it. As she puts on her own pack, she eyes me strangely. "What?"

I realize I'm smiling. Despite the horrors surrounding us, my bone-chilling fear at being back here, I can't help myself. "I'm just glad you're with me."

"I know," she says, and pushes me ahead of her. "Lead the way. Let's find our brothers and get the hell out of here."

I slide the bayonet from my boot, stick the point through the candle, and hold it aloft as we move forward through the narrow cave, toward the cavern I remember so well. "We'll need to mark this corridor when we reach the main cavern. There are many caves, but this is the only way out. It can get confusing down here, especially if we're—"

"Being chased?" Ellie offers.

I nod. "Something like that."

A few minutes later we're at the opening. There's still daylight outside, and the small hole in the cavern's ceiling—marking the old well above—lets enough hazy light through that I can make out the shapes of the wooden benches, the strange items stacked inside the endless shelving, the stone table where I last saw my brother.

Which is empty.

"He's not here," I say, and jog out of the cave and into the large open space. I shoulder my rifle, pluck the candle off the bayonet and blow it out. I toss it to Ellie, then stuff the blade back into my boot.

"Wait," Ellie says, and drops her pack onto the ground at the mouth of the opening. She stands straight and pulls the saber free of its sheath, the sharp tip pointed toward the ground.

"What are you doing?"

"Might as well leave the packs here. They'll mark the exit. I doubt we'll need salted beef or clean britches in the next few hours."

I consider for a moment, then put my own pack down next to hers. I have pouches and bullets for the rifle in a cartridge box on my belt, along with the witch knife. She's right, there's no need to have the extra weight if it comes to a fight. I already feel leaner, faster, and for the first time since we crossed the creek, I feel a swell of confidence, a feeling that we just might get through this alive. We just need to find our brothers and—

"Ethan…"

I turn toward a voice I don't recognize—toward the sound of my name, spoken so softly it could have come from a ghost.

And that's when Ellie screams.

54

At first, my mind refuses to accept what I'm seeing.
It's a trick of the light…
He's sunken into shadow…
I take a step closer. Ellie clasps a hand over her mouth.
His head rises—ever so slightly—so that he's facing me.
"Mason?" I speak his name as a question, because even standing a few feet away from the man I grew up with, I can't be completely sure.

His hands are bound in coils of thin rope, looped over a large iron hook that dangles from the chamber's high ceiling. His arms are skeletal and bone-white, but whole.

I cannot say the same for the rest of him.

His head is shaved.

His eyes have been put out. His ears cut away.

Below his neck and shoulders is a torso, every inch knotted with hideous scars, some still prickly with heavy black stitches. The flesh is concave where larger pieces have been cut away, the skin tightened, then sutured. Below his bony, narrow hips is nothing but a molten mound of flesh where a man's genitalia would be.

He has no legs.

I take another step forward, trying not to retch at the sight of him, the smell of him. He is a sack of poison. Of rot. He is not even a corpse, but a portion of a corpse, reanimated.

It's impossible that he's alive.

And yet, he moves. He speaks.

He knows my name.

I reach out to touch his face, but when my fingers brush his chin he jerks away in terror, the chain he's hanging from chatters like a rattlesnake's tail, echoing throughout the chamber. "Mason, it's me," I say, the words sticky on my dry tongue. "I've come back for you."

His face turns in my direction, but the dark holes where his cold blue eyes once lived see nothing. He sniffs the air, as if he would know me by scent, and there's a mad part of my brain that's relieved she left him a nose to smell through.

"Get me down," he rasps, then drops his chin to his sunken chest, spent.

I look over to Ellie—who weeps openly—for guidance, but she only shakes her head in horror, as if she wants no part of this. I can't say that I blame her.

I set my rifle on the uneven stone floor, grip my brother by what remains of his biceps, and lift him off the hook as easily as one would take a coat off a peg. I cradle an arm beneath his back and walk him to the stone table where I'd last seen him. When he was whole, and human.

I lay him down. Ellie slinks, reluctantly, to the other side of the table, and we both study what's left of my brother. The details of his body are hard to make out in the weak light leaking from the top of the cavern, but what there is to see...I'm not sure I want better sight of.

Without thought of its talismanic power, I pull the witch knife from my hip and cut the cords of rope around his wrists. He exhales in relief. Gently, I lower his arms so they rest on either side of him—it's like handling sticks covered in leather, and I wonder what witchcraft Sarafina has employed to keep his heart beating, his lungs pumping air.

With a flare of hot anger, I long to ask her.

"Ellie's here," I say quietly, bent over the table, studying my brother's face—memorizing all the things I find familiar about him; things she hasn't stripped away.

The line of his jaw, the arch of his thick brows, the slight dent at the bridge of his nose, where it was broken when we were children.

"Ethan," he says, hardly a whisper.

I sense the effort it costs him to speak, so I lower my head toward his, doing my best to ignore the foul smell of his flesh, the reek of his breath. "I'm here."

He turns his head slightly toward me. When he speaks again, the words are soft as a sigh.

"I'm sorry," he says. "I was not a good brother."

I shake my head, swipe away the tears running down my cheeks and chin, knowing he would see it as weakness. "No," I say. "You were the best of them all."

His lips twitch, and I wonder if he's trying to smile.

I put my hand—gently, *oh so gently*—into his. Ellie starts to reach out, then pulls back. Her eyes flick up to mine. "I'm sorry—"

"Ellie," I say.

But she shakes her head, crying her own tears, then turns her back on both of us.

I look down one last time upon my brother, remember what he was. A grown man, full of violence and determination. This carved monstrosity was once someone I loved, that I played with as a child, that protected us in his own way, dark as those methods may have been. I feel a fierce love for him in this moment, and when I reach into my boot, and slide free the bayonet, it's as if I'm pulling out my own heart.

"Archie," Mason says, a near inaudible gasp. "Help him."

"I will," I say, straightening. "And then I'm going to kill her."

His head rolls, as if he's no longer sure where, or who, he is. He takes in a shallow breath, then lets it out. "Take me home," he says, fingers clenched in mine. "I'm in so much pain, and I want to go home."

"I'm sorry."

He frowns, and a low moan escapes from deep in his throat. "I'm so scared," he says. "Please—"

"It's okay, brother."

I set the tip of the bayonet against the flesh just above his heart.

As a soldier, I've been trained for this. I know just the right place, the correct angle to kill with one thrust. For this knowledge, I'm grateful.

"I love you."

"Save me..." he says.

I drive the blade down.

55

Ellie takes the wool blanket from her pack and covers Mason's body.

"He was our blood, and our family," she says.

"Amen," I reply, not knowing what else there is to say. What else there is to do for him.

"What now?" she asks.

"We go up."

I locate my rifle in the dim light, pull the hammer back to half-cock; make sure it's eager to fire. "Stairs are this way."

Clutching the saber, Ellie falls into step behind me as we make our way through the shadowed cavern toward the stairs—the very steps I was dragged down, paralyzed, less than one year ago. Even in the dark we find them easily, and looking up toward the cabin floor I easily see the thin square of light around the trapdoor that leads into the house.

Quietly, we climb the steps. At the top, I press my palm against the door, expecting resistance, thinking it will likely be locked, or bolted.

But the door swings upward effortlessly, soundlessly; the hinges apparently well-oiled and often used. I hesitate only a second, waiting to see that demon's yellow, black-slit eyes staring into mine, the vicious teeth and hawked beak snapping at my face...

But there is nothing but lamplight, and silence.

We climb up and into the house. I continue to study the interior for signs of Sarafina—perhaps cupping a palmful of dust to blow into my face, paralyzing me, or worse—but see no one in the main room. Ellie comes up the steps behind me, glances around nervously.

"Those stairs at the far end," I say, pointing. "They lead to her bedroom." I gesture with the rifle toward the wall to the left. "That far door is the boy's, the middle one where we slept." I glance behind us, toward the kitchen. "That last one leads out back."

The doors are all closed, the stairs leading to the upper floor empty. As we step deeper into the large room, I prepare myself to see Sarafina charging down those steps, spitting curses, her body caught somewhere between human and monster.

Instead, it's the door at the far end of the room that creaks open.

It's Titus—and not Sarafina—who steps cautiously out.

He stares at us for a moment, standing in the open doorway, stoically studying my sister and I, as if we were objects of curiosity rather than intruders. He eyes my sister suspiciously, then those black eyes settle on me, and harden.

"You shouldn't have come back, Ethan," he says.

"Titus," I say, holding my rifle tight but aiming it away from him. For now.

Despite what the priest said, I have no desire to kill him if I don't have to.

"Where is she?" I ask.

"She came into my room while you were below, settling things with Mason." He takes a look behind him, then turns back to us, eyes wide and shining. "She's gone now," he says, and closes the door behind him. A shudder passes through his body.

"Titus?" I say, and slide a finger over the cool metal of the rifle's trigger. "Are you alright?"

"She made me drink," he says, taking a step closer. There's a long knife gripped tight in one of his small hands. "I never should have helped you," he says. "She's been punishing me ever since. And now—"

"Punishing? I don't—"

"She made me drink it, Ethan," he says. "She made me drink it all."

"Titus, I'm sorry." I don't understand what the boy is going on about, but I keep my eye on his blade. "We can help you. We'll take you with us," I say, feeling the lie heavy on my tongue. "I just need to know where she is."

"She's out there," he says, pointing, with the tip of the knife, somewhere behind us. "But you're too late."

"Where, Titus?"

He stifles a yawn, gives his head a little shake. Again, he shudders, then staggers, seemingly unsteady.

"She's out there," he says again. "With Novah. Her and the baby. She's preparing him."

When he speaks of the baby, my heart stutters. It can't be.

After all, he's the father of my child.

Ellie puts a hand on my elbow. "Ethan, what's he talking about? What baby?"

"Hold on, damn it," I snap, waving her off. I take a step toward Titus, lift the butt of the rifle to my shoulder, point the muzzle at his chest. "Preparing him for what?"

Titus smiles, and something moves in his face. Something unnatural; as if fat caterpillars were crawling just beneath his flesh—through his cheeks, forehead, and chin.

"For the offering, of course," he says, grinning wide now.

His small, neat white teeth are no longer neat, or white. They're browned and crooked, and too big for his mouth. He extends the knife in my direction. "She's taking her gift from me because of *you*," he says. "She's taking my gift, Ethan. TAKING MY GIFT!"

He takes another step forward. His skin begins to sag and wrinkle, as if his face were made of wax melting beneath a candleflame. His arms and legs jerk and crackle, and he grunts as he continues walking toward me.

"Ethan?" Ellie says, but I ignore her. We both take a step back.

"Unless I kill you—" he mutters, his voice no longer that of a child, but of a man.

An *old* man.

Suddenly, his black hair sprouts wildly—impossibly—turning gray as ash as it extends down his skull and over his shoulders. A beard fills out along the bottom of his face, and in the next step he's two feet taller than he was but a few seconds ago, his body contorting beneath too-small linen clothes as bones snap and grow, grotesquely stretching his flesh at a shoulder, then a leg—as if his previous body can't recall exactly how it once was and is now doing its best to recreate a forgotten shape.

The buttons on his shirt pop away, his pants rip along the seams. He lets out a low, frustrated growl before peeling away the shirt, pushing the pants to his ankles, then stepping out of them completely.

"Good Lord Jesus," Ellie mumbles from behind me as we both stare at the freakish, naked old man approaching us, his right arm bent unnaturally sideways, the legs skinny and knobbed in all the wrong places. His chest has caved inward and he's arched like the branch of a tree, his spine misaligned and twisted.

"Just have to kill you," he rasps, gasping and wheezing, as if he can hardly breathe.

Then, without warning, he moves faster—scurries toward us in a bizarre, hitching shuffle—the knife thrust toward me, a snarl on his wrinkled, sagging face.

Ellie screams and something shatters against the floor but I don't take my eyes off Titus, from the beautiful boy I'd thought of as a friend. The child who'd saved my life.

As he nears, I see sparks of madness in those familiar black eyes, and I have only seconds to wonder if he's been insane this whole time.

He makes it within a few feet before I come to my senses, raise the point of my rifle, and fire point-blank into his chest.

Blood sprays the wall behind him and his body jerks backward as if pulled by a string. The knife clatters to the floor and his body collapses, legs and arms splayed wide. A long breath escapes his open mouth as his flesh releases the spirit trapped inside.

The drifting smoke cloud of the rifle shot begins to clear. The stink of burnt powder fills the air. I lower myself to a knee.

A hand comes to rest gently on my shoulder, and I reach up and clutch Ellie's fingers, desperate for contact, for comfort.

"Jesus Christ in Heaven," I say, staring at the gnarled, misshapen old man bleeding on the cabin floor.

Ellie steps between me and the body, kneels down in front of me, eyes on mine.

"Ethan," she says quietly, forcing me to focus on her, and her alone. "Tell me about the baby."

Blood pools beneath Titus's true form—or the semblance of what it once was—as I tell Ellie what I know. I tell her about Mason sharing Sarafina's bed, how she'd claimed to be pregnant with his child.

"I thought it was a lie, a taunt," I say, wondering if I believe my own words. I push away the idea of my own jealousy, of Archie's burning hate. It will do no good to try and explain how we all fell in love with Sarafina in different ways, to different degrees. "But now," I say with a tired shrug, "I suppose it's possible."

Ellie chews her lip, something she does when angry. "Why didn't you tell me?"

I shake my head. "Christ, Ellie. Given everything that's happened, I honestly didn't think it relevant. You saw him down there. That's savagery. That's *hate*."

"Maybe he did something to her," she says, looking away. "Maybe he wasn't invited to her bed at all. Did you think of that?"

I look at my sister carefully. "Ellie, I—"

"Forget it," she says, then stands and walks briskly toward the stairs at the opposite end of the long room, saber clutched in her fist.

"What are you doing?"

"I'm seeing if she's home before we go running off into the wild," she says, and begins to climb the stairs toward Sarafina's bedroom.

Cursing, I pull a pouch and ball from the cartridge box at my hip and reload the rifle, replace the ramrod, toss away the old cap and place a new one. I want to be ready to fire at a moment's notice.

If Sarafina is up there, I'll only have time for one shot.

56

Sarafina's bedroom runs the length of the house, its ceiling an A-frame to give it more height than the floor below. The walls are lined with packed bookcases and trunks that all appear brand new; there are wardrobes, dressers, a massive four-post bed draped with loose netting, a drafting table, a desk, and artwork hung on either side of the bedframe—bold, colorful paintings that steal my breath with their beauty. The floor is covered with rich-colored rugs, the likes of which I've never seen.

As for Sarafina herself, she's nowhere to be found.

Ellie walks over to the bed, pushes aside the netting with the sword's tip. "This doesn't look slept in."

"She's not here," I say, wanting to be out of this room, this house. "Let's go."

Ellie studies one of the paintings for a moment, then circulates around the room. She runs a hand across the desk, opens a trunk. "There are men's clothes in here. And jewelry. A fortune's worth." She goes to the wardrobe and throws open the doors.

"Ellie," I say, pleading. I keep one eye on the stairs. I don't like the idea of there being only one exit.

My sister ignores me, runs a hand along the sleeve of a bright blue dress hanging in the wardrobe. "What kind of demon has dresses like these?" she asks, then turns to look at me, a strange smile on her face. "I don't think this is her room."

I frown, not understanding. "Of course it is."

Ellie shakes her head, sheaths the sword. "What I mean is that the woman you met, who wears dresses and bakes biscuits, isn't real. It's like...make-believe. And this is nothing but a place where she plays at being human." She closes the wardrobe doors, looks at the bed. "Have you ever even seen her sleep?"

"How would I have?" I sound defensive, angry, and feel my face reddening in frustration. "What the hell does it matter?"

She walks to one of the room's windows, the cool sunlight giving her a soft glow that tightens my heart with love for her. I notice she still wears that strange smile on her face, one I can't place the meaning of. "I'm just trying to understand what she is, Ethan."

"I told you what she is."

My sister studies me a moment, as if there are stories written on my face.

"I don't think you have," she says. "Not everything."

Before I can reply, she walks briskly past me toward the stairs.

I give the large room a last look around, wanting to sear the details of it into my memory, as Ellie's footsteps drift down the steps toward the main floor. Outside the window I see a meadow and tall, narrow trees—dense as an approaching army—just beyond. The light of the day is fading. Shadows bloom like mold where the sun has lost its touch, and for a moment it seems as if the whole world is rotting away.

Knowing we're out of time, I blow out a heavy breath, say a silent prayer for courage, and follow my sister down, toward whatever awaits us.

When I reach the bottom of the stairs, Ellie is already at the door.

"Ellie, wait."

She gives me a quick, dismissive glance, yanks open the door—then stops in her tracks, mouth open in fear, or shock. She steps slowly backward into the house.

"Ellie?"

But she only shakes her head, eyes locked forward.

I rush to the open doorway, already pressing the Springfield to my shoulder, and step in front of my sister, rifle pointed toward whatever it is that's terrified her.

When I see him, I lower the gun.

Standing at the bottom of the porch steps, staring up at us with wide, wet eyes, is a massive black dog. Or, at least, similar enough to a dog that it's the first word that comes to mind. Now that I realize what it is, I wonder if there might be a better term for it.

For him.

When we meet eyes, he cocks his head, as if curious.

I take a small, cautious step forward, study the animal's strange face, the tall shape of its body, the patchy, newly grown fur.

"Archie?"

There's no doubt. In his partially transformed state, even Ellie sees the truth of it.

He's tall, his limbs knobby and bone-thin. The body is covered in varying degrees of black fur, as if parts had been recently sheared, and other parts left to grow. He has a stub of a tail, which wags slowly.

Instead of paws he has hands, lumpy and covered in bristles, the fingernails dark and pointed.

It's his face, however, that will haunt me forever.

The snout is fully extended, the nose wet and black. The ears are human, but elongated, pointing up from the head; the bottom of his face is a clump of fur burrowing into the neck.

The eyes, however, are all Archie.

Human, and aware.

I take another step forward and instinctively reach out with a tentative hand, as one would with a feral dog they hope is docile. It's only then that Archie's lips spread and his mouth splits, revealing a jumble of long, pointed teeth. A growl comes from deep in its throat, and those long, human ears twitch forward.

"Archie, it's Ethan," I say soothingly, unsure how much more of this I can take. "It's your brother. We're here...Ellie and I...we're here to take you home."

Archie barks once, the sound a horrible amalgamation of beast and man, and then, without warning, he turns and runs off, disappears around the side of the house, toward the barley fields.

"Jesus Christ, Ethan," Ellie says from just behind me. "Jesus Christ."

I nod, not knowing what to think, what to say. "We can fix him," I murmur, unsure of the words even as I speak them, knowing deep down in my heart there's no fixing the creature I just saw—that there'll be no bringing him back home. No making him human.

"We need to find Sarafina," I say. "We—"

Before I finish my thought, a sound carries to us on the breeze, lightly as a leaf blown on an autumn wind.

The distant cry of an infant.

"Come on." I step quickly down the porch steps, Ellie right behind me.

Together, we follow Archie's path toward the barley fields.

Toward Sarafina.

57

We break through the edge of the tall, brittle barley and into the clearing that I'd seen—both in reality, and in my dreams. The giant gnarled tree looks even more ominous in the dusk of the settling day, backlit by a blood-orange sun, its bare arms crooked and reaching, its trunk wider than a door, its roots writhing along the earth like serpents before diving into the soil far below.

Sarafina sits comfortably, her back against the trunk, wearing a white linen dress. Her hair falls loosely over her shoulders, her feet are bare.

There's a baby in her folded arms.

She's never looked more beautiful.

"Ethan, you're back," Sarafina says, her voice smooth as black silk. She keeps her eyes on me a moment longer, then shifts to study my twin, a benign smile on her face. "And you've brought a friend."

I look to my right as Ellie steps forward, saber drawn.

"What a beautiful young girl you are, Ellie. I've heard so much about you."

Ellie says nothing, keeping the sword's tip down for now, brushing the dry grass. Her eyes are fixed on Sarafina, and the child she holds.

I rest the butt of the rifle on the ground and, with my free hand, slide the witch-knife free of its sheath. I raise it, horizontally, so Sarafina can clearly see the markings on the blade.

She purses her lips, as if more annoyed than scared. Her eyes narrow. "Very interesting, Ethan. Did you acquire that from a hunter, or a priest?"

I take a step closer, into the looming shade of the tree, and extend the knife's tip toward the witch; the blade glints, reflecting the day's dying light.

"I must admit," Sarafina says, bouncing the baby in her lap, head tilted back, throat exposed, "I was impressed with the strange iron plate you used to find passage. Some sort of invocation tablet, I assume."

I'm close enough now that I can see the baby clearly. It's naked and tiny—even for a newborn—likely no more than a few weeks old. It's a boy, and has a distinct shock of dark hair for an infant so young. I grip the knife more tightly, knowing that with one lunge I could plant the blade into her chest, or neck.

"We saw what you did to Mason," I say. "Tortured. Mutilated. And now you hold his child as if you were a mother instead of a monster."

Sarafina's eyes flash, her jaw tightens.

"Your brother," she says, and spits on the ground. "If he had simply done what I wanted—given me his seed and then left me alone. But he wanted more, of course, like they all do. He wanted to *dominate* me. To *humiliate* me. In my home. In my bed. Your brother was evil, Ethan. More evil than you know."

Her eyes don't leave me when she says, "Isn't that right, Ellie?" I turn to look at my sister, but she says nothing, keeping her eyes locked on Sarafina. The baby spits and coos, pulls at a strand of Sarafina's hair, the siren of its cries having dissipated with the setting sun.

"What's to become of the baby?" Ellie asks, so calmly that I wonder for a moment if Sarafina has put a spell on her.

"I will offer it to Lilith, along with the organs of the father which, as you've seen, are in my cellar." Sarafina looks down at the child, runs a black-nailed finger down its cheek. "It's the only way for me to be free."

"Lilith?" Ellie says.

Sarafina sighs heavily, seemingly misunderstanding Ellie's confusion. "I wish there was another way, but the night mother wants what she wants. And I've been waiting a long time for the right man to darken my doorstep. And now, finally," she says, holding the child up in her arms, its limbs wiggling like fat worms, "I have a worthy sacrifice."

"Sacrifice!" Ellie says, taking a step toward the child, then stops when Sarafina shoots her a dark look.

"You're lying," I say, debating whether to attack now or wait until I have a better opening. My fingers squeeze the knife's hilt.

Sarafina laughs. "Put down that silly blade, Ethan," she says, turning those hard, dark eyes on me. "You think me a witch? And what...that dagger will protect you? Will hurt me?"

A hard wind blows, the branches of the tree creak loudly, the fat leaves whisper. The light is fading fast, and the air turns frigid.

"Maybe we should find out," I say, speaking more bravely than I feel, and set my feet in a fighting stance.

Sarafina glances back at Ellie, a pitying look on her face. "This is your last chance," she says. "If you ask, I will release you both. Even now, after you've murdered my companion, and slain my hound. Even now, I will have mercy."

"Enough!" I let go my rifle, letting it drop to the ground, and lunge toward the witch, knife raised, meaning to plunge the blade into the flesh of her exposed neck.

Instead of screaming, or begging for mercy, she calmly raises one hand, fingers hooked.

"So be it," she says, and from one step to the next strong hands are digging into my arms, yanking me back, dragging me away from her.

No...not hands.

Branches.

The tree—somehow come to life—grips me with impossible strength, then lifts me high into the air. Wire-thin branches coil around my arms and legs, then more of the tree's rough limbs snake around my chest and neck. My skin chafes and tears wherever the rough wood slides across my flesh, squeezing tighter and tighter. I let out a scream, then clench my teeth as pain consumes me. I drop the knife, freeing my hands to tear at the branches—rough and hard as iron—while fighting to pull air into my compressed lungs as I'm lifted higher, higher.

Sarafina watches stoically from below, her angelic face relaxed, taunting me with a smile. "Really, Ethan. Can't you see the women are talking?"

"Ellie—" I choke out her name as the branches squeeze against my throat.

I can't breathe.

Suddenly, the witch is on her feet, staring up at me. Her skin begins to glow in the sinking dusk, her eyes shine bright gold and her hair lengthens, thick strands flowing away from her like the snakes of Medusa.

"I am Sarafina!" she roars, and the branches crushing me vibrate; blood runs into my eyes, blurring my vision. Her voice rumbles across the gloaming sky like cannon fire and the fabric of her dress rips away as great black wings unfurl from behind her—two, then four, then six.

The baby in her arms begins to scream.

"I am the wife of Samyaza, defender of Heaven, leader of the two hundred." She points at Ellie. "Drop that relic, sister. We have much to discuss."

Without a word of argument, Ellie casts the sword onto the grass and drops to her knees, forehead bowed to the earth in supplication.

No!

More and more branches twine around me, pull at my limbs until I am stretched to my body's limits, suspended high off the ground. Something pops in my shoulder—a sharp burst of pain that makes me gasp. I whimper in fear and agony and my vision tunnels until all I can see are those golden eyes, all I can hear is that booming voice in my head as coarse wood slithers across my face, ripping my flesh—flaying me alive. I try to scream but my jaw is locked tight. Blood seeps from my wounds, runs down my neck and back, into the branches. There's an ear-popping *SNAP* and a jolt of fresh, fiery pain ignites in my right arm and I know a bone has been broken.

I stare down, fighting not to lose consciousness, and watch helplessly as a long, thin branch snakes down toward Sarafina like an extended hand. She reaches toward it, smiles as it intertwines around her wrist.

"Let me tell you my story, sister," she says, as a second leafy branch circles her hips like a snake. "The powerful Samyaza, my beautiful angel, taught me many things, and we were happy. After many years, I bore his child. And this—" she says, kissing the branch woven around her wrist. "This is my son, who I named Novah, for he was turned into something new. When first born, he was part angel, part human. A giant among men. What your scripture calls a Nephilim." Sarafina releases the tree branch and leans over Ellie, rests a hand atop her head as giant wings extend outward, flapping beneath me.

"And then the reckoning came, and God sent his four strongest angels to strike at us, at the world He'd created, at our *children*."

She leaves Ellie and walks beneath me, those yellow, goat-slit eyes studying me from far below as I hang—slowly dying—my body screaming in torment as I gasp for each shallow breath.

"Do you know the story, Ethan? Did your priest tell you how Raphael, Gabriel, Michael, and Uriel came for us? How God, in a childish rage, flooded the earth, murdered the children that I—and others like me—had borne with the angels? It was Michael himself who bound me here, trapped me in this prison.

"When the flood came, the only way to save me, and our son, was for the angels to give their wives great powers. In one last act of defiance, they transformed us into something else, something ancient. Something eternal."

There's a loud fluttering and Sarafina hovers before me, wings whipping the air, the baby nestled in one black arm as she extends the other to grip a branch, grinning madly.

"We became sirens, Ethan," she says, her voice roughened once more—the voice of a beast. "A fact hidden deep inside the pages of your Holy Book. Each of us women were infused with a small part of our lovers. Some, like me, became creatures of the air, so we could fly above the waters that consumed our world. Some became creatures of the sea, so they could breathe, and live, beneath the waves. Our only son—my Novah—was transformed into this powerful tree, whose roots grow deep into the earth, into stone, twining with the very crust of this planet so that he would be strong enough to survive the great flood while I soared high above. Unable to fly beyond Michael's powerful binding, I circled this land while the people and animals below me drowned, along with the remaining Nephilim. When the waters finally cleared, I returned here, to this land. To my son.

"Samyaza, like all of the two hundred, was not so fortunate. He and the others were banished to a place between Earth and Hell. They lie buried beneath mountains, alive but lost, forever trapped by their God."

She runs a long, taloned finger down my cheek, licks my blood with a forked tongue.

"For centuries I have tried to free myself, to tap into a power greater than my own so I could finally cross Michael's pentagram and enter the human world. Be free to leave this place."

Sarafina looks down at the baby nestled in one arm. "But freedom comes at great cost."

Suddenly, the branches release me and I drop to the earth, freefalling a dozen feet or more, landing hard enough to knock out my breath and make me see stars. The impact on my broken arm sends a searing, white-hot pain shooting through my body, and my head spins.

Sarafina lands gracefully between me and my sister, who has not moved. I groan and roll to one side, keeping my eyes on the creature as she shrinks, transforming back into human form. I look away, focused for the moment on my own injuries, dreadfully aware that portions of the skin on my arms and legs—my face—are ruined, ripped away, and that I've lost more blood than I care to imagine.

I have little time left to live.

Looking once more like a woman—naked and perfect against the dark branches and the darkening sky beyond—Sarafina stands over my torn, broken body, and sighs. "You think me evil," she says quietly. "For doing what I must do. But it is you who are evil, Ethan Belle." She presses a cool, bare foot to my face, dips a toe into my mouth and tugs me toward her, so that my drifting eyes are on her alone. "You are the devil in our midst."

I try to reply but my jaw refuses to move. Instead, I groan and close my eyes, defeat and death seeping into my flesh, my mind.

I can only pray Ellie will escape.

"I have much to do before the offering," Sarafina says abruptly. "Our time here is done."

Ellie, I'm so sorry.

The world is swallowed by darkness.

My heartbeat slows and I'm left alone, prone and helpless on the cold ground.

My last thought is the bitter knowledge that my failure is now complete.

58

I open my eyes in the dark.

I have no idea where I am, or what's happened to me. Can't think...

My face is a maelstrom of pain, and there's a high-pitched ringing in my ears, a tremendous pressure inside my head. I remember the war...

Am I in South Carolina? I recall artillery. Buried beneath the rubble of Fort Sumter?

No, wait. Tennessee? Yes, yes! I was at Shiloh...I was running, there was an explosion, the man in front of me blown apart, a flash of white and I'm flying...

No...no...

My sluggish mind slowly comes awake, catches up to reality. And I remember.

Not a battle.

Sarafina. The tree.

Ellie...oh, God.

"Ellie?" I call out for her, but my voice is muffled, my mouth restricted.

Regardless, there's no answer from the darkness. A light appears from far away, a flickering flame moving toward me. As it gets closer, I blink to try and clear my vision. A figure emerges—a woman carrying a lantern.

But something is *off*.

Her face comes into view—Sarafina.

And behind her, my sister.

They're both upside down.

I tilt my head up and see my arms, dangling; hands brushing black, jagged stone. Now that I'm coming alert, I feel the tightness at my ankles, and as the light from the lantern fills the room, I recognize the tables, the shelves, the remains of Mason's corpse.

All of it upside down, because *I'm* upside down.

I use what strength I have to tuck my chin to my chest and look upward, see my ankles are bound together and attached to a large iron hook that extends from the darkness above—the same hook from which my brother had hung.

"Your arm is badly broken," Sarafina says as she moves around the room, lighting wall sconces. "So I bound your ankles instead. I also treated your wounds, along with the worst of the gashes in your limbs. I had to wrap your head in bandages, which may feel strange at first." She turns to glance at me, and despite once more taking the form of a woman, her wicked smile is anything but human. "Novah wasn't very gentle, I'm afraid."

Ellie stands across the cavern, hugging herself.

Holding the baby.

"What are you doing?" I ask, but again, the words don't come out right. I raise the hand of my good arm to my face, touch the tightly wrapped bandages there. I pull at the ones near my mouth and ignore the fresh, searing pain it brings. "Ellie," I say again, this time clearly enough that she turns her head to look at me. "Help me."

"It's okay, Ethan," she says, as if placating a child, then focuses on the baby.

"I'm sorry for the pain I've caused you, Ethan," Sarafina says, now moving to stand directly in front of me. She kneels, her face a few inches from mine, and lowers her voice. "I told you not to come back."

"Thou shalt not suffer a witch to live," I say, quoting the Bible verse I'd read in the priest's book, the one from Exodus. "I'll destroy you, and your powers."

Sarafina cocks her head in a way I find reminiscent of the creature Archie had become. "I'm curious," she says. "Why do you feel that a woman with power is so very dangerous? What is it, in your mind, that makes me evil—so evil that men would hunt me down and burn me at a stake? Or drown me? Tell me, Ethan, if I were a man, would I still be a threat? Or would I be a hero? Someone to fear, someone who garners respect, versus animosity?"

"You use your powers to hurt. Those men you killed—"

Sarafina grips me by the hair, pulls my head toward her. This close I see a flash of gold flicker in her eyes, and I realize it's something that occurs when she's angry. "Are you speaking of the ones I kept from killing you? Those men? The ones who were hunting you?"

"Archie...you turned him—"

"I saved him!" she screams, and the gold in her eyes blazes like fire. Her shout echoes in the large chamber. "That was a choice I left to you, Ethan. That night in the field, *you* told me to save his life, you fool."

I can't think. I can't reason. The pain is too much, there's no sense in her words.

"You sent nightmares," I say, searching for a way through this, to show her what she is.

"Yes, I did that to know your mind," she says evenly, calm once more. "And oh, Ethan...the things I found. But then—"

She moves close enough that I can smell the sweet fragrance of her breath, and whispers next to my ear. "I suppose, at heart, we're all a little bit evil, aren't we?"

I try to speak, to defend my nature, but I can only cough, blood and saliva running over my lips, spraying her chin. She doesn't seem to notice.

"We have a bond, you and I," she says, eyeing me closely, studying me. "You've seen my other form and lived, and that's rare, believe me. Still, I imagine you were never quite the same after that. Humans can only understand so much of what is shown to them by the gods; the rest they must imagine for themselves. And instead of angels, you see monsters."

Sarafina releases my hair, turns away. She lights a few last sconces until the large underground cavern is well-lit, the walls painted with flickering oranges and yellows. Then she points to the stone slab in the middle of the cavern.

"Ellie, my love, place the child on the table," she says. "It's time."

To my dismay, Ellie doesn't hesitate, but walks forward and places the infant, now wrapped in a blanket, atop the stone table.

Right next to his father.

Sarafina moves quickly now. With purpose. She pulls heavy black candles from the shelves and places them around the infant—then lights them, one by one. Moments later, she puts bowls made of gold and silver around the quiet baby. She carries large, sealed earthenware jars from her worktable, opens them, then pours their lumpy contents into the bowls.

"Organs, intestines," she says evenly, as Ellie looks on in wide-eyed horror. "Mason's insides, and...parts of his extremities."

Ellie steps away, face ashen in the room's dim light.

"I would have preferred his heart beating, and not pierced, but I think it will still work. I've tried this a few times before, and have come close on occasion." Sarafina tips over another jar—this one smaller—and even from my skewed vantage point I can easily identify the contents as they spill out.

Mason's eyes.

"Why?" My voice is small and cracked—choked by the bandages, the dryness of my mouth, the searing pain of my body.

"To conjure the night mother," she says. "The child, the spawn of an evil man, and the father's flesh are my offering to Lilith. She is the only one within my reach who is powerful enough to counter Michael's magic, to break the bonds cast upon me by the guardians. I've spawned other infants, and slain many men, over the long years. Of course, some of the men and women who found me were good, and decent. Those are the ones who left this place in peace. Others came to me hurt, or dying, souls trapped in the evil of their lives. Those special few became my companions...like your beloved Archie, whose life I saved. Titus was an exception. An experiment. I suppose I was lonely, and so I made him a child—one who would never age, never grow sick. Never be able to hurt me. He was happy before you came."

"Of course, most arrived on my doorstep with darkness in their souls; with violence in their hearts. Those men became offerings, their children, sacrifices...but time and time again I have failed. Only once has the night mother come to me. Only once has she accepted my offering. But even then she would not hear my pleas. She simply took what was offered then returned to the abyss to feast with her husband, the great serpent, Samael—"

Sarafina plucks a long dagger from the folds of her dress, scrapes its edge against the stone, sending sparks.

"The one you call Satan."

"Ellie!" I croak out, loudly as I'm able while struggling to catch my breath, to think clearly through the pain. I try—desperately—to bend my body, to reach my constraints. But with the broken bones in my arm, it's an impossible task. I can't waste the energy to focus on her blasphemous, impossible story. Angels, sirens, demons...

Murderer, I say.

I must get free.

"God damn it, help me!"

Ellie considers me a moment, her expression stoic. She glances to Sarafina, who says nothing...but pauses, waiting.

As if interested in what will come next.

Finally, Ellie takes a deep breath and slowly walks across the chamber to stand before me. Sarafina makes no move to stop her.

"Ethan, stop. Stop, and listen to me."

I stop twisting, struggling. Panting through the damp bandages, I look up at her as best I'm able until she crouches to one knee, and looks me in the eye.

"I came with you...I came to this place to help you, Ethan," Ellie says. "To try and save our brothers. Save our family. But there's much you don't know. Sarafina kept it from you as a mercy...as did I."

"Ellie—"

"Remember the way father beat me after mother died? How you all ignored it, never defending me, never helping me? It only got worse when you three left me there, alone with him." She pauses, wrings her hands. When she continues, her words pierce me like arrows. "What he did to me when I became pregnant? He killed my baby, and destroyed my body…while my brothers did nothing to stop it."

She wipes a tear from her cheek. "And still I forgave him, forgave all of you. I forgave and forgave and forgave—"

Gently, she places her palms on either side of my head, over the wrappings. I hiss in pain, but meet her eye.

She gazes upon me with something akin to pity…a way I can't identify. It's as if she's looking at a stranger, rather than her twin.

"Sarafina told me more, Ethan. She told me about the boy…the one I kissed when I was a child. The innocence of it was laughable, but you became enraged. Jealous, perhaps, without realizing what jealousy even was. What did you do to him, Ethan? To little Samuel, who had a wonderful laugh, and who cared about me?"

"Ellie, please—"

"What did you do, Ethan?" Her eyes widen, and she no longer looks at me as if I'm a stranger, but as if I'm something foul. Something dangerous.

"My God, what did you do?"

59

I remember finding him there, catching crawfish.

There was no one around, and an uproot of trees clumped at the river's edge blocked us from the view of any passersby. It didn't matter—no one came by there that afternoon. No one who could see us, anyway.

No one within shouting distance.

I pushed him to the ground, his long hair mixing with the loose soil, his eyes wide with shock, then anger. He stood and pushed me back. He was smaller than I was, and I'd learned about fighting from my older brothers. I'd learned violence. I knew he couldn't beat me, and I'd *hated* him for what he did. The fact he'd touched my sister. That he felt affection for her—and received affection in return—stole something from me. Something that was *mine*. The same as if he'd sneaked into our house at night and taken gold from a chest.

I hit him hard, in the jaw, and he fell, then came back at me with a stick. He swung it at my head, connected just above my ear and knocked me down. Later, I'd tell my father that Mason had done it while we'd been wrestling. Mason didn't deny it, and I wondered then if he knew what I'd done.

I think maybe he did. I think maybe he respected me for it.

When I went back at him, it wasn't with a stick, but with a rock in my fist. I clubbed the skinny boy in the temple and he collapsed. I dropped to my knees, pinned his arms beneath them, as if he might fight back. But I knew he was done fighting, knew it because I could only see the whites of his eyes, which had rolled up into his head. My arms free, I brought the rock down on his cheekbone, which broke inward, leaving a gruesome dent in his face. A distorted mask. It terrified me and I didn't want to look at that dent in his face anymore so I hit him with that rock again, and again, and again.

He'd gone still.

Nearby, I spotted a fallen tree, broken away from its rotting stump, split along the middle. It crawled with barklice, beetles, and ants. Because Samuel was scrawny, and short, I was able to wedge his body into that fallen tree.

I remember having to widen the split in places so I could fit all of him inside. I never did get both legs completely hidden, but it was close enough. I pushed the log through the muck and into the river and it floated atop the water, then kept on pushing until the water was to my chin. I ignored the bugs falling off the log, crawling in vain for dry ground over my fingers and arms. I gave the makeshift coffin a final push and watched as it spun lazily in the current then began floating south, past the docks. I continued watching to make sure it didn't catch on something, or that someone didn't holler in alarm at seeing a body…but neither thing happened.

Samuel just kept floating away, away, until I couldn't see the log anymore.

I made my way to shore, found the bloody rock and threw it as far as I could into the Mississippi. It splashed down, cast out a halo of ripples that were swallowed in seconds, as if they'd never been.

"And the boy?" Ellie says. "Tell me about the boy in your boat."

I turn to Sarafina. "How could you know?" I say, the bandages pressed against my lips, smearing my speech.

She only stares at me.

I turn back to Ellie—my head pounding now—the pressure in my face building to a such a point that I feel I'll explode like a grape if they don't release me.

"What does it matter?" I say.

"Ethan—"

"I made him swim," I whisper, and that's the truth.

He was crying when I told him to jump, to jump into the river and head for shore. He told me he couldn't swim, but I wanted him off that boat. He would give me away—I knew he would somehow give me away—and I was *so close* to home. I couldn't have him raising an alarm, or sabotaging the vessel I'd stolen from the docks.

I had no weapon but my bayonet, which I'd pointed at his small chest and told him that he could either swim, or that I'd gut him right there in the boat.

Crying, he'd climbed over the boat's edge and began to paddle toward shore. No more than a quarter-mile. No more than that. I watched him for a while as I floated further away, the current taking me rapidly downriver on its mighty back. I watched—

He was just a small head above the surface and then, from one moment to the next, he was nothing at all.

"When Father took me away," Ellie continues, bringing me back to the horror of the present, "why didn't you do something? Why wouldn't you speak out?"

Because I was afraid, Ellie. Afraid of what you'd done.

Because I was weak. Because I was a coward.

Because I was jealous. Because I was angry.

"I don't know," I say.

But she's already turning away from me, no longer listening. Perhaps not needing to. She knows there are no answers.

"I love you," Ellie whispers. "But I don't know who you are."

"I'm your brother," I say, then I let my body go limp; arms dangling, feet numb, my body and soul drenched in blood and sin. I don't know what else to say, so I repeat myself—speak the only thing left in my heart I know to be true.

"I'm your brother."

60

Sarafina begins the ceremony.

The candles are lit. The baby coos and gurgles on the table, wedged against the meat that was once Mason. Sarafina holds a large piece of white chalk, murmurs in a language I don't understand, guttural and broken—a mix of German and Latin, or possibly a form of Hebrew. She kneels in her linen dress and draws a circle on the stone—at least six feet wide—still muttering her strange prayers.

Inside the circle she draws more symbols. Hanging upside down as I am, it's hard to make out what they are, but I note two long lines with crosses at the ends...some sort of multi-angled design in the middle.

A soft light shines on the stone where Sarafina works. I tilt my head toward the ceiling—toward that crevice where daylight comes through—and see a piece of the moon, bright as a pale sun, suffusing the torch-lit cavern with a silver glow.

When she's done scratching at the rock floor, Sarafina steps back—outside of the circle—and raises her arms, her white dress catching the moonlight, giving her entire being a soft luminescence as she gazes toward the heavens and repeats the same strange phrases over and over again, her cadence rhythmic, the words gibberish to my ears.

The outer rim of the chalk circle is no more than a few feet from where my head hangs, and I long to be far away from it. From this bizarre ritual. I search the room for Ellie, willing her to do something—to *help* me—but I can't see her.

The cavern begins filling with haze, or smoke...

But it doesn't come from the candles.

It comes from the floor.

From the circle.

I blink my eyes, not sure I believe what I'm seeing, because the floor seems to be *dissolving*, as if it were made of paraffin instead of stone, heated by something just below the surface.

Sarafina, arms still raised, begins to chant louder as the floor evaporates and now I'm looking straight down—not at a stone surface—but into an expanding *pit*, a great black maw increasing in size until if fills the entire circle.

Then I see what lies below, and I scream—I scream over and over and try with renewed desperation to release myself, jerking and twisting my body in an effort to reach my feet, to untie the ropes binding me and run, run from this hellish place and never come back.

I must get away!

As I writhe, the floor continues to dissolve, the smoke to rise—and there, at a great distance far below, I see a light. It's as if I were seeing a distant campfire from atop a canyon ridge, the flame no more than a flickering speck in the dark.

I stare in horror as the smoke begins to move around and around, a vortex burrowing downward toward that ever-growing red light in the center of the earth, getting larger and larger as I struggle helplessly with my bindings.

No, not larger, I realize with a deep, desperate groan.

Closer.

The smoke carpets the floor where it doesn't funnel downward and the sound of rushing wind buffets my ears, as if we are—all of us—caught in the heart of a tempest.

Finally, I spot Ellie. She stands across the chasm from me, staring down as I am, a look of naked terror on her face. She spins toward Sarafina.

"Stop this!' she yells over the growing tumult, but Sarafina ignores her, continues chanting as the unnatural pit broadens until I'm not staring into a crevasse but an abyss, an endless dark so bottomless that I know now where it leads, into what damnation I'm caught gazing—

Hell itself.

I cry out again, writhing on the chain like a hooked fish, pain and weakness forgotten, as the flickering red light gets closer and grows larger and now I make out shapes in the hellish glow—lithe, pale creatures circling upward, upward, towards the surface. Towards me.

"Ellie, run!"

She looks to me, skin pale, eyes wide and afraid, and is about to speak...

When a new sound joins the fray.

A howling.

The dogs have come down. The four of them have stopped a few feet from the gateway—for that's exactly what it is, I have no doubt, a gateway to Hell—and they *howl*. I make out the two grays, the big black-haired beast...and yes, Archie, howling right along with them.

The hounds' cries intensify as long, pale creatures emerge from the hole. They circle in the air before splitting up—three wyrm-like demons, skinny as snakes with heads like dragons, feet like children, and eyes...so many eyes, black and blinking as they float around the cavern, over Sarafina's head, weaving around me, around Ellie.

One of the dogs barks and snarls, then snaps its jaws at a wyrm who flies too close. The demonic thing jerks back, then—like a striking snake—coils itself around the dog's body, around its neck, and lifts it into the air, fangs sinking into the meat of the dog's stomach again and again as it howls in pain and then, within seconds, the wyrm burrows *inside* the hound. The large dog convulses in the air and—for a heartbeat—Sarafina slows her chants, eyes twitching toward the beast with a hint of concern, with uncertainty. But then she continues, louder and faster than before. I hear snatches of "Lilith" in those words, and "Samael," but nothing else is comprehensible.

Now a new sound arises from the abyss—a shrill, hateful screech—and the wyrms return to the pit as if beckoned—one covered in the hound's gore—and slip away, back into the twisting funnel, the burning light.

As I watch them go, I see something new rising from the great depths.

Something much larger.

The emerging figure stares up at me as it comes and I want nothing more than to look away, to close my eyes and forget this nightmare, but I'm unable to break free of its hold on me, on those bright eyes, pure as snow.

Lilith.

She's the most beautiful thing I've ever seen.

Her skin is not the color of flesh but alabaster, pale as pure marble. Her flowing long hair is thick, tied in endless braids of gold, her lips red and hungry. Her body, curved and full and taller than any man, is so enticing that—even hanging here, upside down with my body torn and broken—I burn with an unquenchable desire that surges through me like an all-consuming fire. Something more than love, more than lust.

Need.

I reach out my hands, heedless of the pain in my destroyed arm, wanting to touch every part of her. *Taste* every inch of her.

She emerges from the abyss and rises into the air like a goddess from a dark fairy tale, the cavernous room filled with her radiance, her aura of power, her divinity. I groan with a desire borne of madness and she turns toward me, eyes impossibly wide and bright, with a smile that unhinges something deep in my mind.

There's a flash of white—like the firing of a cannon, or the bursting of a star—and I sink into a cold sea of yearning as she turns back toward Sarafina. I hate that her attention is taken from me—*stolen* from me! I know, without question, that I would kill for her, for the night mother, for Lilith.

"Great mother," Sarafina says. "This sacrifice I present to you. This child I bore is a gift for you. This man, who flowed with evil and dark deeds in life, I harvested for you." Sarafina falls to her knees, arms thrown wide in supplication. "Please accept my offering, great mother, and grant me what I desire."

Lilith's bare feet touch down onto the stone floor. She takes a few gliding steps away from the smoking mouth of Hell, toward the table. She reaches out a hand, porcelain fingers long and smooth, and slides a fingertip along the baby's stomach, then laughs.

"A sweet thing." Her voice is chimes in a soft wind. "And what would you ask in return, wife of Samyaza, mother of Novah? You have beckoned me, and I will listen."

"I wish to be free of this prison," Sarafina says.

Even through the haze of my mad lust, I sense the desperation in her voice.

"I wish for you to break Michael's curse," she continues, "so I may leave this place and walk into the world, take myself away from all this loneliness."

Lilith removes her hand from the baby and turns her head toward Ellie, who stands still as a statue at the edge of the light, half-steeped in shadow, watching it all. "The babe is sweet, but the girl is sweeter. Innocent and broken...pure, yet poisoned." She takes a step toward my twin, her voice filled with command. "Come to me, girl."

Ellie takes a step toward the demon, then stops suddenly, as if pushed backward. A bright flicker of light comes from her finger—from the ring—that halts Ellie in her tracks, no more than an arm's length away.

"She is protected?" Lilith spits, venomous with rising anger.

Sarafina hesitates a moment, caught off guard, but recovers smoothly. "The girl is bound to me," she says, then rises from her knees, demanding the attention of the goddess as Ellie quivers in fear.

Lilith shrugs, then—in the way of a petulant child—lazily begins knocking over bowls with a long finger, tipping blood and meat and organs onto the stone table.

The baby begins to cry.

Sarafina watches all of this without comment, even as Lilith plucks something wet—the size of a dark apple—from the stone table and puts it into her mouth, chews quietly.

When she swallows whatever part of my brother she's consumed, she sighs heavily. "I cannot do what you ask, daughter," she says, her annoyance seemingly appeased by her taste of flesh. "Michael's power is too great for me to bend, or break. Much like you, I lost my struggle with the three sent to me after the garden, and was forced to bargain for my own freedom."

Sarafina's mouth twitches. Her eyes flicker bright gold, then settle back to black. "Please," she says. "You are my only hope in this."

Lilith shakes her head, then runs her fingers through the spilled gore atop the stone table, as if debating. "I will take you with me, Sarafina," she says, finality in her tone, as if all had been decided. "In my world you will be free. You will rule the dead who reside there—a Queen of Sheol, a Daughter of Gehinnom. You will be a god second only to me, and have whatever your heart desires."

Then Lilith's voice hardens, and any lust I'd been feeling turns to ashes in my heart, for this, I realize, is her true voice—a voice that reeks of evil, that would consume the darkest night.

"Of course, you will serve me," she says. "In all that I say and do, in all that I wish. You will be sister and slave, companion and lover. You will be my hand. Further, you will serve my beloved, Samael, in all ways. In this manner will you have your freedom.

"This is what I offer."

Lilith reaches down and plucks the baby from the table, lifts it high into the air, its doll-like limbs waving in the smoky light. "And we accept this gift," she says, voice purring and dangerous. "It will be part of a special feast in your honor. Together, we will suck on his flesh and chew on his bones."

She sets it back down, roughly, and the infant begins to wail. Not bothering for Sarafina's response, Lilith turns back toward the gateway. "Come, Sarafina, and bring the offering."

"Wait!" Ellie takes a step forward, the mutilated corpse of one dog at her feet, the others—including my brother—having vanished into the shadows, cowered by the demon in our midst.

Sarafina, startled, gazes at her with curiosity.

"I'll stay," Ellie says, words rushed and breathless, as if wanting to get them out before she can overthink them. "I'll stay with you, Sarafina. Let me be the freedom you desire," she says, then glances at me through the haze.

I shake my head.

Don't…

In three quick strides, Ellie goes to the table and scoops up the crying baby. I notice her pull the ring from her finger and fold it into the child's palm.

"But only if we keep him here, with us. And…" She falters for a moment, as if wondering whether to push whatever luck she feels she's tapped into. "And you must let Ethan live. If you can agree, I'll stay. I'll stay with you forever."

Sarafina appears genuinely surprised for the first time since I've met her. Surprised…and unsure. "Ellie—" Sarafina starts, her voice sounding more human than it ever has, rife with uncertainty.

"Search your heart," Ellie begs. "And then tell me you'd rather be a slave in Hell than a master on Earth. Would you be a servant, or would you be served? Here, with me. I will be all those things you desire. I will be your body beyond the edges of that creek, your surrogate. I will be your mouth, your eyes, your ears. I will be yours completely."

Sarafina thinks a moment. Then she smiles, albeit sadly. "And what of your home?"

Ellie shakes her head. "Home is nothing but another prison," she says. "One to which I have lost the desire to return."

"Ellie, no—" The words fall from my tongue like cinders.

Sarafina walks to my sister, puts her hands on her thin shoulders, then embraces her gently, the babe wiggling between them. She kisses her cheek, then whispers something into her ear. From my inverted vantage point, it's impossible to make out her reaction, but I see her nod, a shimmer of tears nestled beneath her eyes.

After a moment, Sarafina turns away and approaches Lilith, palms held open and out to her sides, as if she were approaching a wild animal. "I'm sorry, Mother," she says, then lowers herself to a knee, bows her head.

Lilith laughs, but there's no humor in the sound.

Without another word she turns and glides back toward the gateway, her feet no longer touching the stone, as if she's had enough of this mortal plain and no longer wishes to feel its cold reality. "Do not beckon me again, *wife*," she says, the last word spat like a curse. "Or you will lose more than a hound."

Before sinking back into the swirling abyss, she looks once more in my direction, but her smile is no longer tempting, her hair and skin no longer beautiful.

She is monstrous.

Her eyes are that of a dragon, her fingers long and crooked claws. "I will see you again, sweet one," she murmurs to me, then transforms into a wisp of smoke that mixes with the rest, all of it sucked back into the vortex, the abyssal hole spiraling forever downward until, within seconds, the pit is erased from this world and the floor is once again stone, now covered in ash.

The baby gurgles in Ellie's arms.

Sarafina steps into the circle and slides her bare foot through the dense ash in a slow, sweeping motion, as if testing its solidity.

I gaze past Sarafina to see Ellie standing behind her, a calm, resolute look on her face. "Please don't do this," I manage, and when the tears flow they climb up my forehead, dissolve into the strips of cloth.

Ellie takes a step closer, looks at me with an indifference that punctures my heart.

"If I'm to be trapped, then let it be by choice," she says, the baby held tightly in her arms—then her eyes flash with something akin to fury, a rage I've never seen.

"And let it be with power."

I shake my head. "Ellie, I'm sorry. Please—"

"Goodbye, Ethan," she says quietly, then turns her back on me and disappears into the shadows. The sounds of her footsteps dissipate, then vanish.

She's gone.

Sarafina, seemingly satisfied that the portal is closed and the demon returned to her domain, watches Ellie's departure, then approaches me. Because of my position, it appears as if she strides across a ceiling, like a bat in a cave.

"Well well well...just you and I now, dear Ethan. And it seems a bargain has been struck." She kneels before me. The pressure in my head is enormous and it's hard to breathe, my chest and throat are thick with fluid. I can hardly suck in even the smallest gasps of air through the wet bandages. "You will return home after all," she says. "And this time, I promise you, there will be no finding your way back."

"No dreams," I ask, ashamed of my pathetic fear.

She considers this a moment. "No dreams," she agrees, then grins widely, savagely.

"And now," Sarafina says under her breath, "you're mine."

Her onyx eyes flicker, then blaze gold, locking onto me with a savage, hateful glare. In one fluid motion she stands and rips away her dress, exposing a naked body that bulges and ripples, as if there were snakes writhing beneath her flesh. Her face elongates, and darkens. Great, leathery wings spring from her back. Dark fur sprouts from her chest, belly, and legs. Her fingers and toes extend into hard talons. She swipes a hooked claw at my feet, slicing cleanly through the bonds between my hanging body and the metal hook.

I collapse to the stone floor—hard enough that the breath is punched from my lungs. Knowing she means to kill me, I reach for my boot just as those long talons clutch my neck, my legs, dig through cloth to pierce my skin. I scream in pain as she squeezes the break in my arm. Before I can fight back, I'm lifted from the ground, the sound of her wings beating the air surrounding us as we rise.

I spare a glance downward, the cavern's floor spiraling further away as we fly higher.

Just as I begin to fear crashing into the ceiling, she pulls me tight to her body—wings wrapped around me like a shell—and we burst into cold night.

I look back one last time to see a shrinking circle of stones— the old well, her doorway to the underground caves.

It's impossible to take a breath as air rushes past—higher and higher we climb, past the treetops and into the starry night, the horizon tilting and spinning as she takes us ever closer to a fat white moon.

"You made a deal!" I yell, my nostrils filled with her animal scent, my vision blurred by fluttering feathers, my ears deafened by the pounding of the monster's heart. "You promised to let me live."

When she speaks, her words are scratchy and thick.

"I told you, boy," she says. "We're all a little bit evil."

My fingers curl around the cold metal at my calf.

I pull the blade free.

"I want to show you the stars, Ethan," she says, madness in her voice. "I want to show you the things that lie beyond your world. I want to open your mind and see it shatter."

I punch the knife into warm fur, feel it puncture the skin and sink into her.

The abomination shrieks in pain...

And releases me.

I plummet downward, the frigid night air blasts against me as I fall toward the treetops. I inhale—one last time—in a failed attempt to scream as air floods my throat, my lungs. The world turns on its axis and I'm spinning, plunging wildly toward certain death.

I crash through a flurry of branches and feel parts of me tear away, clothes and flesh alike. The ground races closer and I want to pray, to close my eyes and beg for my soul. My vision tunnels as I wait to be broken against the rocks below...

A flurry of wings hammers the air. A flash of black darker than any midnight.

I feel a hard blow to my head and the world explodes in a final eruption of light and pain and then I'm consumed, burned through and—finally—am nothing more.

PART SEVEN: AFTER

61

I've lost time.

When I come to, I'm alone.

There's no sign of the creek, of Sarafina's land. I have no idea where I am.

I hear the continuous rush of a nearby river. I'm lying in a bed of dead pine needles, surrounded by fat loblolly, tall and full and imposing. The sun is up, the day young—pale light spreads across the earth like a welcome, or a warning.

I spend a few minutes on the ground, letting my body speak to me, tell me it's alive, that it's functional. I begin to rise, but my arm is an endless well of pain so it takes me a bit to get my knees beneath me, then my feet. I study my surroundings, the location of the sun, and I figure a way south.

South, and home.

I don't know why I'm alive, or if this is perhaps Heaven, or Hell, but I'm too tired to care, too weary to pray. Somewhere along the way I've lost my soul.

And so I wander, a pilgrim adrift through unfamiliar wilderness.

As I trek through the trees, my shattered arm shrieks in agony, my flayed flesh feels as if it's on fire. My face has crusted over with dried blood, and I'm too afraid to remove the coverings that stick to me like a second skin. My clothes are torn and there are places on my arms and legs that will need stitching, but I'm not losing enough blood to fill my boots or halt my hobbled progress toward some form of salvation.

It finally comes when I stumble upon two families making their way toward Jackson. They take pity on me; give me water and what food I can stomach. I'm laid in a horse-pulled wagon and spend the next couple days staring at the sky and the overarching arms of the trees lining the narrow road.

As we near Jackson, I hear the familiar sound of battle. Cannon and rifle fire, men screaming in a great chorus. There's a debate among the families as to the safest route—assuming one even exists. We finally continue forward but are soon stopped by Union soldiers, who waylay our progress. They see me and ask the men if I'm a soldier. They lie, say I'm a nephew who fell down a precipice, that I need a doctor.

Fate has a sense of humor, I suppose, and life can take strange turns; each day we exist are as seeds floating upon a wild stream, flowing one way, then another, our movements powered by something greater than us, mindless forces of destiny, our lives wrested from our control. That sense of humor is never more evident than when the Yankees pull me from the wagon and hoist me to my feet. I scream when one grips the broken bones of my arm and after that they handle me more gently. I'm marched to a field hospital where I'm pressed onto a canvas cot among groaning Union soldiers. Hours go by until a doctor named Poole comes and roughly pulls away my bandages, ignores my cries and tears of pain.

"You look worse than some of these soldiers, now hold still," he says, and pushes a needle into my cheek to sew closed one of the wounds. He then sews my legs and arms. By the time he's finished he's enlisted two men to hold me down, such is my writhing and bucking with the fresh pain. He pours a swallow of whiskey into my mouth and sets my arm. "You're done," he says. "If you want to rest, do it outside, we need the cot."

I'm lifted by the two enlisted nurses—both wearing blue uniforms—and steered outside to a nearby patch of grass and an old Magnolia tree. They sit me down against its trunk and leave without a word.

My life saved by the goddamn Union Army.

How my brothers would have laughed.

The entire state of Mississippi, it seems, is a battleground. Jackson and Vicksburg are under siege, soon to be taken. Natchez is fully under Union control, and the whispers I hear along my journey say that the great river is lost.

Three weeks later, I walk through the front door of my father's house. I am starved. My clothes are rags, my stomach and pockets empty. My pack, resting in an underground cave in an unreachable patch of land, had carried what mattered of my worldly possessions.

I have lost my brothers. I have lost my sister.

I am alone.

My father studies me for a few moments, as if unsure who this stranger is in his house. Then he approaches me, stares hard at my scarred face, my bearing, my emptiness.

"Ethan." He says it like a sigh. Like forgiveness.

And then my father puts his arms around me and holds me tight. I settle into his embrace. For me, the fight is over.

62

TEN YEARS LATER

I lean against the door of the tobacco shop and watch the people walk up and down the street.

I took over the business three years ago, the day my father passed away. After a few weeks, I had the sign repainted to read *Belle's Tobacco*, wanting the family name represented. I also made a few improvements, carrying some of the newer pipes and cigarettes my father had dismissed in years past. I moved the Indian from one side of the door to the other so the entryway would be visible from the docks, had a wall knocked out and a display window put in to show off the manufacturer stands. They get free advertising, and I get a discount on the usual wholesale prices. A good deal all around.

Now that the war is over, things are changing fast around the South. The last of the Union soldiers have long moved on, finally clearing out of the God-forsaken Devil's Punchbowl where those hypocrites kept so many of the freed slaves locked up. Lincoln would have had something to say about that place, I think, had he lived longer than a week past the war's end. But the plantations have let go their slaves, and many work the docks here in town, or up in Vicksburg, or down in New Orleans. Most have gone north.

Once the war was settled things pretty much got back to normal. My father and I regrew our relationship, our mutual grief at losing everything we loved somehow bringing us together. That, and some help from Father McKee, who passed in the same year as my father, in the winter of 1870.

When Ellie and I left home all those years ago, and word got out that we'd gone missing, my father searched for us all over town. It was McKee who finally pulled Jeremiah aside and informed him of all the things I'd been through, and the things he had done to help me try and put things right. He told my father where Ellie and I had gone, and why.

I admit that, when I was first told of this, I was furious. The priest had given me his word, and he knew the last thing I'd wanted was for my father to know my story and to think me insane, or worse.

But the old man knew better than the young man, it seems, and instead of being angry, or thinking me mad, my father was proud of me. He believed every word the priest told him, and every detail of our latest confrontation, which I told him about once I'd regained my strength. I relayed Sarafina's claim of being wife to an angel, about Novah turned from a Nephilim to a tree, about what she'd done to Mason, and Archie. Lastly, I told him how Ellie had chosen to stay, to save the child, and save me. I said that last bit with no shortage of shame, but Father only patted me on the shoulder and nodded. "She made her choice," was all he said about it.

For a while, many folks inquired about Ellie, curious about her disappearance. Father and I decided on a story about her and I traveling to see to our brothers' burial, and that she took sick and passed.

And that was that.

It was easier to dispatch inquiries about my brothers. The war took tens of thousands of men, so there was no arousal of suspicion to affirm they'd been lost in the war. Body and soul.

Ten years later, there's not a person in this town who could claim to have known my sister; only a handful would say they'd shaken my father's hand, and most of those were his customers, who are now my customers.

It's been lonely since the old man passed away. The house is empty except for me and my memories, my dark thoughts. I've taken no wife, for obvious reasons.

No one wants to marry a tobacconist whose face is a bundle of scars, whose arm never healed properly and is now numb most of the time, and useless. Whose eyes—one milky white and blind—have seen the darkest things imaginable.

Yes, even Hell itself, and those who inhabit it.

The men and women who frequent the shop are kind, though, and some even look me in the eye when they pass me coin, as if I weren't a monster.

Nights are the hardest.

The nocturnal hours when I'm not busy with the shop or talking to folks. When I'm home, alone, in Father's old bedroom.

When the dark thoughts take over.

I no longer have the nightmares that once woke Ellie from her sleep—Sarafina kept her promise about that—but I still see ghosts.

Mason, for one, is a regular visitor to my chamber. He sits in the far corner of the room, doused in shadow, and watches me sleep. When I focus on him for more than a few seconds, his eyes light up—still cold and blue as a winter sky—and he grins at me. Sometimes, when I'm feigning sleep, I'll hear his feet shuffle across the floor, feel his cold breath on my cheek as he whispers into my ear that I should *go back*, go back and finish what I started. That I should avenge him. Avenge them all.

After this happened a few times, I fashioned a noose. Father was still alive then, and I was still in the process of healing, physically and otherwise. He came home early from work one afternoon and found me hanging by a crossbeam, and decided to save my miserable life. Another minute, I suppose, and there would have been nothing left to save. He told me he'd had a vision I was in trouble, then raced home to find me hanging. We both cried that night, and I silently cursed Sarafina, knowing it was her cruel joke to keep me alive, and suffering.

Father kept a close eye on me after that.

Now he's gone, but I still have that noose. I keep it coiled in a trunk at the foot of my bed. I've taken it out a few times, inspected its strength, its knots. I like to think I do it out of morbid curiosity, but can't say for sure. Every now and then I'll even put it around my neck and draw it tight. The brittle cord on my throat makes me think of the way that tree grabbed and tore me, sliced me apart. Ruined my face. When I'm done reliving the past, I take the noose off and restore it to the trunk.

Today, though, is a bright, shining day.

A busy summer day in Natchez, and I feel good. I feel strong and, perhaps, even happy. The shop is making more money than it ever did during the war, and I have an eye on expanding the space, possibly adding a drug counter with refreshments. Or, potentially, opening a second location here in town, or somewhere upriver. I have no shortage of ideas, and more than enough time and money to execute them. I'd have to hire some help, of course, because I couldn't do it all on my own. Because that's how I live, how I've *learned* to live, and how I'll always live until the day I die.

Alone.

It's while leaning in the shop's doorway on this sun-drenched, agreeable day—watching the passersby and nodding hello to those who look my way—that I see her.

Ellie.

She's *here*. I spot her walking along the boards across the way, where she knows full well she's in sight of our father's old shop.

I stand up straight, remove the pipe from my mouth and stare, gaping at her, wondering if I'm seeing things. But as she gets closer, there's no doubt in my mind.

It's her.

And she hasn't aged a day.

She's still the same eighteen-year-old girl. But not a child, no. Her head is held high and the look on her face belies her years—an expression imbued with determination, with confidence. She has the bearing of a woman who fears nothing, and no one.

At her heel is a giant dog.

Oh, sweet Jesus…

Archie.

Unlike Ellie, he *has* changed. I take a step into the street, nearly knocking into a messenger boy while gawking at my transformed brother, the creature he has become.

He is no longer the man and beast hybrid I'd seen from the cabin door a decade ago. His paws are now fully those of a dog, not the hands of a man, and his fur has grown in, thick and curly. He has a long, bushy tail, and his face is coated with black, dense hair.

As I step closer, Archie turns his shaggy head toward me and we lock eyes, and I swear to bleeding Christ those eyes are still his own!

Those are the eyes of my brother.

"Hey!" I yell, dodging the throng of pedestrians as my sister walks on—moving past where I stand—without even bothering to glance my way. I stumble further into the street and am jostled by a well-dressed couple carrying packages, then pushed hard by a passing sailor who knocks me to a knee in the mud. I stand, brush myself off. I spot her blonde head at the corner.

She's getting away.

"Ellie!" I cry, and run after her. After them both.

She turns the corner onto Broadway…and disappears from sight.

By the time I reach the bustling intersection she's lost in the crowd. Here, by the waterfront, things are extra busy, the docks plied with goods for steamers, vendors hocking wares, visitors pushing toward the town. I try to give chase, but after a few blocks I give up.

I've lost her.

63

I'm home, and it's late.

I replay seeing my sister on Main Street, but the more I think about that expression on her face—confident, determined—the more I worry.

Why is she here?

It's warm inside the house, but I keep the windows closed and locked and, in addition to the front door, I also keep my bedroom door locked tight at night—a habit that started the day I arrived home all those years ago.

Windows and doors locked. Every night. Without fail.

In the years since Ellie left, I've been able to reacquire a few things important to me. There's a Henry repeating rifle mounted above the bedroom door where my father's old Springfield once rested. It's always loaded, though I take the gun down once a week to clean and oil it. Usually on Sundays. The Henry can fire up to sixteen shots, one every few seconds, without a reload. It brings me great comfort.

Before Father McKee died, he secured me a replacement of the *Malleus Maleficarum* I'd left behind. Despite having a newer binding, the material is the same as the one I'd lost.

I keep it on my nightstand and read from it—study it—every evening before I go to sleep, along with my Bible.

Stuck into the frame of my bedroom door is a squat knife, engraved with the nine crosses, and the nine crescent moons. A *Trudenmesser*. This one has a bone handle and cost me a pretty penny to have it imported from Germany. But expense be damned. If I keep it lodged in that door, no witch or evil spirit can open it. My bedroom, at least, is secure.

All that, and one other thing.

But it is late, my day was long, and I begin to fall asleep.

A sound stirs me.

I turn over in my bed, anticipating a vision of my brother skulking in the corner, grinning. But the corner is empty.

I sit up, listen to the sounds of the house, debate whether the noise came from a dream, or the wind, or...

It comes again!

A *tap-tap-tap*, followed by a creaking hinge, and I realize now that it's the front door being pushed open.

Footsteps enter my home—walking softly—but not so soft I can't hear it plainly amid the still night, the quiet house.

"Hello?" I holler, ready to spring from the bed, pluck the rifle from above the door...but I'm stopped—stopped frozen—when a voice responds.

"Ethan," she says.

Now I hear another set of footfalls on the wooden floorboards, just outside my bedroom door. The *click-clack-click* of long nails.

The dog.

I pull the blankets to my chin and press my back to the wall, my eyes glued to the door. I don't move. I don't make a sound. I wish it away. I wish her and the thing with her *away*. I do not want to see them—here in the still cradle of deep night—coming toward my bed.

Shadows interrupt the blue moonlight seeping through the bottom of my door. There's a shuffling sound, followed by a wet, noisy huffing. The dog—my brother—snorts madly at the gap beneath the door, sniffing for my scent, I suppose.

Or, possibly, for the scent of his dead father.

Scratches!

He paws at the door, wanting passage, trying to claw his way inside! The hound scratches and scratches at my door!

Ellie laughs lightly.

She's just there. On the other side.

"That knife will do you no good, brother," she says, and I watch in horror as the handle of the door twists, then shakes.

Locked, thank the Lord. Locked.

"Go away!"

Ellie laughs again—louder now—and the sound reminds me not of my sister, but of the other one.

Of Sarafina.

It's *her* laugh I hear through the door.

What devilry is this? Is it my sister taunting me? Her mind twisted by her time with the creature? Or is it the other, speaking through her, using her body as a conduit to this world?

Or is it somehow—impossibly—both?

"The shop looks nice," she says. "But you, dear brother? You look old, and broken. If you don't mind my speaking plainly, I'm surprised you're still alive. You have the stench of death on you. It's as apparent as the crooked, scarred nose on your face, if one knows to look for it."

Archie huffs and growls, continues to run his claws against the wooden door.

"He's excited to see you, I think," she says, mockery in her voice. "Archie has been a wonderful companion for us, Ethan. He's quite happy. He eats scraps from our table, and when I'm done with my food, he licks the grease from my fingers. He shits in the woods, hunts his own game and eats it raw, devours the insides of small beasts and fowl as if it were a delicacy."

I hear the dog panting heavily. I wonder if she's stroking his head.

"His mind is still his own, of course," she continues. "He does all these things, but make no mistake, he still knows who and what he is. He remembers every bit of the man he once was. Can you believe it?"

"Please go away," I murmur into the pillow, now clenched tight across my chest.

I'm so afraid. God help me, I'm so afraid.

"We wonder what kind of dog you would be, Ethan. Would you greedily lick yourself? Happy to be alive, thankful to be transformed into something better? You're so miserable, aren't you? With that rope you keep? Perhaps you should return with me, return and live with us. Come with me, Ethan," she says, a hardness in her tone.

The door handle jiggles once more, then settles.

"You would be our favorite pet."

"Never," I say weakly, not having the strength—nor the bravery—to raise my voice.

"You could see our son, your nephew. He's grown so much you wouldn't recognize him, although he does have his father's eyes. Raising him, protecting him, has been a blessing. One day he'll be fully grown, and then he'll be more powerful than all of us. Tell me, brother. Wouldn't you like to come see him? To join us?"

"Leave me alone!" I scream, the cry bursting from my chest like a curse. I begin to weep but hold the pillow to my face so she won't hear it.

"We've seen you in our dreams," she says, whispering the words through the thin wood, as if her mouth was placed close up against it. "We've seen your return, Ethan. It's inevitable. It's fate. But *how* will you come back to us, we wonder? What form will you take?"

There's a slamming against the wood, the hard pounding of a fist.

To my shame, my bladder releases, runs hot down my thigh, into the bedding. I want to cry but can only whimper like a scared child. I despise myself for being so afraid, but the memories flood my mind. I think of that pit I hung over, and the pale wyrms, and Lilith. I think of Sarafina's beauty—the way it called to me—and know I could never resist her if she wanted me. I can only pray to God she does not.

The pounding stops, and there's more laughter. Whispered words.

Now, a second set of nails runs along the door. Higher up than the dog. Sharper. I hear them dig into the wood, run slowly from the top down—gouging, craving to be inside.

"We promised you no more nightmares," she whispers. "But we may yet visit, from time to time. We want to see you again. When it's dark, and you're alone, we'll come back, Ethan. We'll come back and visit you in this cage you've built, sweet brother. This prison."

A few moments of silence pass. My heart pounds hard and painful in my chest and my breathing is labored but then, thankfully, the footsteps recede. Archie whines, but his claws *click-clack-click* once more across the floor as they go. Both sets of footsteps grow quieter as they walk away, away from my bedroom.

Then, blessedly, I hear the creaking hinges of the front door slowly closing, the finality of its latch falling into place.

And I'm alone once more.

I throw the blanket aside and run to the door. I lift the rifle off the pegs, undo the latch, and yank the door inward. I point the gun toward an empty room, moonlight spilling through the front windows, the door shut firm. I run to it and throw the bolt, then spin and check the shadowed corners of the room, just to be sure they are truly gone, and then—only then—do I release a held breath.

Rifle in hand, I return to my bedroom, lock the door, and sit on the bed, anxious and wary. I light the lantern on my nightstand, then open the drawer and remove the leatherbound copy of *Malleus Maleficarum*, hold it tight to my beating heart. I draw strength from its solidity, its powerful words.

I gaze down, into the open drawer, at the shining bayonet that rests there. My lucky bayonet, sharpened and cleaned, a wooden grip now fastened to its base.

Along its sides are deep etchings—carved many years ago by a man well-versed in the ancient arts of angelic lore—the long metal blade now blessed with Hebrew symbols.

The markings of Heaven.

I take it from the drawer, grip it tight in one hand, pray for strength.

For guidance.

Cradling the book, and the blade, I settle once more into bed.

I stare at the closed bedroom door and wait for the dawn—for the warm light of a new day—to come and release me.

To free me from all this darkness.

About the Author

PHILIP FRACASSI is a USA Today bestselling author, as well as a Bram Stoker and British Fantasy Award nominee. He is the author of eight novels, including *The Autumn Springs Retirement Home Massacre*, *Gothic*, *Boys in the Valley*, *The Third Rule of Time Travel*, and *A Child Alone with Strangers*.

His award-winning story collections include *Behold the Void*, *Beneath a Pale Sky*, and *No One is Safe!*

His work has been published in numerous languages, and his short fiction has been featured in dozens of magazines and anthologies, including *Best Horror of the Year*, *Nightmare Magazine*, *Southwest Review*, and *Interzone*.

You can follow Philip on Facebook, Instagram, and Bluesky, or visit his website at pfracassi.com.

www.ingramcontent.com/pod-product-compliance
Lightning Source LLC
LaVergne TN
LVHW040039080526
838202LV00045B/3404